Of Fathers and Sons:

Geoffrey Hotspur
and the Este Inheritance

Evan Ostryzniuk

Book Two of the English Free Company Series

KNOX ROBINSON
PUBLISHING
London • New York

KNOX ROBINSON
PUBLISHING

3rd Floor, 36 Langham Street
Westminster, London W1W 7AP
&
244 5th Avenue, Suite 1861
New York, New York 10001

Knox Robinson Publishing is a specialist, international publisher of historical fiction, historical romance and medieval fantasy.

First published in Great Britain in 2013 by Knox Robinson Publishing

First published in the United States in 2013 by Knox Robinson Publishing

Copyright © Evan Ostryzniuk 2013

A CIP catalogue record for this book is available from the British Library.

ISBN HC 978-1-908483-15-7

ISBN PB 978-1-908483-16-4

Typeset in Bembo by Susan Veach
info@susanveach.com

Printed in the United States of America and the United Kingdom.

Download the KRP App in iTunes and Google Play to receive free historical fiction, historical romance and fantasy eBooks delivered directly to your mobile or tablet.

Watch our historical documentaries and book trailers on our channel on YouTube and subscribe to our podcasts in iTunes.

www.knoxrobinsonpublishing.com

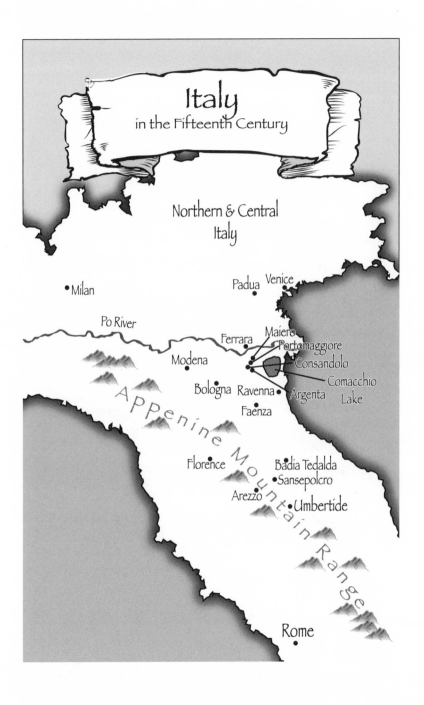

Italy
in the Fifteenth Century

Northern & Central
Italy

• Milan

Padua • Venice

Po River

Ferrara • Maiero
Portomaggiore
Modena • Consandolo

Bologna • Comacchio
Ravenna • Argenta Lake
Faenza •

Florence • Badia Tedalda
• Sansepolcro
Arezzo • • Umbertide

APPENINE Mountain Range

Rome •

CHAPTER 1

Umbertide, Italy
January 1395

The squire Geoffrey Hotspur reaffirmed the grip on his sword and set his eyes to search for a challenger.

A great clash of arms continued to rage on the field below, oblivious to the flank attack he had made to seize the high ground and discomfit the line of knights that was about to charge and win the battle.

But now, as he stood alone on the very crest of the heights, a number of heads turned towards him, most notably that of his lord and master, Sir John of Gaunt, the Duke of Lancaster.

With bloodied sword still in hand and surcoat smeared with the grime of war, England's greatest warrior looked down at the young man with expectant eyes.

Then out of the mess of men and horses a knight emerged to meet him with sword drawn and visor down.

Geoffrey immediately went to the attack.

An upward cut intended to put his foe's sword out of place failed to connect, as the unknown knight pulled himself back at the last moment.

Undeterred by his miss, Geoffrey quickly made a half-turn into his opponent and struck crosswise to slice open his belly.

Another whiff of air.

Expecting a counterstrike, Geoffrey shifted his stance away from the knight and pulled his sword into a defensive guard.

After parrying a possible cut, thrust or cleaving blow, he could pass into yet another turn and close play to keep the man from retreating again.

But no attack came; the knight merely stood in a ready guard.

Geoffrey felt the eyes of the duke on him. He had done well by his lordship with

7

his deed of arms, but the defeat and capture of a knight, and perhaps several others, in a duel could earn him his spurs.

He drew his sword up to his shoulder and advanced quickly, hoping that such a brash move would entice the passive knight to pass into an offensive guard, but as before the man stood steadfast, as though awaiting a proper strike.

Geoffrey furrowed his brow and gritted his teeth.

"Fight, you blackguard!" he yelled as he feinted a thrust, twisted his blade and pulled upwards at an angle, all the while closing.

The knight dodged the blow as Geoffrey expected and with great effort twisted his sword again for a crossing slash.

Geoffrey's eyes grew big as he watched his blade pass cleanly through that of the knight's.

He must be misjudging the distance, and so to clear his vision he blinked several times.

His sight now clear, Geoffrey snatched a glimpse of the duke; he remained stoic in his saddle, as though waiting to shift judgment.

The noise of the battle stopped. Yet more eyes fell on the squire. Geoffrey retuned to the attack, stabbing and hacking with increasing recklessness, desperate to inflict some kind of damage on the knight who continued to step away from play.

Eventually, Geoffrey found himself on the edge of the heights, far away from Gaunt and the battle, confronted by nothing more than a harmless breeze.

He turned around in time to see the Duke of Lancaster riding away. Geoffrey dropped his sword, but just before it struck earth all went black and he woke up.

The dim outline of the roughly hewn beams above him was enough to remind Geoffrey that he was about as far from a battlefield as he could be. Instead, he was lying on a wooden bench wedged into a clay wall in a shepherd's hut. He could indeed feel a harmless breeze, since he saw that his blanket was now on the floor next to him. Morning had arrived.

He had to move. After twisting the stiffness out of his spine, Geoffrey threw himself off the bench, crashed his way through the hut, wrenched open a small window, closed his bright blue eyes, and let the full force of winter's icy breath wash over his face, pour down his open neck, and flow through his thick black hair.

He needed to feel the cold sting on his flesh, the purity of frozen air with its enlivening strike. Although he was unaccustomed to such mountain cold, having been raised in the papal city of Avignon within a stone's throw of the Mediterranean

Sea, the squire was not bothered, and in truth believed that such pure air helped balance his humors.

The intense morning sunlight forced itself through his eyelids and burned away the final images of that strange and dispiriting encounter with the anonymous knight.

This was the second night in a row after a month's interval that the battle near the fortified town of Orte, located many leagues south of Umbertide, had invaded his dreams. Of course, his lordship had played no part in the actual pass of arms and Geoffrey himself had not crossed swords with anyone, let alone a knight, but he had led a successful flanking action against a company of horsemen. The result was a total victory for his side, so why had that radiant moment of glory been transformed into a nightmare? Well, Geoffrey knew why, but there was nothing to be done for the time being.

When he at last opened his eyes to the new day, all he could see was mound upon mound of glittering snow on the ground, in the trees and astride the towering mountains. For the month Geoffrey had been stranded in the hut near the alpine city of Umbertide, howling winds and a steady snowfall had made travel impossible to anywhere but the nearest village. He craned his head upwards and squinted into the deep blue sky, searching for signs of yet another storm. Not a hint of cloud. The heavens were as clear as on that day in April nearly one year ago, when he had been sent away on a strange commission of his majesty King Richard II to Florence to fetch the bones of an esteemed warrior, a commission he failed to complete, much to his shame. Despite the lengthy passage of time, or perhaps because of it, the squire had to fulfill this solemn duty to his lord the duke, to his majesty the king, and to himself or risk at best disgrace.

Meanwhile, his friends and fellow squires had no doubt served a knight on campaign, or even his lordship the duke himself, and were preparing for the next fighting season between bouts of debauchery and gaming. Although he had not received a word from his lordship, or anyone in Avignon, since the day of his departure, Geoffrey was sure they remembered him. He felt the blood well up in his heart at the prospect of missing another chance to earn his spurs and tightened his grip on the window sill until his knuckles turned white. He had been idle for too long – in a foreign land yet – and was anxious with every sinew in his body for another clash of arms. The renewed nightmare and the clear weather might be signs to continue the journey, the squire reckoned. Yes, nothing should prevent his return now. Geoffrey raised his chin and through his aquiline nose inhaled deeply. The time had come to finally complete his commission. It was time to go home.

"Close the bloody window, you daft ass!" The words spewed from a dark corner.

Geoffrey was not distracted. He remained as still as steel, though stooped slightly on account of his great height.

"We cannot afford more wood, unless you are willing to part with that precious sword of yours. I am having a hard enough time keeping what few twigs we have left alive with fire. And then there ---" The words abruptly cut out at the onset of a violent cough, which was followed by a round of sniffling. The darkness stirred and a stocky man wrapped in a blanket staggered towards the hearth.

"I know you can hear me, master squire." Jean Lagoustine raised his hand to shield his eyes from the brilliant shaft of light that sliced through the dimness. In contrast to the squire, he had a full face of beard of an indeterminate color, although if pressed he would describe it as mostly red, like that of Emperor Frederick Barbarossa. His thick nose was bent to the left and his black eyes were barely visible beneath a drooping brow. He was nearly a head shorter than the squire, but a good deal broader, as though his shoulders had been stretched by some infernal device.

Jean too hailed from Avignon, although he was neither English nor a man of rank. In truth, he occupied no specific station, but if a lord were to demand he state his place, he would have to admit to being a villein, a tiller of the soil, or rather a former tiller of the soil, having many years ago made his way to the city to eventually become a debt collector for the notorious Gamesmaster.

He was hired muscle, which was how he had gotten mixed up with this uncertain squire in the first place. The Gamesmaster had expected him to return to the fold once he completed his business with young man of Gaunt. He had, but now he was not sure if he wanted to go back, although he saw he had little choice in the matter – he was nothing in Italy.

"God's dignity! His mind has wandered off again," Jean mumbled. He stamped his feet, straightened his mustard yellow jupon and adjusted his brown woolen cloak so that it would not fall off his uneven shoulders. He looked at the hearth and seeing wisps of smoke rising from it, decided that its stoking could wait.

"I hear you. I *wish* my mind would wander off," Geoffrey said. His voice was clear, but tinged with melancholy. "I was there again last night."

Jean stared at the young man, bathed in white light. "At the battle? Did you slay anybody this time?"

"No." Geoffrey pulled his head back and turned to Jean. "It was the same as always: fighting and fighting, but no blood. I came close this time…well…no I do not think I did." He shook his head.

"Did you see me? I was in one of your nightmares, you told me." For a moment, Jean saw himself on the heights overlooking the field where the battle near Orte had been fought. He had not killed anybody either, which was just as well, but more importantly he had survived unscathed.

"No," Geoffrey said curtly. "I did not see Sergeant Godwin either, but it was the battle, all right. Does that day never return to you at night?"

"I am burdened by many things, but dreaming is not one of them."

"You must. You just do not remember them."

Jean squinted from the light as he walked towards Geoffrey. "That may be, but for all that is holy, I have no use for them. Your problem is that you remember that day too much."

"It was a grand day. My first feat of arms." The pride in the squire's voice quickly dulled, however. The only blood he caused to be spilled had belonged to Sergeant Godwin, companion-in-arms, teacher and compatriot. Geoffrey poked his head out the window again.

"That band of urchins should be arriving soon with the victuals," Jean announced, changing the subject. He pushed himself next to Geoffrey and peered outside. "It is appalling that I should have to pay in advance to those little extortionists for such common fare. So much advantage conferred by familiarity." Jean spat into the snow and shuffled towards the door.

"If you are going to open windows, then I am opening doors." He wrapped himself in his cloak and tugged on the rope handle until the heavy wooden door swung open. Immediately, a gust flung snow in the Frenchman's face.

"Ptui! At least it is not a hail of arrows. God's bones, I will never forget that day." Jean scraped the snow away from the door with his clogs and then stood with arms akimbo and eyes searching the horizon for his breakfast.

Geoffrey was hungry, but he remained distracted by thoughts of finally getting back on the road. This was not the first time he had contemplated leaving a place. After the battle near Orte, he had made plans to reach Florence before the first snowfall via the familiar pilgrim's route called the Way of the Franks, or Via Francigena, and there board a vessel bound for Avignon. But of course he could on no account depart before celebrating the victory with his companions-in-arms, which involved a week-long feast. Then he had been obliged to wait for his small share of the booty. Then he had met a girl. Then another. And then he had discovered that the local taverns kept a backroom for gaming, just as those in Avignon did, and then in his haste to beat the onset of winter he mistakenly took a branch of the Via Francigena that led to Assisi. However, Geoffrey had retraced his steps for no more than a dozen miles when the major snows arrived, forcing him to seek shelter with the *signore* of Umbertide, who was a friend of a close companion.

"Come on, already!" Jean shouted at the forest and then turned towards Geoffrey. "The lord of this wretched land should be feting us in his hall, not letting us starve in a miserable hut."

"His lordship, the *signore* of Umbertide, does his best," Geoffrey said in a plain voice, his face still bearing the brunt of the wind. "Sergeant William Godwin would not have grumbled so."

"Godwin was a grumbler and worse, which explains why the *signore* received us with such mild courtesy! Well, I suppose this sort of hospitality is all what the old sergeant was worth, upon my word."

Geoffrey suddenly grew passionate. "Do not speak ill of the dead, Jean! Godwin saved my life."

"True, true. All the same, though, his name was buried along with him." Jean stared ruefully at the smoldering fire and wondered if his own name might have value one day. For now, Jean Lagoustine was worth something only to the Gamesmaster of Avignon, and maybe to this little English Free Company he had created.

"On a cold and wintry day,
The English Comp'ny came to play,
Tho 'stead of bringing stick and ball,
They doffed their caps to beg from all,
And so as good Christians we,
Bring them food for all to see,
Come out! Come out! Free-e-e-e men!"

The verse belonged to a choir of childish voices, intermittently broken by laughs and giggles. It was the party Jean had been expecting.

"It had better be hot, whatever witch's brew they deliver," Jean mumbled. "Hurry, you fools!" Jean yelled at the children as they trudged through the snow.

The victualing party stopped a few yards from Jean and released a single member to hand over an assortment of clay pots. The moment Jean felt the weight of his new burden, the strain stung his stiff right shoulder and he nearly dropped the wares. He winced and clutched at the pain with his left hand. He had suffered some injury during his year-long wandering with the English squire, yet what his body remembered most was the mighty blow struck atop the same shoulder several years ago by a panicking doctor as Jean tried to extract a delinquent debt payment from him. Since then, he could never align himself properly, with his right side sunk lower than his left and the wound reawakening at the changing of the seasons.

A boy moved to help Jean by cupping his hands beneath the largest pot, but Jean waved him away.

"I am not as bad as all that, lad," he said. "Wait here." Jean took the meal inside and set it next to the hearth, withdrew a small pouch that served as the treasury of the English Free Company and poked around inside. The only sound he produced was that of his fingernail scratching against raw leather. Nothing.

"For all that is holy…" Jean sighed. He looked around and saw his leather satchel lying on the bench. He turned it over and shook it vigorously, releasing a dented tinder box, a handful of rivets, a cloud of dirt, and a few copper coins. Jean collected the coins, sneezed and returned to the door.

"Jean," Geoffrey said. "Have those boys learn if the pilgrim's way is passable and report back as soon as possible."

"Why? You need to visit some village milkmaid before she tires from her chores? Ask her for a few pennies in exchange for your affection, or whatever games you play."

"A little early for such ribaldry, is it not? Nonetheless, I warrant it a good sign for our departure. We are leaving here today."

Jean shot Geoffrey an amused glance and snorted. "You mean like how we were leaving the feasts, the gaming halls, and the taverns over the past four months? Eat first; deceive me later." He handed over the coppers to the leader of the juvenile band.

"I have read the signs. We will not wait for spring."

Jean eyed the squire and determined that he was sincere. He turned back to the door and repeated Geoffrey's instructions, adding in a quiet voice, "And tell me whose been traveling the Way. Got that?"

The boys nodded and their leader held out his hand expectantly.

"Not until you tell me something useful. I am not the village idiot."

One of the girls stepped forward and asked if the squire would hear mass today or tomorrow. Some of the village maids wanted to know.

So that is where he goes, Jean thought. He should have known that Geoffrey Hotspur, man of Gaunt, would frequent both the local chapel and the local lasses. The squire had never confided in him about his jaunts outside the hut and Jean never asked. Only once did he invite the Frenchman to accompany him to hear mass, which had resulted in his suffering the same village children pestering him for pennies and presents. He never went again.

"The master squire has decided to dine with his lordship in the great hall tomorrow," Jean lied.

The girl nodded, but the boy leader gave a knowing smile, doffed his cap and made a curt bow. With a whoop, the children ran towards the wood and began singing an obscene air. When Jean turned around, he saw the squire standing near the hearth, sword in hand.

"The bread is not so stiff as to need be sliced by such a knife," Jean said, "or are you giving your blade a final look before I drag it down to the blacksmith to sell. The coin it would fetch would take us within spitting distance of Avignon, I reckon." Geoffrey's *couteau* was an old and heavy but perfectly balanced broad sword of simple design with a mottled ruby-colored orb lodged in its pommel.

"I still feel agitated from the nightmare. A little training exercise should help bring my humors into balance." Geoffrey adjusted his grip, stretched his leg back and angled the blade to the right. "And if we are in need of silver, you can sell one of our palfreys."

Jean grunted. "Did you forget how I sold the lamer of our horses last month? Of course you did, and what little silver it fetched."

"Indeed? I thought you had tried to run away and those urchins knocked you off the horse and stole it. All the same, it will mean one less beast to feed on the road." Geoffrey turned into another stance and passed the blade over Jean's head.

"So, you mean to say that we are really leaving this palace and heading to Florence? Well, I suppose we must, since in another month I am certain that the bellies of several maids will begin to grow unexpectedly, and even a peasant father has his honor to protect."

"We are, although you can remain here, if you like, and continue complaining to the walls."

"My heart is glad, but let my belly be gladder." Jean peeled the skeins off one of the pots and sniffed. "Smells edible. If nothing else, the locals have yet to give us anything rotten." Jean turned to look at the squire.

"Stop that! The nightmare is over and the meal is getting cold."

Jean turned back and doled out the thick mash of oatmeal and mushy vegetables into clean bowls. He opened another pot and quickly shrank back.

"Ugh! I spoke too soon. Is this jellied meat? Lord, I hope that is what it is. What are you doing now?"

"This is the unbreakable Iron Door guard, although I suppose you cannot tell the difference between an offensive and a defensive attitude, master debt collector."

"I have asked you not to call me that anymore. I am the company treasurer, if you please, and besides, I paid off your debts to the Gamesmaster through that astrologer woman after the battle, although I have had to work hard to prevent you from growing more since then." Jean took the bowls to the ledge on the opposite side of the hearth.

"And *this* is Half Boar's Tooth, which is another stable guard that I can easily pass into, giving me equal chance to strike, counter or parry." Geoffrey shifted his stance and pulled the sword until its hilt was resting against his hip. "Oh, that is right, you are the Treasurer General of our famous English Free Company. Well, let us get this company on the road." Geoffrey chopped the air with his blade.

Jean refused to look at him this time. "Come guard your grub. These vegetables are turning as we speak." He was usually skeptical of the squire's sudden passions, since Jean had seen him pass from ecstasy to despair in a heartbeat, but this time, the nightmares combined with the fine weather ignited a spark of belief.

Geoffrey, now well distracted, sighed and carefully wrapped his sword in its oiled cloth scabbard. He did not particularly like Jean Lagoustine. He was low born, untrustworthy and had deceived him more than once in the past year. Geoffrey was accustomed to the company of fellow squires, ladies at court and retired knights—people of distinguished rank. But this Frenchman had no place. Or rather his place was in the English Free Company, which Geoffrey himself had created at a time of desperation. However, he had noticed that Jean excelled at those dull tasks that related to the keeping of a company of men-at-arms, such as victualing.

The two men ate their gruel in silence.

After Geoffrey emptied his bowl, he looked up and said, "The meat is bad."

Jean froze with his spoon an inch from his mouth. "I know it is bad," he said with quiet menace.

"We should have fresh for our journey."

Jean slammed his spoon down on the edge of the bowl, sending the piece of crockery spinning along the ledge and onto the floor. "You know we have no silver!" he declared with unfettered frustration. "Your lingering in places has cost us the season, half our horses and now all our money! We have nothing left to pawn except for you-know-what!"

Geoffrey straightened his posture. "God will provi---"

"Stop right there! You have been tempting my patience long enough, what with your constant need for company, so you had better not tempt anyone else's, let alone His." Jean pointed at the ceiling. "What we need is to earn our bread, not hope for it." He would have struck the squire with his fist if he knew he could get away with it, but there was no question who was the nimbler of the two. Instead, the former debt collector stuck his fist beneath his chin and frowned.

"There is method in my madness, Jean. We will be on the Via Francigena, which means that the road should be well endowed with shrines and hospices. We should find fresh fare in those shelters, and even if we do not, the humility will serve our souls."

Ever since he had listened to old knights' stories about pilgrimages to Jerusalem, whether as crusaders or humble penitents, Geoffrey had wanted to tread a Way. One time, when he was still serving as a page in the halls of Gaunt, he had tried to run away to Vézelay, the starting point for so many pilgrimages, but he only reached the first village north of Avignon before being caught.

"And besides, we are only traveling to Florence, where I am expected, not to Jerusalem, which is what, a week's journey?"

"More like two weeks, but even so, I do not want to have to beg at every village if you are wrong."

"I will not remain here another day. Do you not want to go home?"

Jean had been ruminating on this very question since the end of the battle near Orte. He could and he should, but he was not sure if he would return. Staying in the hut had long exhausted its charm, yet Florence beckoned. He would decide there. In the meantime, Geoffrey's divine appeal coupled with his own knowledge about holy routes was enough fuel to fire an idea in the Frenchman's chilled skull, an idea that should get them to Florence with the skins still on their backs and a few coins in their purses.

"Come, captain," Jean said as he slapped Geoffrey on the shoulder. "Let us prepare for our departure."

Ferrara, Italy

Eleven-year-old Niccolo d'Este thrust his wooden sword into the sky and puffed out his chest in readiness for shouting his war cry. What should it be? Este? Ferrara? Something clever he had read in Cicero? He could shout 'Whites!', since that was the color of the Este eagle and the name of the host he was leading, but that would sound silly.

What was not helping him decide was the band of a dozen boys his age, all from the best families in Ferrara, fussing behind him as they awaited his signal to advance. Some were giggling, some were lobbing taunts over his head, some were banging their own toy swords against their small round shields known as bucklers.

Niccolo frowned as he tried to concentrate. If he had his way, he would declare an end to this mock battle and have his companions play some other game, one that did not rely on him yelling or running at another group of friends with ill intent. But he had raised his arm, so he could only go forward.

"Come on now! Let us have at them!" one boy shouted.

"My lord, my lord, do not make us bored!" another sang.

"The cold stings deeper the longer we stand here," a third boy complained.

The impatience of his companions irritated Niccolo. He could wait all day for the Blue host to tire of idleness and initiate the pass of arms, but he was the Marquis of Ferrara, as well as captain of this little company of childish knights, and so he had to act soon if he still wanted the boys to follow him. Also, he too was cold. Christmas had just passed and the weather had grown chillier.

Someone shoved him in the back.

"Sorry, my lord *dominus generalis*," the offending boy said. A couple of his companions giggled.

Niccolo bristled at both being touched and addressed by the strange Latin title, but he said nothing. *Dominus generalis!* What did that really mean? Lord the Great? The regency council had conferred on him the honor during his investiture ceremony last year, but its significance was never explained. Niccolo did not think that his father ever possessed that title. At least, he had never seen it on any of the chancellery documents. He would have to ask Donato degli Albanzani, his tutor, to explain the meaning to him later. He could no longer tolerate his companions' mockery of it.

Niccolo straightened his back and reaffirmed the grip on his sword. Although a recent growth spurt had made him half a head taller than the tallest of his companions, he did not feel superior to them – he just did not like to be touched. But Niccolo could not let that bother him now, not with his mother, her maids, and his captain-general Azzo da Castello watching from the loge that overlooked the walled garden in the heart of Ferrara.

He suppressed an urge to look at them and instead focused his eyes on the defenses he was about to assail. It was just a snow castle, but an impressive one. The walls were chest height with a wide bastion jutting from the center and a shallow trench fronting the entire works.

The marquis espied a few boys pouring water along the battlements to ice them up, a nasty trick he had forbidden at the outset of the contest. That annoyed him. He wanted to yell "You cannot do that!" but he knew he would look foolish, petty even. This was yet another obstacle for him to overcome.

Niccolo gave a thin smile. He was troubled enough about having to fight with sword and buckler, since he had little training between the barriers. However, he was a capable rider and could take down a hart with one shot from a crossbow. He excelled at falconry, he was told, but his favorite place was his father's library, where he could sit and read fascinating tales for hours. One of his mother's maids told him the other day that he was already handsome like his father, with a thick head of brown hair, firm chin, straight nose, and narrow, piercing eyes.

Then he had it – an old war cry his father had taught him during a lesson in family history, when the Este clan was a stout defender of his grace the supreme pontiff against the German Emperor.

"For Guelf or none!" Niccolo shouted, and he began to run.

"Huzzah!" the Whites responded, and in ragged order they followed their leader across the frozen field.

He watched the builders drop their buckets and clamber behind the main wall, while the others disappeared inside the bastion. Niccolo frowned; he would not produce a clean pass of arms on the flat field like he wanted, but instead he would have to storm the snowy walls. Well, if the Blues would not come out and fight, he would run them over. This was not a tournament; that would come later.

"Faster!" Niccolo yelled. "Form up against the center!"

Immediately those boys who were strung out on the flanks shifted inwards, turning the line into a wedge.

When the Whites were half way across the field, the Blue captain leapt up and shouted: "Now!" His company arose as one and set their right arms back. In each hand was a fat snowball.

The first volley mostly fell short, as in their excitement the boys short-armed their throws, but one caught Niccolo squarely in the right shoulder. The blow put him off his gait and he stumbled, tangled his feet with those of another boy and fell hard onto the frozen ground. Most of the ground cover had been cleared away by both sides to build fortifications, leaving exposed the packed earth and broken stems of last year's growth. Niccolo was not hurt, though the laughter drifting across the field burned his ears.

"Don't stop!" Niccolo ordered while still on his back, but no one heard.

Seeing their leader down, the Whites became confused. First one boy halted to help his captain, then another, and soon all of them were standing over Niccolo, ducking incoming missiles or trying to intercept them with their swords.

With his company in disarray, Niccolo saw that the defenders were accelerating their volleys, and a few boys had even left the bastion to find better angles for their snowballs. He kicked his feet free and propped up his buckler to give himself some protection while he set himself right. In quick succession he heard the pops of three snowballs against his impromptu palisade. This gave him an idea.

Niccolo swallowed once and shouted hoarsely, "Rally to me, Whites! Crouch beside me, shields out!"

Trained to heed such commands, one by one the boys dropped down and huddled around their captain.

Recalling Vegetius' exposition on Roman battle tactics, Niccolo hurriedly explained what he wanted them all to do. "We can only go forward, and we will advance as a…shape, right into and over top of those…those…other lads."

"What?" one boy asked. "Speak up. What are we to do again?"

Niccolo fell silent. He knew what he wanted to say and in his mind he could see the words of the ancient Latin script. Even the interpretation of his tutor echoed inside his head. Well, if his own voice was failing him, then he would use that of his tutor.

"Tortoise," Niccolo said in a lower register. He hoped the others were as well read as him. A snowball sailed passed and into the gaping maw of the boy who had just spoke. "You, you and you will form the bottom rank with me. We must bind our shields tightly if we are to avoid drenched faces. The rest of you will bunch up behind us with shields overhead, protecting us and yourselves. Understand?"

One boy said, "Great idea!" while the remainder murmured their agreement.

What Niccolo wanted was to fight his opponent on the lists so that he could show his mother that he had learned something from his father's arms master. Knocking over a pile of snow would not do it. "Now, let us form ranks!"

19

Niccolo furtively looked at the loge and caught sight of the woman standing next to and a step behind his mother. Like himself amongst his friends, she was noticeably taller than her fellow maids, which was unusual, since his mother preferred companions that were shorter than her. The woman had joined his court only a few months ago, yet her face and stature seemed familiar, although that could be because he recognized her station. She was attired in several shades of blue and wound her wimple as a turban. Her name was Catherine and the ruby pendant dangling from her headdress marked her as an astrologer.

The missiles were coming in not only hard and heavy, but with suspect composition, for Niccolo felt splinters of ice jab his face when one snowball shattered against his shield. This too was against the rules and it caused him to wonder if the Blues were true companions. While the Whites comprised sons of *racommendati*, men who served the Este through a written bond, the Blues were mostly made up of Este vassals from the *contado*, many of whose families predated the arrival of the Este to Ferrara.

Niccolo let the anger caused by the offense flow through his humors until it fired his fists.

"Closer! Closer!" he shouted quickly. The response was immediate. "Now, advance!"

The tortoise inched forward. Hunched behind and beneath the shields, Niccolo could see little more than a strip of white, but after a short while he felt the volleys slacken and heard the rattle of arms being readied. His maneuver was working.

"At my signal, break company and strike," he said.

The tortoise crept ahead another twenty yards in tense silence before Niccolo saw figures crawling over the battlements. He thought about engaging them now, when they were at their most vulnerable, but he realized that if he pushed them back into their wintry fortress they would be off the lists. He would let the Blues come out unmolested.

"Spread ranks!" Niccolo ordered. He stood straight up and bashed his head against an overhead shield, but he ignored the blow. His companions fanned out on either side of him. Some were knocking their swords against their bucklers and shouting challenges, but they kept close to one another.

The enemy was well disciplined. Each boy carefully made his way over the wall and quickly found his footing on the lists. Niccolo let them take a few paces before he charged at the opposing captain.

Then Niccolo heard a war cry that froze his blood and struck his heart.

"Azzo in Modena!" the Blue captain yelled.

Niccolo dug his heels into the ground within a couple of yards of the offending captain. He could not believe that anyone would utter the name of his mortal enemy, his uncle, a great condottiere who had taken up arms against him with support from the treacherous city of Modena. It would only take a word to the regency council to have the boy and his entire clan exiled from the city and deprived of their lands for such impudence, especially now when Niccolo was vulnerable, here on this frozen field as well as in Ferrara.

The boys clashed, shield to shield. Some on both sides were bowled over upon impact, but it was not long before pairs formed to engage in swordplay. Niccolo, now staring in hatred at the Blue captain, readied himself in the manner the arms master had taught him. He had a clear height advantage, but the other boy had better leverage; he could make a devastating strike from on high, but the Blue captain could thrust more effectively. Bending his right knee forward and stretching his left leg back to produce a stable stance, Niccolo put himself in the most secure guard possible – Iron Door. He would wait to defend an advance by this fool and then counter with both sword and shield.

It was not to be. At first the Blue captain did as Niccolo expected, charging forward to join in close play, but just as he set his sword back he stopped short and kicked a load of snow into Niccolo's face, blinding him long enough to knock the buckler out of his hand with a fierce crossing strike.

Instinctively, Niccolo brought his sword up to guard his face and stepped back. Snow melted on his hot cheeks, leaving rivulets to fill his mouth and crawl inside his arming jacket. His vision blurred, although he still could make out his opponent again drawing his arm in readiness for a center thrust. Was the boy a traitor? Perhaps the toy sword hid a steel blade and the boy was preparing to assassinate him. Several old and respected vassals of the Este had defected in recent weeks. Was his clan yet another? Regardless, the Blue captain had no honor.

Niccolo shook the doubts from his head, but not the fear and hatred from his eyes, and he brought down his sword to counter the vague attack. The sharp clack of wood on wood and the tremor racing up his arm told him that the connection was true. Now, Iron Door was no longer useful. With his opponent's sword put away from his body, Niccolo made a full turn and brought across a counterstrike that cleaved into the Blue captain's right arm. The boy cried out in pain. Niccolo wiped his eyes before following up his advantage by kicking the boy in the shin and moving in to grapple, taking his opponent by the wrist. The Blue captain countered by swinging his shield at Niccolo, but he was too close and the blow bounced harmlessly off his back. Now, reckoning that he could make the boy yield, Niccolo pushed ahead until they collided with the bastion. They wrestled until the force of their violence broke the weakened snow wall, sending them tumbling into a pile of snowballs.

Niccolo was dizzy. He could hear the melee raging around him, the cries of the injured, the specific crush of snow beneath boots, and the clacking of wooden swords. Still filled with anger, the marquis sat up, wiped his eyes and looked around for his foe. He found the Blue captain on his back twisting to pull himself out of the now mashed cache of missiles. Both boys had been disarmed by the dramatic fall. Niccolo saw his weapon lying just a few yards away, but he decided that he could give the Blue captain a thrashing without it for uttering that cursed name. Just as he was about to place his boot on the boy's neck, he heard a deep male voice shout, "Enough! The war is over."

Niccolo swiveled his head and stared hard at the loge, where he saw his captain-general holding up his right hand.

"Everyone to the kitchens!" he shouted. "Niccolo, come here!"

The boys immediately retired. After dusting themselves off and straightening their kit, they did as were told, but not before each in his turn shook Niccolo's hand and said that they would wait for him, including the still reeling Blue captain.

"I am glad the regency council was not here to see this," Azzo said after Niccolo greeted him. "It was a comedy we can do without."

"I will fight much better at the tournament next week," Niccolo declared. There was sharpness in his tone. His humors were still quick with choler and his eyes were burning from the mixture of sweat and anger. He dragged his sleeve across his face and blinked several times. "And blast them anyway, they cheated!"

Azzo laughed and slapped Niccolo on the back. "Rules are to be respected, to be sure, but always be prepared for them to be broken," he said. "Any pass of arms is a damned unsure thing."

CHAPTER 2

Geoffrey was excited to be finally rid of his idleness, yet the joy of soon being reunited with his fellow squires and joining them on one of Gaunt's campaigns was tempered by a number of anxieties, not the least of which was his appearance.

Since he would be riding on a famous pilgrimage route, Geoffrey had to display his station as a squire in good standing with the Duke of Lancaster and show the appropriate humility. His sword was a must, not only for the sake of prestige, but also because it counted as his only weapon. He would sling it on his left hip and make sure that its mottled ruby pommel shone like a beacon, illuminating the Way. The *couteau* had been with Geoffrey since before he had hair on his head, when the good duke discovered him as an infant swaddled together with it.

The squire lifted the sword, kissed the place where the guard crossed the tang, and set it on the bench away from the rest of his gear. He was already wearing both pairs of chausses, brown leather buskins, his linen and woolen tunics, the pourpoint, or padded arming jacket, he brought from Avignon, and the hauberk. Geoffrey did not have a surcoat that would protect his chainmail shirt, so instead he decided to use the light blue doublet he purchased in Assisi last summer for that purpose. A struggle with the doublet's narrow sleeves, however, only led to a ripped lining and a string of curses aimed at himself and the garment.

"Hey, Jean!" Geoffrey called out as the Frenchman was passing, a satchel slung over his higher shoulder. "Do you have a spare tunic? It should be large enough to cover my hauberk, I reckon."

Without stopping, Jean made a dismissive wave and said, "No, I do not have a spare tunic for you to ruin."

"Yours have no markings anyway," Geoffrey shouted as he watched Jean leave the hut. "I might be able to find a penitent's tunic in the village," he said to himself, "or if luck is on my side perhaps an old crusader's surcoat." Geoffrey warmed to this prospect, but the feeling passed when he realized that no one in his right mind would give up such a treasured relic from the reconquest of the Holy Land to a lonely English squire. He would have to leave his hauberk exposed.

Geoffrey shook his head and slid the doublet and a few sundry items into his canvas satchel, but as he was cramming in his polishing kit, his hand struck something hard at the bottom. He gasped when he realized that it was the seal of his lordship, the Duke of Lancaster. When he extracted the brass disc Geoffrey was confronted by a noble figure in full regalia seated on a throne flanked by filigree and the arms of the duke himself. He felt shame that he had forgotten about this one proof of who he was, presented to him on the eve of his departure to Florence by the lord who had not only saved his infant life, but given him a place in his hall. Geoffrey nestled the seal beneath his pourpoint; he would return it to his lordship in Avignon.

Now that his one bag was packed, Geoffrey had to decide what to do with the rest of his harness, which consisted of six pieces of armor to protect his legs – pairs of cuisses, poleyns and greaves – and a helm. Being careful not to repeat his mistake with the doublet, Geoffrey placed the leg harness against his legs without securing them and saw that they would not fit over his buskins. It was just as well, he reckoned, since without a complimentary set of armor for his arms, he would look silly.

He shoved the leg harness into a net. The helm, however, he would cram on over his arming cap and wool hat that one of the village maids knitted for him. It was an older basinet style helm without either a mask or an aventail, but the metal was smooth and solid. Geoffrey frowned at this perfection because it meant the helm had not withstood the blows of battle. Geoffrey furtively glanced around before whacking the dome of his helm against the pommel of his sword.

He stood back and stared at his baggage. Something is missing, he thought. The gear could belong to anyone. That was it, Geoffrey realized. He had nothing that would easily identify him to fellow travelers. Gaunt's seal would not do, of course, since it would be hidden. A pennon would solve this dilemma, but he had neither spare cloth nor rags from which to piece together even the smallest of gonfalons. Then Geoffrey wondered whose colors he might fly – those of his king, his lord, or his own in the guise of the English Free Company. As a man of his lordship John of Gaunt he could display the white ostrich feather; however, he was in Italy by virtue of a royal commission, which implied riding under the gold lion of his majesty King Richard. As to himself, neither he nor the regrettable free company had colors, crest, device or charge of any sort to display. So, he had nothing. As distressing as this anonymity would be, perhaps it was best that way, Geoffrey thought. It was a sign of his uncertain fate. He slapped the flap of the satchel closed and buckled it.

"Are you ready, finally?" Jean shouted from the door. "The sun is bright and the days are short."

"I am ready. These things have to be done properly. I assume you saddled the horse?" Geoffrey laced up the net that contained the peripheral bits of his armor.

"Saint George is fed and watered and anxious to go. Here, now. I hope you are not expecting me to lade your gear. I have done enough for this merry band of ours, and if you think…"

"Enough! You long ago made it clear that you are not my servant, and I would not trust you to get it right anyway. I was well trained in the halls of Gaunt, and so as a squire I know better than anyone how to set gear." Geoffrey slung the net over one shoulder, his satchel across the other, and his *couteau* he tucked beneath his arm.

Jean nodded and waited for the squire to leave the hut. He took one last look around before slamming the door shut.

Saint George was a palfrey, a simple riding horse, brown with a black mane. He was a tame creature, which made it easy for Geoffrey to burden him with yet more baggage. After checking that all was secure, he grabbed the horn and the cantle and set his foot in the stirrup.

Jean snatched the bridle and turned the horse towards him. "Now hang on. Either we both ride Saint George or neither of us does. I am the one who feeds him, after all."

Geoffrey hopped back on one foot a few paces before setting himself right. "Yes, but I groom him. And besides, who is the man of rank between us? How would it look if *I* was on foot?"

"It would look like you were on the Via Francigena, a humble traveler, pious even, where your meager rank means little. But if you want to ride alone, then give me your buskins. The road will be frozen." Jean looked down at his clogs.

"That will not do. I will agree to take turns on the mount, for the sake of harmony."

"My feet will still be cold, and with one of us always on foot, the going will be slow."

Geoffrey grabbed the reins and pulled the palfrey a little away from Jean. "Then we shall ride as one. *That* will be my show of humility. I believe Saint George is strong enough for that."

"Agreed. I will even let you lead."

"As it should be."

Geoffrey mounted the saddle while Jean kept the beast still, and then with some difficulty Jean took his place behind the cantle.

"I feel like a Templar," Jean mumbled.

"A what?"

"A Templar, you know, a knight of the Holy Sepulcher."

"Why would that be? Are you feeling heretical today? I do not understand you sometimes."

"For someone who has spent as much time as you have in noble halls, you have not learned much. The Poor Knights of Christ, I was told, rode two on a horse."

"Hmm…That is true." Geoffrey snapped the reins. "But they at least knew how to ride, so try not to fall off. I have no time for stragglers."

Geoffrey had little trouble finding the trail that led to the Via Francigena, since the boy who had told him that the road was clear said that it went passed the village chapel. They would travel this branch of the Way to the crossroads city of Sansepolcro and from there turn west to Arezzo and then northwest to Florence. The entire journey should take around ten days, they were told, weather permitting.

"I cannot believe that we are the sole travelers," Jean said. "We would do well to hire ourselves to a group of pilgrims to protect them from thieves and bandits. You would be surprised how many devilish men roam the pilgrim routes."

"So, that is your scheme. Well, I would be surprised if anyone would hire one man-at-arms."

"There are two of us here."

Geoffrey guffawed. "Yes, but only one man here is trained in arms. Do you not recall how poorly you fared at pike training, when you were constantly tripping? We were not even practicing in ranks and the field was level. We make a poor lance."

"I believe I acquitted myself very well during the battle. I might not have slain anyone, but I still did the company proud."

"You did not flee, so that is a worthy boast. And speaking of deeds of arms, where are yours? I only see mine."

"My sword is tucked away in my satchel."

"And?"

"And that is all. Oh, I also have studded leather gloves for holding a pike."

"What about your harness? You had a leather jack and some metal bits."

"The helm I had to sell for fodder and the jack was cracking in too many places to count, so I practically gave it away. There was nothing to be done."

Geoffrey swatted away a low-hanging branch, sending snow flying in all directions. They had just passed a milestone inscribed with the words 'Via Francigena'.

"Did I not tell you to oil it once in a while, you fool? Ugh! For the love of all that is holy, if you want to be in this free company you yourself created, you must do things properly. You could have borrowed grease from me."

"No, you bloody well did not tell me anything of the sort," Jean retorted, jabbing a finger into Geoffrey's ribs. "Anyway, I was burdened with greater tasks, like gathering provisions and keeping our parchment safe."

"Ow! Stop that! You know I do not really need you, right? I could without a bother of conscience throw you off and ride on my own. I have the horse, I have the name, I have the arming skills, and I even have a seal that should ease my way."

"Yes, well, my friend, that all might be very well and good if we were in France, where you speak the language and the halls of Gaunt are always within reach, but we are in Italy. I have the words, I have the parchment that makes the English Free Company, and I have…I have…the reckoning skills." He poked the squire again, but from the other side.

"I have gathered new words that have cured the numbness of my tongue. I can make my will known." Geoffrey flipped his hand over his head. "And I warned you not to be troublesome. One more time and you will be eating that parchment of yours."

"Ours."

"Yes, ours. It is I who makes this wretched company, although I will grant that a true company is made up of more than one man, or two, as it is now."

"You are provoking a quarrel, good squire, and we have long hours ahead of us, so I will not joust."

"Very well. Then we shall ride in silence."

As they rounded a bend, the landscape opened to reveal the village commons dotted with sheep and groups of children.

"What are the little beggars doing there?" Jean said. "Had we the time, I would give each of them a sound beating for all their taunts and jibes." Jean scanned the commons for anything that might provide Saint George with some discreet sustenance.

When a few of the children caught his gaze, they called out to their companions and suddenly the tranquil rustic scene transformed into a flurry of activity. Some ran to the stone wall that defined the commons while others scrambled for a stack of sticks set in the middle of the field, but all came away with a prize.

Jean looked on with growing concern as the children, some two dozen in all, approached the road in a single wave. He became genuinely alarmed when they raised their arms to brandish a crude wooden sword, crooked spear or stick trailing a shiny object on a string.

"Oh, bloody hell," Jean mumbled. "Geoff! Hey, Geoff! Be lively. Let us put old Saint George through his paces for a mile."

"What? I see no reason for that." Geoffrey, who until now had scarcely noticed the children or the sheep, turned his head and caught sight of the advancing band. "Jean, ask the urchins how far the next shrine is."

"I think not," Jean said. "They are a tiresome lot."

"Go on and talk to them; they are your companions."

"I do not befriend children, Geoff. They probably want to rob us, now that we are no longer guests of the *signore*." Jean threw an angry glance at the boys and girls, who were almost upon them.

"We have nothing, so what is the bother? We do not owe them anything, and if we did let their parents collect it. And besides, why are they not at home, weaving cloth or pressing olives or doing some such task as suits their stations? Such a permissive land this is."

As the children swarmed to block the road, several of them began to call out in sing-song voices.

"We want to join the English Free Company!" one boy shouted.

"Let us come with you," a girl yelled. "We want to serve a brave and bold knight, such as you!" She spun one of the mysterious shiny objects over her head. Others imitated her, and between bursts of laughter they issued pleas for them to be taken away.

The juvenile parade moved ahead and alongside Geoffrey and Jean, dancing and twirling and waving their arms.

"Are they mocking us?" Geoffrey asked.

"So it would seem, the little bastards," Jean said through his teeth. He lashed out, but he was too slow, grabbing only air. Then, feigning another attempt to his left, he quickly shifted to his right and caught hold of one of the shiny objects.

"Ow! I should have worn my gloves," Jean said. He steadied himself and opened his hand.

"Well, what have you?" Geoffrey demanded.

"A rowel." Jean frowned.

"A what? You mean from a spur?" Geoffrey accepted the object from Jean. He flipped it through his fingers several times as he scrutinized it. "So it is. It is old and rusty, but it is a rowel just the same." He looked carefully at the children for the first time and frowned. "They all have rowels. Ask them their meaning."

"You can speak to them just as well as I can, if your boast is true." Jean poked Geoffrey in the side. "They seem to know you well. What stories were you spinning in the village chapel during your bouts of devotion? I think I can guess."

"Had you ever come with me more than once, you would know, but nothing I said was for your ears anyway." He tucked the rowel into his belt.

"You were praying to be made a knight, were you not? I saw you secret that *couteau* of yours out of the hut on more than one occasion. You should have prayed for the deliverance of silver."

"I prayed for many things. I might have had the honor of knighthood by now had I not become stranded. My spurs are waiting in Avignon."

Jean made a derisive snort, leaned back and looked at the sky. The Lord had granted them mercy by giving full force to the sun, for warmth and light. Perhaps he should have paid more attention to his Christian duties, but attending the squire was service enough for him, Jean reckoned, and penance, and it looked as though he had at least a few more weeks of *that* honor.

"Give Saint George a rest for a moment," Jean said. "I will dismount and beat away this mongrel horde." He reached for his sword.

"Why should you do that? They are only children, for Jesus' sake!" Nonetheless, Geoffrey reined in the palfrey and turned to Jean. "So?"

"So?"

Geoffrey sighed. "Very well. Put away that knife and I will deal with them."

"Do you worst!" Jean slid his sword back into his satchel, leaned back and folded his arms.

Geoffrey stood up in the saddle. "Fine lords and ladies! I am humbled by your affections and attentions. However, should you agree to enroll in my company, know that I offer you only riches in blood, a wealth of pain, and a treasure trove of anguish as the English Free Company fulfills its chivalrous destiny to hack and slash and chop from the world those demonic companies founded by the fiend himself! You will hear no jangle or jape! Do not expect any mirth and minstrelsy!" Geoffrey placed his hands on his hips and deepened his voice to suggest menace. "So, devoted lads and lasses, to those who are with me, lead me to the next sanctuary!"

A great "Huzzah!" went up and they did as they were told.

Geoffrey turned to Jean and smiled.

Via Francigena

The children accompanied the English Free Company and its one horse as far as the first shrine after their village, whereupon Geoffrey thanked them for the escort and told them to go home. The shrine itself was little more than a wooden box with a shelter attached to it, but it was clean and the nuns who patronized the tiny hospice had recently left some bread and dried fruits for wayfarers.

By the time Geoffrey and Jean reached the next shrine, which was not unlike the first, dusk arrived, so they were obliged to spend the night. Both men were disappointed not to have met pilgrims of any rank at either stop, but their spirits remained high as they dined on plain fare. Shortly after dawn Geoffrey and Jean made their devotions and continued their journey.

"That was quite the confraternity you gathered yesterday," Jean said. Again, he occupied the rear position on Saint George. The air was deathly still and snow glittered all around. The freezing cold pierced Jean's lower shoulder, forcing him to spend a quarter of an hour massaging out the stiffness.

"What do you mean?" Geoffrey asked.

"Those urchins who were following us yesterday, of course. Do not tell me you have forgotten them already. You got along with them better than I ever did."

"Oh, I suppose," Geoffrey said laconically.

"I know that when my companions and I ever tormented the lord of the manor, we were well beaten."

"I am not a lord."

"Well, all the same, you are dressed as one."

"I am a man of Gaunt; I have no need to beat village children, nor should I. It would be undignified. After all, if I cannot command a harmless band of ragamuffins to do my bidding, then what good will I be as a knight? Even you must realize that."

"I realize a lot more than you might think, squire, although what you should have done with those children was not befriend them, but rather set them up with a game and taken all their pennies, and their rowels. Well, I suppose you are fated for greater things."

Geoffrey fell silent. He stared at the pale road that wound into the mountains and shivered.

Geoffrey did not want to believe in Fate. From his first day of training as a squire in the halls of Gaunt all he would hear was how a man had to make himself. Spurs were earned by satisfying the knightly virtues, by deeds of arms, and by service to one's lord. A man could not wait for great events to happen to him. However, there must be some meaning in all this, he thought, and he absentmindedly waved a hand in front of him. The Lord must be leaving signs for him; he only had to learn to read them, especially those signs that would lead him to a knighthood. Nothing else mattered. No, that was not true, Geoffrey thought, and he shook his head in disgust. He had a duty to the Lord, of course, and he had a duty to his friends and family. Well, to his friends at least. Geoffrey had no blood family. He was a foundling, adopted by the Duke of Lancaster, John of Gaunt, and raised in his hall in Avignon. There was meaning in all that had befallen him, Geoffrey reckoned, but it could not be an expression of Fate.

So, what of this former debt collector jabbering behind him? He is a rogue and a bastard, to be sure, a liar and a deceiver. He has no place or status, and he is unskilled as a man-at-arms. Even his language is not dependable, being a mash of southern French dialects. Jean Lagoustine might not even be his true name. Nevertheless, Geoffrey could never forget how he had saved his life on that desperate night in Avignon, when he and his closest companion Roger Swynford were set upon by a band of drunken ruffians. The debt of gratitude had since been paid, in silver, no less, with the aid of some games of chance. Also, the Frenchman was to blame for the English Free Company, which he had founded in Geoffrey's name as an unwelcome concession to the strange system of condottieri they had encountered in Italy. He wanted to join the company of a knight, not captain a band of men-at-arms. He would leave both behind at Florence, Geoffrey decided. Still, it was nice to have a companion on the road.

Geoffrey clenched his fist around the reins and grimaced. Those games of chance, he wondered. Hazard, naipes, quek, and a host of others he had mastered. He was scarcely twenty years of age, or nineteen, yet he had spent as many nights wagering as he had in prayer. When was the last time he played for real stakes? Geoffrey squinted at the highest peak and prodded his memory. The game had involved dice – Hazard, probably, since it was his favorite game of chance and he had introduced the Avignon version at Orte. He recalled that the citizens there were preparing for

All Saints' Day, so his final cast of the year 1394 must have been made on November 1. He and Jean had left for Umbertide a short time thereafter.

"...and I could have taken those dice with me," Geoffrey heard when he brought himself out of his reverie, "but I was distracted by a company of mummers, and then the players packed up their gear and went to the feast, but I still had to collect the few pennies that were left on the table..."

"Enough! I want no reminders of our most recent idleness. If you must talk, then choose a matter more suited to our sojourn, like the life of a saint, or a pilgrimage." If no opportunity to wager would present itself, Geoffrey was in no mood to hear about games of chance.

It was Jean's turn to grow silent. After adjusting his lower shoulder, he said, "So, you want to exchange tales, then, do you? To that I can agree. I must warn you, though, that you will not hear a word about a saint from me. I heard enough of them in my day, and they all sound the same, as far as I remember, and I cannot say that I remember much. Our village had a patron saint, like all others, and..."

Geoffrey threw his hand back and caught Jean on his injured shoulder. "I do not want to hear *your* life. Listen: I will go first, and meanwhile you come up with a genuine tale. Agreed?"

"Ow! Bastard! Very well, but yours had better keep me awake."

Geoffrey knew a great many stories and songs; he and his Blue confraternity (the color represented the field of his master's coat-of-arms and fidelity) would perform them often. A saint's life was out. He felt that a romance would not be in keeping with the solemnity of their journey. And while a *fabliau* would be much to his companion's liking, he could not recite such ribald verse without musical accompaniment, since he found the words get tangled up without it.

"Well, come on, then," Jean said. "The crows make more melody than you."

"Give me a moment, or I will start chanting psalms to put you to sleep."

Jean laughed and slapped his thigh. "You find the riding that enjoyable, do you?"

"I did not mean it that way, you oaf. You want that I should make you walk, in the snow and ice?"

"Geoff, Geoff, Geoff! Oh, by the glory of Saint Mary's blessed womb, I have not laughed this hard in months! Ow, my shoulder!"

"I am ready with my tale now, and I will begin when you are set. I can wait."

Jean alternated chuckling with wincing. "Carry on, my lord, or should I say good Sir John."

"Say what you like, as long as you know your place. I was thinking of reciting one of the lays of the Holy Grail, the adventures of Percival, or Galahad, or Gawain. I am quite fond of Gawain."

"I am surprised. I would have thought that you reserve your greatest love for Galahad, or Lancelot."

"You know these tales, then?" Geoffrey asked. He did not believe such stuff was village fare.

"I have heard them," Jean answered with casual indifference. "I quite like the one about the tryst between Lancelot and Guinevere, and the one about Bors and Guinevere, and Lionel and Guinevere…"

"What, what, what? No, there is only one such lay that has at its heart the tragic infidelity of Guinevere, and no others."

"Have you not heard these other songs, then? Ribald is not the word."

Geoffrey was quiet for a moment then mumbled, "Yes, I have heard them. You've put me off now."

"Sing whatever you want. Where will I go, should your voice burn my ears? Choose a song close to your heart."

Any interest in King Arthur or Holy Grail quests fled Geoffrey in haste. Nonetheless, for the sake of raising his own spirits, he wanted to tell of something chivalrous, something that would sharpen his focus on his own ambition of becoming a knight. Looking around him once more, Geoffrey was again struck by the great distance between him and his place in the halls of Gaunt.

"I have it," Geoffrey announced.

"Very good. Now, let *me* have it," Jean said.

"Now it is you, who has exposed himself to ridicule."

"What? Oh yes, that was careless of me. Well, now we are even. Carry on."

"I will speak about that most majestic of kings, Richard the Lionheart, and how he won over the king of the infidels in the Holy Land." Geoffrey inhaled and straightened his posture.

"I am listening."

Geoffrey coughed into his hand and sniffled. "Good King Richard of blessed memory was a man of noble and pious heart, and he was given by our Lord the sacred commission of freeing Jerusalem and the Holy Land from the Saracens, who by deceit and cunning had overthrown the Christian masters to create a dark dominium there." Geoffrey's voice was slow and pronounced.

33

"Sounds good. Continue," Jean said.

"I shall. Pass the skin."

After taking a long draught of water, Geoffrey continued with a list of crimes committed by the Saracens against Christian pilgrims, their desecration of churches and their accumulation of relics for the sake of depriving the faithful from venerating those sacred objects. The longer the list grew, the more emotion crept into the young squire's voice, and the litany of horrors became more terrible, until after nearly an hour of florid introduction, Jean poked his companion in the side and said, "A very nice start indeed, Geoff, but I have yet to hear a word about the mighty Richard, your lord and sovereign. Let us get to it, shall we?"

Geoffrey abruptly turned and stared at Jean, who flinched and clutched his bad shoulder. But the squire's countenance softened, as though he was only just recognizing him.

"I am there," Geoffrey said. He proceeded with a brief history of Richard's reign before getting on with the campaign itself, about his journey to protect his sister, about the travails he encountered during the final passage to the Holy Land, about his capture of Cyprus, and about feats of arms performed.

"How many times had great King Richard suffered in the baking prisons of the Saracen invaders for the sake of his men, his religion, his queen, suffering in which he found the strength to break his fetters and smash the thick walls that enclosed him? He had killed a thousand heathens on his way to Jerusalem to reclaim the Holy Land when no other king could, and only returned to England when his pledge was fulfilled. However, of all the feats the pious King Richard performed, the most famous was not that of arms, but a deed of valor, when the King of England made Saladin, the great captain of the Saracens, a knight.

King Richard had Saladin bathed to recall the washing away of sin through baptism and then, as though his father, ordered that he be dressed in a white robe to show the cleanliness of the body, a scarlet cloak to remind him of his duty to shed blood in defence of the Church and brown chausses to mean the earth in which he would one day lie. Then came the knighting ceremony itself, with King Richard placing on Saladin golden spurs to show that a knight must be as swift as a charger to follow the Lord's commandments and girding him with a sword, whose two sharp edges were to remind him that the knightly virtues of justice and loyalty must go together. They were to fight, as it was their duty, and to this Saladin replied that he was sure of this. As it was told, so did it happen."

Geoffrey bowed his head and slackened his posture.

"Very nice," Jean said. "That tale is new to me."

The rising sound of rushing water distracted the riders, and they soon came upon several village women collecting water in leather pails from a gap in the ice on the Tiber River.

"Saint George is slowing," Geoffrey said. "We should rest a while. The next shrine should not be far, I expect." The day was well past noon.

Jean slid off the horse and stumbled a few yards towards the river before finding his footing. "I will water Saint George and you can go into that wood over there and forage, or maybe catch us a hare for dinner. And then I will tell you my tale."

"I have neither bow nor arrow, and besides, that would be poaching. Ask those women who is the lord of this wood and if any pilgrims have passed recently."

"I am not asking you to slay a hart or a wild boar; that would be poaching. Listen, just scout around while I talk to these women. What say you?"

"I am keen to stretch my legs anyway." Geoffrey dismounted and began skirting the wood, looking for a way in. The snow was not deep, as the boughs carried most of it overhead, but the light was dim, so he trod carefully and kept the road within view.

Foraging was a part of squire training, and his search reminded him of how he and the Blues would compete with rival bands of squires on their outings to collect wild berries and mushrooms, make fires, trap game, and perform a host of other contests. The Blues won their fair share, and he had knelt before his lordship several times to receive a prize from his hand.

About a few dozen paces in, Geoffrey saw purple clumps of frozen berries hanging from bare branches. Jean could boil them up and, if he could get a few cloves from those women by the river, they could brew a nice concoction. God does provide, Geoffrey thought.

The sharp snap of a twig caused the squire to hold still and his hand to grab the pommel of his sword. Without moving his head, he scanned the depths of the wood until to his left he spotted the twitching nose of a hare. The creature did not appear to notice the intruder, and casually hopped deeper into the wood, halted for a moment, then continued onwards.

Geoffrey relaxed. He quickly pinched off a few bunches of berries and followed the hare to see if it would lead him to more.

The creature remained oblivious to the foreign presence, which allowed Geoffrey to easily track him. After about a hundred yards, however, the hare perked up its ears, stood on its hind legs, and sped away like lightning. Geoffrey was surprised, but it was not long before he learned the source of the animal's fear. Voices. He trudged a few dozen steps until he reached the edge of a clearing. Geoffrey ducked behind some bramble when he his eyes fell on a band of armed men, all with swords drawn, confronting a group of unarmed men in penitent tunics.

"Banditry!" Geoffrey whispered. After dropping the berries in the snow, he carefully withdrew from his cover and scampered through the wood until he reached Jean and Saint George.

CHAPTER 3

"The women told me that the next shrine is just passed the wood," Jean said as Geoffrey ran up to him. "They were shy at first, being from the village and all, but I charmed the words out of them. They even said —"

Geoffrey grabbed the sleeve of Jean's jupon and pulled him behind the palfrey. "Brigands!" Geoffrey breathed into his companion's face. "Or bandits. Maybe *routiers*. Heavily armed. Come! We must save them!" Geoffrey again yanked Jean's sleeve, hoping to drag him towards the road, but while the squire was tall, lean and trained to fight, the Frenchman was stout and better anchored to the earth, so he dug in his heels and stood his ground.

"What you on about, Geoff?" Jean slapped away the offending hand and straightened his jupon. "And I see you have returned empty-handed."

Geoffrey composed himself. "I saw a band of armed men threatening some fellow travelers in the wood, pilgrims, by the look of it."

"What are travelers doing in the wood, pilgrims or otherwise, let alone at this time of year? Armed men? They might be foresters, for all you know. Did you speak with them?"

Geoffrey shook his head to loosen his thoughts. "No, no. *I* was in the wood, and I came upon a clearing. They did not see me, but I saw four or five men in full harness with swords drawn. I was deaf to their words, but against them was arrayed a company of pilgrims, judging by their white tunics, and they carry nothing that resemble arms."

"The women mentioned a group of pilgrims, which is good for us, but nothing about brigands prowling around these parts, and I did ask them directly." Jean looked sternly at the squire and clamped a hand on his shoulder, as much to hold his attention as to keep him at bay.

"They might be afraid, they might not know..." Geoffrey shrugged. "All the same, pilgrims are being attacked. My eyes did not deceive. I know a man-at-arms when I see one. We cannot stand aside!"

Jean frowned and pursed his lips. He rubbed his bristly chin while breathing hard. "You say there are four heavily armed men out there?"

"Yes. No, five."

"Are you sure?"

"On my oath. Now, get your sword!"

"We are far too outnumbered to make such a rash venture. Let us have a peek first. Then we will know if we will be killed or not."

"True, but we cannot shrink from a fight, certainly not one that has right on our side. We will retrace my steps and take them by surprise. The pilgrims will support us." Geoffrey felt his blood race and his temples pounded.

"Perhaps, but the snow and ice…"

"We fought together against greater odds. You remember it well, since it was you who joined the fight without asking. You excel at stealth and surprise."

"Yes, but they were piss drunk, it was dark and I knew the territory." Jean well remembered how, against his better judgment, he had entered the fray in Avignon on the side of the two squires against some drunken louts. He also remembered the fatal blow that struck Geoffrey's friend Roger Swynford.

"You are going into the wood with me." Geoffrey drew Jean's short sword from the satchel and slammed it against his chest.

"Oof!" Jean stumbled a few steps backwards. "All right, but we cannot rush in and reveal ourselves. Be quiet and careful."

Geoffrey's longer legs carried him to the wood well ahead of his companion, but Jean was able to catch up as the squire slowed to track himself back to the clearing.

"They are just over there," Geoffrey whispered.

Jean strained his ears and eventually found voices in the distance. He followed closely behind Geoffrey until they reached some scattered berries at the foot of a bramble. The scene had changed, but not by much. The armed band was now standing together before the pilgrims, while a man who appeared to lead them was holding a wooden casket and talking. The men-at-arms were holding their swords out and pointed upward.

"By the Lord's grace, we are not too late!" Geoffrey whispered. "If we set upon them now, we will put down two each and divide the fifth between us!"

Jean examined the scene. "Those men are *very* well armed and harnessed for common brigandage, and look – they have servants." Jean pointed at the horses gathered on the far side of the clearing, where several boys in respectable livery were attending steeds.

"What are you saying? That we should steal their horses and be away? I scarcely think we need to approach from another angle, if that is what you mean."

"Let me listen." Jean strained his ears again, but the voices were still muffled by distance. "Damn! We must be sure about this." He carefully shifted himself so that he could better scrutinize the horses. "I do not see any crossbows, and the two hunting bows I see are unstrung, so we should be safe from those lads at least," Jean mused sulkily.

"I missed the opportunity to cross blades the last time I was in a pass of arms; I will not lose this one!" Geoffrey's voice was terse and anxious.

"You did your deed of arms and was recognized for it. What is this lust for blood? Forget the dream, already."

"You *will* follow me. I outrank you." His body was bursting with wrath.

The squire was right, but not for the reason he assumed. Jean's own survival rested on his ability to keep the man of Gaunt alive, at least until they reached Florence, or perhaps longer. "We should have shields for this," he sighed.

Geoffrey was about to answer when they saw the apparent captain of the band sheathe his sword, move towards the pilgrim leader and reach for the casket. Serious looks crossed all faces.

"This is the moment, Jean! Let us have at them!"

Jean grabbed Geoffrey's arm. "Who gets who?"

"Listen: I will take the right flank and you take the left flank. That should push them together as we set upon them like lightning. We will carve them up as one body."

"But I have nothing but a worn jupon as my harness, which is little defense against the bluntest of swords. Perhaps we should steal some armor from them first." Jean was desperate to find a peaceful and preferably invisible way out of the wood.

"Do not be daft! Listen, surprise will be your harness. Had you a harness in Avignon? You did not. They will be at our mercy before they can set themselves to strike. Look now, how the old man must hand over his silver! That disarms their leader. We go!" Geoffrey kissed his *couteau* thrice before leaping to his feet and crashing through the bramble.

Jean had no choice but to follow through with the squire's plan, but instead of slowing himself by breaking branches, he went around his hiding place and closed from the left flank.

"Yield, knaves!" Geoffrey yelled, "or be cut down without mercy!" He was gripping the hilt with both hands and running with sword set in middle guard – at the hip with point up – so that he might easily pass into an offensive guard.

The armed band immediately backed itself into a defensive circle, while the captain placed himself and the casket he was holding in its center. "Bandits!" he cried.

The moment he was within striking distance of the closest man, Geoffrey cut upwards and knocked the man's sword out of position before turning and passing to strike his neighbor's blade at its middle. The first man, who was struggling to reset himself, ducked as Geoffrey cut crosswise with the intention of drawing blood. The scrape of steel echoed around the glade.

Jean engaged the other two men, but he set himself firmly in a defensive stance so that he would not be easily outflanked, slashed or pierced. He was content to let the squire draw first blood.

"You will pay for robbing pilgrims!" Geoffrey threatened as he struck downwards against his still unsteady first opponent, this time knocking the sword clean out of his hand. "By me now and the Lord thereafter!"

The second man saw an opening to stab Geoffrey, but he was slow, as his hand still stung from the initial blow against his sword, and so he merely scraped Geoffrey's hauberk.

"*You* are the *routier*!" the band's captain shouted. "Yield or be killed!"

Seeing how easily his companions had been discomfited by the tall swordsman, one of the two men confronting Jean passed to attack Geoffrey. Jean and his single opponent, meanwhile, were left to eye one another warily without crossing blades.

"I see only thieves, preying on the weak and defenseless!" Geoffrey yelled back.

The band's captain frowned. "From what land are you, brigand?"

Geoffrey did not answer, for the new man tried to engage the squire in order to give his defenseless companion a chance to retrieve his sword.

Geoffrey nimbly retreated and kicked the weapon towards the old man, who was standing agape no more than a dozen paces away.

"Grab it!" he shouted, hoping that he would give the sword to one of the younger pilgrims.

Instead, the old man placed his foot on the free sword so that none would have it.

"All of you, drop your arms!" he ordered in a voice that was accustomed to giving commands.

"*He* is the intruder!" the captain shouted. "Let him yield!" He released the casket and unsheathed his sword.

Geoffrey, seeing he was about to face the prospect of fighting three swords, decided to dispense with one of them right away. He lunged at the new man, who had overreached in his effort to cover his disarmed companion, bound their blades, and with the leverage afforded by his great height forced the man to stagger and fall backwards. The second man reaffirmed his grip on his sword and brought down an oblique strike against Geoffrey's left arm, but the blow only left scratches on the chainmail and a bruise underneath. However, the blow did put Geoffrey off his stance, and he prudently retreated a step to reset himself.

"Stop, stop!" the old man cried as he waved his arms above his head. "We shall not have the spilling of blood here!" He looked directly at the captain. "I will dock you, should it come to that!"

"Geoff, listen!" Jean shouted. "Declare yourself! Quickly"

The captain looked at the old man angrily, but nodded his assent. "Disengage!" he shouted. "Rally to me!" He stood over the casket, now lying half buried in the snow.

The band did as ordered, leaving Geoffrey and Jean to stand alone.

"Who are you and why do you attack my escort?" the old man demanded.

Geoffrey stared at him, but said nothing.

Jean, seeing the squire's confusion, quickly declared, "We are the English Free Company. We, too, are on the pilgrim's way north."

"That only means you are certainly bandits," the captain said. "*You* yield and I might consider sparing your lives."

Jean glanced at the tree line and then at the boys minding the horses. He would have a strong chance of making the wood before anyone was upon him, especially now that command of the armed band was split between the captain and the pilgrim leader.

"We are not bandits," Geoffrey announced at last, seeing that no one was about to either attack or defend him. "As a man of his grace the Duke of Lancaster, I cannot be."

"Lancaster?! Do not make me laugh," the captain said. "The English were driven from these lands years ago." The captain spat on the ground. "What is your name, boy?"

"Geoffrey Hotspur!"

41

"That is it?"

"That is enough."

"Throw out your seal, Geoff!" Jean yelled.

Geoffrey glanced at Jean. After a moment's hesitation, he delved into his pourpoint and cast out the brass disc at the foot of the pilgrim leader.

The air was deathly still as the old man closely examined the seal.

"Looks genuine," the pilgrim leader pronounced at last.

"Could have been stolen. Gaunt could have sent spies here," the captain said.

"He is also a condottiere," Jean said, pointing at Geoffrey.

"So am I!" the captain rebutted. His companions laughed.

"He was given a *condotta*. We fought at the battle near Orte last year. His name is on it!"

The laughter petered out. The captain and the pilgrim leader exchanged looks.

"And where is this *condotta*?" the pilgrim leader asked.

"With our horse," Jean quickly answered. "Not far."

"That is a different matter altogether," the captain said. "Bring me your *condotta*, if it indeed exists, and then we can talk. Crivelli! Seeing as you are now useless without arms, go with him."

The man who had lost his sword to Geoffrey acknowledged the order with a nod and escorted Jean out of the glade.

"You may sheathe your sword, young man," the pilgrim leader said. "Captain dell'Ischia is in my pay, so he will do as I say."

"The hell I will!" Ischia said. "If I need run him through, then run him through I will! Never let your guard down with an Englishman, condottiere or not."

"My sword remains at the ready," Geoffrey declared. "Who are you, then, if not a load of maggoty brigands?"

"You are not in a position to ask, but I will tell you anyway. We are the Company of the Rose, and I am Captain Giovanni dell'Ischia." The man straightened his posture and looked haughty. "Remember that name, should you live another day."

Although he was well hidden beneath a dark blue surcoat, graying beard and salet helm, Geoffrey could see that the captain was of middling age with a pale complexion, long face, and eyes of great intensity.

"I am Count Robert d'Ivry, magistrate of his majesty King James of Cyprus," the pilgrim leader said. "You are a man of the great duke, you say, yet how is it you prowl about an Italian wood?"

Geoffrey was surprised and for a moment suspicious of the claim, but since no one in either group spoke a word to deny the claim, Geoffrey was inclined to believe in its veracity.

"I am most honored, your lordship." Geoffrey wanted to bow to the high-ranking noble, but he could not let the captain out of his sight. "I am journeying home. His grace awaits me."

Count Robert stepped forward. "You are headed in the right direction, at least. Tell me, young squire, what made you think I was being robbed?"

"He had you at sword point and he snatched your silver."

Count Robert laughed. "You are mistaken. I was inspecting their arms, as I do every morning. I must be diligent with the men under me."

"And the casket?"

"It is a reliquary holding several relics that I purchased on my pilgrimage. I have all members of my company kiss it during the muster of arms."

Geoffrey thought this plausible, but all the same he held his sword in low guard.

Jean and Crivelli returned. Saint George trailed close behind them.

"I-I have confirmed it," Crivelli said as he approached his captain. He was a slight man with plain features and jerky movements for a man-at-arms. "It is a ghost *condotta*, b-but a *condotta* nonetheless, w-well written and with proper seals. We have been attacked b-by Geoffrey Hotspur, squire in the h-hall of the D-Duke of Lancaster and c-captain of the English Free Company." Geoffrey and Jean gave the Italian a curious look.

"A ghost *condotta*?" Ischia sneered. He glanced at the document, which Crivelli was holding aloft. "No money, no share in the spoils, not even a knight of the esteemed duke? How sad!" He laughed derisively before turning back to Geoffrey. "Very well, you are plainly harmless, so you may go. You have no business here." He sheathed his sword. The others did likewise.

Geoffrey's face burned red and he held his sword tighter, but after seeing that the count was not about the share in the ridicule, Geoffrey too sheathed his blade.

"Well, now that we have that bit of nasty business settled," Jean said as he took back his company's only document, however 'sad', "perhaps we should start some other. For the sake of peace between our respected companies, let us dine together."

"You call two men a company?" Ischia asked, sarcasm lacing his voice.

"And you call five men the same?" Jean retorted.

"You only saw the lance heads. The others are at the hospice nearby. Besides, I

43

have three decades worth of fighting experience under my belt, from one end of Italy to the other," Ischia boasted.

Count Robert stepped between the arguing parties and held out his hands. "*I* invite all who stand on this field to share my table. Such needless squabbling catches the ear of Misfortune, and I wish to keep her far from me."

Jean and Ischia bowed to the old man and withdrew to their respective companies.

"How is it that you travel in winter on this mountainous way, your lordship" Geoffrey asked Count Robert. They were walking side by side out of the glade. The Company of the Rose was ahead with their horses while Jean was behind talking with the other pilgrims.

"We have been traveling the Way to Rome, Perugia, Assisi, and many places in between. We started on the Via Francigena last September, hoping to reach Ravenna before the heavy snow set in, when I became ill and had to stop. We could not wait until spring before setting out again, since I am needed by my king."

Although Count Robert walked with the proud bearing of a knight, he was almost a head shorter than Geoffrey and had a lion's mane of gray hair streaked with black and an equally thick beard that hid a small but square jaw. A series of deep scars lined the left side of his face, which were made all the more prominent by his deeply set eyes. They reminded Geoffrey of the duke.

"My situation is not dissimilar. I too suffered a late start on my journey to Florence. I have a commission there on behalf of my lord and his majesty King Richard." The word 'commission' ignited a pang of anxiety in Geoffrey's stomach.

"Our pilgrimage is done, may the Lord bless us. I ask you to tell me about your ventures here in Italy, and perhaps those of his lordship and your fellow squires."

Geoffrey was elated. "I vow to give a full account, your lordship."

Ivry smiled. When the hospice was in view, Count Robert said, "My servants should have everything prepared by now."

What passed for the great hall of the hospice was filled with men-at-arms and pilgrims crammed on benches around a long table. A small hearth at the back was giving off as much smoke as heat, leaving the room overcast, but the air was clear enough for Geoffrey to see the impressive spread of meats, pies, pottage, and wine.

"Come, sit between me and Captain dell'Ischia. A man of Gaunt cannot be left to stand and starve," Count Robert said. He sat down and bid Ischia to shift over a little.

The captain of the Company of the Rose said nothing, but he looked grim and kept his eyes firmly on the English squire.

Geoffrey removed his cloak and sword, handed them to Jean, who was not surprised to receive them, and took his place. A servant set a bowl and spoon in front of him while another handed him a wooden cup filled with red wine. Jean, meanwhile, found a seat next to Crivelli and within earshot of his lordship.

"Take some bread and raise your cup," Count Robert told Geoffrey, "and let us toast to a safe and fulfilling journey. May the Lord protect us!"

"And we you," Ischia interjected.

"Yes, of course," Count Robert said. "Captain dell'Ischia has been telling us of recent events in Italy, but I must confess that I have been in this land for so long that scarcely any of it is new to my ears. What I want to hear, and doubtless the rest of my company does as well, is the deeds of the great Gaunt, as you promised, about his hall in Avignon, and about your own deeds of arms. You fought at Orte last September, I gather."

Geoffrey nodded at Count Robert and saw that all eyes were on him. "I would like to start by thanking you, your lordship, for allowing me to share your table," he began in the loud voice he used when addressing the Blues. "It is a blessing that our paths have crossed, although I again apologize to you and the esteemed Captain dell'Ischia for our…er…misunderstanding earlier."

Laughter rippled around the hall. Ivry slapped Geoffrey on the back and said that so long as no blood was spilled, they were all the wiser for it.

Geoffrey smiled and looked around the table. The pilgrims appeared to be not much younger than their leader, but the men-at-arms were of varying ages, some no older than the squire. They seemed to be the most eager to hear his stories.

"Please continue, squire," Ivry said.

Geoffrey smiled and began to list the virtues of the Duke of Lancaster, as custom dictated, and followed this with a description of his lordship's palace in Avignon. He talked about the great hall with its magnificent hearth and tables that could seat hundreds, the training hall for squires and the magnificent chapels. He came close to mentioning the recent campaigns conducted by his lord and master, but as the words rose in his throat his conscience reminded him that he would be betraying a confidence thusly, so instead he related stories about himself and his fellow squires, his late friend Roger Swynford, and his confraternity the Blues.

The longer he spoke, the stronger his voice grew, so that after an hour Geoffrey felt more confident and comfortable in this new company. No one interrupted him, not Captain dell'Ischia or the host, although from time to time it looked as though

Jean was about to interject. However, the Frenchman more often was holding his own whispered conversations with his neighbors. A familiar warmth encircled the squire's heart, and in spite of his excited words, Geoffrey was relaxed.

The evening reminded him of the few times he had the honor of dining with his lord and patron, the mighty Duke of Lancaster. His lordship always had Geoffrey seated near him, despite his lowly status, for the two of them shared a bond other than lord and squire. Geoffrey owed his very existence to the great man, for it was he who found the orphan Geoffrey, scarcely more than a newborn and screaming himself blue in the rain, on the bank of an overflowing river while on campaign in Normandy. As one of England's most powerful barons was saving the life of a nameless babe, that babe saved the English host, for it was the lure of those frightful screams that allowed the duke to see how a band of French sappers was about to flood his camp and ruin his army.

"You are quite the hearty fellow," Ivry said after Geoffrey finished an account of his winning a contest for swordsmanship. "Eat before my servants clear the table. I cannot let a man go hungry, and with your height I dare say you must be ravenous." Count Robert pushed a bowl full of pottage at Geoffrey, who nodded respectfully at this honor and picked up his spoon. "Now, I invite you join me. We can ride together until our fates diverge, or you may accompany me to Ravenna."

Ischia frowned. "My company is armed well enough to protect you, your lordship," he said. "I need not enroll any more men, and certainly not some English squire."

"Can you be so certain of that, captain?" Ivry said with a smile. "The young English squire proved himself today. Regardless, I see no harm in our traveling together."

"As you wish, your lordship," Ischia said and he seemed to pull a face beneath his beard. "Are there any more of you lot out there?" he asked Geoffrey.

"None that I know about. They should have all left by now," Geoffrey said, avoiding reference to the royal commission.

"And at Orte? I heard Bretons and Germans fought there. Were many killed?"

Geoffrey wanted to give Sergeant Godwin's name as one of the many who fell on that field last year, but hearing the sudden anger that entered the captain's voice whenever he spoke about English men-at-arms, or Breton and German, for that matter, Geoffrey held his tongue.

"Both sides suffered losses," Geoffrey said, "but I did not set myself to reckon the numbers." He shrugged. "All the same, the pass did not bloody too many arms."

"We will hear about that battle another time," Ivry declared. "The wounds are still fresh from it, I fear."

Geoffrey swallowed and turned to meet the eyes of the count. "I thank you for the offer, but my commission beckons, and therein lies my duty above all, so I must to Florence."

Ivry nodded. He took a sip of wine, stroked his beard a few times and set down the cup. "You sound true of tongue, good squire. I myself have a stable of lusty squires anxious to serve me or one of my vassals, and they are every bit as brash and brusque as you." He coughed into his hand. "Should our paths cross again, I would not reject your company."

Geoffrey wondered what it would be like to serve a man like Count Robert so close to the Holy Land.

Taking advantage of a gap in the conversation, Jean looked at Ivry. "My new friend here," he said and gestured at Crivelli, "tells me that you met the Company of the Rose only in Assisi, your lordship. Had you not an armed escort before then?"

Count Robert paused before answering. "I arrived on these shores as a simple pilgrim, not as a man of exalted rank, but at Assisi thieves broke into my lodgings. Soon, the whole city knew who I was, and so I was obliged to hire Captain dell'Ischia for protection. Men of the Romagna are the toughest, they say." He nodded at Ischia and raised his cup.

"Now that we are entering the Romagna, as I am told," Jean continued, "perhaps a stronger escort is needed, at least as far as Sansepolcro? The English Free Company is not currently engaged."

Count Robert stifled a laugh, though Ischia and his men did not, and he turned to Geoffrey and said, "Thank you all the same, master squire, but as good as your sword might be, two more men would only make a difference to my purse. Had you a proper company of at least a few lances, I might have had you share duties with Captain dell'Ischia."

Ischia stared hard first at Count Robert and then at Geoffrey.

"I understand," Geoffrey declared solemnly. "You company is reward enough for our shared journey." He was not pleased with Jean's crass proposal.

The supper continued for another half hour when, after complaining about weariness and lingering ill health, Count Robert and the pilgrims retired.

"You spoke fairly tonight, master squire," Ischia said. "All the same, I would have run you through and not given it another thought had his lordship not stayed my hand. I warn you not meddle any longer in Italy and take yourself with all speed back to your lord. You will find no knighthood here."

Had Geoffrey been in a less ecstatic mood, he might have felt the sting of the condottiere's insult, yet still could not let the words passed without giving a suitable retort.

"My path to knighthood begins wherever I can perform a deed of arms, captain." Geoffrey looked around for Jean until he found him standing with some of the men-at-arms. "Jean! Set out the blankets!"

"You do not have a pavilion or a tent?" Ischia asked.

"Sadly, no. I will sleep in the hall. This will not cause you discomfort, I pray?"

"Not at all. I just hope you are not intending to go to sleep soon. My men wish to still enjoy the evening." Ischia smiled thinly.

"I am not the lord here. By your leave, sir."

"Excellent! Crivelli! Fetch the tables!"

Geoffrey took a sip of wine and was about to approach a senior man-at-arms when he saw Crivelli open a chequered gaming board. Geoffrey's eyes grew wide.

"Captain! Will you be wagering beneath this roof?"

Ischia nodded. "Count Robert does not approve, but he has left the manor, so to speak. Why, do you play?"

"Hazard is my game, but tables are no strangers to me."

Jean took alarm; he too saw the gaming board being laid out. He dropped the bedding and ran to Geoffrey. "You are not thinking of playing, are you? We have no silver, or copper, for that matter."

Geoffrey frowned. He wanted to maintain the mood of confraternity that had blossomed during the evening, and short of drinking or fighting together, he could not think of another way to do so than to wager. "Are you sure you do not have a few pennies hidden away somewhere? Maybe I could exchange my leg harness for some silver for a few rounds."

While Jean was trying to come up with a rebuttal, Ischia stepped in with a proposal. "No need for that, good squire," he said. "*I* will lend you a dozen florins. That is about a novice lance's wage for a month." He opened his purse and began counting coins.

"Thank you." Geoffrey said and bowed. "You are a man of honor and generosity. You do credit to his lordship. But what if I lose?"

"Oh, I trust you will find a way to repay me."

"Of course."

"Are you sure about this, Geoff?" Jean whispered. "What *will* you do if you lose?"

"Listen, my humors will not leave me in peace until I join the game. Too much time has passed since I last challenged Lady Fortuna. Besides, I am no fool at wagering – you know that. These men are new to me, so I will depress the stakes until I learn their methods. Then, I will clean up. However, should a strange thing happen and the silver runs from me, then I will send to Florence for a loan. It is a paltry sum. The royal commission still waits, remember?"

"All right. When the boards are brought in you distract Ischia while I check them for pits or angles or anything that might cause deceit."

"I trust you in this matter. So be it."

"You will be happy to learn that we play with dice, in the French manner," Ischia explained.

"We call this a quek board," Geoffrey said. "And you?"

"Cheque, quek, triquet, it is all the same."

Jean discreetly ran his hand across the surface of the board and found nothing untoward. He nodded at Geoffrey when he glanced his way.

If they indeed played in the French manner, then Geoffrey was very familiar with the rules: the caster throws a pair of dice on the board and must make the number of points they show; the players then bid on the number of pebbles he needs to make those points, with white squares scoring one point and black squares scoring nothing in the simplest variation; the caster accepts whatever bid he is confident he can satisfy, thereby setting the stakes.

"The squire may cast first," Ischia said, "as the younger captain." He passed Geoffrey the dice in a leather pouch that was not unlike the sort he commonly held in the gaming halls of Avignon.

"You are not playing?" Jean asked Ischia.

"I will join later," he said. "His lordship might yet have orders for me."

"Who will enter the lists first against this mighty champion?" Geoffrey boasted and he raised a cup of wine. The casting pouch was warm and supple and felt good in his hand.

The rank and file men-at-arms waited for their lance heads to make a move before deciding. All three except Crivelli declared their intentions to join the circle of play.

"That is all? Well, you do not know me, so I understand your caution, or is it fear? For all that is holy, we shall soon reckon rightly!" Geoffrey rattled the dice and waved the pouch over the board.

"What custom have you for first cast?" Geoffrey asked Ischia. "You are the host."

"We have none, boy, so make your cast before his lordship finds us still playing when he comes in to breakfast," Ischia declared.

Geoffrey nodded and blew into the pouch for luck. He threw a 'seven', the commonest of combinations and a middling result. The first player started the bidding at thirty stones for a penny a hit, which was little more than a jest, since thirty would easily cover seven white squares with points to spare. The second player countered with a bid of twenty stones at double the stake. The third player knocked once to say that he matched the wager while the first player knocked twice to check the bid.

"Eighteen at two-and-a-half pennies a hit," Geoffrey offered. Eighteen was twice his lucky number, and so he figured that would be a good way to start.

Each player knocked in turn.

Geoffrey looked at Ischia. "Must I pitch them all at once, or may I select my own manner of making points?" A designated counter gathered the pebbles, each of which had two flattened sides, for Geoffrey's pitch.

"However you like. We are not as fussy as the French about such details."

Geoffrey stepped back to the white chalk line made on the floor to mark the three-yard distance from the board. He pitched nine pebbles. They landed with a clatter in the middle of the board and none rolled off. Geoffrey raised his head to count his points, but the counter quickly announced, "Five!"

The pitch was a little too good, since he still had nine pebbles with which to hit two squares. An easy win might scare some players into dropping out of the circle. On his second pitch, Geoffrey twisted his wrist at the last moment so that almost half the pebbles caught the edge of the board and fell away. The counter yelled, "Two!"

The other players snorted derisively, but covered their wagers without complaint. Jean, as company treasurer, collected the thirty-five pennies.

"It is your cast again, Hotspur," Ischia declared.

"I cast until I lose, I assume."

"You know this game well."

They continued to play and the stakes remained low.

"Why do you stand back?" Jean whispered to Crivelli. "Are you not bored away from the table?"

Crivelli scratched his temple. He looked at his companions, but they ignored him.

"I-I have n-not played for a while," he said.

"Then now is the time. Go on, speech is a liability in this game, I reckon." Jean smiled and nudged Crivelli towards to circle.

Crivelli hesitated. Again he looked around, and again the only person to acknowledge him was Jean, who motioned for him to join. With an awkward gait, Crivelli went.

Geoffrey continued to dominate the game until a loss on a big wager for few points obliged him to pass the pouch. Then suddenly the stakes jumped, and jumped again, when the pouch came back to him. The men of the Company of the Rose were trying to get even, Geoffrey reckoned, or playing to ruin the new man. Regardless, he had caught on to their wagering strategies and noticed which players had trouble pitching. So, he decided to target one player in particular by making outrageous wagers against him in order to outflank this collective assault against him.

By the time Captain dell'Ischia called an end to play several hours later, a reckoning of accounts showed that the gains and losses nearly matched for all except Crivelli, who had lost twenty silver florins, sixteen of which had gone to Geoffrey, while the squire himself was down four florins in addition to the twelve Ischia had loaned him.

"Not to worry, man," Geoffrey said to Crivelli, whose face was sagging dreadfully. "You will get another chance to win it back, if that is what troubles you." He slapped the dejected Italian hard on the shoulder and called for more wine. Geoffrey then noisily counted out twelve florins and handed them to Captain dell'Ischia, who, Jean noticed, did not look pleased to receive them.

"Will he live?" Niccolo quietly asked Catherine the astrologer. His captain-general, Azzo da Castello, had been struck hard while demonstrating jousting technique at the previous day's tournament and was now lying unconscious in his bed.

"I cannot say. It is in God's hands. Best not to think about it." They were alone in the newly finished study chamber attached to his mother's lodgings. The pungent scents of freshly cut wood and lacquer permeated the small space, but it was quiet.

"Did you know this would happen? Did you read for him?" Niccolo was worrying the edges of the desk with his fingers. The captain-general had been like a father to him in the past year, or as much of a father as Niccolo could imagine.

"No, he never engaged me."

"Maybe if you had, he would not have mounted that horse."

"No one is to blame for the blow. He took the risk, but this is a common thing at tournaments." Catherine's words sounded almost dismissive, but that was because the regency council had ordered her to keep Niccolo calm after they saw how pale he became at the accident. In truth, Catherine was deeply worried that the loss of Azzo da Castello would mean the end of Niccolo as marquis, leaving her with the need to find an escape route.

"I am to blame. I told him to arrange a tournament for me." Niccolo grimaced and looked at the floor. His voice was soft and carried little emotion.

"I told you not to think about. All is in God's hands now."

"You should read for me," Niccolo said nervously. He nodded at the stack of cards perched on the corner of the table near Catherine. "I should know what might happen to me."

"I cannot do that without your mother or someone from the regency council present," Catherine replied quickly. She was sitting opposite him at an ornate oak table inlaid with a marble chessboard.

"I understand that." Niccolo paused before continuing. "At least you did not say that I am too young, or that the results might frighten me. My father's astrologer told me that once, and it always bothered me. I would prefer to know."

Catherine was relieved by these words, although not because of his resignation to her refusal. Rather she was glad he did not know that she was one of his late father's astrologers. She had only returned to the Este court last October at the request of the regency council.

"Oh, I believe man and nature offer plenty to frighten you without my hazarding your future, and the regency council gives enough guidance to set you on a proper course. And who told you that I read for your mother? Have you been playing at servant by listening at doors? For shame! Just because I am marked as an astrologer does not mean I cannot do otherwise. I am just a humble maid to your mother." Catherine caught Niccolo's eye, but he averted her gaze, even though the room was dim with the window shuttered.

"Nothing frightens me," Niccolo said curtly. He snatched his hands away from the desk and shoved them into his lap. Even though he was wearing his thickest woolen hose, fur-lined boots and his father's old mantle, he felt cold. He scanned the room and wished his mother had installed a hearth. When his eyes again fell on his companion, he wondered how she could sit so still and erect for such a long time. "I am weary of the city, and this keep. I want to go riding. I invite you to accompany me. Do you ride well?"

"Alberto Roberti and your mother told me to keep you company here, although I thank you for the invitation." Catherine fixed her hazel eyes on the boy. He would have to wait another year or two before his voice was restrung for manhood and he was only just starting to lose his baby fat, judging by the looseness of his clothes. She too was anxious to leave the study room, as well as the castle, despite its luxury. Although she was careful not to show it, Catherine was uncomfortable. She was not accustomed to the company of children.

"I do not mean at this moment, mistress astrologer. I mean after the rebellion is crushed." Niccolo paused. He felt his humors churn every time he said the word 'rebellion'. "Alberto can lead the campaign against my uncle. I know my father trusted him."

"He is the head of your regency council. I doubt that he would be able to fully devote himself to both duties."

"True. He is always either holding counsel or finding documents for me to sign. Maybe I should ask Master Donato to be my captain-general. He is a wise man and I have seen him in the saddle."

"I doubt he would accept such an honor. As wise as he is, his place is in the study hall, not on the battlefield. He can captain your learning, but that is all."

"I was jesting." Niccolo made a thin smile.

Catherine smiled back and thought about what to say next. She was not familiar with the martial qualities of the Este captains, vassals and *raccomendati*. The light seemed to grow dimmer as silence descended on them. She was not there just to keep the marquis company. At her arrival at court, Alberto Roberti instructed her to learn the boy's disposition, about his suitability to rule the lands of the Este and Ferrara. His mother, naturally, could not be fully trusted on such a matter, while his tutor could only gauge his intellect and the arms master would determine his prowess on the lists. So, they appointed her as maid to her ladyship, a station she resented but for the silver they lavished upon her. It was a sign of trust, which she appreciated, but the contract bound her to the Este court, a court that was unstable.

"You are fortunate to be blessed with so many fine captains," Catherine said.

"I am. We should have Uncle Azzo in chains before Easter." Niccolo raised a clenched fist in victory.

"You might be married by then," Catherine said and smiled. She wanted to keep him distracted from thoughts about his wounded captain-general. "You are almost of age. Perhaps then your uncle will leave you alone."

Niccolo scrunched his face. "*That* is something my regency council would be sure to tell me." Then he suddenly sat up and stared at Catherine. "You have not been forbidden to speak with me about the false claimant, I see," he said quickly. "Most others have, including my companions."

"So, that is why you attacked that boy with such ruthless abandon the other week. I understand, but it really was bad form. You started out so well." She leaned towards him and placed her hands flat on the table.

Niccolo stared at the newly revealed hands for a moment and then imitated the gesture. "You are right. It was the shock of the words, I believe, that released my fury. In truth, I remember little of my assault."

"You recovered well. That I remember. I think your arms master had mixed praise for your performance, such as it was." Catherine had indeed been impressed by how the young marquis was able to rally his companions, especially as eleven-year-olds were not accustomed to listening. The boy could lead when he wants to. "How did you treat with him afterwards?"

"Treat with whom?"

"The Blues captain, of course. You struck him very hard and he had broken the rules."

"Oh, we were fine in the kitchens." Niccolo fell back into his chair and looked up at the paneled ceiling. "He apologized and showed me the big bruise I had made on his arm."

"So, you were no longer angry with him?"

"I don't think so. It was as I told you, that I barely recall my fury on the field. His family is an Este vassal with land and privileges deep in the *valli*, unlike those traitorous fiends from Modena and the western *contado*. I read about them in the survey father made and they did not refuse investiture."

Catherine knew that the offending boy had not been punished for his indiscretion because, she reckoned, the Este needed the goodwill of their vassals now more than ever. The family even had been invited to sponsor knights at the recent tragic tournament.

"I counsel you not to think about Modena or investiture," Catherine said in measured words. "It will heat the yellow bile in your humors and cause you to become more choleric."

Niccolo snorted in derision. "How can I not think about them? I have suffered no greater humiliation than on that day. I am the true marquis by right of blood – even the supreme pontiff says so! – yet those blackguards conspired to overturn the will of my father and tell me to my face that I cannot be who I am!" Niccolo snatched his hands away from the table and began to count on his fingers. "Their names and faces are burned onto my memory: Ato di Rodiglia, the Flesso brothers, the Sassuolo brothers, the Modenese bastard Lancellotto Montecuccoli…"

"Stop, Niccolo!" Catherine nearly leapt from her chair. She could see that the boy was starting to shake from anger. "Calm yourself! Would Donato tolerate such an unprovoked outburst? I daresay not!"

Niccolo heard the woman's words as though she was calling him from the opposite end of a great hall. He had lost himself in the memory of that fateful day six months ago when a band of vassals, instead of accepting investiture of Este land from his hand and declaring anew to faithfully serve the Este, refused. They refused to recognize the regency council led by Alberto Roberti, they refused to abide by the concord they had signed with his father, they refused to see him as the heir to the Este inheritance. They would not accept investiture from a mere boy, they argued, or rather they could not, since they were already Este vassals. When Roberti had insisted, the rebels declared that it was against tradition, and so they could now give their fealty to who they want. Within a week, they had taken up arms against him.

"I will call the regency council if you refuse to control your humors," Catherine warned and she slapped the table.

The sharp crack of flesh against wood made the rebel vassals disappear. Niccolo's face softened and he dropped his hands to his sides.

"I am sorry," he said quietly. "I should have spared you the painful details."

"You should read instead."

"*You* should read for me," Niccolo pleaded. He returned to the table.

"I said 'no'."

The boy sighed. "If you will not, someone else will. Ferrara is a big city."

"And the Este court is small, which means your mother will know about your little venture before the final card is laid."

"I can read them myself," Niccolo argued playfully, and he reached across the table. Catherine swept the cards into her lap before he could touch them.

"Enough! I can do nothing without the consent of your mother or the regency council." She had not meant to be so curt, but no one was allowed to touch her cards.

Niccolo's eyes flashed in anger, but the spark quickly faded and he dropped his head onto his chest.

"We could play a game," Catherine suggested. A game could prove to be a useful test of the boy's cleverness as much as a distraction. Catherine did not want to have to sit in silence or make idle conversation with the child. She was weary of sitting. It was one of the most difficult aspects of reading astrology she had been forced to master.

"Chess?"

"No. I do not know that game well enough."

Chess bored Catherine, but the neat arrangement of black and white squares reminded her of quek, a simple game of chance a naïve French debt collector had once shown her out of boredom or vanity. Or was it the tall English squire with intense blue eyes who had shown her? He loved wagering, she recalled, while his lowborn companion preferred arranging for him to wager. Catherine suppressed a smile as she thought about Geoffrey Hotspur and Jean…Lacalmar, was it? No matter. She had taken from the debt collector what he owed to their mutual associate, the Gamesmaster of Avignon, who was still looking for him, she was told, and a little bit for her trouble. What struck her most about the squire was his devotion, whether to his lord, the Church or his sword, and because of that she could trust him, Catherine reckoned. She also figured that she could trust the debt collector because simple avarice ruled his humors, making him as common as a cartwheel. Lagoustine! Catherine nearly shouted, as she finally remembered Jean's surname.

"That is disappointing, but I will play any game you suggest." Earnestness returned to his voice.

"We shall play quek," Catherine announced. She quickly went over the basic rules, as far as she could remember them.

"No, I have never played that. My companions and I sometimes do a pebble-tossing game in the great court, but the purpose of that is to knock pebbles out of a circle, or move your own closer to the center. Is quek popular where you are from, mistress astrologer?"

"No, quek is a northern game." She would not be drawn into a conversation about herself. "We can play by either English or French rules. The English version is simpler while the French play with a gaming die." Catherine looked around, hoping to find a place where a set of dice and wagering tokens might be kept.

"Which would you prefer?" Niccolo asked.

"That depends on whether we can find the necessary gear. How well do you know your mother's lodgings?"

"I could ask the steward to bring what we need."

"The time would pass too quickly before it arrived."

"Will coins do?" Niccolo stood up and went to a small writing desk. He reached around the back with one hand and braced himself against the edge with the other.

Catherine watched until she heard the pop of a spring and saw a hitherto unmarked drawer jut out from the side of the desk.

"Hah!" Niccolo exclaimed, and after easing himself down to the floor reached into the newly exposed drawer and pulled out an assortment of gold coins. "How about these instead of pebbles?"

Catherine peered into the open hand and nodded. "I should think so, yes."

Niccolo dumped the rough equivalent of several years of a carpenter's wage onto the chessboard. "How many do we need?"

"Let us start with ten." Catherine rose from her chair.

Niccolo counted the requisite number of gold florins, shoved the remainder off the board and took his place next to the astrologer. "We must use the smoothest pieces. Mother will be upset if we chip the table." He held out his gold-laden hand.

Catherine responded likewise and waited for the boy to pour the coins into her hand, but instead he clasped her wrist and gently placed the money against her palm. She quickly withdrew her arm and stepped to the side to create an open space between them. "Let us move back a little. We cannot make this too easy on ourselves."

They soon felt their backs against the cold oak paneling. Catherine wished she could melt through it.

"So, how shall we score? Mother does not like me wagering, although I sometimes do so with my companions." Niccolo leaned towards Catherine and whispered, "The Blues captain and I bet on the battle you witnessed the other day."

"Then you had better take to the field again, since that pass ended in a draw."

Niccolo shrugged.

"I will tally the scores in my head," Catherine declared.

"I have a slate in my chamber. I can run and get it."

"No, let us pitch now."

"Shall we pitch by piece or in one throw?"

"Which would you prefer?"

"How would the rules have it?"

Catherine sighed. "We can make the rules. You will learn that soon enough. Let us try pitching as a lot and see how that goes."

"Inner squares are worth two points, outer squares are worth one, right?"

"Right. Throw."

Niccolo took one step forward, looked intently at the chessboard, and lobbed ten gold florins high into the air. All landed on the table, but with such force that half of them bounced and rolled over the edge. Niccolo ran up to the table.

"This makes me sad. I must be honest and count only three points." He collected his coins from on and around the table before returning to Catherine's side, closer this time. "You heard me say 'three', did you not?"

"Yes, of course." Catherine had never played quek herself, but she had a good wrist for dice. Nevertheless, she was not about to show up her charge under any circumstance. All but one of her coins struck the edge of the table and dropped to the floor. Again, Niccolo ran to calculate the score.

"Are you sure you want to know the result?" Niccolo asked. He turned and smiled.

"Just tell me. I can remember small numbers as well as large ones."

"One point, and even then the coin is just touching the white square. Does that count? Must not at least half of the coin rest in the square proper?"

"Well...let me think..."

"I will let you have the point." Niccolo gathered Catherine's money and returned it to her.

"Thank you." She looked down at the boy. He will be taller than his father, she reckoned, and he moves well despite his young age. Niccolo had been arms training for only a few months, so his poor showing in the snow was not unexpected. Even so, at least he had looked like he knew what he was doing.

They pitched coins for about half an hour when Niccolo's interest began to wane.

"Are the French rules any different?" he asked.

"We would need dice, like I said, and the points are set using them. Or the player simply tries to land the dice themselves on the white squares and tallies the points won by counting the spots on the face that show up." Catherine was sure she had the Frenchman's words right. He did not know much, but games of chance did fall into his narrow range of understanding.

"We must try that version the next time we are together," Niccolo said. His tone shifted to uncertainty. "In the meantime, let us wager properly. I am ahead on points now, but what purpose does that serve?"

"No, we should not." Catherine glanced at the door.

"Just one cast. It is boring otherwise."

Catherine gave the boy an exasperated look. "What would we wager?"

"A reading."

"I will wager telling your mother how poorly you behave. I have her ear."

Niccolo frowned and sat again at the opposite side of the table. He began to place his florins in a pattern on the chessboard.

A messenger announced himself at the door and stated that his lordship was to attend a meeting of the regency council with haste.

CHAPTER 4

The day broke with an eerie silence, as no cocks crowed and no children sang. A light snow that had just begun to fall seemed to hesitate before striking the ground. Even the servants were reticent while they pulled down the pavilions and packed the gear. The eastern side of the Via Francigena remained in darkness while the western side enjoyed scattered illumination through the broken clouds. The only meaningful conversation taking place near the hospice was Jean convincing Tommasino Crivelli to lend him a horse in exchange for gaming tips from the squire. All three companies – pilgrim, Rose and English Free – were on the road within an hour.

Giovanni dell'Ischia arranged the column, placing two of his lances at the head, himself and Robert d'Ivry in the center, the servants and baggage wagons after them, and finally Crivelli and another lance at the rear. He advised Geoffrey and his companion to ride near the end of the column, for their own safety, he argued.

"You did well last night, Geoff," Jean said as he caught up with the squire, "However, I must say Ischia seemed none too happy when you gave him back his money. I wonder what that was all about? I know he bears some sort of grudge against the English, but that might just mean that he has good sense." Jean bounced awkwardly on his mount and constantly winced.

"I cannot say. Maybe he still resents my intrusion. I embarrassed him before his lordship, I suppose, and his lordship showed me favor. Regardless, it cannot be helped," Geoffrey argued as he took stock of the company around him. Count Robert was a few lengths ahead, he noted.

"All the same, we must be mindful that he does not drive a wedge between us and his lordship." Jean pulled his coif tight against his ears.

"Between *me* and his lordship. By the way, your offer at dinner nearly spoiled the evening. And what could Captain dell'Ischia say? I am not enrolled in his company and the road is wide enough for all of us. Most importantly, though, is that Count Robert has invited me to ride with him."

Jean frowned. "The mood was hardly affected. All the same, I should have approached someone in Ivry's retinue first."

Another rider fell into step with Geoffrey and Jean.

"H-how goes it, my friends?" Crivelli said. He was kitted out in a long hauberk, arm and leg harnesses of the latest style, and a light green woolen surcoat. Since his tapering salet helm was dangling from his saddle, on which he sat awkwardly, Geoffrey and Jean could plainly see his brown eyes, youthful complexion, stubby nose, and receding chin.

"It goes peacefully, thank the Lord," Geoffrey answered. "Your captain seems to have everything well at hand. However, I neglected to ask him about the road ahead. I assume he has made inquiries of the local folk about its condition and the like."

"A-all is well, f-from what I hear, m-master squire. You are a mighty player. I would do well to learn from you."

Jean looked at Crivelli and shook his head to indicate that now was not the time to accost the squire.

"I have no doubt," Geoffrey said. "You suffer from an affliction of the throat, do you not? Forgive me, but I do not want to mistake an accent for something more sinister."

"I-I am all right when I whisper," Crivelli said, lowering his voice. "My mother fell just before I was born, which I am told is what caused my stutter." He smiled wanly.

"Well then," Jean said, "you can ride next to me. I have excellent hearing."

"I hope *you* do not," Geoffrey said to Crivelli. "He says nothing but rubbish." He jabbed a thumb at Jean. "Why are you not riding with the rest of your lance?"

"I could only get one man to follow me, and he lies ill in one of the wagons."

"I hear that the Romagna convulses with men-at-arms," Jean said. "You look well-equipped to attract a few to your banner."

Crivelli jerkily shifted himself on his saddle. "Captain dell'Ischia did not give me enough time to recruit. He formed the Company of the Rose only in December, saying that there was good money in a winter campaign."

"You could have refused," Jean said. "With all due respect, escorting a Cypriot lord is not much of a campaign, is it?"

"My family must provide him with one lance when demanded. We rent some of his land."

"Sounds proper," Geoffrey said. "Any passing of arms since then?"

"None. We marched from Sansepolcro to Assisi; the captain told us that Perugia was under threat again, so we hoped to find a *condotta* with his grace the pope, since he is the *signore* there, but all was settled before we arrived. Then we found his lordship."

"I dare say Lady Fortuna is as cold to you as the winter," Geoffrey said and he chuckled.

"Alas, yes," Crivelli said as a snowflake fell into his eye.

The Tiber River remained to their left and the steep forest stretched across the mountainside continued to their right. A snow flurry came and went in an hour, but it was not strong enough to slow the column, although Geoffrey found it difficult to keep his eye on Count Robert.

While Jean and Crivelli conversed about things that did not interest him, Geoffrey grew anxious as he awaited the call from his lordship. He thought about sending Jean to eavesdrop, but that would be inappropriate and undignified, Geoffrey reckoned. Instead he decided to replay moments from the past evening, when he held the attention of the count, to try figure out where he stood.

A servant approached Geoffrey as the column was passing into a wider section of the road and informed him that Count Robert bid they ride together. Immediately Geoffrey set off, weaving between carts and mules, until he found the noble figure of the Count d'Ivry.

"Master Hotspur," Count Robert said, "you are most prompt."

"My lord trained me well." Geoffrey looked for Captain dell'Ischia and found him at the head of the column talking with a scout.

"Yes, I heard so much about the great duke last night that I feel as though we have been companions for years." Ivry smiled.

For a moment Geoffrey thought the count was referring to *him* as an old companion, but a spasm of reason informed him that, of course, his lordship had meant the Duke of Lancaster.

"It fairly warms the cockles of my heart to recite the deeds of arms of my lord and master," Geoffrey said. "There is more to tell."

"You have done duty by your lord, and I shall remember, but I find myself in a voluble mood, boy, and since I cannot give you a place in my retinue or a *condotta* to escort my company of pilgrims, in exchange I offer you a few words of my own, about deeds of arms done in the East. What say you?"

Geoffrey bowed his head. "That is more than a fair price, my lord. I am all ears."

To Geoffrey's surprise, Count Robert began with a story about the fall of Acre, the last of the cities held by Christians in the Holy Land proper, a hundred years ago. With a strong and passionate voice, his lordship recounted how his grandfather had fought until the city's final hour before setting sail for Cyprus so that he could continue the war against the heathens there. However, he died before a campaign to reclaim the lost lands could be organized, a fate that also befell Count Robert's father, who had collected a treasure trove of silver, gold and relics in anticipation of a grand invasion.

Ivry then told about his own upbringing in the court of his majesty King Peter of Cyprus, and how his life and the lives of his fellow squires were dedicated to preparing for battle with the heathens until finally, in 1365, King Peter mounted an expedition against Egypt. The invasion was a success, and Count Robert performed many feats of arms beneath the walls of Alexandria, for which he was made a knight. Then, with the news of their success spreading throughout Christendom, they waited for more bands of knights to join them.

"That was a remarkable triumph of Christian arms against the heathens," Geoffrey said. He could see the proud young knight beneath the count's gray beard and mottled cheeks. "In the great hall of my lord an old knight once recounted his taking the Cross at that time, but he was never able to bring the words of those deeds to life with such force as you have, your lordship."

"My family has always been dedicated to the recovery of the Holy Land, master squire. The first Robert d'Ivry was a companion of Godfrey of Bouillon and was one of the first Frankish knights to enter Jerusalem. He was enfeoffed with land taken from the infidel and died defending it. William d'Ivry took the Cross a hundred years later in the company of King Richard the Lionheart, who granted him land and villages in Cyprus. His blood courses through my veins."

Geoffrey's ears perked up. "Indeed?"

"Yes, like how the Lionheart might have won Jerusalem, we too could have swept the Saracens out of Egypt had we a few more men and horses. Unlike so many others before us, we campaigned well because we knew the land and learned the way of war of the enemy, and the Lord favored us for a while. However, when his majesty, may God rest his soul, reached out to France, England, Castile, Milan, and Florence, and to his grace the supreme pontiff himself to join him, they foolishly tarried, and so the Lord withdrew his favor."

"That is troubling. Forgive me for saying so, your lordship, but are you sure?"

"God helps the righteous, Hotspur, but not if the righteous are stupid. How else to explain these ultimate defeats despite the justice of the cause?" The count's voice became tinged with bitterness.

"I would like to take the Cross myself, one day," Geoffrey said. He straightened his posture and raised his chin.

"I believe all knights should make that vow. I have, and so have my men. I patronize the Knights Hospitaller, you know."

"Does your son hold fast in Cyprus against the Saracens, your lordship?"

Count Robert shook his head. "I have not been blessed with a son, sadly. Only a daughter, Marguerite, and she does hold fast in Cyprus."

Geoffrey mouthed the name 'Marguerite' and thought it beautiful.

"Tell me, master squire," Count Robert began. "Has your lord ever taken the Cross? You said nothing about such a noble deed yesterday." He looked into Geoffrey's eyes.

"He fought in Spain, I know." Geoffrey thought hard. No, no one had ever recited deeds of arms performed by his lordship in the Holy Land. He found that curious.

"No matter. I am sure he has made the vow. What about the condottieri you have met? What is their view on taking the Cross? I must confess, I only met a few during my Way, since they tend to shy away from shrines and pilgrims."

Geoffrey shook his head. "We never discussed such things, your lordship."

"What is your opinion of them, then?"

"They are rogues and bastards, on the whole." More emotion crept into Geoffrey's voice. "I trust them as much as I would trust a Jew, and few of them rank as knights, it seems. Still, they can fight. I have witnessed a few fairly perform feats of arms."

"Tell me."

Although he was loath to expound on the virtues of condottieri, Geoffrey wanted to keep Count Robert's ear, so he spoke about the German Conrad Prosperg, who was his captain-general at the battle near Orte and a soldier he admired for his decency and skills in arms, the hard-bitten Italians Ceccolo Broglia and Brandolino Brandolini, whose inseparability on and off the field made them a potent force, a drunken but capable Catalonian captain of crossbowmen, and a duplicitous condottiere named Giovanni Tarlati of Arezzo.

"I heard that this Tarlati was slain near his native city, by Broglia and Brandolini, I believe," Count Robert said.

"It is just."

"So it would seem. Do you recall how these condottieri were paid? I must admit, this strange system of commissions has me curious."

"I confess ignorance on that account. I would have to ask my master victualer about that." Geoffrey frowned. He was surprised that such an esteemed lord would concern himself with such a base matter.

They talked for another hour before Count Robert, seized by a bout of coughing and shivering, said, "Master squire, should you find your commission in Florence quickly ended, my offer of a place in my company still stands, perhaps even as an armed escort, since we will be passing through more dangerous territory. But now I am tired, and I release you. You will sit at my table again in Sansepolcro."

Geoffrey returned to Jean's side. He was excited and without asking if his companion was interested gave Jean a full account of his conversations with the count.

"Well done. I must ask you something, Geoff." Jean lowered his voice and sighed. "You are not planning to pledge fealty to Ivry, are you? I know he is a great lord and all, but I do not wish to be flogged by Gaunt for not getting you home."

"Look, I know better than to fly to the nearest lord and offer to become his man. As grand as it would be to fight the heathens in the Holy Land, I must wait to be invited." Geoffrey had embarrassed himself on more than one occasion with a precipitous declaration of service in the past year. "And above all, Florence and the royal commission await me. That is a vow that cannot be broken."

Jean nodded in satisfaction. "How much did he offer?"

"For what?"

"For serving as an armed escort, of course."

Geoffrey shrugged. "He did not say. The going rate, I suppose. What does it matter?"

Jean shrugged. "I like to know these things."

"His lordship has a few questions for you about that, but I expect he will send a servant around to collect your words."

Jean craned his head towards the skies and squinted. "Considering all this talk about taking the Cross, maybe the count is here for something more than to stare at a bunch of dusty relics, Geoff. He might be looking to recruit men for a new campaign. Why else would he want to know about condottieri?"

"I have thought that possible too. His lordship did tell me how poorly the other nations reacted to his king's victory in Egypt. Wise man that he is, his lordship must be planning well ahead of the game." Geoffrey glanced at Ivry. "I hope I never have to wager against him!"

"Just do not commit yourself." Jean changed the subject to distract the squire from the idea of taking the Cross. "Did he mention his children?"

Geoffrey straightened his posture. "He did."

"A son and a daughter, or so Crivelli says. They are in Cyprus. So, if you are hoping he will adopt you as Gaunt once did, you will be disappointed." Jean chuckled.

"Perhaps his lordship will invite me to fight alongside his son. I expect he must be of age."

It was dusk by the time they reached Sansepolcro and Captain dell'Ischia shouted for the column to stop.

"The gatehouse seems better guarded than usual," Ischia said to Count Robert, "and I see a lot of men-at-arms about. Crivelli! You have the lightest horse. Inform the captain of the gatehouse of our approach and learn the meaning of this ado. And be sure to give him my name, not yours, and that of Count Robert, of course!"

Crivelli did as he was told and galloped off. As they were waiting, Geoffrey trotted ahead. Jean followed.

"We will have to pay for lodgings now, and with all these soldiers around they will not be cheap." Jean looked at the men-at-arms warily. "I should ask Crivelli about that, since he is from around here."

"Good idea. I shall be dining with his lordship in the meantime."

The pang of anxiety grew stronger as Geoffrey thought about his arriving in Florence to finally complete his commission and his imminent parting with Count Robert. He clutched his stomach and swallowed. The company of his lordship and Ischia's men-at-arms had successfully distracted him from what he might encounter in that city of merchants, but the day of reckoning was almost upon him. Would anyone from the original party still be there? Would he learn of the duke's anger towards him? Would he be obliged to do the most humiliating tasks as punishment for his tardiness?

Geoffrey pulled off his helm and coif and stroked his hair. Perhaps they would be glad to see him, he thought. He had a few amusing tales to tell, let alone he sort of fought in a pass of arms, so he might be able to charm his way back into the good graces of his lordship, or whoever was still representing his majesty in Florence. The young squire was suddenly filled with uncertainty. Of course, he had to go. Geoffrey was then seized by an urge to ask Count Robert to divert himself for a few days and accompany him to Florence, to give an account of the squire's good character, he supposed. It was a silly idea, Geoffrey knew, yet the fantasy eased his anxiety a little.

Crivelli returned, but before he saw his captain gesture that they should converse away from the others, he announced, "The city is in chaos! Azzo da Castello has been killed!"

Soldiers and servants alike began to murmur.

"Indeed!" Count Robert said. "And that is enough to put a city into panic? Was he killed here?"

"You know the man, your lordship?" Geoffrey asked.

"By reputation. He is the captain-general of Ferrara. Or rather, he was, it seems." Ivry frowned and stroked his beard.

"Ferrara is so near, then?"

"No, the city is closer to Ravenna, across the mountains. All the same, his death is important."

Geoffrey was about to ask another question when Ischia leaned towards him and said, "Enough! Do not pester his lordship. This has nothing to do with you, and should you wish to learn more, visit a tavern! I must keep this company together, for his lordship's sake. Uncertainty reigns here. You can find your own way in, Hotspur."

Ischia ordered his men to flank the pilgrims, pushing Geoffrey and Jean out of the column. Count Robert looked back and gave a reassuring nod to Geoffrey, while Crivelli agreed to meet Jean later to collect the promised gaming tips.

While the captain of the gatehouse was respectful to Giovanni dell'Ischia after he identified himself and his party, he stopped Geoffrey with a whip and a stern look.

"Free lances need to pay to get in," the guard captain said.

"I am a squire and man of his lordship the Duke of Lancaster." Geoffrey showed the man his seal.

"And?" He looked around. "You do not have much of a retinue. What is your business here?"

"We are on our way to Florence."

"Then you do not need to be in the city. Look, a lot of you free lances have arrived and more are coming every day. You can sleep outside the walls with the rest of them."

"I am not a free lance," Geoffrey declared. "I am with Count Robert d'Ivry. You just let him pass."

"I was told otherwise. You say that you are a man of Gaunt. Yeah, I know who he is, but that makes not a lick of difference. You can find a warm hut down thataway." The guard captain pointed to his right.

"He is also a condottiere," Jean said, and he began fumbling for the parchment.

"Indeed? Well, which is it? Man of Gaunt, man of Ivry, or captain of men?"

Geoffrey was frustrated not only by the gatehouse captain's refusal to let him pass, but also by the realization that he might have to play condottiere again. His lordship's seal was proof enough for men of exalted rank, so he could appeal to the *signore* of this city, but that would take time, if this blackguard would permit the appeal at all, and he would have to wait outside the walls in the dark anyway. Damn it all!

"I am a condottiere," Geoffrey heard himself say. "I am heading to Florence, to collect the rest of my company, which is in Florence." He did not meet the gatehouse captain's eye.

Jean registered a stunned look on his face as he found the *condotta*.

"What have you to vouchsafe your claim?"

Jean showed the *condotta*.

"Fine, fine, you may pass."

Jean and Geoffrey rode along the main street towards the center. Jean waved a hand at the groups of apparently indifferent people carrying baskets, sacks, pails, and assorted bundles in a calm manner and said, "This does not look like chaos to me."

"No, indeed." Geoffrey grimaced at the dull scene. "Avignon is thrice as lively when his grace is *not* in residence. All the same, I will stay close to the pilgrims, since they are as strangers here as am I."

"You mean stay close to Count Robert," Jean whispered.

"And what of that? He is most important."

"So are finding lodgings."

They turned into a large square, where a great mass of people forced them to rein in their mounts.

"Lord's mercy!" Jean exclaimed. "Now, this is more like Avignon. How are we to wade through this sea of…of hats?"

From their elevated position, they indeed could only see a densely packed array of the most exotic headwear, from the lowliest workman's coif to the merchant's red biretta to the grand chaperon of the nobleman, as well as crisp white wimples of all sizes and shapes, but most of all they saw the steel helms of men-at-arms.

They eventually tracked down and trailed behind Ischia's company at a discreet distance until they saw them turn into the courtyard of a large hospice. Several monks appeared and began collecting the baggage, while a steward escorted the pilgrims into the main hall. After identifying a landmark, Geoffrey turned his horse and began riding back the way he came.

"Are we leaving already, Geoff? Pray, let us wait for daybreak."

Geoffrey ignored his companion until, after a few uncertain looks down several alleys, he declared, "Aha! This is the sign for me!"

Jean looked around and saw a gently swinging plaque.

"The White Hart," Jean pronounced. "You can read that? Your Italian is improving."

"I saw it earlier. You said we needed to find lodgings, so here they are. The same charge belongs to an ale house I frequent in Avignon." Geoffrey dismounted and peered into a window, where he saw a small number of patrons sitting quietly and drinking. "Not too lively, but we shall see to that."

Geoffrey spent a few moments observing the interactions between the patrons and innkeeper to learn the local ale house customs before seating himself at a small table as far as from the hearth as possible. He admired the clean stone walls and sparse furnishings that surrounded him, as well as the sturdy table, which he knocked twice to attract the attention of a serving maid. He looked around for the arms of the landlord, hoping on the off chance that the inn belonged to an English lord, but he only found a series of tapestries depicting a great hunt. His eyes were on a mounted man about to shoot a white hart when Jean sat next to him.

"You have chosen well, Geoff. We can afford to stay. It is cold on this side of the hall, though. Now, I understand why this table was free. Let us move to the long table over there." Jean pointed towards the hearth with its blazing fire.

"I am comfortable here." Geoffrey continued to stare at the tapestry. As a page in the halls of Gaunt, he was once made a beater during a hunt by his lordship. He tried to remember if their quarry had been a hart or a boar.

A serving maid arrived and asked if they wanted strong or weak ale.

"Strong, of course," Geoffrey said. "Jean?" He pointed at the girl.

"The same," Jean said.

"No, pay her. I ordered for both of us."

Jean nodded, dipped into his purse and set a few thin, silver coins on the table, which was a large portion of Geoffrey's meager winnings. The maid took two and left.

"I noticed that you have made a friend in that stuttering Italian fellow. He does not look all that fair for soldiering, though. Is he from a good family?" Geoffrey asked. The tapestry and the memories it conjured was making him anxious about leaving Count Robert and returning to Duke John, and so he wanted some distraction.

"Who? Crivelli?" Jean grimaced and shook his head. "So far, I have found him to be an honest fellow, though the others in his company seem to have little respect for him."

"He is not titled, is he? He would have sat closer to Count Robert at the hospice if he was." Geoffrey leaned back and sipped his ale. He looked around, hoping to find a fellow squire, a peer, who could tell him over a pint of ale and with a lively maid on his lap about the local customs of knighthood and chivalry.

"I do not know, although he has never performed a deed of arms, as you would say."

"He poorly handles a sword, but maybe your friend can hold a lance. Tilting might be his game."

Jean grunted his approval "I see a spit of pork has been set to roast. We can afford such hearty fare now."

"You may order, but I will save my appetite for dinner with his lordship. I will have some more ale, though." Geoffrey knocked again. He glanced at the tapestry and instead of hart and hunter he saw a scene from his bloodless nightmare. Geoffrey shuddered and turned away.

"I shall."

After the serving maid set down new tankards and Jean ordered enough meat for two, she asked if he and Geoffrey were German, since she could not place their accents. When Jean asked why she must know this, the maid answered that the White Hart was popular with men-at-arms from Germany, and their captains often left instructions for them.

Geoffrey and Jean scanned the hall and noticed that the patrons looked different from the usual tavern clientele. Complexions were fairer, features thinner, and clothing distinctly northern in style. Jean cupped his ears to help him overhear a low conversation at the long table.

"They sound German," Jean said. "What do you think, Geoff?"

"They could be. I wonder if any of them know Conrad Prosperg?"

"That is true! Prosperg was German through and through, and I believe he said after the battle that he was going north. God's bones, you are blessed with quite the memory!"

The maid coughed. Jean wondered if he should disguise their origins. However, it was possible that someone, namely Geoffrey's royal commission to Florence, had left a message for the squire, so he decided to tell her the truth, but only if she would tell him to whom the White Hart's guests belonged. The maid shrugged and explained that most of the German men-at-arms were enrolled or hoped to enroll in the company of Corrado Altinberg. Jean asked her to repeat the name several times until he figured out that the condottiere's true name was Conrad of Heidelberg.

The door opened and an icy gust swept over Geoffrey and Jean. They looked across the hall and saw Crivelli stamping his boots. He bounded over when he saw them.

"At last, I found you!" Crivelli said as he sat down.

"So, what news, Tommasino?" Jean asked.

Crivelli looked around and then pulled out a pair of bottles and three wooden cups from beneath the table. "The captain's best wine," he whispered.

"This is your lord's stock," Geoffrey whispered.

"In a sense. It comes from my family's vineyard, so I am entitled."

Jean and to a lesser degree Geoffrey were convinced of the justice in this.

After opening one bottle and pouring out three measures, Crivelli launched into an account of what he had learned about the death of Azzo da Castello and how the struggle for the Este inheritance was drawing condottieri and men-at-arms northwards.

"For the love of all that is holy, who holds a tournament in the middle of winter? No doubt his horse slipped on some ice and he was thrown from his mount!" Jean exclaimed.

"Oh, I do not agree with you, Jean," Geoffrey said. "A winter exercise should be all for the good. A man must learn to fight in all seasons."

"The tournament was organized at the last moment," Crivelli continued, "so that none from the rival Este clan could show up and challenge Niccolo to a pass of arms. A bad sign for all."

"Should a child rule, though?" Geoffrey said. "Is this Uncle Azzo such a poor knight that he cannot take the boy's place until he comes of age?"

"The other cities will not let him because he is close to the *signore* of Milan. Everybody fears Milan."

Geoffrey shook his head. "It is not for me to understand. However, if the uncle wins by conquest, he will have the right to take the seat, and the inheritance with it. Or do such customs not apply in Italy?"

"Th-they do," Crivelli answered. "B-but with so many men churning up the fields around Ferrara, I would not wager on either side to win. The death of the esteemed captain-general has left the young Marquis of Ferrara exposed, and I am as sure as night comes after day that his uncle will soon attempt to discomfit him. Azzo da Castello was a great condottiere, feared as much as respected."

"You are on the side of this marquis…Niccolo, I believe is his name," Geoffrey said.

"May the devil take him! The Lord will protect he who belongs in Ferrara. No, at issue is that the marquis will be looking for a new captain-general. Every condottiere worth a *grosso* will be making a bid for that lucrative rank."

"And what about Count Robert?" Geoffrey asked. "I know a *condotta* is not a blood oath, or fealty, but to break it would cause your captain's reputation to suffer, no?"

"His *condotta* is finished when we reach Ravenna."

"Are you warning us or giving advice?" Jean asked.

Crivelli looked surprised. "N-neither. We are travel companions, and companions-in-arms, and so I am compelled by that bond to tell you this."

"Are we to pay for this knowledge?" Jean narrowed his eyes in suspicion.

Crivelli shook his head.

"You think Ischia will make a bid for captain-general of Ferrara?" Jean asked.

"The captain?" Crivelli looked over his shoulder and then spat to the side. "Doubtful. Ischia's name is not big enough, at least not as big as his father's was. I do not know what sort of commission he will look for in Bologna."

"You will follow him all the same?" Jean asked.

"Where else would I go? Besides, he will only enroll Italians, especially those from the gentry, which helps me keep my place in the company."

"Why only Italians?" Jean asked. "A good man-at-arms is a good man-at-arms, as far as I can reckon." He poured himself more wine.

"A good company must comprise good gentry," Geoffrey said. "Your captain is sound."

Jean turned to Geoffrey and said, "So, you would rather fight alongside a fat, drunk lord than a lean seasoned pikeman, would you?"

"A fat, drunk lord would not take the field," Geoffrey answered, "at least, not more than once."

"And that wisdom is drawn from your many years of campaigning, has it?" Jean said.

"It is a reasonable assumption. I have heard many tales of battles won and lost, and not a few from well-heated old knights, yet none uttered a word about a lord entering a pass of arms in a state that warned against it."

"Bah! I know a few knights myself, Geoff, and I can—"

"Let us drink to the successful completion of our commissions!" Crivelli suddenly proposed. "Raise your cups!"

Geoffrey and Jean immediately suspended their debate and downed their cups.

"I have more news, which will affect your fates," Crivelli said after he wiped his mouth with his sleeve.

"Indeed?" Geoffrey and Jean said in unison.

"Many of the men-at-arms in this very hall were recently involved in some heavy campaigning around Arezzo. Two of the companies there belong to old friends of yours: Ceccolo Broglia and Brandolino Brandolini."

Jean froze when he heard the names. He and Geoffrey had been partially responsible for defeating them at the battle near Orte last September.

"I suppose they still maintain large companies?" Jean asked.

"They are in the pay of Milan, so you can assume that, yes."

"They will know me," Geoffrey said. "Florence must come to me."

Jean and Crivelli raised their eyebrows.

"Or, we could send a message to Florence, to the…what is it called?" Jean turned to Crivelli.

"Signoria," Crivelli answered. "The ruling body of the commune of Florence. They are a haughty lot, so do not expect them to come to you, master squire."

"A message should get through, I should think. Yes?" Jean again turned to Crivelli.

"If you send it with a Sansepolcro rider, it should arrive. Those captains have no quarrel with this city, and considering how many condottieri have passed through Sansepolcro in recent days, they would not dare sever communications and make more enemies."

"So be it," Geoffrey announced. "I can wait here for a few days."

Crivelli took a sip of wine, glanced at Jean and then said to Geoffrey, "Now, how about revealing some of your gaming secrets, master squire?"

"Come back tomorrow. I am off to share his lordship's table."

On the first day after Geoffrey had bid a fond farewell to Count Robert d'Ivry, the squire made a tour of the churches, chapels and shrines of Sansepolcro, offering at each station a prayer and a few coins for charity. He grew steadily anxious through the day, which he was only able to ease by a steady intake of ale. On the second day, to distract himself he spent most of the daylight hours sorting and polishing his gear, visiting armorer's row to see what wares they had on offer, and asking about the local lords, while at night he filled his belly with White Hart fare and introduced himself to several veteran men-at-arms.

"The lot hails from Bavaria," Geoffrey said when Jean inquired about his new friends. "They would not disclose their intentions, although they invited me to play at tables." He pointed at the men in question. "Now, give me the company silver."

Jean looked around Geoffrey and saw how one of the Germans was opening a hinged wooden board while another man was dumping a load of black and white pieces onto the long table.

"We are playing for a penny a point." Geoffrey started to feel excitement rise in his chest, stirred by a recollection of his great gaming victory over the combined efforts of the Rose Company.

"I will not play, but I will watch." Jean rose from his stool. After snatching a few glances at the German men-at-arms and taking note of their copper coins, serious demeanor, and well-worn kit, Jean figured that they would be playing for low stakes.

Once Geoffrey showed himself to be a hearty fellow, the Germans became more affable, and even stood him and Jean a round of ale. Vespers was over, which gave license for other patrons to set up their own boards. More men-at-arms came into the White Hart, mostly Germans, until the place was awash with ale, laughter and foreign curses. Geoffrey continued to play at the long table, and Jean noticed that he was winning more often than losing. His gaming skills, enthusiasm, and gregarious nature intimidated the other players, which was causing them to make obvious mistakes. However, they appreciated his affability, and so were well disposed towards the young squire.

On the third day near the hour of compline, a messenger from the *podestà* of Sansepolcro arrived at the White Hart Inn to inform Geoffrey Hotspur, squire of his grace the Duke of Lancaster, that Florence was not expecting him, that the royal commission had long departed, leaving no instructions concerning a squire belonging to the said duke, and that the Signoria had not received a message, missive or other communications from his grace or his majesty King Richard that bore the name Geoffrey Hotspur. He had been forgotten, if not forsaken.

CHAPTER 5

Geoffrey sat in his usual place far from the hearth with a tankard of warm ale in front of him. The maid had brought it an hour ago, but Geoffrey had not so much as looked at it. His eyes were fixed on the tapestry, on the white hart that was about to go down, and his left hand was wrapped tightly around the hilt of his *couteau*.

The anxious pang in his stomach was gone, replaced by a dull, heavy ache. Geoffrey had not said a word since he received the fateful message, not to the messenger, not to Jean, not to the Germans who invited him to join their games. He sat alone, in his blue-gray doublet and leather buskins, his hair, now grown to the nape of his neck, was pushed straight back, revealing furrows on the youthful brow. He was not missed. He had never seriously entertained the idea that the royal commission would wait for him in Florence in its entirety, but to abandon one of their own without leaving so much as an instruction was unconscionable. It drove home just how far on the edge of his lordship's circle he was.

When he first heard the message Geoffrey could not understand the words, but after he heard it a second time a storm of such force rose within him that his body trembled and Jean had to escort him to the table. With humors churning wildly, a rush of emotions clouded his reason enough that Geoffrey became deaf and dumb to the world around him. The hall lengthened and the door that led to the street seemed a mile away when he saw the messenger leave.

Yet, he was still a man of Gaunt. His lordship had not renounced him, as far as he knew. He was the man of a great man, and so he would act like it. To hell with the royal commission! To hell with the lowly Florentine merchants! To hell with waiting to be asked to return! The white hart of the tapestry started to prance. Its wound healed and the beast began to trample the dogs and beaters encircling it. The trembling stopped and a wicked scowl appeared on his face. He grabbed his tankard, downed the ale in a single draught and tossed the empty vessel onto the floor. He hailed the German men-at-arms, who were playing at tables, and demanded he be given a place with them.

The Bavarians welcomed the squire with a great cheer, which grew louder when Geoffrey dumped the contents of his purse onto one of the quek boards. When the innkeeper, hearing the sudden commotion, rushed over to ask Geoffrey to remove his sword, he growled, threw a coin at him and demanded he bring a round of his strongest ale.

"And what is this pathetic penny-a-point stakes, you sons of whores!" Geoffrey cried in a mix of French and Italian. "Let us play like men, not children!" He grabbed the tunics of several men-at-arms and shoved them together near one board. Geoffrey then began pointing and yelling at others to come here and to go there, to raise this wager and to double that stake.

While some seconded Geoffrey's authority, others became annoyed by the bullying and began to threaten him. Jean reached Geoffrey just as a veteran German sergeant grabbed him by his doublet and began yelling something in his native tongue. Geoffrey shouted curses back, but since he was holding a tankard in one hand and clutching pebbles in the other, he could not grab a fistful of cloth in his turn.

"God's balls!" Jean said as he struggled with the squire. He could see the gaming fury in his eyes. "Come away from here!"

Jean had no soothing words for Geoffrey. He was out of ideas. Unbeknownst to Geoffrey, the fateful message included the answer to a query Jean had made to Gamesmaster's Florentine associate: he was to return to Avignon, with or without the squire.

The innkeeper rushed to the spat, and together with Jean they pulled the two sides apart. While the innkeeper argued with the German to keep the peace, Jean hauled Geoffrey away from the games.

"For the love of Christ, Geoff, have your wits fled you?! Are you trying to get us killed or get us thrown out?!"

The choler in the fiery squire was keeping his blood so quick that his head swam from the heat. "This silver came from gaming, and so it will be spent on gaming. That is the law, master victualer. And I have yet to throw out."

Jean frowned at this confused response. "That does not answer my question. Listen, let us take ourselves away from here and discuss…"

"No! This is my home now!" Geoffrey slammed the tankard and pebbles on a nearby table and produced a handful of coins from his doublet. "I keep winning this.

Here. Take some and buy yourself a proper harness already." He grabbed Jean's wrist and slapped the silver onto it.

"You should take this to a brothel and fuck the choler out of you, or whatever demon has possessed your soul," Jean said, although he dumped the coins into his own purse.

"The whores can come to me. Someone must come to me after all my wandering." Geoffrey suddenly grew quiet and he glanced at the white hart. "Listen. At the approach of dawn, be good and guide me to a chapel." He clapped Jean's bad shoulder.

"And then we shall talk?"

Geoffrey ignored the question, spun around and returned to the games.

Through the night Jean watched his troubled companion like a hawk, stole coins now and again from the reckless squire and kept an eye on the Germans so that they would not cheat him. When the first cock crowed to announce the dawn, he dragged an exhausted Geoffrey Hotspur to a nearby chapel and dropped him beneath a tapestry of Saint Sebastian. As he looked down on the disheveled squire, Jean thought about their options, or rather his options, and came to the ironic conclusion that they only had one way to go.

"If we leave now, we should be able to catch up with Count Robert within a day," Jean said. They could not stay in Sansepolcro. The path to Avignon can just as well go through Ravenna and Lombardy.

Geoffrey's eyes were closed, but he had heard. "What do you mean?" he slurred. "I am the duke's man, and so I cannot pledge my sword and my life to another lord, however esteemed." He raised his hand, but a lack of strength caused it to fall back to the floor.

"Of course, but you told me that his lordship offered you a place in his escort to Ravenna. You shall take him up on that offer, as the captain of the English Free Company."

Geoffrey opened one eye and stared at Jean. The Frenchman was fuzzy, but he recognized the yellow jupon. "True. But what about lances?"

"Leave that up to me."

"Very well. Now let me pray." Geoffrey shut his eye and fell fast asleep.

Jean let Geoffrey sleep until noon. In the meantime, he collected enough of the money owed to the squire from the previous night's games to settle accounts with the White Hart Inn and offered a deal to the remaining debtors: false enrollment in the English Free Company until Ravenna in exchange for cancellation of their debts. Three Bavarian lances took it. Jean then bought provisions, packed their gear, purchased a palfrey for himself, and had Saint George reshod. He had looked for new armor, but anything he tried on did not fit, pinched his shoulder, or restricted his movements. He had no time to have a harness tailored, and so he resolved to find a good leather jack somewhere on the road. Instead, he bought himself a thick woolen cloak and a matching hood.

Jean also learned that to catch up with Count Robert's party, they would have to endure some hard marching through the mighty Mountains of the Moon to reach the headwaters of the Marecchia River, and from there follow the valley through the heart of the Romagna.

Dusk had fallen and they had nearly reached the Viamaggio Pass when Jean decided that Geoffrey was alive enough to be told about the ghost lances.

"His lordship will see through the ruse," Geoffrey said. He spoke quietly and without emotion. His head hurt and his voice was hoarse. "He inspects arms every day, if you remember."

"I do remember, and the Germans have promised to look convincing. Their captain awaits in Bologna, so what is this little ruse to them?" Jean nodded at his new companions and they nodded back.

"All the same, deception is deception. What if I take his silver and then bandits fall on us? Will the Germans fight?"

"They would have too, if only to defend themselves. They have their captain's reputation to think of, as well as their gear. Geoff, we will be a large enough group that no one will dare attack us, so do not worry."

Geoffrey sighed and gently shook his head. "This is a bad sign," he whispered.

"Listen, you are the captain of a company composed of actual lances now, so act like it. They owe you money, so they will heed your commands."

Geoffrey was too emotionally tired to argue with Jean, but all the same he thought about the clever arrangement the Frenchman had made. True, he now led some men-at-arms, more or less. He felt some pride and responsibility in that. Still, the idea about taking the Cross was very close to his heart, and if his lordship was indeed secretly recruiting men for a war against the heathens, that was a sign he could not ignore.

Both Geoffrey and Jean pushed themselves and their companions to march hard, so they were able to catch up to the Ivry party at Badia Tedalda, a fortified town overlooking a jagged valley located near the start of the navigable part of the Marecchia River. Count Robert had just sat down for dinner when the English Free

Company plus about a dozen German lances marched through the gates. The *podestà* announced them.

Surprised to hear the name 'Hotspur' so soon, Ivry immediately granted Geoffrey an audience on the porch outside his lodgings.

"My lord," Geoffrey began. He knelt before Count Robert with his head bared. "I am here to accept your offer as your armed escort." Quickly and with few words he told about the fateful message from Florence.

"It was an oversight, I am sure," Ivry said. "Well, now that you are here, I must keep my promise. Have you any lances to fill out your company?"

"We have, my lord," Jean said. "Three." He pointed at the Bavarians, who waved back and doffed their helms.

Ivry raised his eyebrows. "Well done, my boy." He called for his steward to draw up a *condotta* for Geoffrey Hotspur and the English Free Company.

"Are they formally enrolled?" The voice came from behind Ivry. Captain dell'Ischia pushed his way through the pilgrims he was escorting and stood next to his lordship. "Where is their *condotta*?"

Geoffrey looked at the captain and then at Jean.

Jean removed a sheet of parchment from his satchel and displayed it for all to see. "They signed it themselves, next to their names," he explained proudly.

Ischia scrutinized the document. He made a wry smile and announced, "This is that ghost *condotta* from last year!"

"So what?" Jean said. "I wrote out the names, figures and…and…terms of service on the back." He frowned and looked at Count Robert for support.

Ischia shook his head. "That is not done, or at least the first *condotta* must be properly voided. Also, is it notarized?" He glanced at the parchment. "No, clearly it is not."

Geoffrey jumped up. "If these men declare that they follow me, that should be good enough!"

"Not if you want to be paid, master squire," Ischia said, "and be recognized. They can shout your name to the Heavens, but in our eyes you will remain an orphan squire, albeit one with a few friends."

"Calm down, Captain dell'Ischia," Ivry said. "That is true, Hotspur. I must respect the custom here. However, you may again ride with us, but that is all."

"Thank you, my lord." Geoffrey bowed, but he was not as content as he appeared. He had been embarrassed, and his lordship would remember.

As the Ivry party filed back into their lodgings, Crivelli whispered to Jean, "You should have had the document notarized."

"Sorry, Geoff," Jean said. "It would have worked, but for Ischia. I have rarely seen such jealously in a man, and over you, of all people." He was fully expecting the squire to punch him, and so had joked in order to deflate the tension. However, Geoffrey just inhaled that cold mountain air and slowly exhaled.

"At least his lordship did not turn me away," Geoffrey said quietly, although he was already thinking about how he might get close to his lordship. He had lost the royal commission, and he would be damned if he would lose the favor of the Count d'Ivry.

Geoffrey turned and went in search of his German companions; his humors were quick and he wanted life around him. He found them a local ale house near the main square, along with several members of the Company of the Rose. Geoffrey kept his eye out for gaming boards, dice or even cards. When he inquired as to the whereabouts of those marvelous instruments of hazard, the Germans replied that they had decided not to unpack them, since they were lodged deep in one of the carts.

"Are we just to sit here and drink?" Geoffrey cried.

One German man-at-arms suggested singing.

"I like the sound of that," Geoffrey said. "And musicians. We must have music." He asked the innkeeper about the possibility of hiring musicians, but he showed little enthusiasm for wandering up and down the cold, snowy streets in search of something that would not benefit him.

Geoffrey waved him off and began asking the Germans about songs. However, he could not understand theirs and they his, and the Germans themselves could not agree on a cycle, so the effort died amidst conflicting melodies.

"Are the brothels closed?" Geoffrey asked sharply.

Someone said that the town was too small to have one.

"Nonsense! Let us search ourselves. That should be an easy quest."

Another man suggested that the squire sit down and keep quiet.

Geoffrey ignored him and gave an imploring look to one of the men he knew.

Someone else told Geoffrey to propose something himself.

Geoffrey fingered the pommel of his *couteau* as he tried to come up with a suitable diversion that would need little time to organize. His sword gave him the answer. "A tournament!"

The Germans looked at him as though he was mad.

"Well, why not? The light still shines, the winter has kept us out of practice, and just outside lies a nice square that should serve well as the lists. Come now! Are you afraid that I would force all of you to yield? You may choose the arms!"

A brief discussion produced a resolution that the English squire's proposal was indeed a good idea. The veteran German men-at-arms wanted to evaluate the skills of the raw recruits while others wanted to test the fit and strength of their harnesses in a proper pass of arms.

Geoffrey's enthusiasm was infectious and his will ruled the day. He immediately set about organizing the tournament, and in consultation with his companions decided that it would comprise three events: pike, of which he would be the judge, since he took himself out of that competition, sword and buckler, and broad sword. The crowd dispersed to arm themselves, while Geoffrey went to the main square and began defining the lists with piles of snow.

Jean followed the squire. Although he was not keen on a tournament, recalling the sad fate that had recently befallen Azzo da Costello, Jean was glad to see the squire so lusty and in fine spirits. Still, now that he was sober Jean wanted to keep Geoffrey's mind off the unfortunate message from Florence.

"Will you have prizes?" Jean asked.

"Prizes? Yes, there should be prizes! Perhaps some token from Count Robert. He must witness this pass of arms."

"Why do you not play for pride, boasting rights? I am not sure how much you should get Ivry involved in this. He did not call for a tournament."

"Even so, he should be assured of my prowess. If not for a prize, then go ask his lordship to judge the tournament." Geoffrey shifted a pile of snow and looked around for a pole or something that might serve as a barrier. Geoffrey spotted a stack of tree branches beneath a gallery. "You want to play, Jean?"

"No, of course not. However, I am not sure – hey!" Someone knocked Jean's shoulder, causing him to stumble. He looked around and saw a group of Germans with all points armed trotting passed him.

"Listen! Let us determine the prizes later. They do not matter now. You can be a judge too, or a herald. The tournament is on!" Geoffrey greeted the Germans.

"Very well, I will be a judge." As he headed to the pilgrims' lodgings, Jean thought that perhaps he was right, and his victory here improves his standing with the count. There could be money in such a display.

Geoffrey quickly determined the sides with a vertical slash of his hand between the twelve assembled lances and named them the Guelfs and the Ghibellines. Geoffrey himself would take the side of the Ghibellines for the sword events, he announced. After establishing a few rules for pike play, he stepped back.

Cheers went up and a few even dared yell the old war cries. Each team gathered at its side of the square, formed ranks and waited for Geoffrey to start play. When someone asked what the prizes would be, Geoffrey yelled, "A kiss from Captain dell'Ischia!"

Geoffrey gave the signal and the push of pike began. As the men-at-arms struggled to force the other side to give, Jean returned.

"Well?"

"His lordship said that he would watch, but because he is a pilgrim, he cannot in good conscience participate."

"More is the pity. I will judge this event then. Will you be the judge for swordplay? I should be in both events."

Jean closed his eyes and nodded. He had no experience in such games, but he could not imagine that it was particularly difficult to judge: someone strikes; someone falls.

When it was clear that the clash of pikes had reached an impasse, Geoffrey called for time and ordered the sides to withdraw and prepare for another pass. As he stepped back, his eye caught some movement in the loge of one of the wealthier houses on the square. It was Count Robert and a couple of his fellow pilgrims.

Geoffrey neither waved nor gave any indication that he noticed them, yet with as much discretion as he could muster, he squinted hard in their direction.

The Ghibelline side, which was composed mostly of Bavarians, easily won the second pass. The sides then agreed to make the contest a best-of-three, but during the third round a Guelf lance lost its footing and was nearly trampled by the irresistible Ghibellines. The three men of the fallen lance sustained some bruises and dented armor, but what was worse was that Captain dell'Ischia stepped onto the lists, his body bursting with wrath.

"Hotspur! This contest must end now. Has the *podestà* given you permission to draw arms on the square?"

Geoffrey had never thought to ask anyone other than the men-at-arms about passing arms. He was not the lord of this town. However, the tournament participants answered for him by shouting that Geoffrey *was* the *podestà* as far as they were concerned, and if they could not practice their skills amongst themselves, they would do so against the citizens of the town.

Ischia, seeing that his own men were amongst those supporting the English squire, said nothing.

"Judge the swordplay for us, captain," Geoffrey suggested. "You are a man of experience and wise counsel. We need you."

Ischia deemed the offer an expression of sarcasm, but did nothing to counter it considering the immense support the squire suddenly enjoyed. "I will not judge, but you are responsible and will pay if this farce boils over!" He retreated to a gallery and watched.

Geoffrey smiled and furtively glanced at Count Robert.

The sword and buckler event followed. Each side selected five champions and Jean stepped in as judge. His team wanted to put forward Geoffrey, but he changed his mind at the last moment and declined, saying that his best skill was in broad sword play, although the truth was that he wanted to give everyone a chance to compete and to continue organizing. So, he captained the Ghibellines, advising each contestant before he stepped onto the lists.

Jean did his best to judge, deciding to score points only when someone cried out in pain from a hard strike. The Guelfs won the event, three victories to two, but Geoffrey was not discouraged. He ordered that the ground be cleared for the final event.

Geoffrey looked up at the sky. "We should have enough light to continue. Let us play this way: eight men a side, and the winners of each pass will continue to fight until we have one champion. What say you?" Geoffrey drew his *couteau* and held it outstretched.

The answer was never in doubt. The teams took some time, however, selecting their combatants, searching for the best swordsmen.

"Anyone who draws blood will be disqualified and made to pay a fine," Ischia declared from the gallery.

Jean seconded the order. Seeing how he was darting back and forth between the men on his team, Jean recognized more than a hint of the gaming fury in Geoffrey. He hoped he would not kill anyone, least of all Ischia's men. The captain did not look to be the forgiving type.

"Then why not join us to ensure your command is obeyed? You declined to judge our play," Geoffrey taunted.

Jean cringed and looked at Ischia.

Ischia's eyes grew big and he drew himself up to full stature. "Bring me my sword," he ordered one of his servants. His voice was laced with quiet menace.

Two pairs dueled at a time, one on either side of the barrier, since dusk was fast approaching. The *podestà* appeared at Count Robert's side, but was impassive. The initial rounds passed quickly, for it turned out that the Germans were poor swordsmen on the whole.

All were as much in awe of Geoffrey's sword as in his skill, and more than one man-at-arms asked to see it. He would not let anyone handle his *couteau*, though, yet between rounds he was happy to expound on its virtues and hint at a powerful relic lodged in its ruby-colored pommel.

Ischia proved equally adept at discomfiting his opponents, so as the final glimpse of sun disappeared behind the mountains, Ischia and Geoffrey faced each other in the final.

"He prefers thrusts to crossing strikes, Geoff," Jean whispered as he gave the squire a cup of water. They were standing on the edge of the square beneath Ivry's lodgings.

"I know. I have been watching." He gulped down the water in a single draught. He felt hot inside and out. "He likes twisting his blade and he never sets himself in low guard."

"Can you make him yield?"

"Of course I can, now that I know his style. We do not fight in that manner in Avignon."

"You will take care not to…" Jean searched for the correct term. "…over strike?"

Geoffrey frowned. "What do you mean? Are you an arms master?"

"All I am suggesting is that you not rush in. You do not have the advantage of surprise on your side this time."

"Is he watching?" Geoffrey wiped his sword with a special oiled cloth.

"Would it help you if I said 'yes'?"

"Why must you respond to a question with another question?"

"Do not get irate." Jean looked up at the loge. "Yes, he is watching."

Jean called for play to begin. Geoffrey and Ischia approached the trampled middle of the square and bowed to each other. The men-at-arms, their numbers now swollen by a fair number of citizens, crowded in a circle around the lists.

"Out of respect for the mighty Gaunt, I will not kill you, squire," Ischia whispered. "The moment I make you yield, though, you will leave this place."

"His lordship holds pride of place here, captain, not you, so your words carry no force with me. I am not trying to replace you as leader of this party, so why do you hold me in such low esteem?"

"Because you upset things. Now, set yourself." Ischia raised his sword and stepped back.

Geoffrey put himself into a low guard, holding his *couteau* at his hip with the blade pointing at his opponent's head. His strategy had been to make a pass that just touched blades, perform a half-turn, rise into a high guard and bring down a cleaving blow that would either knock the weapon out of his opponent's hand or put him so far off his stance that Geoffrey could either knock him down with another blow or move in to grapple. Ischia was old, so he should avoid grappling, Geoffrey reckoned, but he also recognized that the captain's quickness made up for his physical weakness, plus his experience had to be considered. Geoffrey would look to cut crosswise after he parried the deep thrust.

Ischia advanced quickly with a series of short steps, feinted to his right and made a middle thrust to keep Geoffrey's sword down. Geoffrey refused to give ground, so he parried the thrust not once, but twice. The thrusts were not as deep as he was expecting, so he moved to close, hoping that with his height advantage he would force Ischia back. Then he would sweep across and maybe force him off the lists.

This did not happen. The Italian held firm and maneuvered his blade beneath Geoffrey's while bringing his own guard low to gain the advantage of leverage. Geoffrey was expecting him to twist his blade, so he reaffirmed his grip and waited for the moment when he could get his own blade below and drive his opponent's up and away from his body. However, when Ischia bound their blades, he gave Geoffrey a mighty kick in the thigh that put him off guard and forced the point of his sword down. Ischia turned to Geoffrey's exposed side and angled his sword point at his neck. A single prick and the contest would be over.

Geoffrey saw the danger of his position and knew that he would not be able to right his blade in time to parry the inevitable thrust or offer a kick of his own. A glint of red from the now exposed pommel flashed in his eye. It was a sign. Geoffrey heaved his shoulders and brought the pommel against the blade that was slicing towards him.

A sharp clang seemed to echo against the distant mountains and the crowd cheered. Geoffrey recovered his stance, righted his sword as he turned into a high guard, and believing that Ischia could avoid a crosswise cut, he instead brought down a cleaving strike against the thick forte part of Ischia's blade near the hilt. The captain was stuck. The force of the blow reverberated throughout his body and he slackened his grip, preventing any attempt at a parry or counter-thrust.

Geoffrey closed to grapple. He grabbed Ischia's wrist and forced his sword's point into the ground. He tried to step on the blade, but Ischia managed to drag it out from beneath the sole of Geoffrey's buskin. However, before he could lift the sword, Geoffrey put all his might into a short strike he hoped would knock the weapon out of the captain's hand. Instead, the *couteau* shattered it.

The square went silent. The crowd first looked at the duelists and then at the Frenchman for a judgment. None was forthcoming. Ischia dropped the remnants of his sword, grabbed his right arm and stepped back. He was breathing heavily and wincing in pain. Not knowing what to do, Jean turned to the loge, hoping that Ivry might help him.

Geoffrey looked up as well, followed by the crowd, and finally Ischia made an unspoken appeal to the count.

"By any custom, the squire Hotspur is the winner," Count Robert declared.

Jean raised his arm and called an end to the contest.

Several people ran up to Geoffrey to congratulate him, including the captains of the false lances, who offered to formally and properly enroll in his company.

Geoffrey reveled in the adulation. "All may join me!" he cried.

Jean appeared beside the squire. "Let us find ourselves a notary," he said and shook his hand.

Bologna

The regency council had made a stunning miscalculation, one that even the young Niccolo understood all too well. Within days of having sat with the body of his late captain-general as it lay in state in Ferrara's main cathedral, his uncle had outflanked his army deployed in the western *contado* and taken the cities of Argenta, Consandolo and Portomaggiore in swift succession, the last of which lay within striking distance of Ferrara and was the key to controlling the southern and eastern *contado*. All that saved Ferrara from siege was the swift march of the city's garrison – a company of Breton men-at-arms that his father had hired after the 1385 revolt – to a key crossing of the Po di Primaro River just north of Portomaggiore, where they blocked Azzo's advance.

At the same time, the condottiere Giovanni Barbiano and the Polenta brothers of Ravenna tried to force the Po River in the east, hoping to cut off Ferrara from the lucrative *valli* and thus starve him and the ruling council of money needed to fund his army, but the Este river fleet remained loyal and beat off all attempts to force the river.

As the situation stood now, Niccolo's maternal uncle Alberto Roberti and the vassal Pio and Boiardi clans were defending what was left of the western *contado* with their own retinues; the old German condottiere Conrad Landau, whom the late Azzo da Castello had hired, commanded six hundred heavy men-at-arms in the northern *contado* to protect Ferrara from invasion out of Azzo's homeland in the Polesine region; the Bretons under their captain Jean de la Salle had made their camp in the town of Maiero just north of Portomaggiore; the Este river fleet was patrolling the rivers and canals of the *valli* in the east; Ferrara itself was being defended only by Niccolo's retinue of several hundred mounted men-at-arms, drawn from the oldest and most trusted Este vassals. He wondered how many were now thinking of joining the rebels. Meanwhile, the German condottieri Corrado Altinberg and Ugo Monteforte, also Castello hires, had been ordered to attack Azzo where they could, but they were campaigning in distant Tuscany, and they would need at least a week to return. In short, Niccolo had enemies on all sides with faint hope of relief.

Niccolo and his regency council had survived this test of arms, if only just, and his forces were stretched to near their breaking point and without the guidance of a captain-general. So, it was only a matter of time, just about everyone assumed, before Azzo would recover his strength and make another attempt to take Ferrara. The powers that supported his right to rule – Florence, Venice and Padua – assumed this too, which had provoked them into calling a peace conference in neutral Bologna.

This was why Niccolo was sitting in his lodgings near the hall of the *podestà* with Catherine the astrologer, while the regency council and his mother were flying about Bologna looking for allies, shoring up support and interrogating spies. The shutters were open and Niccolo let his face be whipped by the cold winds.

"I say let stupid Uncle Azzo bash his head against the gates of Ferrara," Niccolo said. "Then his men will see what a fool he is and let me alone." Niccolo felt trepidation tinge his own voice. He looked down from the third-floor window and saw women and men-at-arms scurrying around. None looked up at him. He wondered if anyone would catch him if he leapt out the window.

"And I say close the stupid shutters, Niccolo. I am catching a chill, as will you, and then how fit will you be to rule?" Catherine pulled her mantle tighter around her shoulders. She already had ordered her maids to pack, should worse come to worse.

Niccolo grabbed the window jambs and leaned forward. "If I jump, God will save me, if I am the true heir." A swirling gust pushed him back.

"Stop being silly and get down from there." Catherine stood up. She sounded like a mother and it made her shiver. Regardless, she was the boy's guardian now, and there was nothing she could do about it short of fleeing the Este lands. She also knew that most of the Este vassals were unreliable, so no one else could fill that role. The death of Azzo da Castello and the loss of Portomaggiore had put doubts in many people's minds about the solidity of Niccolo's rule.

"I will get down, but I will not close the shutters." Niccolo stepped away from the window and ambled to a chair across from Catherine. He was wearing court attire, a gold braided doublet and full sleeves, calfskin boots that were cold on his feet, and a cape that was fastened with an immense broach engraved with the Este arms of the crowned white eagle. His mother had told him that he should always be prepared for when they might need him.

"Thank you, my lord," Catherine said. "Now read what the regency council sent you."

Niccolo put his hands on either side of the parchment stacked in front of him and glanced at a book of Cicero, which was his preferred reading, lying open on the far table. He struggled to tear his eyes away from it.

"I wish I could speak like Cicero," Niccolo said as he stared at the tome, "but I cannot."

"I cannot either. All the same, that is for later."

"Why would you need to speak like the ancients?"

"Am I not worthy?"

"You are, but you are an astrologer. You conjure futures for people. What need have you to recite grand words?"

"I do not conjure, Niccolo. I read what the signs show me. But you are right; I do not give speeches." She stared at the boy and wondered if he would survive the week. Rumors of murder plots and conspiracies to overthrow Niccolo and his regency had become more frequent at court and on the streets of Ferrara in recent weeks. Members of court were eyeing each other more warily than usual, Catherine had noticed, and the castle guards appeared to be new every day. Neither she nor anyone else had told Niccolo about this, but Catherine believed that the boy must sense the rising tension around him.

Niccolo smiled shyly. He liked to hear her say his name, although he would never tell her so.

"The ancients never had vassals." Niccolo's tone was serious. "Donato told me, and then he showed me in some books of his. I should just get rid of the lot, or make them all sign *accomandigia* so they can be *raccomendati*. I like the idea of a simple bond on parchment – you protect me and I protect you. Then I would not have to bother with investiture." Niccolo made a dismissive wave with his hand.

"A grand scheme, my lord, but I fear one that would break too cleanly from custom. I doubt the old Este vassals would ever agree to such a reduction in privileges. And while I know little about the ancients, I do know they respected tradition and custom. Besides, who would serve you personally? Who would fill your retinue? Do you want to empty your coffers and *pay* in silver everybody around you? Put this scheme to the esteemed Donato and see if he does not share my counsel."

Niccolo sighed. "Perhaps. Do you know how many vassals I have? Over seven hundred! In sixty-two groups! I read the census my father took. If I were to ask for hospitality on each of their fiefs, I would need more than a year to visit them all! It is all too much."

Catherine wanted to laugh, but she held her tongue. The boy was already filled with so much knowledge, yet nearly empty of experience. That made him fanciful and volatile.

"You are young," she said. "Your father ruled them all, as did his father, and so will you. You must be patient. Now, I suggest you return to your reports."

"Let us play at tables," Niccolo said. "These reports mean nothing to me, and even if they did, the council will have already made all the decisions they want." Just touching the parchment made Niccolo anxious, since they reminded him of the threats to his rule, maybe to his life.

"No quek today," Catherine said loudly. "The next session convenes in an hour, where you will have to say in your own words the reasons for your right to rule."

So far, Catherine had observed that Niccolo held himself well at the sessions. He was quiet and looked nervous, which was to be expected, but above all he had listened to the regency council's suggestions when obliged to answer the few questions put to him and had not let his emotions run away with him. In short, he was the epitome of dignity. However, that seemed to carry little weight with the arbiters of the dispute – the *podestà* of Bologna, the papal vicar of Bologna, and three lawyers from the local university. Each side had challenged the other's legitimacy to inherit Ferrara, and so far, if Catherine's sources were correct, the arbiters believed that each side was right in equal measure: the forced investiture of every Este vassal by a minor was indeed without precedent, although not strictly against custom, while Azzo belonged to a branch of the Este that had renounced its right of succession to the core Este lands several generations ago, although he could claim the inheritance by right of conquest.

Just as equal were the respective alliances: Niccolo's trio of supporters easily balanced Azzo's backers, Milan, Modena and Reggio. Catherine held little hope that the dispute would be resolved peacefully in the coming days. Rather, she believe that, with the condottiere hiring fair in town, both sides were more interested in using the interlude to gather as many captains as they could before recommencing hostilities. At the moment, her side was well behind, and so she had better prepare herself for defeat.

"So be it!" Niccolo shouted and he sat at the desk. He was not angry, but all the same he was hoping that the astrologer would sit next to him, though she had never done so. He grew excited when he noticed her rise from her chair, but his heart sank when he saw her close the shutters and return to her place.

As Niccolo read, he could not help thinking about the great audience in the session hall. Meeting some of the most powerful lords in Lombardy nearly terrified him, which had made his head swim and put a knot in his stomach. He wondered if he would not be more comfortable speaking with Uncle Azzo privately, each with not more than one advisor by his side. However, that was a foolish notion because Uncle Azzo was a great captain and had seen many things, while he had been nowhere and done nothing.

And besides, the regency council would never permit it. They would not consult with him; they just gave him lines to read and an astrologer for company. Niccolo wondered how his father had handled such threats. He had trouble imagining him.

"Tell me about my father," Niccolo asked as he turned over the last page.

Catherine shuddered. "You have finished reading?"

"Yes." He held up the overturned leaf. "I heard the groomsmen in the stable say that you knew him, before he died."

"Read them again."

"Did you know him?"

"You are old enough to remember your own father, Niccolo. Why do you need my memories of him?"

"So, you did know him!" Niccolo slammed his palm on the documents and flew to Catherine's chair.

"You have your own memories, so play with them." The line of questioning was making Catherine uncomfortable. She was not sure how much she should tell the boy, if anything. She looked around the room for something with which to distract him.

"In truth, I remember little. I remember he was old, although he had kind eyes, but little more." Niccolo slid his hand along the armrest until it was touching Catherine's sleeve.

Catherine did remember Alberto d'Este. She also recalled Uncle Azzo, for whom she read after a banquet once. The encounter happened shortly after Alberto had crushed a conspiracy against him, about five or six years ago, led by a number of the Este's oldest vassals. Uncle Azzo was never implicated in this affair, but all the same he did nothing to help his cousin. At the banquet Alberto had lauded Azzo as a great captain and noble lord, while Azzo in return had raised his glass to the longevity of the Este clan in Ferrara. As to the reading, her conclusion was that he would lead a long and prosperous life, but with little fame or notoriety. And he paid well.

"He was a great man and you should always honor his memory," Catherine recited.

"Why do you tell me nothing? No one tells me anything. They just say to wait and wait, dress and read and wait. Where is my arms master?"

"What do you want with him?" Catherine, concerned by the abrupt change in the boy's demeanor, sat up in her chair and dragged her hand off the armrest.

"I want to train." Niccolo began whipping the air with his sword hand. "The regency council cannot hide from me that I must fight. I know I can. I have read about battles won and lost, and you saw me the other day with my confraternity. We would have won had the battle not been called off."

"Snow is not steel, and books are not bastions. You will be called when you are needed." When she saw that the boy was about to protest, Catherine said, "I will not hide the truth from you, Niccolo. You are the *signore* of Ferrara and the head of the Este clan, but you are not ready to lead. Do you understand the word 'regency'?"

Niccolo closed his mouth and narrowed his eyes. His stiff body slackened a little, but he balled his hands into fists. "Yes," he said coldly. "I understand the word. It has become uncomfortable for me, and I shall soon outgrow it."

Niccolo went to the main window and opened the shutters. Expecting a cold blast of air, instead he received nothing. The sky was clear but for a flock of ravens circling in the distance. The echo of their caws was the only sound he heard. Looking into the square below again, he counted more men-at-arms than citizens.

"You will, and get away from that window before someone shoots you out of there. Is that what you want?" Catherine was exasperated with the boy, but she would not touch him.

"What I *want* is to ride. Or read my book." He glanced at the Cicero. Niccolo smiled. "Let us play a game. You read the words of the noble Cicero and then I will recite them back to you. I wager that I can repeat the words without error."

Catherine sighed. "We will do this: you prove to me that you have fully and attentively read the reports by telling me the most important bits in them, and then we will read Cicero together."

Niccolo closed the shutters and returned to his seat.

"You may start when you are ready," Catherine said.

Niccolo began to breathe hard. The caws of the ravens seem to grow louder. "Will they kill me?" he whispered. Niccolo did not look up from the page.

Catherine stared at the boy. He did not look frightened, but she noticed how his shoulders would occasionally shiver.

"I have not the gift of foresight, Niccolo. I cannot answer you."

Niccolo looked up and gave Catherine a thin smile.

"Your honesty comforts me. Please, stay."

They heard a violent rapping on the door, followed by the rattling of armor and the turning of a lock. A man-at-arms entered the room and said, "The next session is about to get underway, my lord."

CHAPTER 6

Both Captain dell'Ischia and Count d'Ivry forbade the convening of any more tournaments, even if they were organized by the local lords, for fear of injury. Nevertheless, a good humor had been established within the diverse group, especially considering the growing stream of worrying news they encountered as they followed the Marecchia River north to Rimini.

Men-at-arms were on the move as word of the peace conference at Bologna spread, so almost every knight, pikeman and crossbowman of the poor mountain villages of the Romagna were arming themselves, founding companies and marching the same direction as the Cypriot pilgrims and their escort. The Montefeltro lords of Urbino, Malatesta of Rimini, Manfredi of Faenza, Sforza or Pesaro, Polenta of Ravenna, and Ordelaffi of Forli were recruiting new men to swell their ranks. Jean took note.

Count Robert called on Geoffrey's company infrequently during this time, as both he and Captain dell'Ischia would often search out the local *signori* and condottieri to learn more about the mobilizing companies in general and about the progress of the war for the Este inheritance specifically. This confirmed Jean's suspicion that Ivry was laying the groundwork for a campaign against the enemies of Cyprus, and so he was happy that the count appeared to be losing interest in the squire.

Ischia, meanwhile, refused to speak with Geoffrey and barely tolerated his presence at dinner, but that did not stop the squire from ordering his newly increased company to stay close to Ivry, so he was often within the count's sight.

At Rimini, the group split, with most of the German men-at-arms bands taking the old Roman Via Aemila northwest to Bologna and the rest heading directly north to Ravenna by the Via Popilia. After another two days of riding, Ivry and his company reached their final destination.

A wave of exultation washed over Geoffrey as he passed through the gates of

Ravenna, and as he sat tall in the saddle of Saint George he nodded proudly to any citizens who took notice of him. He had fulfilled his commission to safely bring Count Robert d'Ivry to his destination. Now, the young squire was considering making a new one. The fateful message from Florence was still searing his heart like a burning coal, but rather than douse the heat with drink or acceptance, he used the pain as a point of focus for what he might do. Geoffrey inhaled the icy gale that blew in from the Adriatic that might carry him to the Holy Land.

"One night," Jean said when he met Geoffrey in the Black Hart Inn after the squire had dined with Ivry, "then we ride to Bologna." He had collected the balance of pay from his lordship and was not content to spend it on foolish luxury. So, after convincing the Germans to remain with the English Free Company until they reached at least Bologna, depending on what they find there, he found cheap lodgings and fine ale. "The hiring fair is well underway and the innkeeper told me that war is expected to ignite again near here the moment it closes."

"All the more reason to stay," Geoffrey said. Each man had a tankard of ale before him, but Jean's was almost empty.

Jean cocked his head and frowned. "What you mean? Are you expecting the war to come to you? I am no condottiere, but I am certain such things do not work that way. Also, no one is hiring in this city as we sit here."

Geoffrey took a tentative sip of his ale. "As I am sure you have noticed, since being nosy is a part of your nature, his lordship and I have spoken at length on many matters, most of which are close to both our hearts. Tonight was no exception."

Jean opened his mouth to speak.

"Hold your tongue, please! I plan to take the Cross. For a while I was uncertain, but his lordship embraced me as we parted, as he might a son."

"You jest at my expense, and the slight is well deserved," Jean said in a voice that cracked from uncertainty. "Very well. Two days here, and then we must be off. It is only proper." He downed the remainder of his ale and waved for the serving maid to bring him another.

"I make no jest, knave! His lordship and I agreed to meet at compline hour in the chapel next to his lodgings, where I will make my declaration. Cyprus is very much under threat and the Ivry family, as well as all the other defenders of Christendom, needs our help. I expect we set sail when the weather clears."

"Did the count invite you?" Jean asked sharply.

"No, but…"

"Then you are not taking the Cross and you are not setting sail for Cyprus. Gaunt will not let you, for one, and for another you have not enough silver to allow you passage, complete your motley harness, sustain you on that wretched island, and provide you with lodgings. Can you be certain Count Robert will even accept you? Why do you wish to embarrass yourself?"

"Listen! You said yourself that his lordship is recruiting men for a holy campaign."

"I said that he *might* be recruiting, or planning to recruit in some distant year. And Gaunt? The royal commission is gone, but your lord and master remains."

"His lordship the duke will be proud of my decision, as word of my deeds of arms against the infidels makes its way to Avignon and England." Geoffrey placed his hands flat on the table and leaned forward. His eyes glistened with intensity.

"You are assuming too much. You have been long away from court and his lordship expects you to return, deeds or no deeds. And besides, I do not recall either pope calling for men to take the Cross, or your king either, for that matter. A one-man army will do precious little damage to the Saracen hordes."

"It is a man's heart what tells him when to take the Cross and perform his Christian duty to his brothers in faith."

"Are those your words or Ivry's?"

"We are of one mind in that belief. Time has no meaning in the eternal battle against the enemies of Christ. The English Free Company will be welcomed. Others will follow. Of that I am certain. I will have a merry band when I convince the German lances to follow me, and with your skill at victualing, we should…"

Jean's eyes grew wide. "Whoa, whoa, whoa, master squire! You are not expecting me to accompany you on this ill-conceived venture, are you? There is no cross for *me* to take, I tell you!"

Geoffrey frowned. "You must come. You are the captain-victualer, or whatever, of the English Free Company. I lead the English Free Company. I say we take the Cross and make for Cyprus. Therefore, you are taking the Cross." He pounded the table with his fist to emphasize his point.

Jean snorted. "So, suddenly the English Free Company is important to you! Who is the knave now!?"

"Count Robert has made it so."

Jean was breathing hard through his nose, and after one great sniff, he said more calmly, "As much as I appreciate your delicate reasoning, you do not want to do this, Geoff."

"Why?"

Jean blinked a few times and squinted at the timbers overhead. His right shoulder started to hurt, so he took a great gulp of ale. "The money, as I said. Even if the Germans are swayed by your passion to take the Cross, we cannot afford to sustain our merry band, as you call us, for more than…maybe a few weeks in the East. Think about your own king, Richard the Lionheart, and how he pledged his lands for the sake of campaigning in the Holy Land. You told me those tales yourself."

"I reckon we can stretch the silver. Count Robert told me that we would be welcomed at the hospice of the Hospitallers, which his family patronizes, and provisions are cheap, he says. We can also forage." Geoffrey folded his arms across his chest.

Jean shook his head, trying to think of a decisive reason that would kill the squire's quest. "Men greater than you have fought for years, decades, in the Holy Land, yet heathens remain in Jerusalem. You want to spend the better part of your life there?"

"I do not expect to conquer the infidel in a day. However, once I win my spurs, as a knight in good standing I will attract others to fill my ranks."

"Ahh, so that is what this is all about. A knighthood!" Jean cried. "I should have guessed. And here I thought that the source of the reckless act lies in your soul. Rather, your head is doing the thinking for you." Jean sneered and clapped his hands.

Geoffrey swung his right fist and hit Jean square in the temple. Both tankards went flying, spraying ale as far as the next table.

"You are lucky I am not wearing a gauntlet!" Geoffrey shook his hand and then called for more ale.

"And you are lucky I am not wearing a helm!" Jean rubbed his bruised temple, but he did not check for blood. Experience told him that the squire had not opened his skin. "Was that payment for my words about the knighthood? I am doing the accounts tonight, so I need to know."

"Were you not so slow of pace and wide of girth, you could have been a jester of the highest order."

"Verily, 'tis true, my lord. But setting such comedy aside, you must be as honest with yourself as with me. I know your ambition, Geoffrey Hotspur, and it is as common as a cartwheel!"

Geoffrey made another fist, but quickly relaxed his hand. He now could not afford to drive the Frenchman away. "I will not deny it. I am a squire and a man of Gaunt, after all. However, such an honor does not stand in the bottom rank of my desires. I have long thought about taking the Cross, but only as a dream, but his lordship has made it real, and so it cannot be hastily discarded."

"You hate sailing, Geoff." Jean paid for another round of ale. He nodded at the company's three German lances that had just entered and gestured that he and the squire should be left alone for the time being.

Geoffrey froze and stared ahead. What the Frenchman said was true. Perhaps an overland route to Cyprus existed…

"And where is your tabard? Have you sewn a cross on a surcoat? Of course not – you do not own one. Have you decided on the color? You are certain to enlist in one of the orders." This detail gave him an idea about how he might undermine the squire's rash venture.

"I have convinced you then, you will come? I expected nothing less. Your days as a debt collector are far behind you!" Geoffrey clapped Jean's good shoulder.

Jean closed his eyes and slowly nodded. "You are my captain, and the English Free Company needs me. But we still need livery. I will talk to Crivelli. He seems to know a lot about clothes and fabric and the like."

"I shall talk to the Germans and give them the good news." Geoffrey made as if to go.

Jean reached across the table and touched Geoffrey's arm. "I can do that. I will need to enroll them anew anyway, and they will need to sign and I will have to find another bloody notary. Meet me back here when the bells toll for vespers."

As he walked the streets of Ravenna, Geoffrey thought about the glorious moment when he will first draw blood from a heathen. But how would he do it? By pike? By sword? Naturally, his ideal was to charge into battle astride a mighty destrier with couched lance and a shield bearing his arms, tearing through enemy ranks and sending them to flight. He could see himself doing just that. After all, he had trained for it. However, he had yet to earn his spurs, and the English Free Company must aid in that.

Geoffrey was feeling some guilt about not returning to Avignon, to the hall of his lord and master, but as his lordship the duke himself had told him, a man must make himself and take every opportunity to display his prowess. Also, Geoffrey reasoned that he was not yet a proper vassal of the duke, just a member of his household, and so his following the Count d'Ivry could not be considered a violation of any oath. He was at peace with his decision.

After scouting the chapel near the hospice of the Hospitallers, Geoffrey returned to the Black Hart to find Jean already seated in the same place. He looked around the hall. "Are the Germans not here? Have they refused me?"

"They are hearing Mass, and, no, they have not refused you." Jean smiled. "Come. The tailor awaits us, and he does not plan on keeping his shop open until sunrise."

"So, Crivelli has come through for us? He is to be commended. I truly do owe him some gaming tips!"

Jean stood up and led Geoffrey by the arm into the cold, snow-swept street.

While Jean tucked his hood beneath his chin and hunched his shoulders, Geoffrey let the swirling snowflakes melt against his open neck. His heart felt light, though it beat fiercely, and his sight enjoyed renewed clarity.

"We are here. The finest tailor in Ravenna," Jean announced as he pushed a door open.

Inside they found the tailor, several of his assistants, and Crivelli.

"He has all manner and color of fabric, Geoffrey! Have you decided on your Cross?" Jean asked.

"I have not, but I should think red would be proper, or white."

"Why not blue, to match your doublet?" Jean suggested.

The tailor then explained how the blue cross is usually worn by Galician and Portuguese knights of the Cross, and so would not be proper.

"Very well. Cut the captain and squire a red one."

"Or how about I decide?" Geoffrey said.

Jean nodded and retreated to the back of the room. While the tailor and his assistants went to work measuring Geoffrey, the floorboards suddenly vibrated from the sound of muffled cheering.

"What the--?" Geoffrey looked down. "Are we standing atop the bowels of hell, for all that crying?" he joked.

The tailor chuckled and with a sly grin explained that he sometimes rented out his cellar for the playing of games of chance.

Geoffrey raised his eyebrows. "This is a fine evening for such hazards. What games are in play tonight?"

The tailor said that quek was the preferred hazard on this eve.

"Jean! Find out if the stakes are worth my while!" He turned back to the tailor and said, "By your leave, master tailor."

The tailor nodded and continued his work.

Jean tramped down the stairwell, but he soon returned.

"It is a heady air down there, and the host is not keen on admitting a stranger," Jean said, "but when I told him you were taking the Cross, he could hardly refuse you."

Geoffrey descended into a dank, dimly lit cellar with a low vaulted ceiling, where he was greeted by several men of soldierly ranks, some of whom he recognized as belonging to the Company of the Rose. He hailed them in return and began asking about the stakes.

The quek board was crude and uneven, and Geoffrey noticed the great number of pits across its surface. However, his eyes told him that they must be the result of extensive wear, not made deliberately for the purpose of deceit, which meant that every player was equally disadvantaged.

"They play by local rules," Crivelli explained when Geoffrey asked. "There is a 'hit' ceiling, and if the player surpasses it, he has to pay out."

Geoffrey understood immediately. He had to be very careful about his pitches. "How high is the ceiling?" he asked in a loud voice.

"One hit," Crivelli answered.

Geoffrey smiled and nodded. "Jean! Give me the silver and remain with tailor. You must be my ears for compline. I fear these walls are too thick to admit sound."

Jean nodded and did as he was told.

"W-will you g-give me advice on w-wagering?" Crivelli asked.

"It is the least I can do," Geoffrey said.

The stakes steadily grew as the game ground on, from mere pennies a point to full *grossi*, as the players challenged each other's fortitude. The tailor would bring down tankards of ale from time to time, which refreshed the gaming enthusiasm before the oppressive air of the crowded cellar made everyone dull.

Sweat poured down Geoffrey's arms and back, and the constant jostling with fellow players around the table made him more aggressive. He had to focus hard on this tight game, not wager out of turn, keep his hand steady for casts, and watch the other players for weakness and uncertainty. Whether low or high cast numbers, the hit ceiling complicated wagering strategy. Every pot was heavily loaded with silver; every pot could put one or more players out of the game. Loans were given and promises made, threats were issued and taunts growled. The spark of interest in Geoffrey was soon fanned into a glowing flame of gaming fury.

Hours passed.

"The bells for compline have peeled," Jean said plainly from the head of the stairwell. In truth, they had rung an hour earlier.

Geoffrey did not hear. He shouted at one of the players to mind his cast and not bump the table.

Jean pushed his way through to the squire and clapped a hand on his shoulder. The gesture had no effect.

"You should ready yourself for your pledge, Geoff," Jean said more loudly.

Geoffrey cocked his head. "What? What is that you say?" He turned his head and looked at Jean as though he was seeing him for the first time after several years. "Good Lord!" he shouted. He looked down and the mass of silver in his hand, at the table and back at Jean.

"Shall I go to the chapel and inform his lordship that you will attend him shortly? You need to make yourself presentable. Your doublet looks as though it has just endured a tournament."

"Yes, yes. Good man. I must finish this round."

Jean glanced at Crivelli and nodded. Suddenly an argument broke out between a couple of players over the reckoning. The senior player called for all wagers to be cancelled. More arguing erupted, drawing Geoffrey in to help resolve the dispute. After observing the scene with satisfaction, Jean left the tailor shop.

The tailor descended half way down the stairwell and shouted at Geoffrey that he had finished his surcoat.

Geoffrey turned around and saw snatches of a red cross glistening in the flickering light of the torch. "I will go," he announced. "The rest of you carry on without me. I have won my fair share tonight."

Several players looked at one another and then at the squire, wished him well and declared him a good fellow.

"I will come with you," Crivelli said. "Your tips only kept my losses low, although I thank you all the same." He quickly gathered his gear and followed Geoffrey up the stairs.

The tailor had neatly folded Geoffrey's new garment into a square, and as he was handing the package to him instructed the squire on how the cross should face up when it is being blessed and to set his sword and spurs at the hem.

Geoffrey grabbed the surcoat and bounded out of the shop in great strides. Crivelli followed close behind. The damp chill of the winter night clutched at Geoffrey, freezing the sweat against his skin. The moment he walked through the side door of the chapel he frantically looked around, but his lordship was nowhere in sight. Geoffrey dashed down the aisles, peeped around corners and peered behind curtains.

He accosted a priest, who said that he had seen several men of rank that night, but they had long gone.

"Why could he not wait?" Geoffrey said to himself. He turned and stared hard at Jean. "Are you sure you called me at the onset of compline. I seem awfully late. I trust you about as far as I can throw you."

"I-It was as he says, master squire," Crivelli confirmed. "I heard the bells too."

Geoffrey glanced several times between the two men. "Why did you not send me away from the tables, then?"

"That is not my place," Crivelli answered quietly. He looked down.

"That last round took you a long time to finish," Jean said and shrugged. "I could not interfere and risk my neck. Those were some tough players down there."

Geoffrey tore at his hair and began pacing up and down the aisle. "God's dignity, I am lost! No, wait, I can still appeal to his lordship." Geoffrey raced to the side door.

"Geoff, wait!" Jean cried. "It is late! His lordship will not receive you, or he will be angry." But Geoffrey did not hear. Jean picked up the surcoat the squire had dropped and went after him.

Geoffrey flew passed a group of men-at-arms, who were too busy arguing with several of Ivry's pilgrim companions to stop the squire, and burst into the hospice, nearly knocking down the clerk who was minding the door.

"I demand an audience with his lordship, Count Robert d'Ivry!" Geoffrey shouted at the stumbling clerk.

Jean and Crivelli filed into the small hall a few moments later.

"You have no need to trouble that poor man, squire." The voice of Count Robert emanated from a shadowy corridor. "I have been waiting for you." He stepped out of the darkness and into a space of light cast by an ensconced oil lamp. He was wearing a thick, richly embroidered robe and a coif, and had in his hand a stick that could have been mistaken for a crozier, which gave him the air of a Byzantine bishop.

"My lord!" Geoffrey said as he doffed his hat and bowed. "I failed you at the chapel. Forgive me!"

"I was not at the chapel, Hotspur," Ivry said. His voice was weak and his face showed deep anxiety.

Geoffrey looked up.

"By the order of the *signore* of Ravenna, Obizzo da Polenta, I am not to leave this hospice. I am, in effect, under arrest."

Each man in the hall looked at one another with incredulity.

"What for, my lord? I cannot believe that attempting to recruit men to take the Cross, however secretly, violated any law. It is not…not…Christian!" Geoffrey said.

"What?" Ivry coughed into his hand and wiped his eyes. "I am not here to find knights to fight in the Holy Land, well, not directly. No such campaign has been declared. The truth is that I am here to offer my daughter's hand in marriage to the Marquis of Ferrara, Niccolo d'Este."

Geoffrey's mouth dropped open.

"You are soon to travel to Ferrara then?" Jean asked.

"Did you not hear me? I am trapped in Ravenna. The Polenta have sided with this Azzo d'Este. I cannot be touched because of my rank, but they insist I leave Italy before the spring."

They heard shouting and the clatter of arms in the courtyard.

"That will be Polenta's men." Count Robert drew close to Geoffrey and whispered, "Do this for me, if you are devoted. Find the marquis and tell him that I wait for him."

A dozen men-at-arms piled into the hall. Their sergeant ordered Geoffrey, Jean and Crivelli to leave immediately or be thrown into prison. They complied.

Jean took the squire by the arm as they walked through the wet streets. "Do not despair, Geoff. Your anguish will retire with the moon, and in the morning all will be well. Here, let us get you a warm bed and a nice whore. I cannot think of anything better, other than a pail full of silver, maybe." Jean smiled to buttress his levity and peered into the squire's eyes. His diversionary plan had failed, but the squire was strangely not troubled by the count's refusal of him. There was meaning in that.

Geoffrey held himself calm and erect. The muscles in his face tightened into a serious expression. His hand dropped to the pommel of his *couteau*.

"We leave for Bologna in the morning," Geoffrey said resolutely.

"What did Ivry say to you?" Jean asked.

"That he would let me take the Cross another time," Geoffrey answered. "A campaign is being discussed, he promised, though he could not say when the call to arms would be made." He did not look at the Frenchman; his eyes were on the citadel.

Geoffrey was heartily welcomed by the clientele of the Black Hart Inn, and he was immediately swept up the stairs and into a lavishly decorated hall, where a feast was well underway, complete with musicians, dancers and an array of girls. The recently enrolled German lances were in attendance, and they greeted Geoffrey as their captain, as well as the tailor who had sewn him his surcoat, which he found odd.

"Everything is here, except gaming, Geoff," Jean said, and he slapped the squire on the back, "and no curfew. Enjoy! This was to be a celebration of your pledge, but now it is just a celebration!"

"My taking the Cross has only been delayed, Jean. I have pledged to God. Remember, Emperor Frederick Barbarossa waited until his late years before joining King Richard of blessed memory in the Holy Land."

"Well, let us worry about now, shall we?"

"Let us not worry at all." Geoffrey looked around the hall and caught the eye of several maidens. "Did you not invite Captain dell'Ischia and his stammering friend to this banquet? We were boon companions on the journey here, after all."

"Boon companions! You nearly struck down Ischia, and I daresay he wanted to kill you, Geoff." Jean snorted derisively. "You are not even drunk, yet you already speak with generosity."

"We had an honest pass of arms. I would have been insulted had he not stirred his dark humors when we crossed swords. I respect his need to keep order."

Jean could only shake his head at the squire's sanguine response, but he was not about to argue the point when there was fine ale to drink and good company to meet, so all he said was, "All the same, Ischia and Crivelli will not come."

Geoffrey just had a drink thrust in his hand when a tall maid with French features, including dark narrow eyes and full lips, approached and picked up a thread of conversation with the squire. She begged him to tell her about his deeds of valor, about his skill in arms, and about his free company. Other maids came to listen, and soon Geoffrey was sloshing ale on the floor as a result of his broad gestures and speaking in a loud almost ecstatic voice. He danced, even though the airs were unfamiliar to him, and caroused as though he was in the squire's hall of the Duke of Lancaster in Avignon, where his confraternity would put on feasts of a more modest but similar nature.

After several hours of merry-making, Jean found Geoffrey on a padded bench with the French maiden, who had evidently fallen asleep on his shoulder. He sat down next to the squire and rested his head against the cool wall behind him. It seems that the banquet was serving well as a salve for the squire's rejection.

"This will not cost as much as you might think," Jean said. He had imbibed his fair share of ale, but he was far from drunk. "The girls are on their own, so to speak."

Geoffrey shrugged his free shoulder.

"We should have enough silver to get us to Bologna in good order and well armed."

"What did you do with my surcoat? If you returned it, I will have my boot on your arse until you retrieve it!" Geoffrey stuck out his leg. The French maiden moaned softly.

"I am keeping it safe for when you rightly need it." This much was true. "You are probably too drunk to understand this, but I got word that the hiring is fast and furious for the Este war, and not for garrison duty, and so we should easily get on with a caravan traveling west. Rumors are piling up like firewood, but it seems as though everyone but the pope has a stake in the outcome, including the emperor."

"The emperor!" Geoffrey jerked slightly, nearly causing the girl to lose her balance. "Are you sure?"

"No, of course not – they are only rumors. However," Jean dropped his voice to a whisper, "where there is smoke, there is fire, as they say."

Geoffrey patted the sleepy girl on the cheek. "Where is your companion, or have you done with her already?"

Jean was gratified by the return of lust and wit in Geoffrey's humors, and so he was willing to serve as an object of ridicule as long as he could get the squire out of Ravenna. He congratulated himself on arranging this feast, convincing the Germans to stay with the company, and getting Crivelli to help him deceive the squire.

"I have not even started with her," Jean said, "though I am spoiled for choice."

"Do not dally! Take one, and then another, if you are not satisfied."

"For dancing?" Jean said with feigned naiveté.

Geoffrey laughed. "Yes, well, looking at your poor threads, dancing might be the best you can hope for with these damsels. When will you get rid of that hideous jupon? You should have taken advantage of our visit to the tailor."

Jean smiled thinly.

The French maiden awoke and immediately began pawing Geoffrey, playing with the buttons on his doublet and cooing in his ear. Without a word, Geoffrey pulled his companion for the evening off the bench and led her to his room.

CHAPTER 7

Niccolo stared straight ahead. Uncle Azzo was sitting in the large chair far to his right, although it was not far enough for Niccolo to feel comfortable. His mother and Alberto Roberti were just in front of him seated on one side of the table that stretched almost the length of the hall of the *podestà*.

The representatives of his allies and enemies, the arbiters and several neutral observers occupied places further down. Catherine was standing behind him, or at least she said she would – he would not dare turn around to make sure. Above and around him the galleries were packed so tightly that the wooden railings were bending outwards. The accompanying noise reminded Niccolo of a beehive. The *podestà* of Bologna, who was moderating the proceedings, had called for quiet on more than one occasion, the most recent being when Roberti announced that he had a new captain-general, the *signore* of Faenza, Astorre Manfredi, a condottiere as respected for his military abilities as resented for his chronic duplicity. Until an hour before the session, the regency council had not been sure if Manfredi would accept the white baton of captain-general.

Niccolo was not expecting to speak at this session, but now that his military situation had changed for the better, Roberti had decided to buttress this sudden strength with a brief speech by the young marquis himself. He saw the *podestà* look at him and with a silent gesture gave him the floor. As Niccolo slowly rose, his heart leapt in his throat.

"The die has not been cast!" Niccolo declared in a clear and steady voice. He hoped he would remember the words written for him by the regency council. With his eyes forward and focused on nothing but a wooden pillar propping up a gallery, he continued. "Mighty Caesar has yet to cross the Rubicon! The war that will plunge eastern Lombardy into anarchy can still be avoided. My uncle has already been asked, with all due courtesy, to disperse his companies and return to his rightful place, to accept investiture at my hand, as is my right, and I call on him again with my own voice to recognize his folly, and I will forgive him."

The din in the galleries swelled. Who was he to forgive Uncle Azzo, or anyone for that matter? Only the Lord forgives. He could not see the aged captain and veteran of a dozen wars bending at the knee and bowing his head to him in submission. Did the regency council really expect this? To regain his focus, Niccolo thought about the esteemed Cicero.

"I and my allies, Florence, Venice and Padua, will take his refusal to do so as a declaration of war, during which no quarter will be given!" Niccolo did not like the sound of this last line when he had read it the first time, and he liked it even less now that he had spoken it. He found too much certainty in the declaration. When he had defeated that rival confraternity of boys in the snow just a couple of weeks ago, it had been because he had changed his plan during the battle.

"My war chest is full and the ranks of my army are filling so fast that I have had to find more parchment on which to compose their *condotti*. I have informed all my vassals of their duties to me. I know both by heart, so that none might deceive me!"

Without averting his gaze Niccolo extended a hand in Azzo's direction and began listing the number of healthy and sick men fighting under his uncle's banner, the length of service of his captains and the deployment of his men. He followed this revelation with a recitation of former vassals who he declared anathema, including inventories of the respective property the regency council would confiscate.

Just as his voice started to falter, Niccolo bowed to the now silent audience and sat down.

"Well done!" whispered a voice from behind.

Niccolo was relieved that the voice belonged to Catherine. He had been so nervous before the session that he had nearly wet himself, but her reassuring words had brought to him enough calm that he was able to enter the hall without tripping or fainting.

"What did my father do, when the citizens of Ferrara wanted to throw him over?" Niccolo had asked her as the maids were making the final adjustments on his clothing.

"I was not there. I met your father a few years after that."

"How did he rule, when you were reading for him? You should tell me."

"The ruling council, not to mention your mother, would have my head if I were to advise you without their consent. Ask them."

"I am never given the chance to ask. They all tell me what to say, and I say it, but it is not natural. I am certain no one believes me when I speak." Niccolo remembered how he began picking at one of his doublet buttons.

"No, you cannot be certain of that. However, they do listen. In some ways, you are much like your father, Niccolo, and some of those traits made him a good ruler. He understood the value of knowledge, like you do." Catherine had smiled, which he hoped was sincere. "But he knew much more than what could be found in his dusty library. For example, I remember him constantly receiving parchment from his factors, which contained so many columns and numbers that I thought they were about astrology, and so were meant for me! But no, those leaves of parchment held knowledge about all the Este lands, the vassals, the merchants, and all the duties owed to him. And he used that knowledge, like you did during your snowy battle last month, when his enemies tried to bring him low."

"How did he do that? I had remembered my Vegetius, but if I just had a load of numbers, I am not sure what I could have done with them."

"Those numbers represented men, money, land, and a host of other details. And they were indisputable, because your father made them so. He was not a great orator, although he spoke well enough, but when he would say anything his words would always bear the ring of truth, because all the numbers and knowledge he would recite were true. He crushed the conspiracy against him because he understood which treacherous vassal did not have the silver to sustain him, and he knew which land to occupy that would give him and his army the most provisions. That is how your father outmaneuvered those who planned to overthrow him."

"If the vassals were so traitorous, then why did he not sweep them all aside and replace them with *raccomendati*?" Niccolo remembered staring at the astrologer and thinking about why a vassal's wealth might mean so much, yet he detected a connection.

"I cannot speak for your father, but he was a great respecter of custom and tradition. Also, remember that not all vassals rebelled. Had he broken that sacred bond with all of them, I doubt you would have had much of an inheritance."

"I remember my father as not being very strong." Niccolo heard the guards stomping around outside his chamber. "I mean, I recall him being a big man, but he was always tired, and he always had doctors and bleeders around him."

"*I* remember him as a strong man. He was a fine rider."

This observation pleased him. "Did he slay anybody? He must have slain some of those who were plotting against him. I know I would have."

"Would you really? If you found yourself with a little sword pressed against the neck of a man whom you had forced to yield, could you make the final thrust and end his life?" Catherine made a stabbing motion against Niccolo's neck. "Paint that image in your mind and think. Close your eyes."

Niccolo had closed his eyes and saw his companion the Blue confraternity captain. "It would have to be an enemy," he said after a while.

"Of course, but must it be a mortal enemy?"

"What does 'mortal' mean?"

"He wants to kill you too, and will not stop until he has done it. Could you slay a man on a battlefield, a man who is unknown to you and is only fighting you because it is his duty, not his desire?"

These words had affected him. "A traitor is a traitor! They must be killed!"

"What about Christian charity, Niccolo? What about granting mercy. There will always be someone out there wanting to take your place. Would you kill them all?"

"Yes! It is what they deserve! I am the true heir to the Este inheritance."

"That may very well be, but are not friends better to have than enemies? I cannot see you riding day and night ridding your lands of all you hate. This sounds very much like your poor scheme to remove all vassals."

"I do not hate." Niccolo was holding his fists so tightly that their knuckles had turned white.

"What about that boy you thrashed for calling out your uncle's name? Would you have killed him, had you a metal blade instead of a wooden one?"

Niccolo opened his eyes; Catherine was no longer smiling. "I wanted to at the time, but now I no longer hate him. He had to be punished though."

"That is good. I do not believe your father slew very many people. He did not need to. Do you understand?"

"I think so."

"At the next session you will show confidence in your knowledge about your enemies, as well as your friends. Looking as though you possess great knowledge is half the battle. Someone will feed you the rest. Ask and continue asking until you get what you need. You are the Marquis of Ferrara, after all!"

Niccolo tore his gaze from the post when he heard the *podestà* loudly announce that Azzo d'Este was asking for a recess. He then saw Roberti and his mother get up and he quickly found himself being escorted out of the hall.

The condottieri hiring fair was mainly held outside the walls of Bologna, although famous captains were allowed to rent lodgings within the city proper.

Neither Geoffrey nor Jean had ever seen anything like it.

The frozen field was alive with tents and pavilions of many colors, like a flower garden in full bloom. The scene reminded Geoffrey of the tournaments he and his fellow squires had been allowed attend near Avignon. Then, he had been put to work assisting any knights Gaunt was sponsoring, and so had only seen the backside of the events, flitting between the tents of blacksmiths, carpenters, grooms, and the like, but today he could ride passed the pavilion of the most famous knight.

Geoffrey spotted a group of boys carrying pikes and for a moment he saw himself in their midst as a young page, minding his grace's gear as he prepared for a tournament.

Crivelli was their guide to the hiring fair. Despite his open dislike for the squire Hotspur and his offset companion Lagoustine, Captain dell'Ischia had not opposed their riding together, although he never spoke to them or offered them hospitality during the whole of the two-day journey from Ravenna. As they passed through the camp, Crivelli pointed out which pavilion belonged to which condottiere.

"Th-that massive one with red and white stripes b-belongs to the Barbiano family. They are a t-tough lot, and th-there is no question that their agents will be all over the city. The b-blue and gold chequered pavilion next to th-that is the Polenta family, I am sure, since I saw their crest in Ravenna. Oh! See that yellow and black series of small pavilions?" Crivelli extended his arm across Jean.

"Yes, I see them," Jean said.

"Corrado Altinberg. The G-Germans should be here in f-full force, since none of the T-Tuscan cities want to hire them this year. I do not see the Gonzaga anywhere, which is a bit odd, since Mantua is a neighbor of Ferrara." Crivelli stood up in his saddle and scanned the field. "N-No, they are d-definitely not here, at least as condottieri, and th-they are sure to have one or t-two men inside. The dark blue and yellow pavilions, though, definitely belong to the Polenta. I would not mind enrolling in one of their companies," Crivelli whispered to Jean. He continued identifying arms, pennons, gonfalons, and charges until the party reached the registration booth.

Jean leaned over to Geoffrey and said, "He is very knowledgeable. You would not think so to look at him, but I have no cause to doubt his word in these trifles."

"These colors are not trifles, Jean," Geoffrey admonished. "Not knowing the colors means not knowing the family, and that means insulting the reputation. I remember at one tournament when a herald put up one pennon and called the name of a knight belonging to a different family. The tournament steward dismissed him on the spot, but not before having the squires of the offended knight beat him without restraint. Can you remember them all?"

"So, I am representing the English Free Company then?"

"Of course." If he was to keep secret his commission from Count Robert, Geoffrey had to let Jean show that the English Free Company was looking for work.

Jean nodded and dismounted. After briefly conferring with the Germans, he approached the registration booth and stood behind Crivelli, to whom Captain dell'Ischia had delegated the same task. Jean peered over his shoulder when the time came for the Italian to give the name and strength of his company, present credentials in the form of executed *condotti*, declare intentions to engage in which kind of service, and a host of other details. Jean had not realized, although it was perfectly reasonable, that the English Free Company would have to state its arms specialty, whether escorting, sapping, river fighting, scouting, raiding, foraging, or plain old field service as knights, pikemen or archers.

The declaration of intentions also meant that anyone in need of such services could find him and Geoffrey. Jean knew what service Geoffrey would prefer – anything that would allow him to perform deeds of arms before esteemed witnesses. He also had the three German lances to consider. Geoffrey had impressed them enough to enroll in the company, and so he could not risk disappointing them by accepting a poor paying and dull commission. And he needed the money. Jean decided he would have the English Free Company protect a big caravan that was traveling westwards – soon.

"Did you make your mark at the booth, Geoff?" Jean asked as they pushed their way through the crown of condottieri.

Geoffrey was flipping between his fingers a wooden token he had been given embossed with the arms of the city crossed with those of the *podestà*, which allowed him to enter and exit Bologna at will for the duration of the hiring fair.

"I did," Geoffrey said. He also had asked where the Este peace conference was being held. He had no idea what Niccolo d'Este looked like or how he might meet with him, or even how he might convince the marquis that he, an English squire, represented the esteemed count, since his lordship had not been allowed the time to give him his seal or write him a letter of introduction. It was a problem Geoffrey had been mulling over since Count Robert had given him the commission, a problem he had to resolve alone.

"So, you will act like a condottiere and be the captain of the English Free Company?"

"Do not give voice to such things, however true they might be. Let us find a pavilion so that we might camp with the rest of the knights here."

"Humph!"

After making a number of straightforward suggestions on how they might procure the necessary trappings of a new condottiere company, Jean decided to put their fortune in the hands of the Germans to buy a pavilion and find a dry place to put it. He also hoped that these tasks would bind them closer to Geoffrey and the company.

"I should offer my sword, and the lances of my company, to be precise, to the greater captains at this…this…hiring fair," Geoffrey said. Such a scheme might get him an audience with people close to the marquis.

"That is not how things are done here, Geoff," Jean said. He stared at the bustle around him and especially kept an eye out for pickpockets, whoremongers and debt collectors who might harass them. He put on a scowl to ward off anyone who might consider the squire easy prey, despite his impressive height and noble bearing, and kept one hand on his purse at all times.

"Then how are they done, Jean? You tell me, since you are a master procurer at these fairs, and have served as quartermaster, victualer, swordmaster, and constable in the finest armies in Christendom." Geoffrey was wearing his finest attire, including his doublet, the better of his woolen hose, which was steel gray in color, a wide belt with his sword affixed, polished buskins, and a pointed chaperon that would have been the height of fashion in Avignon, but was considered passé where he was now. Fortunately, the large number of Germans attending the fair diluted whatever foreignness Geoffrey exuded.

"You aim for ridicule, but you strike well passed the mark, squire. Listen, this is a fair like any other, which means we keep our eyes open and our mouths shut until we find what we want."

"And what is that? I have suggested slicing to the bone instead of carving around the gristle by making directly for the main captains, but you want to do *what*, exactly?"

"The main captains, as you call them, are hardly likely to be seen dealing for themselves. They will have agents, and we will have to find them."

Geoffrey thought that logical, but he would insist on an interview.

Jean was feeling frustrated, since he was not sure what to look for. Crivelli might have helped him on this account, but the Company of the Rose had their own business. Then he saw a row of stalls that seemed to offer no wares but some worn books and a load of parchment. No signs were hanging near them to suggest their guild, but nailed to the lintel above each stall was a crest, some of which Jean recognized as belonging to the families of the condottieri Crivelli had pointed out earlier.

"With who should the English Free Company enroll, do you think, Geoff?" He made a broad sweep with his arm. He could not distinguish between condottiere and merchant booth, but Jean supposed that one might be dependent on the other or they shared space. The confusion bothered him and he instinctively clutched his weak shoulder.

"With a lord and knight, Jean. Someone respectable." Geoffrey wanted to keep up the ruse of caring for as long as possible.

"That much I know." Jean sighed.

Geoffrey tried to recall if anyone, Crivelli perhaps, had mentioned who was on whose side. He did not wish to give himself away.

Jean saw the arms and crest of the Polenta family, but ignored that stall for fear of Geoffrey somehow being returned to Ravenna, although according to Crivelli the Polenta captains were both lords and knights. He then saw sitting cheek by jowl the recruiting booths of the Obizzi, Boiardi, Correggio, and Cantelli, all of whom were respectable condottieri. Further on Jean noticed that the leading German captains had their stalls close together. He looked around for any English or French arms he might recognize, but found none. Groups of men were clustered around each stall, and Jean soon learned that soliciting advice from passersby was useless, leaving him and Geoffrey to guess where to start.

"Let us start at the beginning, since you know about as much as I do," Geoffrey said, pointing at a crimson shield blazoned with a white chevron, the arms of the Boiardi.

Jean and Geoffrey had to work to shove their way to the front of the queue. This was one occasion where the squire's impatience, let alone his strength and height, served them well.

"Well, that could not have gone any worse," Geoffrey said as he slammed down a tankard of ale. "Now I know why the Gamesmaster hired you for your brawn and not your brains."

They were sitting in the Roasted Hart Inn, a shoddy-looking tavern built into the city wall that served weak ale, diluted wine and nothing else. The only offers they had received came from several petty condottieri, who also had yet to find commissions, to join forces and share provisions, and no caravans. Jean had to admit that he was out of his depth in this game. He had been slow-witted in responding to the many pointed questions the recruiters had asked, did not understand several others, and had difficulty reading the sample *condotti* shoved under his nose. And with the crush of other soldiers trying to gain the same ears, interest in the English Free Company quickly waned and Jean lost confidence.

"You were no better, with all your petty questions about the captains and their families, and who is staying where," Jean said. "You are not a king, or a prince, or anybody in particular. Are you expecting to be invited to attend court somewhere just because you are a man of Gaunt?" Jean took a violent swig of ale, causing some to dribble from the corners of his mouth. "For all that is holy, you cannot go about playing the grand lord and expect the recruiters to take you seriously."

Geoffrey was content to let his companion misunderstand the purpose of his 'silly' questions, for he now knew where the marquis's lodgings were and who was on his side.

"Then I will go to the hall of the *podestà* and you can continue complaining to these walls," Geoffrey said and he slurped the last of his ale. He had to see what all the fuss was about with the Este inheritance, and it might help him figure out a way to meet with the marquis.

"Fine! The bitterness of my gall needs no further irritation!" Jean shouted as Geoffrey left the tavern.

To calm himself, Jean decided to engage in the routine practice of inspecting prices. He expected them to be high on account of the hiring fair and peace conference, so he knew he had to be careful with his limited means, especially now that he had to buy for three German lances in addition to himself and the English squire. The debacle at the hiring stalls had dented Jean's confidence in his ability to negotiate, so he made sure to visit all the stalls in the market and to remember their prices.

A crude calculation gave Jean a sum that would cover the victualing cost of the English Free Company for about a month at best. They had a pavilion and they had horses. Geoffrey and the Germans could be counted on for the full complement of arms and armor – just, but he had yet himself to consider. That was not quite true. For some time Jean had been wondering whether it was worth his while to buy a respectable harness and a decent sword, or halberd, which he preferred, if he had to fight. He knew he should get something, if only for his own protection – he had been fond of a thick black leather jack adorned with a hundred metal studs he used to wear in Avignon. However, such an arrangement would make him eligible for service in a lance, at least in the squire's eyes, he was sure, and from a lance to a battlefield was a very short distance in his own eyes. Well, if the silver was short, then the silver was short. The absence of a fortune meant that Lady Fortuna was smiling on the former debt collector for once.

Jean was passing through the main gate when the captain there told him that he was wanted at the Roasted Hart Inn – something about underpaying for ale.

"Must be those Germans," Jean mumbled. However, he had seen for himself the inflated costs of just about everything in Bologna, so he was not surprised. At least the captain had not mentioned anything about owing for victuals or whores.

When he arrived the innkeeper ushered Jean into a small room near a stack of casks and closed the door behind him. It was dark but for the weak light cast by an oil lamp on a table.

"The squire's boy," someone said. It was a woman's voice. Jean closed his eyes the moment he recognized it.

"How long have you been following me?" he growled. He opened his eyes. "Since Umbertide? Ravenna?"

"Do not flatter yourself. You rank low on my list of concerns." Catherine opened the flue of the lamp to feed more oil to the wick. The pitiful flame grew bolder and soon became a healthy ball of light. "I see you are as ugly as ever, master debt collector, although I can scarcely call you that now, can I, since you have long been away from your place."

"You of all people cannot speak to me about 'place'! And how did you know I was in Bologna? Do me that favor, at least, although I have nothing in exchange. I have no intention of crossing your path again, mistress astrologer." Jean looked around the room for other guests, but he found none.

"And yet you have, you and the English Free Company. I read the registration roll for the condottieri hiring fair. The name almost leaps off the parchment. How is the squire Hotspur? Performed many fine deeds of arms? Seduced a village worth of maidens? Wagered away all he owns?"

"Nothing of the sort, I assure you."

"No, I would have heard about any such worthy exploits."

"Does the Gamesmaster know you are here?" Jean scrutinized the astrologer. She was fairly well attired and no longer wore her badge of rank – a ruby pendant.

"He should. However, you should know that he is still looking for you."

"You can pay him off with all that silver you took from me when we parted last. You owe me more than a few florins from that fortune."

"That fortune, as you call it, was barely a weaver's wage, so our accounts are closed and all debts paid. He wants you back. You are bound to him, and the Gamesmaster of Avignon does not like things out of order, as you know. You are in contact with him, I assume, after all this time?"

Jean frowned. "Are you his associate here?"

"No, I have no commission from him, and before you ask I have not informed his associate in Bologna about your presence. And neither have you, I gather."

"What do you want?" Foolishly, Jean realized, he had not even thought about making contact with any of the Gamesmaster's associates or partners. He could have done so in Ravenna, and now he was caught. He cursed himself as strongly as he did the astrologer.

"Can I not simply inquire as to how you and the squire are faring in this land without arousing your suspicion?"

"Geoffrey can receive you in his command pavilion to exchange courtesies. So, what do you want?"

Catherine raised her eyebrows. "To deliver a message."

"And what message is that?"

"I just told you, Jean Lagoustine. Yes, I remember your name."

Jean doubted that was all, or even if that was her main reason for making herself known to him. Regardless, he considered sending a reply through her to the Gamesmaster. But what would he say? Yes master, I am coming home? No master, I have little to show for my journey with Gaunt's squire? He would think on it.

"Thank you. How much do I owe you for the warning?"

Catherine made a dismissive wave. "Will you be attending the evening session of the peace conference? Hotspur would enjoy it, certainly."

"We have been hired, so we must prepare for our departure, and no doubt the squire will want to pray a while beforehand. We cannot spare the time."

"With whom?"

"A merchant caravan," Jean lied and then added for good measure, "from Parma."

"Then I wish you well. The Gamesmaster has many associates in these northern

115

cities, so be mindful." Catherine rapped thrice on the table, which brought the innkeeper to open the door and escort them out of his premises.

Geoffrey's height and willingness to shove his fellow spectators aside allowed him to find a good view of the hall. The session had just got underway. Geoffrey pestered his neighbor in the tightly packed gallery to identify the leading men in the hall until he relented. Geoffrey stared at Niccolo d'Este the moment he found him in the big chair on the dais. He saw that the young marquis was dressed to play the part of a warrior, although the gold brocade and lavish sleeves suggested a display of wealth as well as of prowess. Of course, no one would be fooled into believing that this little man without a hair on his chest could lead an army on his own. Geoffrey remembered that when he was a lad of about the marquis's age, he was still training to be a squire and had only just begun to lead his confraternity.

The hall went quiet when the *podestà* of Bologna rose from his and raised his right hand. He looked at the papal vicar, who was still sitting, to be sure that he was in agreement with starting the session. He was. The *podestà* then gave the floor to Azzo d'Este.

"My esteemed lords. I and my fellow lords of the Marquisate of Ferrara and Modena heard the heartfelt offer of my forgiving nephew and his council, but we have not considered it." Azzo's words were slow and measured, and pronounced with a well-seasoned voice that inspired confidence.

The gallery began to hum.

"We have not considered it because we do not recognize the right of Niccolo d'Este to make it. However, he is right in that the Rubicon has been reached, and I have no desire to cross it and cause the Este inheritance to be ruined." Azzo paused and extended a hand towards Niccolo. "So, for the sake of peace, order and family harmony I am making an offer myself. I will serve as regent for Niccolo until he reaches the appropriate age, not exile him, and find him a wife. In exchange the regency council must disband, cancel the *condotta* made with Astorre Manfredi, revoke the order for investiture, recognize the *libertà* of Modena, and surrender half of the Este lands to me for the duration of my service as regent."

Geoffrey's ears nearly burst from the laughter and cries of indignation that erupted around him.

"Why does he not just ask the regency council to lift their robes and bend over," Geoffrey's neighbor sneered.

"You believe that it is a poor offer?" Geoffrey asked half seriously.

"He will trample the boy. It must be a provocation."

The representatives of Milan and Modena shouted their support for the proposal while many in the galleries jeered it. Geoffrey wondered if not everybody around him was against *any* sort of peace. Of course, many in the audience were condottieri looking for work, he reckoned.

A member of the regency council stood up and began yelling at someone sitting on the other side of the table. Niccolo's mother appealed for calm, but her voice would not rise above the din as more representatives tried to make their angry voices heard.

To Geoffrey, it seemed that some on the young marquis's side were in favor of the offer, or at least wanted to discuss it. Others he saw giving instructions to their aides or messengers, who scurried out of the hall. The *podestà*, meanwhile, was trying to establish order by banging his stick on the floor and calling on the representatives to return to their places.

"My lords!" Azzo yelled. "Listen! I make these demands not out of greed or to avenge any injustice my father and his father might have suffered when they renounced their right to Ferrara. No! I have been called upon by the great lords of Ferrara to *preserve* justice. I have been called upon to ensure that the Este are not destroyed by a cabal of over mighty vassals. We must return to the bonds that were set long before the death of the respected Alberto d'Este. Otherwise, Ferrara will be torn apart!"

Niccolo turned to look at his uncle for the first time and saw that he was smiling just as the Blues captain had smiled when he cried his name. He was a stranger, just as everyone in the hall was a stranger. At once Niccolo wanted to flee to his horse so that he could ride through the *valli* and hammer his uncle back into his seat. His face was burning and a knot was growing in his chest, but he reminded himself that it was his duty to remain in the chair in the great hall in Bologna and listen to what his foes had to say. He steadied himself by thinking about Catherine and Cicero, but the vile words of his uncle continued to ring in his head until he could no longer endure it. Just as Azzo was about to make another pronouncement, Niccolo stood up and thrust his arms upward.

"My lords and citizens!" he shouted. The hall grew quiet. "I am outraged! As the anointed *dominus generalis*, the Este lands are indeed mine to grant to whomever I feel is deserving and to whomever I trust to serve me faithfully. Azzo d'Este is not that man! I would be committing a grievous insult to my noble father were I to accede to this pretender's demands!" Niccolo began to breathe heavily and his head started to swim, but he would not relent. "We all know that Caesar *did* cross the Rubicon and plunged Rome into civil war. It was in his nature to do so, and he was justly rewarded for his presumption. My uncle has no interest in justice, or *he* would have called this peace conference instead of *my* allies. If he truly had the interests of the family at heart, he would not have set his companies on the Este lands and cities and cause their ruin. He wants to seize all for himself against all sound judgment! Down with the tyrant!"

The hall was suddenly filled with war cries, laughter, insults, and declarations of support for the young marquis. One man fell over the gallery in his exuberance, prompting more chaos. The *podestà* was clearly angry and tried to approach Niccolo, but even around the long table order had disintegrated as representatives, arbiters, guards, and spectators jostled to prevent access.

Azzo, surprised by his nephew's passionate outburst, called for his retinue and stormed out of the hall.

Geoffrey tried to follow the marquis as his retinue was leading him away, but the crowds were too thick for even the tall squire to cut through. He decided to leave the hall and meet with Niccolo at his lodgings, but when he arrived he found that guards had surrounded the building and would not permit even the briefest message to the marquis, let alone grant an unknown English squire an audience with him.

Geoffrey melted back into the crowd and began his march back to the pavilion. Under no circumstance would he allow himself to fail the count. A pang of anxiety struck him. Perhaps he could gain entry by stealth, at night, through an unguarded window, and find the marquis before anyone would see him. He had performed such a deed many times in Avignon, whether to return unnoticed to halls after curfew or to visit a maid, but it was always done in concert with his fellow squires. He would need the Frenchman's help to execute such a scheme.

Geoffrey found Jean alone seated on his blanket. He was staring at a spot on the fabric wall that to Geoffrey looked like any other spot of the fabric wall.

"Jean! I must confess something to you."

"Hmm? What?"

"There is something you should know about why we are here." Geoffrey cocked his head and began to wonder if his companion was drunk.

"Here? Yes, we should remain here," Jean mumbled. He continued to stare ahead.

Fed up with the lack of due attention he was receiving, Geoffrey walked over to Jean and slapped him hard on his bad shoulder.

"By Jesus's noble passion!" Jean cried and he grabbed his stricken shoulder. "I should fine you for that!"

"What? Not run me through or slit my throat during the night?"

"You would like me to try, no doubt! I am not such a fool!" Jean stood up and ambled around the pavilion.

"You were mumbling like one. Listen! Calm yourself and hear me. Are you drunk?" Jean slowed his pace and then sat down on a chest.

"If only." Jean sighed "Now, you hear me. It is about the company."

"No words about the company." Geoffrey sliced his hand through the air. "You should know something about the Marquis of Ferrara."

"Why should I know anything about the boy-marquis? You went to his peace conference, so you should have learned something there. I have been busy dealing with company matters and you should know that—"

"Enough about the company! Well, no, the company must be a part of this."

Jean, his wits having finally returned, leapt up and stared hard at Geoffrey.

"What has happened? You did go to the hall, did you not? Are we to have another tournament?"

"No tournament, and I was at the session. What is with you, Jean? Should I strike you again to bring sense to you? You can tell me all about the company later, if it is that important, but for now keep your mouth shut a listen to me. I must tell you about the marquis and the session and my commission—"

One of the Germans burst into the pavilion and declared that Azzo d'Este had been murdered and that his nephew was to blame. As a result, the *podestà* had disbanded the peace conference and ordered all condottieri to take their men-at-arms beyond the *contado*. The young marquis is every bit at ruthless as his father, the German concluded.

"Well, that hardly affects us, now, does it?" Jean said glumly. "If nothing else, victual prices should come down. Just make sure none of you lads gets caught up in this mess. You warn them."

The German nodded and went out.

"That is remarkable!" Geoffrey said. "I did not think he would make good on his threat! He must have had quite the father!"

"So, it is true? The boy murdered his uncle?"

"I did not see it, but his words were like daggers!"

A dark figure wearing a bulky robe and a deep hood that shaded the face entered the pavilion.

"Who are you and what do you want?" Geoffrey said.

Jean did not have to guess; he could already smell Catherine's perfume.

Catherine pulled back her hood. "I need your help," she said to Geoffrey. "Master Hotspur, I can trust no other at this most dangerous time."

Geoffrey was astonished. He blinked several times to make sure that the woman was the astrologer he had met the year before on the road to Assisi.

"No formal greetings?" Jean said. "You are looking well." He would not reveal their recent meeting to Geoffrey so long as she did not.

Catherine nodded. "We have little time. You have heard about the murder?"

Geoffrey put on a stern look. "We have. If you are involved, I will ask you to leave."

"We are not, not me or the marquis. This is a ruse, I believe. Only the most stupid would commit murder with so many soldiers and lords around. The *podestà* wants to detain Niccolo, so even if the truth comes out, Azzo will be well on his way to seizing Ferrara. His army is bigger than ours, although more men were coming to us when this happened."

"Clever," Jean said. "Dangerous game, but clever nonetheless."

"What do you want from me?" Geoffrey asked.

"Help me get the boy away from here. Your company was not hired by either side and you are not known."

"Where is the boy now?" Jean asked.

"Will you help us?"

"I would not know where to go," Geoffrey said. He thought about his commission from Count Robert, but he had been told to speak with the marquis directly.

"Hide him in the caravan. Parma is neutral. Your *condotta* will confirm it!"

Geoffrey frowned. "Parma? What are you talking about? We–"

Jean grabbed the squire's arm and grimaced. "I lied about that. We have nothing."

"You...! I should have known." Catherine sighed and put her hands on her hips. "Nonetheless, you are free. Take us to the camp of our captain-general. It is not far, but we need some swords and strength to get there. You will be paid. The Este are not poor peasants."

"If he is the legitimate heir," Geoffrey said, "then his mettle should be tested in a pass of arms, not in a city prison. I am with you, Catherine." Geoffrey picked up his sword and kissed it thrice before bowing to the astrologer.

Chapter 8

"We need to decide on a scheme and swiftly," Catherine said in a low voice. "I do not know how long the regency council will hold out against the *podestà*."

Geoffrey and Jean leaned in to hear her over the cacophony of orders being shouted and gear being packed, as men-at-arms obeyed the command of the *podestà* to quit the city.

"What do you mean 'hold out against the *podestà*'?" Geoffrey asked. "Is the marquis under siege?" He was sitting on a folding stool the Germans had bought, hands clasped around the tang of his *couteau* and chin resting on its pommel.

"In a manner of speaking. The regency council has appealed to the papal vicar of Bologna to intercede on the marquis's behalf and tell the *podestà* to let him depart unmolested. In the meantime, the *podestà* has posted guards around the lodgings to prevent anyone from leaving."

"How did you get out then?" Jean growled. His melancholy had intensified since his forced admission that the English Free Company had no commission, giving him a look of intense dissatisfaction.

"I never went in. After the session collapsed, the boy's mother bade me find allies who would help defend them. That was before the *podestà*'s order about the men-at-arms. And before you ask, Captain-General Manfredi has already departed with his company, so he cannot help us."

"So, we are your last resort," Jean said flatly. He sighed and looked at Geoffrey, who was still staring at the astrologer.

"Call it what you like," Catherine said curtly. "I have no time to debate with you."

"You will not await the papal vicar's decision? Is he not important?" Geoffrey asked.

"Bologna is a vassal of his grace, so the vicar's word *is* important, but the people elected the *podestà* to administer the city, and keeping the peace falls under his jurisdiction. The gentry and merchants support him too. In truth, the appeal was made for the purpose of delay, so that a means of escape could be found. I am certain the papal vicar will fall on the side of the *podestà*. So, again, I appeal to you that we do not tarry in brewing our scheme." Catherine turned her hands over in a plea gesture.

Geoffrey frowned. He thought about his pledge to Count Robert d'Ivry. "I am not inclined to raise my sword against the lord of such a city without just cause, but I see one here. His lordship the marquis should not be kept against his will in such a…rude manner, and I am willing to spill blood for the sake of it!"

Catherine was taken aback by these heated words. "I am not asking you to lay upon anyone, Hotspur. The marquis has enough lords arrayed against him to be in want for more, especially the supreme pontiff. Rather, we need your stealth, not your sword."

Geoffrey raised his chin. His first thought had been to lead a company of men-at-arms and extract the marquis by force – the *podestà*, as an elected official, was nothing to him, but now it seemed something cleverer was needed. "Then you must help."

"Of course, I will help," Catherine said. A loud crash followed by whinnying and shouting reminded everyone about the chaos outside the pavilion. "Now, to the scheme."

Geoffrey looked at Jean, who took the hint.

"We need to get the boy out of there," Jean said. His tone grew serious. "He is a boy, right?"

"Yes," Catherine said.

"Many guards?"

"I saw a few that the *podestà* sent, but I expect more have arrived. Ours are defending the main door," Catherine explained.

Jean rubbed his chin and put his right eye asquint. "Other doors, windows, arrow loops?"

"Windows on the third floor. That is all. Small courtyard at the back, but it is sealed. I was thinking of taking him along the rooftops to some sanctuary. No one would shoot at him, since he is a marquis, and the darkness would cover us."

"Maybe not, but the ice might cause him to fall and break his neck," Geoffrey said. "And how would you cross such a delicate bridge in womanly attire?" He gestured at Catherine's green velvet gown, which was showing beneath her robe.

Jean looked up. "She would come with us?" He pointed at Catherine.

"I cannot let the boy out of my sight, and I doubt if his mother will join us."

"No one from the regency council will be with us?" Geoffrey asked.

"Doubtful. And besides, if the young marquis is gone, the others do not matter. We need someone we can trust, and I trust you, Geoffrey." She laid a hand on his shoulder.

"At least we have the night," Geoffrey said.

"And the confusion," Jean added. "The streets should be packed not only with men-at-arms abandoning the city, but also landlords and whores and victualers chasing after them to collect their silver. The *podestà* should have thought about that before telling the soldiers to get the hell out." Jean snorted.

"Maybe we could dress his lordship up as a man-at-arms, or some person of low station, so that the guards would not notice him?" Geoffrey suggested.

"Is that how you avoided beatings by the fathers of all those maidens you seduced, Geoff?" Jean quipped. He could not resist flinging the clever barb at the squire and the effort raised his spirits a notch.

"I never had to. You saw how fleet of foot I am when I crossed swords with Captain dell'Ischia."

"He is too small," Catherine quickly said, "and I am certain a guard would recognize him. He attended the sessions, after all."

"True," Geoffrey said. "And no doubt they would accost him as he left the lodgings."

Silence descended on the pavilion as the trio sought to fashion parts for their scheme.

"You say he is small in stature and in girth?" Jean said slowly and he cocked his head.

"Not small, but he is a child. Why? If you have an idea, now is the time to share it."

"One time in my previous station, I was sent to collect some silver from a merchant's wife. She was not at home, but I decided to wait, since she had to return some time. Shortly after I sat down, a couple of servants rolled a barrel passed me towards the front door, saying that they were going for ale. The barrel looked a little heavy to me, so I kicked off the lid and out poured the lady herself." Jean pursed his lips and looked at his companions expectantly.

"You want us to roll the marquis out into the street?" Catherine said. "What is to say that a guard does not kick off the lid, like you did?"

"Of course, we will need to do more than that. Geoff! You can cause a scuffle and while the guards are distracted you, mistress astrologer, can roll out the barrel with the marquis into the street. Then I will push through a flat handcart laden with beer casks and collect him before anyone is the wiser!" Jean tried to raise his hands over his head in triumph, but his bad shoulder allowed only one arm to achieve its purpose.

"We will need more than that," Catherine declared. "We also must have signs or gestures to bring accord to this scheme."

"I agree," Geoffrey added, "but it is a good start." He looked at Catherine. Her mention of 'signs' reminded him of her station. "Do you still do readings?"

She nodded.

"Good! I will approach the lodgings of his lordship and demand you be given to me."

"What!" Catherine exclaimed.

"Because I want my money back for a bad reading. I will play drunk, if I have to. Then, when Jean arrives with the cart full of casks, I will feign falling, or start a fight, so that I accidentally overturn the cart. As the barrels are rolling free, you push out his lordship and get his barrel mixed up with the others. You, Jean, quickly gather him and all the other barrels and run like mad. I am sure you can find a cart and casks at that miserable inn we visited. What was it called?"

"The Roasted Hart. You are expecting a lot," Jean said, "but it can be done. Where would I run to, though?" Jean rolled his shoulders to measure their strength.

"There is a place beneath the western wall of the city near the river that is partially hidden by trees where we can meet," Catherine said. "Your Germans can keep their horses there and find two more for the marquis and me. Most men-at-arms will be leaving by the northern and eastern gates, so we should be about as safe as we might hope to be."

Jean turned to Catherine. "How did you come upon this secluded place? Were you planning your own escape perchance?"

Catherine gave Jean a hard look. "We all need several passages for leaving lest we become stuck. One would be a fool otherwise. You and the squire know many ways out of Bologna, do you not?"

Jean felt his cheeks warm. "Still, I fear someone will notice a strange barrel tumbling out of the door behind you. We need to add even more distraction, something to muddy the waters, so to speak."

"True." Geoffrey said. "Despite the ruckus, someone will notice the door opening and stuff leaving it. Are you well received at court? Could they easily be rid of you?"

Catherine straightened her back and narrowed her eyes at Geoffrey. "The boy and his regency council trust me, if that is what you mean. I have a place with them."

"Yes, but could his lordship's household convincingly despise you from the windows and the door of the lodgings?"

"More precisely, we want to know if they would be willing to pelt you with debris," Jean added.

"And the rubbish would mix with your barrels and the one containing the marquis," Catherine said. "I see. I suppose I could convince the household to cast me out. They should, since I must be with the marquis."

Jean frowned. "All the same, knowing how close you are to the boy, someone in the crowd might see a ruse in all this fuss and check the barrels or throw you back into the house." In truth, he was thinking about the Gamesmaster's partner in Bologna. The fewer people who knew about the departure of the astrologer Catherine, the better for both of them.

"I will not allow you to take his lordship without me. *The regency council and his mother* will not allow you to take him without me. I will be convincing."

"I believe you, yet you will not be able to hide your station from the guards," Geoffrey said. He sighed and looked around him.

"They might not dismiss the court astrologer," Jean said, "but they would cast out a troublesome strumpet." He smiled slyly and brought his finger up to his nose. "You can play a whore, can you not, Kate? I know you have the attire for it. Just paint your face a little more than is your custom and Geoffrey will call on you for some offense or another."

"Fie!" Catherine spat. "May the Devil poison your seed!"

"Have you a better scheme, woman?" Jean leaned in so close to Catherine that their noses were almost touching. "We are out of time and no one is asking to bed you for silver."

Geoffrey put a hand on each of his companions' shoulders and pushed them apart.

"It is a fine idea on the surface, but who in God's name will believe that *I* would need to visit a whore? This city is blessed with many a fair maiden. The schemes are equally disadvantaged."

"Kate can be a dear whore, which is why you will feel that you have been cheated. In short, she looks better than she fucks."

"Maybe I robbed him," Catherine suggested, "and took refuge with one of the Este maids."

"Take your choice," Jean said. "I have no doubt that you will play the role haughtily. Are we agreed then?"

"You had better collect the right barrel, or you will be hunted down like the cur you are!" Catherine said through gritted teeth. "I am agreed."

"Let it be so," Geoffrey concurred.

The trio heard scratching along the wall of the pavilion, and when they turned towards the sound they saw a shadowy but very animated figure. Then shouting in German erupted and the appearance of more lively figures.

"Those might be our men," Jean said. "I must see what the trouble is. I need to tell them about our scheme anyway." He left the pavilion, sword in hand.

"I must go," Catherine announced. "Be wary about trusting the Frenchman, Geoffrey. I know the two of you have been companions for more than a year, but despite his rough appearance and coarse language, he is cleverer than you might think."

"What are you not telling me, Catherine? At least I know where he is from. I know nothing about you. I will accept your advice at face value, for on my oath reason does not ready you to make falsehoods on this night, nor Jean, for that matter."

Catherine nodded. "Be at the Este lodgings in one hour," she said and slipped into the night.

"It was Altinberg's men," Jean said as he swept into the pavilion. "They were claiming that we have some of their gear, but I set them straight. I also told our men that we have enrolled with Manfredi and that the Parma caravan commission is off. They were delighted." Jean tossed his meager possessions into his satchel and threw it on top of his bedding.

"When were you going to tell me the truth about the Parma caravan scheme, Jean? Had you another plan to get us out of Bologna, like Catherine counseled? And what about my lances? They might have killed you had they discovered the truth" Geoffrey kicked his gear towards the pavilion entrance.

"Oh, for the love of all that is holy, stop carping like a fishwife! You want the truth? Very well. I had no plan, and you did not have one either. Now, we have a commission, so let us get on with it!"

After Geoffrey and Jean explained the scheme to free Niccolo d'Este, Marquis of Ferrara, to the three German lances, Geoffrey selected half of them to accompany him and ordered the others to find a couple of horses, make a rope out of their pavilion and find the appointed place beneath the western wall.

Once everyone understood the scheme, Geoffrey, Jean and four men-at-arms threaded their way through the surging crowds to the Roasted Hart. At the door, Jean sent two of the Germans to search for a handcart and ordered the remaining two to wait in the street for a discreet length of time before following him and Geoffrey in and sitting at a table nearest the casks. He would give each of them further instructions in due course.

"So, how do we plan to steal the barrels and the handcart?" Geoffrey asked after they sat down. They had selected a table that offered a clear view of both the stack of casks next to the small room where Jean had first met Catherine and the bar. The inn was quiet compared to the tumult of the streets, with a handful of regular patrons nursing their ale and mumbling to each other. They scarcely noticed Geoffrey and Jean.

"Oh, that should be easy enough," Jean said. He waved a hand in front of him. "You see those casks? I wager your fancy doublet that the door to the cellar is not more than a few steps from them. That is how it is in all the Gamesmaster's taverns, and I expect that custom holds true here. One of us will sneak into the cellar and toss a few empty barrels outside to the Germans, which means me, I suppose. No one should notice us, what with how lively the streets are, and it is not like we will be returning them, now, is it?" Jean twisted his body and glanced at the timber above the casks. "I reckon the door is right below that worn bit on the main beam. That would be where the pulley hangs."

"Fair enough." Geoffrey looked at the main beam and then at the rest of the hall. "This miserable place is dim enough to hide your stealth while I keep the innkeeper busy, or the serving wench."

They grew silent as the maiden in question brought their flagons of ale.

"Yeah, she is an ugly one," Jean mused. "Good luck to you there, Geoff." Jean took a swig and frowned. "I must say, master squire, that I am surprised by your enthusiasm for this venture. I thought that you would have wanted to return to the halls of Gaunt with all speed, caravan commission or no caravan commission. Despite what you might think, I do understand how returning this lord to his rightful place would serve your need to display your prowess, yet, if I may be permitted to use a gaming term, you do not have a stake in the outcome. Or have you warmed to the English Free Company finally?"

Geoffrey stared at the Frenchman without a hint of emotion and wondered when and if he should give voice to his secret commission from Count Robert. He soon would have to tell Catherine the astrologer, since she had the ear of the regency council and was placing great trust in him. Geoffrey was still not sure he could trust the Frenchman, and not only because the astrologer had planted the seed of doubt in him. Jean had lied about the Parma merchants, he had a history of deceit, and no doubt he saw this venture simply as means of bringing silver, and so Geoffrey could well believe that the former debt collector and villein would sell his secret to the other side. He, too, had no stake in the outcome of the war for the Este inheritance.

"Chivalry dictates that I take this step," Geoffrey declared. "His grace the duke would approve, I am sure, but this venture is about more than just prowess. The boy is being cheated and has sought my help. I cannot in good conscience deny it. Also, as you yourself said, my lances want to stay, and I owe it to them to secure their livelihood, now that they are with me."

"With the English Free Company," Jean corrected. The tardy Germans entered and sat where Jean was expecting them to.

"Yes, and so I cannot deny my responsibility. They are good lads. And besides, I daresay crossing the mountains into France will be a damn sight harder than was marching to Ravenna. The passes might still be closed, if I reckon rightly." Geoffrey slurped a stream of ale. "And what about you? I know you are desperate, but you seem to be in no hurry to return to Avignon. The Gamesmaster must be missing you by now, although that wonky shoulder of yours will not ease your service with him."

"My reasons are the same as yours, Geoff. I am wedded to the English Free Company, the Germans trust me and the weather might not allow me back home for a while. Of course, judging by what snow I see and wind I feel, a clear path away from Bologna is not assured." Jean waved his tankard at the window. "We will get the boy to where he belongs, collect our money and then decide on our next venture."

Jean was now anxious to switch the thread of conversation. "Do you trust the astrologer? She is too clever by half, by my reckoning."

"We no longer have a choice now, have we? We made the pledge."

"We can still abandon the scheme and get out as fast as our mounts will carry us. In truth, we have enough silver to take us across Lombardy." Jean took umbrage at the squire calling him 'desperate'. The Gamesmaster had taken him on when he was desperate, and he would never again allow himself to be at the mercy of another man, or woman.

"I believe she is just about as desperate as you, Jean, so that gives me grounds to trust her, at least until we are safe."

Jean smiled. "That is the logic of a man who has been there before. You know, I am almost curious to hear stories about your life in the hall of squires. Even so, no matter how desperate she is or how closely she is bound to the Este, I will have my eye on her. She has no lord, no husband, no place, and she practices magic. Speaking of desperate, the Este must be to have invited her to court."

"Astrology is not magic, Jean. She does not conjure. His grace the duke keeps astrologers at court. And besides, I have taken silver from more than one of them in the gaming halls of *your* lord and master, and if they could indeed conjure then I daresay they would have made the dice do their bidding. She does not worry me."

Geoffrey was sincere on this account. Catherine the astrologer did not worry him, but she did unsettle him a little. What Jean said was true; neither of them knew her origins. She looked a little Moorish to Geoffrey, which stirred nothing in his heart or beneath his tunic, since he was partial to fairer maidens, although he admired the balance of her features.

After a moment Jean said, "Do you really think this will work? After the scandal in the session hall and then this murder, who knows what boy she will bring out! I just pray she will not throw us to the wolves."

Geoffrey looked Jean squarely in the eyes. "We will be armed. The Germans will follow me, and while I have no wish to spill blood on this eve, I will not let my sword remain idle should I be deceived."

Jean was convinced. At the same time, he believed that the squire would rather die than be humiliated after giving his word, which would bring Jean down with him.

The scraping of a bench along the floor distracted Geoffrey and Jean. They glanced at the Germans; they were fidgeting.

"I think we had better set the scheme to work," Jean whispered. "The time has come, I reckon."

Geoffrey nodded. He got up and stomped across the hall to the far end of the bar, where the serving wench was waiting for the heads to settle in a pair of newly poured tankards, and in his most charming manner possible began to inquire about the various ales the inn had on tap.

With the maid distracted and the innkeeper somewhere out of sight, Jean got up and sauntered towards the casks. As he was passing by the two Germans he told them to block the view of the patrons while he searched for the cellar entrance and then to follow their captain when he left the inn.

He was right about the door in the floor. Taking a final look around, Jean pulled on the iron handle with his good arm and lifted the door just enough for him to slip beneath it. The ladder consisted of only a few rungs, and so Jean quickly found himself in a cold, dark, dank cellar.

Knowing that the only way out was to find the loading doors, Jean warmed his hands by rubbing them together, held them outstretched and slowly turned on the spot until a sliver of freezing air caressed his palms. He followed this guide until he touched wood. Jean smiled and he blindly examined the doors until he found the latch. He drew the bolt and pushed the twin doors outward.

Jean looked up and saw the Germans, who were hugging themselves and stamping their feet next to a large handcart.

"Hello, lads," Jean said and he waved them down. He noticed they were in full harness, though the armor was mostly obscured by vast gray cloaks that went passed their knees, and had broad swords strapped to their hips.

One of the Germans jokingly asked if they should take a full barrel, since they were there.

"Only if you can drink it in one draught," Jean quipped. "I need to look as though I am returning empties to the brewery." He put out the pike-handling gloves he had tucked into his belt. "Now, let us be off!"

They met Geoffrey and the other Germans across from the third-storey window Catherine had said opened into the marquis's private chamber.

"Bloody hell!" Geoffrey said. "That is more than a few guards. It looks like the pope's men have arrived too."

Jean counted over forty men-at-arms milling about in front of the Este lodgings. Several wore the keys of St. Peter on their right breasts, which marked them as belonging to the papal vicar. A few by the door wore the Este white eagle on a blue field, which Geoffrey and Jean assumed were the marquis's men, while those showing a white badge with a red cross, who were the most numerous, came from the *podestà*.

"You had better be convincing, then," Jean whispered. He looked around and took note of the many citizens rushing up and down the street. The snow was coming down thicker than when they had first set out from the pavilion. "You will not have a chance to draw your priceless *couteau* against this group."

"You just take care of the cart and keep your eye out for the *other* barrel." Geoffrey looked up at the window. "Still closed. She had better have convinced his lordship and his advisors. The longer we stay here, the greater the chance of us being noticed."

"And freezing our arses off. Come, let us force the scheme. Make your claim to the guards."

Geoffrey felt Jean shove him in the back. He looked up at the window and then scanned the rest of the lodgings. The house was built to withstand the stoutest of sieges, Geoffrey thought as his eyes fell on the door that would soon expel Marquis Niccolo d'Este. He hoped his Italian was good enough to convince the guards of his claim. He did not want to have to identify himself as a man of Gaunt to keep their attention. This was one time that anonymity became a virtue.

"Look!" Jean whispered. "The sign!" He pointed at the window. One of the shutters had swung open.

Without a word Geoffrey nodded for the Germans to follow him. The squire strode with purpose through the ragged crowd directly at the door. He was about to push his way passed the line of guards when one of them belonging to the *podestà* put his hand on Geoffrey's chest. He identified himself as the sergeant in charge of the guard detail and said, "This is not a gate, soldier. You have no business here."

Geoffrey put on a fierce countenance and looked down at the man. "But I do! I was cheated by someone who has wormed her way into the Este household and I demand restitution!" He brushed aside the man's hand.

"None shall pass. If you have a claim against someone in these lodgings, take it up with the *podestà*, if you like. Now, be on your way." The sergeant's fellow guards closed around him, which prompted the Germans to do the same behind Geoffrey.

"Time is not my friend tonight," Geoffrey said. "My company is already saddled and leaving as we speak. Let me through! I will make my claim at the door and no more." Geoffrey flashed a freshly minted *grosso* in front of the guard's eyes.

The sergeant shook his head and gestured for the squire to be gone.

"Very well! If nothing else, then allow me to pass on a message. It involves a strumpet who now sullies the marquis's court. I doubt that his lordship knows about her, but I will be damned if her servants do not!" Geoffrey flipped the *grosso* into the air. The guard caught it.

"Make it brief," the sergeant barked. By this time several guards belonging to the papal vicar had shifted closer to Geoffrey to listen in.

"The whore—" Geoffrey cut himself short when he realized that they had not settled on a false name, since 'Catherine' might arouse suspicion. He thought fast and blurted out the only other female name that came to mind. "—Marguerite, and I paid a pretty penny for her too. She did not complete the…er…task that I set her to before she fled with my silver. I only want what I am owed, and I am sure the Este would be glad to get rid of her."

"I daresay you are right." The sergeant laughed and told one of the Este guards to give the message to someone in the lodgings.

While they waited, Geoffrey glanced up at the window again. The shutter was still open and still no one was standing there. He also noticed the papal vicar's guards consulting with one another.

"Are they sending her out?" Geoffrey asked after the messenger had returned.

"I should not think so," the sergeant said. "No one is allowed in or *out* of this house. You can wait here for a reply."

Geoffrey froze. "But she must come out! She owes me!"

The sergeant shrugged.

Geoffrey turned around and began a casual conversation with the Germans. He tried to keep their voices low while he thought about how he might get around this sudden obstacle, but the pikemen spoke loudly and without restraint, such that they drew the attention passersby. This gave Geoffrey an idea.

"And I will be damned if let that overmighty strumpet take advantage of a man of Gaunt!" Geoffrey shouted. "She must answer for the insult that I have suffered! She must serve faithfully!" With long strides he passed along the length of the line of guards until he was below the open window. "Come out of there, whore, and give me my due in the manner befitting your station, or I will come in and wring your neck!"

The papal vicar's guards shifted to prevent Geoffrey from scaling the lodgings, should he dare attempt it. The Germans, meanwhile, understood immediately what their captain was up to and began shouting encouragement at him and the window. One man-at-arms "accidentally" bumped into one of the *podestà's* guards.

The sergeant rushed to Geoffrey and grabbed the sleeve of his doublet. "Away with you, knave, or I will arrest you!"

"You will not have to, if you get them to hand her over to me!"

The Germans reached for their swords. Everyone tensed.

The sergeant, now worried that the confrontation might lead to bloodshed and eventually to his own arrest for not keeping the peace, released Geoffrey's sleeve. "Listen, soldier. If I can get the strumpet to give you your money back, will you leave this place? She can throw it out to you from that window." He pointed upwards.

Geoffrey had not anticipated this. Of course, he could not administer proper justice to his false claim, but there was no reason why Catherine should leave the house if only money was involved. Yet, what was money to him?

"I do not want the silver," Geoffrey explained. "I paid her fairly. I demand that she serve me as she promised! I am not some poor Sir John who must keep his sin hidden. I will not let my reputation suffer. You understand, eh?"

The sergeant frowned. "You said you are in a hurry. Whatever act of *homage* you are expecting from her cannot be done until before the gates close anyway."

"All the more reason to throw her out now!" Geoffrey yelled. He hoped that Catherine and the Este household were hearing him and would adjust the scheme accordingly. "She can serve me on the road. I am not fussy!"

Geoffrey's speech may or may not have been heard by those inside the besieged house, but it did attract the attention of several onlookers. Tensions in the city had steadily risen during the Este peace conference, intensified by the presence of a large number of men-at-arms, so citizens were looking to vent their anxiety. So, some started shouting curses at the hidden astrologer while others demanded that the marquis quit their city. Then the crowd heard a tumult from within the Este lodgings.

A maid appeared at the third-storey window and shouted, "We are removing the whore Marguerite! Be ready to receive her!"

Several citizens and guards moved towards the window under the assumption that the strumpet was about to undergo defenestration, but the Este were much kinder than that. After a series of shouts and screams, the main door of the lodgings flew open and in its stead appeared a disheveled Catherine. She had indeed painted her face to reflect her pretend station and changed into a black and red velvet gown with wide sleeves and a low neckline. Her hands gripped the jambs as a pair of servants struggled to push her out into the street.

"No, no, no!" the sergeant cried as he raced back to his original post. "You cannot let her go, you fools!"

"She is no longer welcome in this household!" someone yelled from behind Catherine. "She has been found out!"

All watched as Catherine was nearly bent backwards by the pressure being exerted on her. She shouted denials and even kicked behind her a few times. A crash was heard and a cloud of snow rose between the line of guards and house wall. The crowd looked down and saw the shattered remains of a wooden box; they looked up and saw a couple of servants preparing another missile for launch. Then came a heavy thump near the open window, and yet more servants appeared bearing rubbish for disposal on their besiegers.

Everyone but the guards laughed at the spectacle. The sergeant and the head of the papal vicar guard detail shouted at the Este servants to desist or face dire consequences, but they were ignored. More bits of wood and crockery started to fall, mostly near the still open doorway, while the servants, as though in chorus, demanded that someone take away the strumpet.

Geoffrey and the Germans added their weight to the burst of violence by struggling with the guards and encouraging the Este servants and Bolognese citizens alike to help him get the woman.

Jean and his handcart rolled out of the shadows.

"You might as well let her go, sergeant," Geoffrey cried, "because I am taking her one way or another!" He felt the pull of his *couteau* on his hand, but he held it back with a clenched fist.

While the sergeant's face was turned to Geoffrey, the servants feigned successfully casting Catherine into the street. She fell face first into the snow. The moment all eyes turned to her, the Este guards crowded the door, notionally to prevent Catherine's return, but in truth to block the view to a servant, who was furtively rolling a barrel out after her.

The sudden surge in the crowd's laughter caused the troubled sergeant to turn and see the prostrate strumpet. Geoffrey rushed to seize her, but the *podestà*'s guards blocked his path. The papal vicar's guards, meanwhile, were not sure what to do. The moment the sergeant had his hand on Catherine's arm, a torrent of rubbish rained down from the rooftop and the window. The Germans moved to defend their captain, resulting in pushing and shoving.

Jean, meanwhile, could not get through because the hilarious show was keeping the mass of citizens rooted to the snow. Frustrated, he nudged a few backsides, but to no avail. He decided to wait for Geoffrey or the Germans to bring the brawl to him and loosen up the crowd.

Geoffrey steadily pressed the guard towards Catherine, all the while shouting "She is mine, she is mine!" He glanced at the crowd in the hopes of finding Jean, but instead he spotted the extra barrel lying on its side in a shadow near the doorway. It seemed no one else had noticed it, but Geoffrey was sure that such good fortune would not last for long.

By now the sergeant had pulled Catherine, who was grasping at some of her belongings that had been thrown out after her, onto her knees and was exhorting her to return to the house. She pretended to slip and fell back on her knees, dragging the sergeant down beside her.

Jean could catch only glimpses of the action, but he had seen enough to realize that they were losing their chance to collect the marquis. There was only one way to rescue the situation, he reckoned. Taking a firm grip of the cart, he planted his feet, bent his knees and leaned forward until he felt a familiar pull on his hamstrings. Then, with all the force he could muster he launched himself forward and yelled, "Out of the way you sons of whores! I got a delivery to make!"

Man, woman, child, Jean knocked them all down in a mad dash for the marquis's barrel. He could not make a beeline for it for fear of revealing the scheme, so when he had broken through the now even more agitated crowd, he straightened the cart so that it was parallel with the street and hoped his companions would see his maneuver and some to him without arousing suspicion. Instead, the crowd took over their task. Jean's rude violence had angered enough men that several began to kick and rock his cart. The moment had come. Jean furtively pulled the knot that held the barrels in place while at the same time feigned taking a blow from a citizen, causing him to overturn the cart himself.

A few casks simply tumbled a few yards before becoming stuck in the snow. Others rolled up to and passed Catherine, who was still struggling with the sergeant. The Este guards moved just enough away from the marquis's barrel to give Jean a path to it. While angry citizens abused the loosed barrels, Jean began to rant and rave at them, racing from one cask to another in an effort to save them. He was nearly hit by falling debris, but he succeeded in reaching the important barrel.

Not wasting time to check its weight, Jean quickly rolled the barrel to the cart. As he cried "Shove off!" and "You all will pay dearly for this!" to the offending men, he righted the cart and began loading his spilled freight in between warding off blows to his attackers.

The sergeant and his men were too busy with Catherine, Geoffrey and the Germans to notice the spillage. However, the papal vicar's guards were not, and so they cautiously worked themselves around the melee towards Jean.

Jean had been in this position before. One time in Avignon he was hauling away a load of valuables in lieu of a debt payment from a member of the papal household when a company of his grace's men-at-arms came to stop him. So, he did now what he had done then: he punched the nearest citizen as hard as he could in the face and then ran like hell with the cart in the hope that the pursuing crowd would be slowed by its numbers. With fists beating at his back, Jean had the strength to withstand the fury and push the cart down that street and away from the Este lodgings.

At last, the sergeant gave up. The door was closed and bolted; the citizens remained riotous; the papal vicar's men offered no help. He had not enough of his own men to guard the Este lodgings and hold the astrologer, the tall condottiere and his four men-at-arms. He ordered his men to fall back.

"You can have her already," he said to Geoffrey, "but I do not want to see any of you near this house again!"

"You have my word!" Geoffrey declared and he caught Catherine when the sergeant threw her at him. Then, with Geoffrey holding fast to her one arm and one of the German's grasping her other arm, the English Free Company dragged the struggling Catherine passed the returning papal vicar's men. They were empty-handed.

CHAPTER 9

Jean was surprised by how far he could run while pushing a handcart weighed down with beer casks through snow-covered streets, although he acknowledged that fear of capture always makes the legs grow stronger. He had stopped in an empty alley when he felt certain that the pursuing men-at-arms and angry citizens had long given up the chase. His legs started to tremble and a searing pain sliced through his bad shoulder. Jean let go of the cart-handles and collapsed against a wall. He was gasping for breath and the cold air knifed through his chest.

Jean threw off his pike-handling gloves and began poking at the pain when he heard a muffled cry coming from the cart. He looked around before asking, "My lord?"

A sharp rap against oak informed Jean that he had got his man, or rather his boy. He heard more incoherent noise and another strike against wood in response to his query.

"Hang on a moment!" Jean said. He coughed a few times and then inhaled deeply. "You are not dead, so just settle down in there!" After putting his gloves back on Jean levered himself up against the wall and staggered towards the cart. "Now, which one are you?" He began prying off barrel lids until he found the marquis.

Niccolo looked up and found himself staring into a broad moon of a face half covered in beard. "Are you a friend of Catherine?" he asked in a mousy voice.

"Friend might be a strong word for our acquaintance, but yes, I know the astrologer woman."

Niccolo continued to stare at the stranger. Catherine had told him that a noble squire with icy blue eyes was coming to deliver him from the hands of the *podestà*, but this fellow more resembled one of the bricklayers who worked in his castle in Ferrara.

"Well, are you coming out of there or not?" Jean said. "You had better not ask me to carry you from the city!"

Niccolo blinked a few times. Catherine and his servants had been careful to arrange him comfortably in the barrel, placing his knees against his chest and giving him a thick wooly cap to protect his head, but all the bouncing and jarring had twisted his body enough that he felt himself oppressed on all sides. He wriggled his shoulders and pushed against the bottom with his feet, but nothing came of it. He tried to pull his arms free from between his knees, but he only succeeded in scraping the backs of his hands against the oak.

"For all that his holy..." Jean mumbled and without any forewarning grabbed Niccolo by the collar of his doublet and yanked him out of the barrel.

With uneasy steps Niccolo clambered off the handcart and hopped onto the ground. After straightening out his doublet and adjusting his cloak, he turned to Jean and asked, "You are not Geoffrey Hotspur?"

"I am Jean Lagoustine, master victualer and...um...senior treasurer of the English Free Company, commanded by Geoffrey Hotspur. You are the Marquis of Ferrara, the true one, I mean."

Niccolo's face registered doubt about the stranger's claims, but he was in no position to voice uncertainty. He looked up and down the alley, and seeing no men-at-arms waiting for him, he exhaled and relaxed a little. "Where is Geoffrey Hotspur?"

"We shall be meeting him shortly," Jean said as he instinctively checked the remaining barrels before adding, "my lord."

Niccolo looked around again. "Where?"

"I know where. Come, let us go." Jean grabbed Niccolo by the arm and took a few steps before stopping himself short. He realized that he did not know where he was or even in what direction the western wall might be. The last thing he wanted to do was make a wrong turn and end up back at the Este lodgings.

Niccolo looked up in terror at Jean and tried to shake himself free. "You are one of Uncle Azzo's men!" he cried. "You look villainous enough for that!"

Jean tightened his grip on the boy's arm only to feel it slip away. "What? No! Listen, do not make me stuff you back into that barrel. Just..."

Niccolo broke away, but after running behind the cart, he grew confused and could not think of escape route.

"Come away from there, you fool!" Jean said in a low voice. He took a few steps towards the boy. "Think! Why would your uncle want to steal you from the *podestà* of Bologna when he would be better off knowing you were trapped here? Listen! Time runs from us. How well do you know the city?"

Niccolo thought about his situation and drew the same conclusion as the villainous man. He would trust him for now, knowing that he could escape him if need be.

"Well enough," Niccolo said. "My confraternity and I would visit often."

"Confraternity? Very well. Lead us to the western wall at the place where it is closest to the river. There, you will meet Geoffrey Hotspur. And the astrologer."

Niccolo walked passed Jean and at the first intersection peered around the corner. The street was dark and empty, but he could see far enough to recognize that it led to the square of Saint Domenico, which meant he was facing east.

"We are close," Niccolo said. He returned to Jean.

"We cannot take any broad streets," Jean warned.

"True. Let us go." Niccolo threw on his hood and walked away from Jean back up the alley. As he was passing the handcart, he stopped and reached into his barrel.

"I told you once that I am not carrying you, on the cart or otherwise," Jean declared.

Niccolo ignored him and withdrew a square package.

"Jewelry? Silver?" Jean asked.

"Cicero," Niccolo answered and he tucked the book beneath his arm.

The pair encountered few people as they twisted and turned through the increasingly narrow maze of alleys, since the taverns, inns and brothels had finally expelled the few remaining men-at-arms in this impoverished quarter of the city. Soon they reached the western wall and followed it for a few dozen yards until they saw Catherine, now wrapped in a grey cloak, standing at the base of a set of stairs.

Niccolo ran to the astrologer the moment he saw her. He wanted to throw his arms around her, but instead he bowed.

"I am glad you are safe, mistress," Niccolo said.

"We are not safe yet." Catherine pointed at the battlement looming high above them. She looked at Jean when he finally reached them. "Anyone follow you?"

Jean slipped off his coif and used it to wipe his brow. "No. I outran them all. Anyone sound the alarm?"

"Not yet. Now, quickly up the steps! Hotspur and his band are waiting on the other side."

"The English Free Company?" Niccolo asked.

Catherine stared at the boy for a moment before answering, "Yes, that is the one. I will lead and, Jean, you follow behind his lordship. Take care not to slip on the ice."

"Mind your dress," Jean said. "You might need it to earn some silver on our journey."

"Save your breath for the climb down, debt collector. You might need it to live."

Catherine placed her left hand on the wall to steady herself and began to climb. Niccolo re-secured Cicero beneath his right arm and followed closely behind her. Jean was slower to climb. At the top they found a strip of cloth wrapped around a merlon. Niccolo looked down and saw nothing.

"Where is the tall squire?" Niccolo asked Catherine. He was nervous and took Catherine's hand.

"He is down there, I promise you," she answered. "So is a horse for you."

Catherine turned to Jean and said, "Now, hold fast to your expensive rope until the marquis and I reach the ground."

"Hotspur made you captain, now, did he? He is too generous by half." Despite his griping, Jean checked the fabric for tears, tightened the knot and wrapped his hands around the length nearest the edge of the wall. "The boy first."

Just as Niccolo was taking ahold of the rope, they heard a dull thump.

Catherine looked down and saw Niccolo's book. She sighed. "We have to take it with us."

"Why? Just kick it over," Jean said.

"No! I need that!" Niccolo cried.

Jean picked up the tome and thrust it at Niccolo. "Find a secure place for it then, quickly!" he ordered.

Niccolo tried to shove the book inside his doublet, but it would just slipped out. He tried again, with the same result.

"Give it here!" Jean snatched the book away from Niccolo and crammed it into his yellow jupon, where his belly held it fast.

Catherine froze and stared at Niccolo. "My God! Can you climb?"

"The Whites and I often scaled the garden wall," Niccolo said, trying hard not to let fear slip into his voice. "I will not fall." He was frightened, but he wanted to remain calm in front of Catherine. Niccolo again grabbed the cloth rope, clambered over the battlement, placed both feet against the wall, and began to work his way down into the darkness.

"Nimble lad," Jean said.

Catherine ignored the remark and looked over the battlement. After hearing Niccolo's muffled shout that he had reached ground, she went over herself.

The first thing Niccolo saw after he announced his safety was a pair of blue eyes shining through the falling snow.

"My lord marquis, I am Geoffrey Hotspur, squire of his grace the Duke of Lancaster, at your service." Geoffrey was holding the reins of Saint George and Jean's palfrey, but he released the palfrey in order to doff his cap and bowed his head.

"Of the English Free Company?" Niccolo stepped forward. He was astounded by the squire's height.

Geoffrey sighed. "The same. You are not alone?"

Niccolo told about Catherine and the stout carter.

"Your horse is waiting, my lord." Geoffrey looked up and saw Catherine's cloak billowing towards him.

"You have done well," she said to Geoffrey after resetting her cloak and wimple, making sure that Niccolo was fine, and examining the horses.

"I am a man of Gaunt. I must complete my commissions," Geoffrey replied.

Once the trio was mounted, they saw Jean hit the ground.

"What took you so long?" Geoffrey asked. "Were you praying up there?"

"No, just taking a piss. I had to give time for the others reach ground, did I not, or had you plans to catch them as they fell?" Jean rubbed his hands and looked around for Catherine and the marquis. "All here?"

Geoffrey pointed at the outlines of the Germans, Catherine and Niccolo in amongst the trees. They were ready to ride.

"We must be away," Geoffrey said.

After Jean had climbed into his saddle, Geoffrey turned to Catherine and said, "Lead the way."

Catherine stared at the squire and blinked. "We go to Faenza," she finally stated. "It is Manfredi's city, so he should be there."

"Should be?" Jean asked. "You mean you do not know?" He snorted in derision. "Must I plan everything? Still, I agree with Kate. I heard that Captain Altinberg was making for that city."

"Why do we not return to Ferrara? The castle my father built is stronger than any other in Italy and my retinue is lodged there," Niccolo suggested and he pointed towards the Ferrara road.

"Azzo might have blocked it," Catherine said. "His army had to cross the Ferrara road to reach Argenta. Manfredi's company was to clear it, but I doubt if he had enough time. They could be fighting there as we speak."

"Is this true, my lord?" Geoffrey asked.

Niccolo was surprised that the squire would confer with him about such an important matter. All the same, he did not know the answer and he said so.

"Then we must ride to Faenza," Catherine said.

"Very well," Geoffrey said with conviction. "I assume you know the way."

"The city lies east of here," Catherine said.

"And you know by which road?" Geoffrey asked.

Catherine hesitated.

"I know by which road!" Niccolo declared. "I have ridden to Faenza."

"And do you also know who holds that road?" Geoffrey asked.

"Bologna does, at least as far as Imola," Niccolo said.

"I expect all men-at-arms are marching northwards anyway," Catherine added, "so it should be safe."

"Are you sure?" Geoffrey asked.

"Yes. I have read the maps," Niccolo said with pride.

"Then, by your leave, my lord," Geoffrey confirmed.

The road that coursed the wall of Bologna was deserted as far as the junction with the northern gate, where they saw clusters of men-at-arms still packing gear or desperately trying to coax bullocks into dragging their wagons through the thickening snow. Jean threw his blanket over the marquis in order to hide his expensive cloak. He then ordered one of the Germans to ride apart from them and under the guise of looking for Conrad Altinberg ask to whom the stranded men-at-arms belonged.

"We should ride in the shadows so they do not notice us," Catherine suggested and she gestured at a string of trees lining the opposite side of the road.

"We will ride straight through them," Geoffrey said with conviction. "They are too busy to pay us any mind and we can pass more swiftly." He turned to Niccolo. "What say you, my lord?"

Niccolo looked at Geoffrey in surprise. He glanced at Catherine, who had her eyes on him as well, as though to beg for assistance, but she seemed at a loss for words as well.

"Straight through?" Niccolo answered in a weak voice.

"So be it," Geoffrey confirmed.

"I agree as well," Jean added. "We must be swift and confident."

When the German returned from his scouting mission, he reported that the men-at-arms in question belonged to the rearguard of Azzo d'Este's company, but he also learned that Conrad Altinberg himself had come up through the Romagna instead of northern Tuscany, as was expected, and was already near Faenza.

"This is a good sign," Catherine noted. "They must still be on our side."

"Then I am doubly sure we are going the right way," Geoffrey said. "You can read signs better than any of us here, mistress astrologer."

Jean noticed how this news raised the morale of the German lances, and immediately he was worried that they might abandon the English Free Company for their former captain.

"Come!" Jean said. "Let us be away! Manfredi awaits his lord!" He spurred his horse, making it lurch through the snow.

Geoffrey kept Catherine and Niccolo close and motioned for two of the lances to flank him on either side a few horse-lengths away and for the third lance to trail behind as they approached the crossroads. They kept a steady pace and avoided eye contact with anyone. Geoffrey was right; no one troubled them as they passed.

However, the accumulating snow made for slow-going. The horses constantly snorted and shook their manes and otherwise showed their displeasure at being goaded to plow through the uncertain ground. After Saint George gave one particularly hard jolt, Geoffrey glanced at the marquis to see how he was getting on with his unfamiliar mount and was impressed by his deft handling of the creature. Niccolo sat tall in the saddle, had a firm grip on the reins and moved well with the horse.

"So many roads," Geoffrey said as they passed several turns in close succession. He shook his head.

"Are you certain of the way, Niccolo?" Catherine whispered.

"Of course! The Ferrara road is two miles back and the Molinella road, which leads to Portomaggiore, is just to our left," Niccolo declared confidently, but in truth, he was not so sure. He was straining to the see landmarks and milestones on which his memory depended. Chills flowed down his arms and his stomach turned at the thought of getting lost.

After another two hours of riding, Niccolo reined in his horse.

"Are we close?" Catherine asked.

Niccolo stood up, shielded his eyes from the incessant snow and scanned what he could make out of the horizon.

"I know that place over there. The Este lands start just a few miles north of it."

143

Niccolo pointed at the dim outline of a small wood. "We should send a scout to check that Uncle Azzo has not occupied it."

"We should keep together, my lord," Geoffrey said. "Sending a rider alone in this weather is not a good idea."

Niccolo deferred to the English squire.

The wood was further than they thought, and so they only reached the cluster of huts sheltered behind it after several more hours of hard riding. Without a word the Germans fanned out around the huts with swords drawn. This act bothered Geoffrey, since he had not given them orders to scout the village, but he calmed himself with the assumption that this was customary amongst veteran men-at-arms, so he let them be.

Jean dismounted and without telling anyone pounded on the door of the largest hut. When a burly villein of middling age armed with a sour expression opened the door, Jean demanded to know if they were on the Faenza road.

The man stated that his hut indeed stood on the Faenza road, but it mattered little, since the road was so deeply hidden by snow that it might as well not be there.

Were they not so tired, the group might have cried in despair or stomped around in anger, but instead they stared expressionless at the villein.

"Will you give us refuge?" Catherine asked the man. She would not use the marquis's name. "We have silver to give."

The man looked over the weary party with caution until he saw Geoffrey and the Germans. He nodded and stood aside. Catherine spilled a few coins into his hand and soon the company found itself crowded inside the main room of the hut sipping hot cider.

"How far to Faenza from here?" Geoffrey asked Niccolo.

"Without the snow, no more than a day," the marquis answered. "With this weather, I cannot say."

"Well, if we cannot travel far, then Manfredi cannot either," Catherine mused. "I will ask our host if he has seen the condottiere."

"Do not be a fool, Kate!" Jean exclaimed. "He might be in the pay of Azzo d'Este or one of his captains and will betray us."

"I have thought of that," Catherine said haughtily and then whispered, "With the squire here, we can easily silence the villein, if need me."

"I have a better idea." Jean also lowered his voice. "Let us ask him about all the great lords and condottieri who might have ridden past here. With the war back on, it is only right and proper that we ask, for the sake of our own skins."

Catherine agreed and together she and Jean went in search of their host.

Geoffrey stared at the marquis as he thought about what to say to the young man. He had met knights, counts, dukes and even a prince once, but never a marquis. They ranked below counts, he reckoned, but it was a respectable station nonetheless. This worry about courtesy led Geoffrey to think about the escape from Bologna and the tumult of the past few days, the ruckus in the session hall and the subsequent striking of tents and flight of men-at-arms. To Geoffrey, a very dark cloud was still hanging over those confused events, and now that he was finally at rest, this cloud began to trouble him. Geoffrey nodded as he finally found the words he wanted.

"Your lordship," Geoffrey began in French, which was not only more comfortable for him that Italian, but it ensured that the master of the house did not understand them. "That is the proper address, is it not?"

"It is." Niccolo stared back at the squire.

"I must ask you a question that concerns this scheme, but one I fear might offend you."

"If it is an honest question, then it cannot offend me." Niccolo sipped his cider.

"You speak well. I shall ask." Geoffrey sipped his own beverage before straightening his posture and inhaling deeply. "Are you in any way responsible for the murder of your uncle, Azzo d'Este?"

"That is an honest question, master squire, and the honest answer is – no. The declaration of his death took me by as much surprise as anyone else. Truth be told, I very much doubt he has been murdered."

"You doubt that? Then why was the bailiff after you?"

"It was the *podestà*, but no matter. If Uncle Azzo had been slain, then his company would have remained in Bologna to seek justice, or take revenge, regardless of any order from the *podestà*. No, I believe his aim in this likely deception was to ruin the peace conference and embarrass me. He saw no advantage in it, I assume."

Geoffrey raised his eyebrows. "I suppose we shall know soon enough. If on your honor you say that you had no part in such a devilish scheme, then I must believe you, your lordship." Count Robert and his belief that the marquis would make a suitable husband for his daughter came to mind.

"I suppose we shall. We already know about Captain-General Manfredi."

"True."

"We could not trust the *podestà* once he blockaded my lodgings, since we feared he might be a part of the false murder scheme. Everyone – my regency council, the

Venetian and Florentine ambassadors – everyone told me to flee Bologna as swiftly as possible."

"Did Catherine?"

Niccolo frowned. "Everyone, except for her."

Jean and Catherine returned. While Catherine's expression was unchanged from when she left the room, the worried look on Jean's face told Geoffrey that something was amiss.

"So?" Geoffrey asked.

After they had sat down, Catherine whispered, "Manfredi is not ahead of us or behind us."

"What do you mean? Has he been captured?" Geoffrey glanced at Jean.

"No one knows," Jean said. "At least, no one around here. Neither Manfredi nor any of his men have been seen on the Faenza road for days, which means before the peace conference." He sighed and rubbed his bad shoulder.

"He might not be captured," Catherine said after she saw the fearful look in Niccolo's eyes. "My guess is that he flew straight to his company, leaving Faenza to fend for itself, if need be."

"Can the city fend for itself?" Geoffrey asked.

"Oh yes," Niccolo said. His voice wavered a little, but he soon got it under control. "It is well-stocked and in good repair."

"So, what do we do now?" Jean asked. He scratched his nose and squinted, turning his mouth into a frightful grimace.

"We cannot go back," Catherine said. "The *podestà* must know about the escape by now."

"So we must press on," Geoffrey argued. "West, south and north are out, leaving east." Geoffrey looked at Jean for support.

Jean shrugged and nodded in agreement.

"I am with Master Hotspur," Niccolo declared. He appreciated the authority in the squire's voice; it reminded him of his father.

"And the master victualer of the English Free Company agrees with you," Jean declared. "We go to Faenza. There! It is decided."

Niccolo raised his head and smiled.

"Now that our destination is set, how shall we fashion ourselves for the journey?" Catherine asked. "The master of this house was easily corrupted not to ask questions, but we might not be so fortunate at our next encounter."

"What do you mean?" Geoffrey asked.

"Are we to go to Faenza as three German lances, the Marquis of Ferrara, an English squire, a court astrologer, and a failed debt collector, or should we do something that will not alert anyone to our presence on the road?"

"True enough," Geoffrey said. "I have noticed that word travels especially fast in this land. What do you propose?"

"We are the English Free Company," Jean interjected, "and as you well know, the Company does not have a *condotta* with either the marquis or his uncle, or with anyone, so we should hardly merit notice."

"And his lordship?" Catherine queried. "What rank does he hold in your sad company?"

"Oh, he can be anything," Jean answered. "My apprentice, a groom, maybe."

Catherine shook her head. "That is not good enough. We need a proper disguise."

"I agree," Geoffrey said, "but what?" He was not keen on hiding his place as a man of Gaunt, but humility was one of the primary traits of a knight. "Pilgrims?"

"We are not so attired," Catherine said, "and our German companions might raise suspicion, should we meet any men-at-arms. Villeins?"

Both Geoffrey and Jean showed looks of contempt mixed with disgust.

"Merchants?" Jean suggested as he stroked his beard and squinted at Geoffrey.

"What are we trading?" Catherine asked. "And again, our garments will betray us."

"A family!"

All eyes turned towards Niccolo.

"You, Master Hotspur, can pretend to be *signore* something-or-other, one of my vassals," Niccolo explained. "I can give you a name later. With your sword and your harness, anyone will be convinced. Catherine, you can be his wife. I will be your son." Niccolo smiled and looked from one person to the other.

"That might work," Geoffrey said. "However, I must confess that my accent is sure to give me away."

"Catherine can speak for you," Niccolo said. "She speaks very well."

"That stands to reason," Jean mumbled. "But what about me? If you say 'manservant', then I –"

"Exactly!" Niccolo cried.

Jean groaned.

"What else could you be?" Geoffrey asked. "Had you bought yourself a proper harness and sword like I told you to, then you could have played an Este vassal too." He turned to Niccolo and asked, "My lord. Who am I that is your vassal?"

Niccolo yawned and blinked several times. He looked at Catherine, who simply looked back. "No one famous, but someone who is still loyal to me. There are many."

"It must be somebody respected and of high prowess," Geoffrey said, "so that none might stand in my way."

"It need be somebody with a purpose, I reckon," Jean said, "so that nobody suspects your purpose. Why are you taking your *family* to Faenza, Geoff?"

"Both are needed," Catherine argued and she turned to the marquis. "Know you of a vassal that is loyal, not particularly well known but with a solid reputation, young, of course, for the sake of the disguise, but would have cause to travel in winter?"

"And generous to his servants too, while we are asking for the impossible," Jean said.

"Hold your tongue, fool!" Catherine spat. "You know nothing of this land."

"Well, I remember seeing Faenza on a list of cities my father compiled that traded fish, salt and oil with the eastern *contado*," Niccolo said slowly. "Several vassals from that area were a part of the 1385 rebellion, and so as punishment my father plundered the *valli* they held."

"One of these vassals could be visiting Faenza to negotiate a contract to supply victuals to Captain Manfredi," Jean suggested.

"He would send a factor to do that," Niccolo countered.

"And why would he take his family?" Geoffrey asked rhetorically.

"He could be bringing his family to safety," Catherine proposed. "The war has spread to his dominium, let us say, and if this vassal conducts a regular trade in Faenza, he would have every reason to seek protection behind its walls."

"I am convinced," Geoffrey declared. "Let it be so."

Niccolo made a mental list of his vassals in the eastern *contado* and eventually began to mumble a few names that could serve the scheme. "How about the lord of Voltana? His lands lie not far from here and contain many *valli*."

"Have you ever given this man an audience?" Catherine asked.

"He was at the investiture. I held his hands in mine. I do not remember his face, but I know he is tall and the regency council thinks highly of him."

"Is he young, like me?" Geoffrey asked.

"I think so. He is married."

"That will have to do," Catherine said. "We do not have the time to discuss every candidate-vassal. I can no longer keep my eyes open for want of sleep."

"Agreed," Geoffrey said.

"And the Germans?" Jean asked in a despairing voice. He would not argue the point.

"Well, they belonged to Altinberg once, did they not? So, it is natural for them to return to their master," Geoffrey explained.

"And now I suppose, as your servant, you want me to tell the Germans about our marvelous plan?"

"If you would be so kind," Geoffrey said and he gestured towards the door.

Argenta

"So, you are alive then?" Ischia declared the moment the door closed behind him. He roughly brushed some snow from his shoulders and stared hard at Azzo d'Este. "Was the assassination attempt genuine of feigned?"

"Brusque as always, Giovanni. That is all to the good. I do not need you here any longer than is necessary," Azzo d'Este said as he scratched his neatly trimmed snow white beard. He was wearing a crimson pleated jacket and a simple arming coif, since the old condottiere did not like the heavy turbans most of his fellow captains now favored. Although the sharpness of his movements indicated that he was stronger than his age might suggest, his drooping eyelids and sagging cheeks gave him a tired appearance.

"It was not my idea, truth be told," Azzo continued. "Giovanni Barbiano learned that Altinberg was moving quickly north, and so he thought it necessary to ruin the peace conference before he and Manfredi linked up. The boy's outburst at the last session gave enough of a pretext to put the scheme to life."

Ischia gave no indication that he was remotely impressed by this sequence of events. He merely doffed his wide-brimmed hat, handed it to a servant and sat down opposite Azzo at the large table that dominated his command hall.

"Alberico's brother? Have you made him your captain-general?" Ischia asked in a half-mocking tone.

Azzo gave Ischia an angry stare. "Of course not! I have simply taken him on as counsel. He is in conflict with Astorre Manfredi over some town or other near Faenza, and so he should render good service to me. Regardless, if the feigned assassination plot threatens to hurt my reputation, I can always say that Barbiano was acting on his own in the hopes of getting a commission from me."

"I suppose," Ischia said as he sighed. He looked skeptically at Azzo. The Barbiano was a powerful condottiere clan and had to be respected, but the sudden appearance of Giovanni Barbiano on the side of the pretender to the Este inheritance suggested that Milan might be taking a definitive side in the conflict, since Giovanni's older brother – the same Alberico – was the captain-general of Giangaleazzo Visconti, the *signore* of Milan. The result, Ischia reckoned, could be war across the breadth of northern Italy, which would draw in yet more foreign captains and men-at-arms. His stomach turned at the thought.

"Your supposition on this account is of no interest to me, Giovanni," Azzo said sternly. "What I want to know is what you have been doing for the past month." He pointed a finger at Ischia. "I gave you a simple commission that even you could fulfill, and yet not a word."

Ischia's look darkened. "You could have received me in Bologna instead of playing games with Barbiano, if my words are so important to you."

Azzo took a long draught of wine. "You have my attention now."

"Ivry is in Ravenna," Ischia said plainly.

"And?"

"And, I arranged for Polenta to keep him there." A hint of pride crept into Ischia's voice. "He took refuge with the Hospitallers, but he is not going anywhere."

"So, he knows I sent you. That was not my intention. A conflict with Cyprus is the worst possible outcome from your venture!"

"Enough! He did not suspect me of anything. He played the humble pilgrim and I played the honest armed escort."

"Are you sure? Those in the Outremer are a clever and devious lot."

"I am sure. Your name was never mentioned."

Azzo scratched his beard again and looked off to the side. "Did he make contact with Ferrara?" he said at last.

"No. I always had a man watching him and his company, and not once did they engage a messenger or did anyone sneak away."

"And how many in his company?"

Ischia gave a number.

"And he held no secret counsel with anyone between Assisi and Ravenna?"

"No. In truth, he was very open in his counsel, such as it was."

"What do you mean by that?"

"Well, to buttress his role as a pilgrim from the East, he would often discuss his desire to recruit men to take the Cross."

"Indeed? That is amusing, although perhaps someone will reignite a holy war against the heathens. That could be why he chose to stay with the Hospitallers. I hear they are desperate in the East."

Ischia shrugged.

"Did he find any recruits?"

"None."

"So, it was just the two of you throughout the journey?"

Ischia became silent.

"Giovanni?"

"We were on a branch of the Via Francigena, so a few travellers fell in with us from time to time, but no one of consequence."

"Just pilgrims?"

"Just pilgrims." Ischia felt a pair of icy blue eyes on him.

"This is good. Anything else I should know?"

"A simple commission leads to a simple report. I offer no other details." Ischia neither smiled nor grimaced, and his tone betrayed no inflection. To a stranger he would have sounded tired, but in truth the captain was holding back invective.

"You can offer an army of details, if you want to, Giovanni," Azzo said. "We have known each other for twenty years, I reckon, and you would not be a captain today if you could not see what is what. Would you like some wine to warm your tongue? The weather turns ever colder." He gestured for a servant to give Ischia a cup.

"Keep it for yourself," Ischia said and he waved the servant away. "Pay me and I will buy my own victuals."

Azzo tapped a stack of parchment. "I did promise you a *condotta* for when you returned. What are you calling your company again?"

Ischia told him.

Azzo chuckled. "That old name, eh? You do know that such titles are out of fashion, do you not? And besides, someone might mistake your company for the true one and be disappointed."

Ischia bristled at these words. Thirty years ago the first Company of the Rose was the largest and most feared band of mercenaries in Italy, but it had eventually come to ruin as a result of internal discord and external jealousy. He remembered how his father, Simone, had talked about it with a mix of pride and contempt, and more memorably about the day the great German and English captains of the company refused to renew his *condotta*, leaving him to found his own company, which was not successful.

His father never told him why he had been unceremoniously dumped, but over the years Ischia learned that its principal captain at the time, the English condottiere John Hawkwood, did not like Italian captains, a piece of knowledge that led Ischia to conclude that his father had been too good a captain, and so Hawkwood got rid of him for fear of competition. After serving for several years in one of Alberico Barbiano's companies, Ischia decided that he would avenge his father's sullied name by taking the Rose name and fashioning it for Italians.

"When I take the field, no one will mistake my company for anything but a valiant and disciplined Italian band of men-at-arms, Azzo."

"We shall see. How many men grace the Company of the Rose?"

"A dozen." Ischia had enrolled several free lances in Bologna.

"That is all? So many years in the saddle and you can only boast of a dozen lances? You make me sad, Giovanni."

"Had I not run your errand for you, I would have more. And I will find more once I sign my *condotta*." He reached over the table and tapped the stack of parchment where Azzo had.

"Perhaps. Anyway, you will have time to search high and low for men, since I can only offer you a *condotta* in the spring."

"What!" Ischia leapt from his chair, knocking it backwards.

Azzo merely raised his eyebrows and gestured for Ischia to sit back down. "Calm yourself, man! You must have enough silver to last you through the winter, unless you somehow lost the generous stipend I gave you last autumn, so you cannot claim that you might starve. For the love of Christ, look at the weather out there! My winter campaign is over. I plan only to garrison those cities that I have taken."

"This will not do, Azzo," Ischia said menacingly. "Other companies signed *condotti* with you in Bologna when the snows began. What will you do with them? Take the parchment back?"

It was Azzo's turn to rise from his chair. "I would be wary of taking such a caustic tone with me, old friend. I signed who I had to sign, and that is all you need to know about that. Listen: my host is large enough at the moment for me not to worry about adding another dozen lances to it." Ischia moved to interject when Azzo raised his hand and said, "Hear me out before you say something you will regret. I have another commission for you, since you are so anxious about rejoining me, and this one will pay more than the last one. Will you hear me out?"

Ischia gritted his teeth and nodded.

"Very well. I have always told you the truth, Giovanni, and so I will confess to you that Barbiano's ruse has caused me as much disadvantage as advantage. Namely, the confusion his scheme caused swallowed up the boy marquis."

Ischia righted the upended chair and slowly sat down. He showed no precise expression that might lead Azzo into believing that he was interested in this new venture or that he was accepting his words at face value. He trusted the Este pretender about as much he trusted anyone else, that is, not at all.

"I heard that the *podestà* of Bologna arrested him, but the papal vicar swooped in and stole him back," Ischia said.

Azzo sipped his wine and rocked his head several times. "That is one rumor. Others say that he escaped Bologna by crawling through a chimney and hopping from roof to roof until someone in the pay of the Visconti captured him. However, the *signore* of Milan has assured me that he does not have him and does not know where he is. Neither do the humiliated *podestà* and papal vicar, for that matter, while none of my men saw him with Manfredi when they were fighting on the Ferrara road. In truth, no one knows where he is."

"So?"

"So, you get to find him."

"Manfredi must have him, surely."

"That is doubtful. My men got a good look at the remains of Manfredi's company as they fled to Ferrara and my spies report that Roberti and the regency council have been very quiet. No, he must still be near Bologna, or maybe trying to reach Manfredi's dominium around Faenza, although I have no idea who his companions might be."

"And you want me to find him and bring him to you."

Azzo placed his fingers tip to tip. "Yes and yes. In truth, Giovanni, you are the best tracker I have. You found Ivry in Assisi, after all."

Ischia had no interest in being a tracker, armed escort, garrison sergeant, or any other undistinguished rank in Azzo d'Este's or anyone else's army. However, if the money was good, then he could swallow his pride for a little while longer.

"You prepare a *condotta* for the Company of the Rose as a full and equal member of your host with all the necessary clauses and I will find your boy."

Azzo nodded. "However, you will not be a part of the war council."

"I would not dream of it. Besides, I do not think I would be able to stand the sight of all those Este vassals that are clinging to you like grapes on an autumn vine."

Ischia chuckled. "You just put me in the main battaile when you bring Manfredi to commit to a pass of arms."

"Without question." Azzo plucked an apple from a tray and began peeling it with a small knife. Then, looking surprised that Ischia was still in the room, he looked at the captain and gestured at the fruit.

Ischia shook his head. He had not eaten all day, yet he was not hungry; his worrying about *condotti* had robbed him of his appetite.

What about Ivry?" Ischia asked. "Should I continue to track him too?"

"No need. If you say that Polenta has him, then I am content, while the old Hospitallers should not cause trouble."

A messenger entered the pavilion and whispered to Azzo, who responded with a series of nods.

"Several of those Este vassals that you loath are begging for my attention," Azzo announced, "so assuming that our affairs are concluded, you may leave."

"You know, now that I am thinking about it," Ischia slowly said, "why not give me an *accomandigia*? You owe me two *condotti* already, so why do I not exchange them?"

"You want to become my *raccomendato*? You do not have the land in the Ferrara *contado* for that."

"No, but you will be seizing so many fiefs after your final victory that you will have land to spare. Those of the Roberti alone would satisfy a hundred men."

"You are getting far ahead of yourself, Giovanni. Spend your time thinking about this commission." Azzo nodded at the door.

Ischia smiled as he rose, shook Azzo's extended hand and donned his hat. He was on his way out when he stopped, turned back to his old companion-in-arms, and asked, "Have you enrolled any Englishmen in your host?"

Azzo frowned. "I should not think so. Very few Englishmen still around these days, as far as I am aware."

"So, you did not sign any foreign captains in Bologna?"

"No. With so many Este vassals coming to my side I hardly need to. Why?"

"I just do not care for the English. Cannot trust them." Ischia made a crooked smile, tugged his hat and walked into the falling snow with the squire Geoffrey Hotspur on his mind.

CHAPTER 10

The party had to wait for a couple of hours after first light before setting out because the broad expanse of snow beneath the dim gray heavens masked all landmarks. Even the trees offered barely a peak at their branches beneath thick piles of white. When he finally found the first milestone, the master of the house led his guests to the main road.

"This will be very hard going," Jean said as he surveyed the faint road ahead and behind him. "We will be lucky to stay on the road at all."

They were the first travelers that day, judging by the absence of tracks, and the snow came up to mid-calf on the horses. The snowfall had stopped just before dawn.

"Well, we are going all the same," Geoffrey declared. He inhaled deeply, and the cold air filling his chest enlivened his senses.

"We should put the strongest horse in the lead," Jean suggested. "He can break a path for the others. We should not fear an attack on such a dreary day as this."

"I think you have the strongest animal, master victualer," Niccolo said as wiped sleep from his eyes. He was riding alongside Catherine.

Everyone looked at Jean's mount and declared that this was so. The Germans were riding lively palfreys like Geoffrey's, but none were as stout as the horse under scrutiny, while Niccolo and Catherine were astride sleek riders.

"You had better wrap yourself well in that cloak, Jean. I know how you hate the snow," Geoffrey said and he proceeded to order the column, placing himself and the marquis in the middle. Catherine would ride behind them.

"If I am a part of your household, my lord, you should provide me with one," Jean said. "It is your duty, and I know how important duty is to you." Jean raised his eyebrows in expectation.

Geoffrey smirked. "What you say is true, but only when we reach Faenza."

The riding was rough for the couple of miles and the party had to stop at regular

155

intervals to find the milestones, which were often hidden beneath the snow, to ensure that they were on the right road. The land was flat on either side of them with only the occasional copse or cluster of half-buried huts to break the monotony.

"Do you know where we are, my lord?" Geoffrey asked. He was nervous; the lack of clear visibility troubled him greatly. Also, he was conscious of their steadily approaching Count Robert d'Ivry. He was duty-bound to pass on the count's proposal to the marquis, but in the absence of his regency council – or any counsel for that matter, the astrologer notwithstanding – gave him pause to wonder about where and when.

"I have traveled this road many times," Niccolo lied. He had ridden it twice, but he did not want to disappoint his companions.

"Indeed. Besieging castles, were you, my lord?" Geoffrey said.

"I wish I had been, but truth be told I was usually in the company of the Whites."

"The Whites?"

"Yes. My confraternity. We are called the Whites. Come to think of it, the son of Voltana is a member. Maybe that is why his name came to me."

Geoffrey smiled. "I am the captain of the Blues, back home in Avignon. We cried 'havoc' in the hall of squires more than once, I can tell you."

"Captain! Your family is so esteemed that you are a captain in the court of Gaunt?" Niccolo asked.

"Family? No, I was elected by my fellow squires, although it was not without a struggle, my lord."

"Elected?"

"Of course. The is the English custom. Were you not elected?"

"I am the marquis. I founded the Whites, so I am its captain. No one suggested otherwise."

"I see. The Blues holds a few sons of mighty lords. A couple of my companions will inherit fine titles one day," Geoffrey said with pride.

"Will you, master squire?"

Geoffrey fell silent. "Of course," he said plainly, but after a short pause he added, "I will earn my rank, though, as any good man should."

"So, you are not the first born, then? That is just as well. You are fortunate that your father sent you to Gaunt."

"There is no greater man than his grace the duke. I miss him dearly." Geoffrey thought about his rejection at Sansepolcro and his heart began to beat faster.

"As I do my father."

"He must have been a great man to have had so many enemies. His grace likewise is always defending his lands, but the Lord blessed him with good health and a steady hand. Your uncle must be a rogue and a knave to try throw you over, my lord." Geoffrey was genuinely interested in Niccolo's father and to hear about his campaigns.

"He is indeed," Niccolo said quietly.

"I understand that you would rather not think about him, but it will do you and your cause no good to forget about him, even for a short while."

"Perhaps. In truth, Azzo is the head of another branch of the Este that forsook Ferrara many years ago, but he is my uncle all the same."

Geoffrey frowned. "Then his claim to your inheritance must lie on soft ground. Your vassals should rally to you, if they are not corrupted. Although, I am told this Azzo has performed impressive deeds of arms…"

"Yes!" Niccolo interrupted. "His cause is a false one, yet he works to undermine me by flinging mud at my father for wanting a son."

Geoffrey stared at the marquis through the swirling snow until he understood the true nature of his provenance. No doubt the Church had legitimized the boy's birth, Geoffrey assumed; otherwise he would have no following. Even so, Geoffrey knew from the stories of the old knights that an ambitious and faithless lord will use any excuse to challenge a new ruler.

The revelation brought forth a memory from his first days in halls, when some of the older lads would call him the bastard son of such-and-such a lord on account of his lacking a family. At first, Geoffrey was confused by these taunts, since he could not understand how those boys could slander the names of good families, but when he finally understood that they were trying to humiliate him with base and baseless assumptions, and that his own orphan status was meant to be a source of shame, he reacted by knocking the stuffing out of a few of them. However, this did little to lessen the name-calling, and what was worse the brawls hampered his attempts to make friends. The taunting ceased only when Geoffrey forced his tormentors one by one to yield during arms training and admit their own lowly status. He had won their respect.

"Did your father ever come to blows with his cousin?" Geoffrey asked.

"Never, that I know about. There is an agreement within the clan that none will trouble the other and that they will come to each other's aid to repel any outside threat."

"You witnessed the vow?"

"I read the parchment. It goes back many years. What about *your* father?" Niccolo asked. He was no longer comfortable talking about his family. "I have read about the wars between England and France, but I have yet to hear about them."

Geoffrey was not sure how to answer. He had often thought about who his parents might be, if they were still alive, if they were searching for him, and a host of other questions. He did not want to lie to the marquis, if only not to fall in dignity in his lordship's eyes, but he was not sure of the truth either. So, he simply avoided it.

"I have so many stories from his grace the Duke of Lancaster that they overshadow all other feats of arms!" Geoffrey declared and he launched into an excited exposition of Gaunt's role at the Battle of Poitiers, when he captured King John and forced the chivalry of France to yield.

Niccolo listened intently. The English squire's enthusiasm for these tales impressed him and from time to time he would interrupt Geoffrey to demand more details. The squire duly obliged, but as he moved on to chronicle the exploits of his majesty King Richard and his father Henry, Niccolo began to lose interest and instead asked Geoffrey to speak about his own adventures.

"Like what? I must confess, my lord –"

"Call me Niccolo. She does." Niccolo pointed at Catherine, who had been listening in on the conversation for most of the day.

"Very well, Niccolo. I must confess that the list of my deeds of arms is short. I only took the field for the first time last year." Geoffrey was reluctant to talk about Orte, as it reminded him of his failure to draw blood. However, the marquis himself came to his rescue.

"Then tell me more about the Blues." Niccolo's voice echoed the squire's earlier enthusiasm.

"The Blues?" Geoffrey chuckled.

"After they elected you captain."

"Hmm…where to begin… Would you like to hear about some of our contests? Our victories were many."

"Anything!"

Geoffrey thought about what would interest an Italian marquis and settled on a jousting tournament his confraternity held with the Gold Lions confraternity. However, that story was brief, but the recollection of friends and companions past made Geoffrey feel good, if a little wistful, so he set himself to recounting other competitions.

His voice strengthened and soon he was talking to Niccolo as though he was just another squire. Geoffrey became so absorbed in his own stories that he scarcely looked in the boy's direction and was deaf to his occasional comments. When he undertook a detailed account of a contest for who could bed the newest tavern maid, Catherine cut him short with a loud cough and a question about the road ahead.

Geoffrey blinked and looked at Catherine as though he was seeing her for the first time. Eventually, he read her hard stare and nodded.

"My mount seems to be slowing," Catherine said. "We should stop."

"If we stop now, we must stop for the evening," Geoffrey said. "This light is not unlike what the Blues suffered during one winter foraging exercise. We waited too long and got caught in the dark as we set out on our return journey."

"You will tell me more later, Geoffrey," Niccolo said. His voice was merry. "I see what should be a crossroads just ahead."

"We should find an inn there," Catherine noted.

"We would be safer in a stable," Geoffrey suggested. "It should be warm and I would not have to play the vassal."

Catherine's eyes widened. "I am not spending the night in a stable, squire. Besides, it will be too cold for Niccolo." She did not notice that she had used the marquis's given name.

"I will be fine," the boy declared. "My cloak and chausses are thick."

"No you will not. Do you remember how you left the shutters open in your chamber and nearly caught a chill?"

Geoffrey spotted the shape of a milestone and reined in Saint George. He dismounted and brushed the snow from the inscription.

"Yes," Niccolo said after he read the milestone, "we are almost there."

Jean trotted up to Geoffrey and asked about the distance. The squire answered and then told him that he, the marquis and Catherine were discussing where to spend the night.

"I suppose you will cast your lot for an inn," Catherine said.

"Of course," Jean answered. "The stables will be empty."

"Plundered by the companies?" Catherine asked.

Jean shook his head and gestured at the sky. "The weather. I wager that the villeins have brought their beasts into their huts with them to protect them and themselves from the cold. Straw alone will not keep us warm, should we give in to such foolish notions."

Geoffrey and Catherine exchanged glances.

Niccolo," Catherine said. "Ride with the Germans and lead them to the nearest inn."

Niccolo followed Jean to the head of the column and the party continued onward at a slow pace.

"He is a serious lad," Geoffrey declared as he and Catherine rode side by side. "And he rides well. How is he with a sword?"

"I would not know," Catherine answered.

"You do not attend his training?"

"Why should I? I am not his arms master. Or his mother."

"So, what is your place with him? You cannot be his nursemaid, since he is nearly fully grown."

"Fully grown? Are you mad? He has a ways to go to reach manhood, Geoffrey. How many blows to the head did you suffer on the field last year?"

"I suffered nothing on that field." Geoffrey's voice was shot with resentment. "You still have not answered my question."

"Does it matter? You would not have so quickly agreed to help us had you not trusted me."

"That does not enter into it. As you are an astrologer, I can only trust you with certain threads."

Geoffrey thought back to the previous year, when he first met Catherine the astrologer. In the rush to escape Bologna and find the road through the snow, he had simply accepted her as a familiar face, which was a welcome sight, but now that they were alone together, the woman assumed a stranger presence. She helped him once, when a host of doubts besieged him. She taught him not to be presumptuous about this world, that signs and omens bear several meanings that are known only to the Lord, that trying to decipher them is a fool's game. In short, she told him that he should stick to his duty and leave the thinking to others.

Geoffrey glanced at Catherine, who had her eyes on the marquis ahead. Her face was unlike any other he had encountered in his nineteen years. It was neither round and ruddy like that of a village maiden nor long and pale like that of the ladies who attended court in Avignon. Rather her skin possessed a bronze hue, similar to that of several tavern maids he had encountered in Italy, yet somehow different, richer, for want of a better word. Geoffrey wondered if she was from the East, since he recalled that Count Robert's face was dark for a man of high rank. Such women

OF FATHERS & SONS

had reputations for cunning, Geoffrey recalled, and an ability to find a place in a luxurious court.

"I understand," Geoffrey said at last. His voice betrayed innuendo.

"You understand what?"

"You knew his lordship's father. No one, however desperate, would make an astrologer guardian of a marquis."

Catherine thought about denying the charge, but should the squire speak to Niccolo about her, she might be obliged to admit to him more that she wanted. So, she decided to douse the flame of curiosity by telling a boring piece of the truth.

"That much is true," she said. "I read for the late marquis a few years ago. He was indeed a wise man and a fine ruler. He respected my art, which served him well."

"So, that is what we are calling it these days, my sultaness," Geoffrey said. "Is he really yours, then?" He winked at Catherine and nodded at the marquis.

"Fie! I see that Italy has not refined you in the least, squire. You spend too much time with your coarse companion. I warned you about him. His tongue turns to lies whenever he opens his mouth. I have met his kind before. You should have returned to Avignon when you had the chance!"

Geoffrey grunted. "Now it is my turn to admit 'that much is true'. My regrettable *companion* serves me well enough, upon my word, but once this commission is fulfilled, I can leave him and be home in time for the spring campaign season."

"You should have enough silver in your purse to complete your journey," Catherine said.

"You excel at diversion, mistress astrologer, for you still find a path around my thorny questions. You are not a member of his lordship's war council, perchance? From what I understand of the situation, much help is needed to fend off the pretender."

"No, I am not a member of any council. My sole commission is to return his lordship to safety." In truth, Catherine was not sure what she would do once the boy was back with the regency council.

"And the late marquis?"

"You will not egg me on, for I am not so encumbered by sin." Catherine inhaled and tucked back a lock of hair that had fallen out of her wimple. "It was as I said and no more. Niccolo's mother is a Roberti. She is alive and well and awaiting his return in Ferrara. Or, to put it in words that will ease your vulgar understanding, my skirts are always closed and ankles locked together."

"As you say."

Anxious to steer the conversation in another direction, Catherine said, "You speak the truth, however, about his situation. Manfredi needs men. The peace conference was ruined before he could sign the full slate of condottieri, so you might find a place with him, should you wish it."

Geoffrey lolled his head back and forth. "That would be a pleasant invitation, should I hear it from the captain-general himself, but I am weary of these condottieri. They are not suitable companions, however skilled in the art of war they might be. I shall perform deeds of arms elsewhere." However, he caught a note in the astrologer's words that pinched his ears.

"Do you mean to say that all might not be as it should with this Manfredi? I have not been without *some* refinements in this land. I understand about his lordship's troubles with disloyal vassals, and I also know that condottieri must declare themselves with ink and parchment rather than a proper oath of fealty, so you are saying that those captains who have agreed to pursue his lordship's cause might…not?"

"I am not privy to the complete list of men he will have under arms."

"God's balls, woman!" Geoffrey cried loud enough for several heads to turn in his direction. "What about this Achtunburg we are meeting? Has he signed?"

"Altinberg, Geoffrey, and I can hear to well enough despite the snow in my ears without your needing to shout. That condottiere has been with his lordship since last year and has proven his worth. He started marching towards Manfredi's gonfalon the moment he called him."

Geoffrey began to worry. He would have to confer with Jean, but he recalled that *condotti* were like fruit: after a while they spoil and become worthless. His own ghost *condotta* had been ripe for but a few weeks. Perhaps the marquis knew more about this; they were his men, after all.

Darkness fell upon the party as they entered the crossroads and they had no trouble reaching a wayfarers inn. Catherine gave the name 'Voltana' to the innkeeper, who seemed convinced, while the few guests paid Geoffrey and his company no mind. The Germans entered separately in order not to draw attention.

"No men-at-arms," Jean whispered to Geoffrey as they passed through the front hall.

"They might be elsewhere, but I agree, that is strange, all things considered," Geoffrey answered.

"I saw none on the streets either, or their banners. I would ask about that, but we must stay low."

"I noticed that too. In weather like this, I would chastise the captain who had his men camp out in the fields. My guess is that Altinberg is still in Faenza, if he made the city at all. That road through the mountains would slow the swiftest of armies."

"Should we ask?"

"No. At least, not now. We will talk again in the morning."

They climbed stairs to the second floor, where they had rented two rooms: one for the lord of Voltana and his family and one for his servants. The men would alternate keeping watch during the night. Geoffrey's turn came after the bell for compline tolled. Making sure that he had all points armed and his *couteau* firmly in hand, he wrapped himself in a blanket and sat down on a wooden bench overlooking the stairs. All was quiet, but for the distant scratching of the innkeeper's quill as he did his accounts, when Geoffrey saw a glimmer of light grow from behind him.

"Are you there, master squire?" Niccolo whispered.

"Of course, my lord," Geoffrey whispered back. "Did Catherine send you to check on me?"

"I told you to call me Niccolo. And no, she did not."

"Then how is it you slipped by her. You do know that a chamber pot lies beneath your bed, if that is your purpose."

Niccolo placed the candle he was holding in a sconce and sat on the bench next to Geoffrey. "Nothing of the sort. I cannot sleep, despite the weariness of my eyes, yet Catherine can."

"I am no healer, but I fear the cold might be affecting your humors. Warm mead should put things right. I suffer from the same affliction from time to time." Geoffrey looked down the corridor and then at the stairs to see if anyone might be lurking there.

Niccolo said nothing. He just stared into the darkness and sat with his back pressed flat against the wall.

"That was a marvel of a speech you gave in the hall in Bologna," Geoffrey said after several moments of silence. "You convinced me of your right to rule, I will admit, and were you ever to invest me with land and privileges, I would be honored to serve you. For the life of me, I cannot understand how anyone can refuse you."

Niccolo felt heaviness in his chest. He swallowed and frowned at the candle.

"They said it defied tradition. You heard my uncle, but it was much worse at the

163

ceremony last year when over one hundred vassals declared against me." Niccolo shivered.

"Forgive me for asking, Niccolo, but is there any truth in what your uncle said at the peace conference? I find customs contrary in Italy."

"Somewhat. From what I understand, my father told the regency council to have all seven hundred Este vassals present their charters for investiture, whether they had already accepted them from the hand of my father or his father before. This had never been done before. And they were to gather at once in the great castle in Ferrara to do this."

"So, you were to break the bond of your liegemen and then make it anew. I see nothing wrong in that. I have heard of kings making like demands when they take the throne."

"Yes, but those who now act to overthrow me say that I am not of age to invest anybody except those in my confraternity! The humiliation of that day was so great that I cannot think about it without feeling my ears burn."

"Still six hundred loyal vassals should give you advantage."

"So it should seem, but most of them are small men, whose services do not extend to arms."

Geoffrey nodded and he wondered if the Duke of Lancaster had so few knights under him. He thought not.

"You know, the Blues had a very impressive investiture ceremony for new members. Remind me to tell you about it sometime." Geoffrey smiled and nudged Niccolo.

"It is the lords of Modena what causes all this trouble," Niccolo continued. "They never liked our being the *signore* of Modena and make it their purpose to justify breaking their bond with us. Blackguards, the lot of them!"

"I hear their women are ugly and their men cannot hold their ale," Geoffrey joked. Niccolo chuckled. "I hear the same thing," he said.

"Then we had better get you as far away from that cursed city as possible. However, we must keep our wits about us. Therefore, I must ask you this: does Conrad Alpin… Altinberg know you?"

"He knows who the true Marquis of Ferrara is. What an odd question."

"I saw you sitting in a chair in a hall in Bologna, which is how I am able to trust my eyes to recognize you. We are traveling in disguise, and so we will need to convince."

"Then no, I have never seen him and he has never seen me."

164

"And you trust him? Now, *I* find that odd. And before you explain all about your *condotti* parchments, know that I am familiar with that custom."

"The regency council has taken on the duty of engaging condottieri on my behalf, just as it has assumed so many other duties." Niccolo sighed.

"Well, you might have many wise men counseling you, and so it is not my place to insult them, yet all the same I should think that in your position you would need to make a firmer bond – one of flesh pressing flesh – to ensure the loyalty of those who serve you. You are sitting on a very hot seat, Niccolo."

The boy stared up at the flickering image of the English squire. He had shaven his face and combed his dark hair behind his ears before taking up his post, which allowed Niccolo to see for the first time the sharp outline of his features. He looked younger than Niccolo had at first supposed, and more serious.

"I shall do that when we meet him in Faenza," Niccolo said quietly as he worked to understand the full meaning of the squire's words.

"Has this captain campaigned for you? I understand he is coming from the south, from beyond the mountains." Geoffrey gestured to his sword.

"In Tuscany, yes."

"But in your dominium, for you directly?"

Niccolo thought for a while before answering that Captain Conrad Altinberg is a close companion of Captain-General Astorre Manfredi, and that his campaigning in Tuscany was to block other condottieri companies from joining Uncle Azzo.

Geoffrey shook his head. "Can you be certain that this German captain is fighting for *you*, for *your* sake?" He pointed a finger at Niccolo.

"The regency council says this is so."

"Has he at least signed to serve you?"

"That is what I am told."

Geoffrey jerked his head back. "*That is what I am told?!* Does this regency council do your bidding, or do you do its bidding? You are the marquis, my lord. You should know such things."

Niccolo's face turned hot. "That is not your concern, master squire. You must get me to Faenza and that is all, although I will ask you to accompany me and Captain Altinberg to join my captain-general, wherever he is."

"It is my concern, because if I deliver you into the hands of someone who has not sworn to serve you, my commission will be ruined!" The moment Geoffrey said 'commission', the image of Count Robert d'Ivry manifested itself in the darkness before his eyes. The journey was now even more uncertain and Geoffrey began to feel unsettled. He could not in good conscience delay his speaking the truth about why he had gone to Bologna. Delays had cost him dearly in the past, perhaps even his place in the halls of Gaunt. It was a sign for him to tell all.

"Has the regency council decided your future?" Geoffrey asked.

"I no longer wish to talk about them. Tell me about the maid in Avignon, the one from the contest."

"I no longer wish to talk about them either, but I cannot lay this matter aside. Have you been betrothed?"

"Have I been what?" Niccolo's eyes grew wide.

"A lord must have a wife, and a part of your troubles lies with your father, I am told, and his lateness in marrying your mother."

"I am too young for all that. I do not even have a knighthood."

"And maybe your father thought he was too old, yet all the same it must be done."

"Are you married, Geoffrey?"

"I am not the matter for discussion." Geoffrey paused before carefully enunciating, "Would it not be in your interest to wed a woman of high rank?" He felt strange playing matchmaker for such exalted persons at a Cypriot count and an Italian marquis, and a shiver went down his spine at the thought of his presumption.

Niccolo answered in a sarcastic tone. "I will ask the regency council when I see them."

Geoffrey took a deep breath, squinted down the corridor and turned his full face towards the marquis.

"You may not need to. I have another commission on behalf of a great lord, one who has a serious and considered interest in you." Geoffrey then told Niccolo about Count Robert's offer of his daughter for marriage, as well as numerous flattering details about the count himself, and how he was trapped in Ravenna, which answered the question about why he could not make the offer in person in Ferrara. As proof of his words, Geoffrey gently extracted the count's seal from inside his doublet and handed it to Niccolo.

Niccolo accepted the device and tilting it back and forth so that the brass disc could catch the uncertain light, he stared at the charge and read the Latin inscription.

"Is this in earnest?" Niccolo said as he traced the charge with his finger - fleur-de-lis and lion rampant. "I have not heard the likes of it."

"It seems you have heard little, although you cannot be wholly faulted for that.

His lordship did not wish to give prior notice of his arrival until he was certain that he might reach you."

"Why are you telling me this now? Does Catherine know, or your companion?"

"Set aside your suspicions, Niccolo. Neither of them is aware of my commission, and I tell you this because I see many uncertainties about our meeting with the German captain at Faenza." Geoffrey put on a grave expression before saying, "I suggest we amend our journey and make for his lordship the count."

"But Ravenna is against me. I will be taken prisoner there every bit as likely in Faenza!"

"Count Robert can give us sanctuary. We only need a day in the city proper for him to convince you of the veracity of his offer. And look at us! We are a jolly family! And do not forget that my company is always on guard."

Niccolo shook his head. He hardly knew the squire. "We should tell Catherine. She has given me exemplary counsel in recent weeks."

"And suffer another long-winded discussion? Do you remember last night? Such needless talk robs us of time. You are the marquis. You decide which way we go."

Niccolo felt cold shivers flow down his arms again. The English squire had already done great service for him, he thought, and he seemed so certain. "She will know we are deceiving her when she sees that we are not on the road to Faenza."

"Not if you are reading the milestones. You know the way better than any of us. You lead, Niccolo, and we will follow."

Niccolo fingered the hem of his cloak and then scratched his thigh. The candle in the sconce was burning very low, he noticed, although he also saw an oil lamp holding a small flame in the sconce next to the squire. He thought about that day in the snow against the other confraternity, when he had to decide how to go forward. Now it struck him that it was never a question of 'if' he would go forward, but 'how'. There was never any thought about fleeing the field or calling time. Niccolo smiled at a picture of Faenza with its snow-covered battlements and little men-at-arms shivering in their icy helms.

"I suppose it is my decision," Niccolo said at last. "Altinberg will go to Manfredi whether or not I meet with him in Faenza, and Ravenna does offer an easier path to Ferrara through the eastern *valli*…" He trailed off as uncertainty enveloped him. Not the regency council, his mother or even his companion Catherine had ever called on him to make a decision. Even on that juvenile battlefield in January all the initiative had been his.

Niccolo rubbed the Ivry seal as he weighed his options. Here was a solid object; he had nothing from any of his condottieri.

"You do not know if you can trust me," Geoffrey said. "I understand. Here!" He stuck out his hand for Niccolo to shake. "I am your man for this journey. As a man of Gaunt, I give you my word that I will lead you faithfully. If you want that we continue to Faenza, then hither we shall go. If Ravenna be our destination, I will escort you there."

Niccolo looked at the extended hand and felt his own hand drawn to it. The squire's eyes were steady and intense, even in the weak light. "If I elect we go to Faenza, we go to Faenza?"

Geoffrey nodded.

Niccolo clutched the seal of Ivry. "Should we tell Catherine and the others?"

"I recommend we do not complicate this scheme."

"Then let it be Ravenna."

CHAPTER 11

Giovanni dell'Ischia sat at the counting table in the front hall of a shopkeeper, from whom he had taken over his lodgings, sorting and re-sorting the money that remained to the Company of the Rose in anticipation of the following month's disbursements.

He was alone, since he served as the company treasurer as well as its captain, and in a foul mood on account that he was about to set out in the depths of a snowy winter instead of resting and preparing his men for the spring campaign. The only thing that lightened his darkened humors as he shifted an old silver *grosso* to the clipped coin pile was the thought that soon he would have the opportunity to meet and teach that presumptuous English squire. The squire would then learn that Italy was a far more dangerous place than he thought it to be.

Ischia was certain that the boy-marquis's escape from Bologna was aided by that meddlesome squire for two reasons: no one had yet laid claim to the deed and the squire was close to Count d'Ivry. However, he could not for the life of him remember the squire's name. He was a man of Gaunt, which Ischia recalled him continually declaring during their sojourn on the Via Francigena. However, the captain knew someone who would know the fool's name.

Ischia called manservant, who was busy packing the captain's satchels.

"Get Crivelli in here!" Ischia ordered. "And when he is on his way, check that his gear is set. That wretch has transformed tardiness into a skill."

While he waited for the head of the weakest link in his company to report, Ischia finished his coin sorting task, entered various disappointing sums into the company accounts book and then leaned back in his reluctant host's chair and waited.

He drummed his fingers on the counting table several times and stared at a square of light made by the oil skins that covered the single window. Time was fleeting. The other trackers Captain Azzo had hired to find the boy were likely on their way – the wrong way, Ischia was certain. No one suspected, as far as he knew, that the boy had been taken to Ravenna. He had told only the captain-general about the Cypriot count and his intentions. All believed that the boy and his confederates were picking their way along the paths and trails between Bologna and Ferrara, had gone west to meet with his loyal vassal Roberti, or were making their way to link up with Conrad Altinberg in Faenza. He, meanwhile, would head straight for Ravenna and to the hospice of the Knights Hospitaller. From there, Ischia supposed that the boy would take a ship to his ally Venice, if Polenta did not somehow stumble upon him, and then work his way back to Ferrara with Venetian help.

Tracking was loathsome work, Ischia thought and he spat to his right. He had accepted the first commission only for the sake of some ready money and the opportunity to recruit lances from deeper in the Romagna ahead of other condottieri. Still, he was curious how the English squire might have become involved with the Marquis of Ferrara in the first place. No Italian man of rank would have conspired with an English squire to steal such an important person, Ischia reckoned. Those Este must be desperate, and he doubted that the fleeing band had more than a handful of swords with them. Therefore, his men should be enough to settle matters in quick order. He would bring the boy back in chains and claim his prize of a lucrative *condotta* with the new Marquis of Ferrara; then the war could go on…

Ischia stiffened. *Why* would the war go on if Niccolo d'Este was in the hands of his uncle? Of course, the boy's mother and his most devoted allies, and perhaps Venice and Florence, would continue to fight on his behalf should he be lost to his rival, but in Ischia's eyes the capture of the Este bastard would be like that final flake that sends a rooftop snow pile crashing down into the street. At the very least, Azzo was less likely to require the services of the modest Company of the Rose. He would collect his silver and have to find another campaign to join.

The return of the young heir to his mother, however, would definitely keep the war for Ferrara going. As things stood, the condottieri Giovanni dell'Ischia was not especially devoted to the pretender Azzo d'Este, so he was free to enroll with whomever he wanted, according to condottiere custom. Ransom the boy to he who will pay the most, sign a healthy *condotta* with one side or the other, hire more lances, and watch the Company of the Rose grow into something that overshadows its predecessor!

A sharp rap on the door awoke Ischia from his reverie.

"That had better be you, Crivelli!" Ischia barked.

The door opened and in stepped the expected guest, but he was not given time to utter the simplest of greetings.

"Are you ready to leave? You had better be. I remember being stuck on that sad farm you call an estate for a whole day while you decided how to pack your gear." Ischia got up and walked around the table to confront Crivelli.

"All m-most th-there, Captain." Crivelli glanced at the silver and open accounts book and wondered if the captain was himself not prepared to start his commission.

"You should be done, Tommasino, but that is not why I called for you. You were close to that English squire, were you not?" His voice was larded with menace.

"English squire?"

"*Captain*. Address me properly or I will fine you. Gentry or not, you will respect my law when you are enrolled in the Company of the Rose."

"I-I understand, captain." Crivelli was genuinely abashed.

"Do you. Well then, speak!"

Crivelli looked at his captain as though he had two heads.

"The English squire," Ischia prompted.

Crivelli nodded. "We are n-not friends, captain, s-so our bond is w-weak."

"His name."

Crivelli gave it.

"Hotspur, yes…that is not a bad name. All the same, I will ruin him. He certainly gave you something to remember back on the Via Francigena. I pray you have made proper use of your time here and done some arms training."

Crivelli grew hot in the face, but he would not contradict his captain, if only because what he was saying was true. "I-I better knew his m-master victualer, Jean Lagoustine."

"The slouching Frenchman? Well, what about him?"

Crivelli gave a broken account of the English Free Company, including where they had served and what arms they carried, and he concluded with some speech difficulty by suggesting that as a lance they could serve well in the Company of the Rose.

"Never," Ischia said and he frowned. "I do not know them and they are not Italian."

"B-But the Englishman is, as you have reminded m-me, an excellent s-swordsman and the Frenchman is as t-tough as nails, if his s-stories are t-true."

Ischia struck Crivelli on the shoulder with the side of his fist. "I have told you once who is the captain here and the next reminder will be more painful."

Crivelli said nothing. He merely clutched his left shoulder and winced.

"Never mind the stories," Ischia said. "What can you tell me about them and the Count d'Ivry? I recall that he and the squire spoke often, although about what only the Lord knows."

"Well, captain, I-I did listen in on a f-few of their conversations, although th-they never talked about the Este war, if th-that is what you are after, or anything about the events here in the n-north."

"I am asking you about what they *did* talk about – not what they did not." Ischia made a fist.

"T-Taking the Cross," Crivelli answered plainly.

"What?"

"His lordship would often s-speak about his n-native Cyprus, but the s-squire was m-most interested in the wars against the S-Saracens in the East. I believe he is thinking about t-taking the Cross to f-fight on behalf of his lordship." Crivelli consciously omitted their meeting at the tailors in Ravenna.

Ischia grimaced and glanced to the side. Such a thing would make this Hotspur devoted to the count, he reckoned. Ischia was now more convinced than ever that the boy was heading to Ravenna.

"And I am fining you one week's wages for poor discipline," Ischia said at last.

"P-Poor discipline? B-By right I may offer counsel. I m-might owe you s-service, but I am not your s-slave, captain." Crivelli choked back the bitterness in his voice; he did not wish to openly defy his superior.

"You have not set your gear properly, Tommasino. I will no longer tolerate your lateness. Everyone else is ready to go."

"My gear is s-set."

"I know it is not. You are dismissed." Ischia went to the accounts book, lightly touched one of his recent entries, and judging that the ink was dry closed it.

Crivelli was unsure whether to leave or continue arguing with his captain, but he already knew that Giovanni dell'Ischia was not a man to be swayed by the strongest of arguments, let alone by arguments given to him by someone for whom he had scant respect. Crivelli felt this attitude keenly, but it would have bothered him less if his captain was more distinguished – or even distinguished at all. Regardless, he had no choice but to follow this old man and pray that he would be given an opportunity to prove himself.

"Why are you still here?" Ischia asked.

Crivelli nodded and left the shop.

The servant appeared behind Ischia and coughed.

"Well?"

"His gear is set, my lord."

Ischia raised his eyebrows. "Indeed? Perhaps he is learning, although I am sure he has missed something." He nodded at the accounts book. "Clear this away and finish packing. We are to away."

Ischia looked around the shopkeeper's humble hall and wondered if he would be back. Regardless, he would need bigger lodgings, whether in this camp or the other one a few miles to the north. Every condottiere cherished his own notion of the ideal *condotta*. Some preferred long terms of service, others negotiated for good land and titles from the hand of a great captain, while yet others dreamed of clauses that catered to their companies' strengths. Ischia wanted pride of place. He wanted to see the gonfalon of the Company of the Rose flying at the head of a campaign army.

Azzo d'Este, Astorre Manfredi, either captain-general should recognize and respect Captain Giovanni dell'Ischia as a condottiere of rare prowess. With enough silver he could buy the best armor and hire the strongest lances, but he reckoned that without fame that silver would not come easily. At his age he had no time to earn his spurs in other condottiere companies and thereby gather a following of fine men-at-arms. He had started well under Alberico da Barbiano those many years, participated in a few battles, but he made the mistake of returning home after the great plague swept through his village and carried off his family, when he attempted put his estates in order and find proper service in Florence. Ischia saw these failures and more as signs that he should return to the sword and pike for his livelihood. Now, he had to stand at the head of the queue, in the bottom rank of the main battaile, with all points armed and at the ready for a great pass of arms, regardless of how many men he might have in his conrois.

However, which captain-general was more likely to write this clause into the *ad bene placitum* of his *condotta*, that supplemental though no less important part of the document? Manfredi was arrogant, though practical, Ischia knew by reputation, although he had never fought with or against him. Azzo would be more amenable to the idea, but Ischia could not be sure he could trust him after their most recent meeting, and his army held so many proud former vassals of the young marquis that he feared such negotiations would be far too protracted for his liking. Of course, there was Niccolo d'Este himself. Should he rescue the boy, the marquis could hardly deny him any prize he might ask for.

The captain scratched his bearded cheek several times. He should go for a trim before departing; otherwise his face might freeze from all the ice that would cling to his bristles as he raced eastwards towards the Adriatic. After spitting on the floor, Ischia snatched the small purses of silver from the table, shoved them into his doublet and left.

"I smell the sea," Catherine declared. She daintily sniffed several times and looked over the horizon. With the sky still overcast, although no snow was falling, she found it difficult to orient herself. She reckoned that they were traveling in a vaguely eastward direction, but she knew that Faenza was a landlocked city, and therefore should be enveloped by a different odor.

"So do I," Jean said. He was riding alongside the astrologer in the middle of the column, since Geoffrey and Niccolo insisted on assuming the vanguard. They had been on the road for more than half a day and had not met a single scout or wandering lance, he realized.

Catherine whipped her reins and trotted to the head of the column.

"My lord!" she cried. She would not use the boy's given name in front of rank-and-file men-at-arms.

Geoffrey heard the woman and turned Saint George to block her advance. Niccolo and one of the German lances, who had slipped just ahead of Geoffrey, continued for a few paces before stopping.

"What troubles you, mistress astrologer?" Geoffrey asked. "We must press on to reach the city before dark."

Catherine tried to maneuver her mount to go around the squire, but the drifts were too thick and she only succeeded in spraying snow across her skirt.

"Ugh!" she spat. Her horse began to rear, but she quickly regained control of her mount and brought him back into the column. "And which city might this be, Geoffrey? I fear you have led us astray."

"The boy leads well," Geoffrey said plainly. "He has shown no hesitation in reading the signs." Niccolo was already within a few paces of Geoffrey and Catherine.

"And we are heading to Faenza?"

Geoffrey said nothing.

"Niccolo!" Catherine shouted. "Tell me the truth. These milestones show the distance to Faenza, do they not?" She pointed at a stone pylon standing waist-deep in snow at the side of the road.

Niccolo glanced at the milestone and then at Geoffrey. He opened his mouth to speak, but Geoffrey decided to answer on his behalf.

"The stone says 'Ravenna'," Geoffrey said resolutely. "His lordship fears that Faenza is an uncertain venture, but that Ravenna promises…greater advantage."

"'Greater advantage'? What folly is this, master squire?!" Catherine sliced the air with her hand. "Never mind! His lordship will answer for himself!" She urged her mount forwards until the muzzles of three horses were snorting into each other.

"Captain Altinberg might not be with me," Niccolo said quietly.

"Speak again, your lordship," Catherine said, "I cannot hear you."

Niccolo repeated his words in a louder voice.

"I do not understand. Who told you this?" Catherine instinctively looked at Jean, who, troubled by their unusually long wait, was now just behind Geoffrey.

Niccolo again looked at Geoffrey. "I do not know him and I never saw his *condotta*."

"Nonsense! And what is in Ravenna, besides your enemy?!" A shiver swam up Catherine's spine at the shock that the English squire was not as honest as she thought he was.

Geoffrey pulled his shoulders back and raised his head so that he looked down on all around him. "His enemy there shrinks like a violet in the shade before the great ally and likely father his lordship has waiting for him in the city of Ravenna. A man of his majesty King James of Cyprus, Count Robert d'Ivry, has invited his lordship, the Marquis of Ferrara, to discuss a union, and that is all I can tell you. His lordship, Niccolo, committed me to his cause and I will fulfill this pledge."

Catherine's jaw dropped open. As grand as the squire's speech was to her ears, she could not understand a word of it. Jean, however, did.

"I knew it!" Jean cried. "I bloody well knew it! I knew that…that bloody Byzantine…buffoon said something to you. I should have poured a dram of spirits down your throat and got it out of you, but I…I just deceived myself! By Jesus's noble passion, you are leading us to ruin, Geoff!" Jean slapped the withers of his horse several times, which distressed the mount enough for it to whiny and stutter step several times.

Geoffrey threw a fierce look at Jean and said, "You! Get back into ranks! You do not know Count Robert as I do, and this is the only road we can travel. His lordship has spoken, so I need not explain his reasons to you, nor does he, as the marquis, but all signs point to our meeting with the Count d'Ivry and ensuring the victory of the true heir to Ferrara!"

"Speak plainly, squire!" Catherine said. For the first time since joining the Este court she felt as though she was losing control of her situation, and this angered her. "Who is this Count d'Ivry and what does he want with Niccolo?"

"You do not know the Count d'Ivry?" Geoffrey said. Perhaps she was not from the Outremer after all, he thought, if she did not know the storied name of his lordship. After giving a brief history of the Ivry family, Geoffrey said, "And the results will serve both lords well."

Catherine felt frustration welling up in her breast, but despite the squire's dissembling words, she understood that an offer of marriage was somewhere involved. She looked at Niccolo and said, "Is this truly your decision? This squire, a man not of noble rank, did not force you somehow to submit his will?"

"No," Niccolo answered resolutely. He felt a strong need to defend Geoffrey from unjust accusations. "The decision was mine. I know the way." He looked at Catherine intently, hoping that she would submit to *his* will and not undermine his decision to take counsel with the English squire. He placed his hand on the copy of Cicero he still kept in his doublet.

Jean sighed. "We cannot go back now," he mumbled through his teeth. He was seething from Geoffrey's conspiracy.

Catherine said nothing, but she agreed with the Frenchman. She was now dependent on Geoffrey Hotspur and she resented it to the full. Catherine tightened her lips and remained very still.

"We are still a family," Niccolo said. In the ensuing silence he could hear the winds blowing over the snow-laden fields. "We will pass through the gates of Ravenna without trouble."

"We will make it so," Geoffrey said after seeing the stunned and doubtful faces around him. "We will indeed."

Geoffrey tasked Jean with telling the Germans about the change in destination. Since they had pledged to follow him, they could not now go to Faenza, and instead they were to enter Ravenna separately as a group of free lances and find lodgings in the Black Hart Inn. They were only two miles away from the main gate, so the time had come for them to assume their disguises, which meant Geoffrey leading his 'wife' and 'son' ahead of his 'steward', who was responsible for their baggage.

"The men are not happy about this deception of yours, Geoff," Jean said after he returned from his commission to the Germans, "but I reassured them that the English Free Company would travel to Manfredi and enroll in his host. We are continuing to Manfredi, are we not?"

"Without question," Geoffrey said. "I will not leave his lordship so close to his enemy longer than is necessary. That would be foolish."

Jean stared at the squire and wondered if he was not more interested in the old man trapped in Ravenna than in the boy whom he pledged to escort to safety. This was a double game that Jean was not sure Geoffrey could handle, so as usual he had better stay close to him.

Catherine was silent for the remainder of the journey. Niccolo turned to her several times with the intention of conversation, but her stern expression and forward focus put him off. He hoped that she was not too angry with him and that she would not think of remaining in Ravenna when they set off again for Ferrara.

However, Niccolo was glad that the English squire had helped him to concentrate his thoughts and make a firm decision for the sake of his rule. She should appreciate that, especially since he recalled her telling him just a few days ago that he should question everything, and that he was the marquis, when all was said and done. When he no longer needed the regency council, Niccolo thought, he would appoint Geoffrey and Catherine as his counselors.

The 'Voltana family' reached Ravenna by mid-afternoon and had no trouble passing through its gates. Catherine did most of the talking with the guards, easily convincing them of her and her husband's noble birth. They rented lodgings that suited their mock stations near the Hospitaller hospice. The Black Hart was out of the question, since the innkeeper and maids there were sure to recognize the English squire and his French companion. Jean suggested that they not unpack their gear, should they have to flee at a moment's notice, and so after a quick meal and an inspection of their lodgings, the 'family' set out to meet with Count Robert d'Ivry.

"We should be doing this at night," Jean said as they rounded a familiar corner into the street of the hospice.

"Like that last time we were here?" Geoffrey said. "Tell me, Niccolo: are the Voltana knights in good standing? Did any of them take the Cross and serve in the Outremer?"

"I know the elder Voltana served my father in campaigns against his fellow vassals

177

and *raccomendati*, so he should have been knighted, although I doubt any from Voltana took the Cross. Why?"

"If the Voltana are little more than glorified fishmongers, then they would have no reason to visit the Hospitallers, would they? As a knight of some distinction, however...wait, I know how we can approach them without arousing suspicion. Niccolo, my boy, I want you to serve in a noble household in the Outremer!" He clapped Niccolo on the shoulder so hard that the boy's knees nearly buckled.

All three adults looked furtively around for any sign of men-at-arms belonging to the lord of Ravenna or likely spies loitering in the shadows. The snowstorm that had blown in from the Adriatic seemed to be keeping everyone indoors, however, so the party tramped the remaining few yards to the hospice's main door. Geoffrey knocked.

The noise seemed to startle Jean. He grabbed Geoffrey by the arm and said, "Quick! Hide your face!"

"What? Get off! This is no time for modesty. I am not sending the boy to get tonsured."

"The same clerk as before might answer, and I am as sure as I will be damned that he will raise the alarm if he recognizes you."

"True. And when we are inside?"

"We will be under the protection of the Hospitallers, and so it will not matter."

"Or we can demand to see the senior knight who runs this place," Geoffrey added and he pulled the hem of his cloak up to his nose.

A watchman neither Geoffrey nor Jean had ever seen opened the door and ushered in the 'family'. Geoffrey was about to tell him what he wanted when Catherine broke in with the story of wanting to send their child to the East.

"We heard that a respected man of exalted rank from the Outremer has taken lodgings with the Hospitallers," she said. "We seek an audience with him."

The watchman bowed and mumbled that he would have to ask someone about such a request and ambled away.

Geoffrey gave Catherine an angry look before he remember why he had to keep his mouth shut more often than he would like.

Few Hospitallers were resident in the Ravenna hospice, but Geoffrey was able to confer with an affable old brother-knight who had become friends with Count Robert since his arrival, and so he easily acquiesced to the 'lord of Voltana's' request.

They found his lordship in the library, which was a small room that looked onto the cloister, wrapped in a blanket and seated in a large chair next to the hearth. He was dressed in a long, quilted, ruby-colored robe and a white turban.

At first, Geoffrey thought his lordship was asleep, judging by how his chin was resting on his chest, but then he coughed so violently that the flames in the hearth seemed to recoil in fright.

"Greetings, my lord count," Geoffrey said. He pulled off his arming cap and pushed back his hair. Count Robert looked paler than he remembered, but then again he also remembered that they had spent most of their time together on horseback out in the elements, where Nature painted their cheeks ruddy and eyes bright.

Ivry turned and looked at the 'family' without a hint of recognition, but once he scrutinized the squire's face his cheeks moved upwards to show that a smile was forming beneath his beard.

"Geoffrey Hotspur the English squire!" Ivry said. "You have returned faster than I anticipated. This is indeed a wonder, and I know your honor would not allow you to return unless you had completed your commission, so let us not stand on ceremony. Out with it! What did the marquis and his regency council say when you delivered my offer and my seal?" He stood up and embraced Geoffrey. "And I see you have collected some new companions along the way. He stepped back and nodded to Catherine and Niccolo.

"I have fulfilled my duty better than I had hoped," Geoffrey answered. "I have brought his lordship to hear your offer in person, so that it might not be mistaken." He gestured to Niccolo and introduced the Marquis of Ferrara and heir to the Este inheritance.

The smile fell from the count's face.

"My lord," Niccolo said, "the squire speaks the truth. I am Niccolo d'Este, son of Alberto. I am told that you came to this land for the purpose of meeting with me and to propose a union between our two houses. Am I correct to assume this?" Niccolo bowed.

Ivry made the customary greetings, but not with enthusiasm.

"This was not a part of your commission, Hotspur," Count Robert declared. His voice was stern but otherwise uninflected. "I cannot protect him here, and nor can the Hospitallers, should Polenta wish to invade this place. I instructed you to inform him that I would be waiting for an *answer* in Ravenna, but not for you to actually bring him here in the midst of such obvious dangers."

Geoffrey should have been crestfallen by the count's response, but he knew that his decision had been the right one, and that he was fully capable of getting them out of Ravenna when the time came.

"No one knows he is here, my lord," Geoffrey said, and he went on to explain the recent events in Bologna, their uncertainty about the loyalty of Conrad Altinberg and their eventual road to Ferrara.

Ivry alternated looking at Geoffrey and Niccolo, with the occasional glance at Catherine. When the story was over, he turned to the astrologer and asked her what role she had in this strange play.

"My lord, I was instructed by his lordship's mother to counsel him on several matters important to his well-being, and so I can claim that I am a member of the regency council of the Marquis of Ferrara." If Geoffrey was telling the truth about this incredible offer of marriage, then Catherine wanted to gain the count's confidence to ensure its veracity. "With all due respect, my lord, for the sake of the Este and Ferrara, I must ask that you confirm the presumption of Master Hotspur that you are making a marriage offer for your daughter to his lordship, the marquis."

"I am and you may be a witness to it." Ivry rang a bell, which swiftly produced a servant at the door. "Fetch the silver coffer, at once," Ivry ordered. He then asked the visitors questions about their lodgings, how long they planned to remain in Ravenna and about the state of the war, especially about the peace conference in Bologna. The count received his news filtered through several tongues, and so he could not wholly rely on any single source for the truth.

The servant returned and placed a silver coffer on a table. Jean recognized it as the small chest that Ischia dropped into the snow during their first encounter.

"While I appreciate the great efforts you have spent on my behalf," Count Robert said to Geoffrey, "I must now ask you to leave us so that the marquis and I may speak as peers."

Geoffrey bowed and took his leave, followed by Jean. Catherine stayed. They decided to wait in the kitchens, where they could eat, drink and keep warm.

"I ought to beat you for deceiving me so," Jean said after they had filled their plates and found a place against a warm wall. "What if I had made different arrangements for us?"

"You mean like being hired by a merchant caravan? Listen, Count Robert gave me this commission in the strictest confidence, so his words were never for your ears, and considering the number of times you have tried to pull the wool over my eyes, I could hardly trust you with a matter of such high importance."

"Can you at least confirm for me if we are continuing to Ferrara? I know I asked you once already, but I need to hear it again. As the treasurer and secretary of the English Free Company, it is *my* duty to prepare the company if it is to march in one direction or another. I fear the Germans will tire of you, Captain Hotspur, if we do not soon find a proper host for enrollment."

Geoffrey slurped his pottage, wiped his mouth on his cloak and poured himself a goblet of red wine from the jug provided by a Hospitaller brother-knight. "Of course, we are," he said. "I have completed the commission entrusted to me by his lordship the count and soon I will complete the commission entrusted to me by his lordship the marquis! My men will understand."

Geoffrey felt his breast swell with pride in his humors quicken with renewed vitality. He was now confident that he would come full circle and soon return to the halls of his lord and master, the Duke of Lancaster, without shame or dishonor.

Jean noticed how Geoffrey had used the words '*my* men' when referring to the three German lances. He took this as a good sign that the squire was warming up to the idea of being a proper captain.

"I shall have to tend to the Germans soon," Jean said almost to himself. "They should be at the Black Hart by vespers."

Geoffrey nodded. He was staring at an old Hospitaller surcoat hanging above the doorway. It was black and the white cross blazoned on it was stained – with blood, Geoffrey assumed. His return to the knights' hospice was no accident, he reckoned. It allowed him to finally fulfill a commission after so many months of failure, and very likely another one.

Geoffrey wondered if his majesty King Richard the Lionheart fought alongside Hospitallers in his quest for Jerusalem. He would have to again read the chronicles to learn the truth of the matter, as he had in the monastery during his time as a prospective novice. There, he had once had the good fortune of being asked to copy several letters from one blessed manuscript about the great king's adventures, which he treasured. That scrap of parchment should still be lodged with the paltry remains of his gear in Avignon, if they had not been pilfered, Geoffrey thought.

Jean looked at his companion and followed his line of sight to the surcoat. "You think that is blood?"

"I would wager on it. The Hospitallers will not rest so long as a single heathen remains alive or has surrendered the Holy Land."

"Has the dream visited you again?" Jean dipped a piece of bread into his pottage.

"What? Oh, *that* dream." Geoffrey tore his eyes from the surcoat and stared into his goblet. "No, it has not, or if it has, the thing passed without notice. The weather and my duty to the marquis make me weary at the end of the day, although I am sure not to sleep tonight."

"You will go in search of a gaming hall? I know you have not seen the face of a table-board for some time, but it would be foolhardy to risk your discovery–"

"Enough! I am not after a game tonight, although you have shot close to the mark, for it is because I fear discovery that I will not sleep well tonight. I understand the dangers of coming here, Jean, despite what you may believe." Geoffrey took a draught of wine, which felt good sliding down his gullet.

"I suppose you want me to share the watch with you," Jean said. He was relieved that the squire had the good sense to cool his gaming fury to a low flame. All the same, his other worry about the squire and his passions now rose to the surface. "You will seek another audience with the count?"

"If his lordship will do me that honor, yes."

"Should you not stick close to the boy, I mean his lordship the marquis? He must return to our lodgings tonight. The longer he is with the count, the greater the chance that the brother-knights will see through your ruse and cast him out, at best, or inform the local *podestà*, at worst."

"I cannot see the brother-knights betraying us. They are Hospitallers – not Templars."

"I can, if they learn how you have deceived them. That order is a tight one and they do not wear violation well. How do you think the Gamesmaster keeps his company from collapsing? You know that other men in the gaming trade came before him and failed, do you not? No, I suppose your ears are closed to such stories. Well, he has rules, like the Dominicans, and no one dares break them for fear of… well…you can guess."

"I do not have to guess. I remember how your master wanted to cheat me just because I refused to pay him silver in the manner of his choosing. I told him that I would pay my debt to him. That should have been good enough. Instead, he sends his dog to follow me around and bite my arse from time to time." He pointed at Jean and smirked. "But the dog is far from home, now."

"*Best* dog, I will have you know. But that is all over. I am dead if I go back now."

"You could have returned to Avignon at any time. Instead, you choose to linger in this strange land and suck on the teat of my goodwill for as long as your conscience allows you, as much as you have one."

"*Goodwill teat*?! That teat was good and dry before I laid eyes on you, Geoff, and if anyone has been milked it has been me, by others so that we might have a crust of bread to eat." Jean snatched his goblet and downed its contents. He had an urge to throw the vessel at the suspended surcoat, but instead he chose to slam it on the table.

"You are too heated, Jean. You should be bled. Regardless, I value you as a companion. You are a born master victualer."

Jean was content to let the matter drop, especially once he realized that the squire's words were not altogether untrue. Without Geoffrey Hotspur he would still be beating debts out of foolish and corrupt men in Avignon, or dead. However, he also calmed himself with the knowledge that without *him*, Jean Lagoustine, the squire would be in dire straits, or dead.

"If Ivry does grant you an audience tonight, be sure not to commit yourself to any new commissions. Or rather, do not commit yourself to *anything*."

"Mercy of God, go get yourself bled! Or better yet, prepare our gear and horses for travel." Geoffrey feared that the Frenchman's carping would darken his humors, which he felt were now very well balanced.

"Rest assured, that will be done. Still, I still do not see how we will get around all those condottieri and their companies to reach Manfredi, especially now that we will not link up with Altinberg."

"Niccolo knows the way."

"Niccolo?"

"His lordship has allowed me to address him so."

"I should hope so. He is still a boy."

"All the same, he knows his dominium, and he will lead us through it."

"And the trail will lead to Captain Astorre Manfredi?"

"If that is the will of the young marquis, then of course."

CHAPTER 12

Geoffrey was anxious to ask Niccolo all about his meeting with the Count d'Ivry, but as the quartet returned to their lodgings Catherine walked between them and would say nothing herself.

Thwarted of conversation, Geoffrey bled his frustration by absorbing the scene around him, but the paltry city life scarcely held his attention. The bells began to toll for vespers, yet the call was bringing few citizens into the frozen streets to observe the divine office. Even the taverns were attracting few patrons. He found some amusement in the gusts that would occasionally sweep down the rooftops and crash into the snow, sending up great white clouds that chilled the faces of those unlucky enough to be caught by them.

They passed the chapel where he was to have met his lordship on that desperate night and he wondered if he should hear mass there. It would be only right. This led Geoffrey to thoughts about the tailor and his gaming cellar. If he could find a spare hour or two, it might be worth his while…no. Wagering would not do, considering how they had to merge with the shadows to ensure the marquis's safety. He had better keep his mind safely elsewhere.

At the door to their lodgings Jean excused himself and proceeded to the Black Hart Inn. The others went inside.

"Well, did his lordship deceive me about his purpose here or not?" Geoffrey said as he threw his cloak and cap on the table. He smiled broadly to put Niccolo, who had already reached the hearth, at ease.

"We have the count's confidence," Catherine said in a serious tone. She had been forced to enter the room behind Geoffrey after he had pushed passed her in the corridor. "We must respect that, master squire, so neither I nor the marquis shall disclose to you the details of our discussion." She looked meaningfully at Niccolo, who recognized her call for discretion.

184

But Geoffrey was too excited to let it go. "For the love of all that is holy, come on! Let us share some wine and make a celebration of it."

"You are not giving Niccolo any wine, Geoffrey," Catherine ordered, "or me, if that is your scheme. There will be no loosening of tongues on this night."

Several vulgar quips nearly leapt from Geoffrey's throat at the astrologer's careless turn of phrase, but he choked them back down, lest in a fit of pique she would take the marquis to her room and lock the door behind her.

"I am nothing if not a master of discretion," Geoffrey declared and placed a hand on his heart. "Whatever land, silver or titles that might be involved are of no interest to me. What I want to know – and I do not think this is too much to ask – is about the girl."

If Geoffrey expected Niccolo to grin alongside him, he was sorely disappointed, for the marquis wore a pensive look and the flames flickering in the hearth seemed to have enchanted him.

"Good lord!" Geoffrey cried. "Is she truly that beautiful?" He peered into Niccolo's impassive face. "I dare say she is! Did his lordship show you her portrait? Well, this still calls for some sort of banquet. If we are not to have wine, ale or spirits, then some sweet meats must be brought in, and I will not hear you say, m'lady, a word against a jug of mead." Geoffrey stuck his head around the door and called for the landlord to prepare a meal.

Catherine had neither the strength nor the will to stop Geoffrey. After hanging up her mantle she moved next to the hearth and wondered how she would explain their adventure to Niccolo's mother. Meeting with Captain Altinberg or returning directly to Ferrara would have been acceptable courses of action, but this long route and unplanned meeting with an Eastern lord will require some extraordinary speech, particularly the part about how a strange English squire took over the venture. If this Count d'Ivry's offer of marriage held great promise, she might not have worried, but as it was, the old man had blustered more than the winter winds.

Thinking about the count, Catherine was convinced that Geoffrey had allowed himself to be seduced by his smooth rhetoric and exotic home, for it was her opinion that Robert d'Ivry was desperate. The offer of his daughter was true and the size of her dowry would be impressive, but his words came so easily and with such precision that they convinced Catherine that they had been recited many times before. In short, Niccolo was likely one in a queue of potential husbands for the girl. The marquis needed an alliance, marriage or otherwise, to help secure him in Ferrara, but any negotiations with the Cypriot count were sure to drag on for too long to be beneficial.

Catherine could see that Ivry was more clever and calculating than he led on, since she had known such men before. She could not see the regency council dismissing his offer out of hand, but at the same time the council almost certainly would set it aside until the crisis with Azzo d'Este was resolved. An offer of marriage from an Outremer count more impressed someone like the young squire Geoffrey Hotspur than the experienced and practical men who governed Ferrara.

Geoffrey returned, rubbing his hands together in anticipation. He dropped himself onto a chair and renewed his interrogation.

"So, aside from the words that you cannot repeat to me," Geoffrey said, "what else did his lordship tell you? You were together for some hours."

Finally, Niccolo turned away from the fire and looked at the squire, whose obvious joy nearly startled him.

"His lordship spoke about many things," Niccolo said slowly. "He told me about Cyprus and about the Ivry, going all the way back to Normandy."

"Did he tell you about the time he took the Cross and campaigned against the heathen in Egypt? That is a fine story, and one that I was honored to hear from his lordship himself!"

"No, he did not, but he did talk about Jerusalem and the schemes to retake the holy city from the Saracens. The Ivry are related to the Kings of Jerusalem, he told me."

Geoffrey raised his eyebrows and slapped his thighs. "This bodes well for you, my lord. Conquer the city and seize the crown! From marquis to king! What a marvelous thing that will be. And you will need a captain-general to help keep your army in good order." He winked and nodded. "I am already a captain of men."

Catherine started to worry that Geoffrey's enthusiasm for fantastic schemes would infect Niccolo. Already she could hear rising inflections in the boy's voice. It was time to dump some snow on the squire's fervor.

"But you are not even a knight, Geoffrey," Catherine said. "Captain or not, a royal army must be led by a man of rank. And besides, you are pledged to serve the Duke of Lancaster, whose lands are found on the opposite side of the world."

"That is true," Niccolo said as though this was a revelation to him. "You are not a knight. And your company is small."

Geoffrey waved his hand dismissively and said, "All in good time. The young marquis here is not yet married and I have yet to perform many deeds of arms. I will earn my spurs and I will earn them soon!" He tugged at the pommel of his *couteau*, which was still strapped to his waist.

Niccolo laughed. "*I* will make you a knight, Geoff, if I defeat and ruin my uncle."

Geoffrey looked at the marquis with steel intensity. "Do not make that pledge light of heart, my lord."

"My word is my bond."

"Before we lay siege to Jerusalem," Catherine said, "let us first secure Ferrara. Shall we depart at first light tomorrow, squire?"

"Agreed. I will speak with Jean later tonight, after compline. I wish to listen to a service and pray, since I have not made my devotions for some time."

"Have you decided how by which route we must travel?" Catherine asked. "I suggest taking a vessel to your ally Venice."

Geoffrey cringed. "Not a boat. The weather is uncertain, the water is cold and almost certainly word of the Voltana family wanting to sail to Venice will swiftly reach the ears of our enemies."

Catherine gritted her teeth. The squire was right.

"We shall ride through the *valli*," Niccolo answered.

"The what?" Catherine said.

"The eastern wetlands of my dominium. I know them well, since I have ridden through them before and seen the maps my father made of them. It is rich in fish and eels, reeds and salt, but poor in dry land for armies to cross."

"But for a few horses, it should be safe," Geoffrey added. "I expect that most of the marshes will be frozen over."

Catherine sighed. Again, in the absence of reasonable alternatives, she could do nothing but acquiesce to the planned route. Besides, the sooner they leave, the better, no matter how.

The clatter of crockery and voices of servants in the corridor informed the trio that the evening's repast was near at hand. Geoffrey again sprang to the door and arranged for the meal to be laid out near the window away from the fire so that he could be cooler. He poured three cups of mead and saluted the marquis's good fortune and impending victory in the war against his deceitful uncle.

"So, what *does* she look like?" Geoffrey asked Niccolo after they began eating. "I should think his lordship would have brought a portrait of his esteemed daughter with him."

Niccolo blushed.

"By your leave, my lord, let me hazard the fine features of your wife-to-be." Geoffrey wiped his mouth with his sleeve and leaned back in his chair.

"You may," Niccolo said. He sipped his mead and started to cut up a mince pie Geoffrey had thrown onto his plate into very small pieces.

"The lady Marguerite must have very fine features, and I daresay her complexion would be as pale as that of her Norman ancestors, although she was born in the East. And there is something about her eyes, is there not, Niccolo?" Not waiting for the boy to answer, Geoffrey took another swig of mead and continued. "I cannot see her hair, though. If her mother was of local birth, then I would say it must be dark. I recall that her mother returned to the bosom of our Lord several years ago, so I do not suppose his lordship mentioned her all that much. But the eyes…"

"Her hair is flaxen," Niccolo announced.

"Well, all the better for you then," Geoffrey nearly shouted. "If her hair is as pure as gold, so must her heart be. At least, that is what I reckon, although I have never been engaged to a proper lady. I know a few raven-haired maidens, and they are as dark in temperament as they are in their locks, a result of black bile seeping into the hair, a healer once told me. I recall one night in the gaming hall of…I believe the Blue Boar Inn…when one such immodest lass put herself up for a wager."

"The fire is low," Catherine suddenly announced. "It requires stoking."

Geoffrey looked at the astrologer and then at Niccolo, whose cheeks had become very red. "You are right," he mumbled and went to the hearth.

"I believe the regency council and Niccolo's mother will approve of the Lady d'Ivry," Catherine said, hoping to end the vulgar discussion of the girl.

"I dare say they will," Geoffrey declared. "They would be hard pressed to find anyone as distinguished, short of a daughter of *my* lord and master. Of course, they have all been spoken for." Having prodded the flames to leap higher, Geoffrey returned to his stool. "I expect your father would have approved as well," he said to Niccolo.

"My father would have arranged a suitable marriage for me," Niccolo said. "Would you not say so, Catherine? You knew him."

Catherine stiffened, but her face betrayed no discomfort. "I only read for your father, as I have told you."

"Then you would know better than the two of us," Geoffrey said. "I do not underestimate you, mistress astrologer. Niccolo tells me that he remembers little of his father. It is your duty, as the old marquis's former servant, to tell him what you know. The boy has many duties to master."

"I was not his servant; he simply invited me to attend his court in the guise of the station that I am."

"But you served him," Geoffrey said.

"I read for his lordship, and he paid me. When I was satisfied that I need not do more, I left. Servants cannot just up and leave their masters at will." For the first time that night, Catherine took a draught of her mead.

"Yes, Catherine," Niccolo said, "would my father have approved of this union?"

"It is not for me to say. However, he always believed that the Este need not be restricted to a narrow piece of land wedged between Padua and Bologna. He was a builder, your father, as well as a knight of great prowess. He never confessed to me his plans for you, Niccolo, but there is no doubt they were in keeping with his high ambitions."

"A knight of great prowess, you say?" Geoffrey said. "Niccolo! Why did you not tell me this? Then it is for certain that you will lead your host in a victorious pass of arms against your uncle! What for you need a captain-general or regency council?"

Niccolo drank his mead and began to eat with more enthusiasm. The color had left his cheeks and his comfort with the English squire had returned.

"Was your father a condottiere or a knight, Geoffrey?" Niccolo asked.

Geoffrey unbuckled his sword and with both hands held it between him and Niccolo.

"This was my inheritance, Niccolo. You will not find a finer blade in all of Christendom. Now, look at the pommel. Look at the ruby stone held therein." Geoffrey turned the *couteau* until the stone caught the light and glinted crimson with flecks of gold. "Have you ever seen anything like this?"

"No," Niccolo answered in a quiet and awestruck voice.

"Of course you have not, my lord, and nor has anyone else. It is an ancient stone set in an ancient blade. How much blood has this *couteau* drawn?" Geoffrey shook his head slowly. "Even I cannot answer that question. All I can do is honor all those who once held this mighty arm by making sure it is used in a manner worthy of its great heritage." He drew the sword back and gently placed it on the bench by the table.

"I have my father's sword," Niccolo said, "but it is in Ferrara."

"Then I am sorry for you. What arms *have* you brought with you?"

"None, I am afraid, other than a short sword, which is new."

Geoffrey grimaced and leaned back so that his elbows rested behind him on the table. Although the mead was a weak brew, what little potency it possessed had entered the squire's humors, making his eyes glassy and his muscles relaxed. They both were orphans, he thought, he and the Marquis of Ferrara, although he wondered which of them was the worse off. Niccolo had known his father for a few years, it seemed, but had only lived long enough to fashion a powerful legacy for his son to maintain.

That was all to the good, but who would grant him spurs when the time came? The Count d'Ivry could. Geoffrey, however, had no recollection of either of his parents, let alone an uncle who despised him, but he had the singular advantage of serving one of the most powerful lords in Christendom, the Duke of Lancaster and Guyenne, who had put him through a year with the Cistercians, received him as a page at his court, and now had him training in one of his better squire halls. The next stage was for his grace the duke to arrange for Geoffrey to serve a knight in good standing in the field.

He is a fine boy, this Niccolo d'Este, Geoffrey thought. He rides well, speaks well and has shown a little of the prowess that should make him a good knight. Geoffrey frowned at the thought that he might fall under the influence of women and vassals, or worse be ruined by an uncle whose legitimacy was not justified. The issue will be decided in a grand pass of arms, Geoffrey reckoned, and the boy should be given his chance to prove himself there.

A gust of wind screamed down the street, banged against the shutters and made the fire shudder when it shot down the chimney. Catherine went to the window, peeled back the oiled sheepskin and peered through the slats.

"Another storm has blown in," she announced. "Yet more snow. The clouds are tinged with red, which is the sign." The bells for compline began to toll.

"That is no reason not to attend chapel," Geoffrey said. "This is a test of our fortitude." For a moment he thought about having another drink, but feeling the lightness of his body, he turned over the cup and stood up.

The door latch rattled and in walked Jean.

"Do *not* go into the street, for they are nigh well impassible," he said as he brushed clumps of snow from his shoulders. Jean pulled off his hood, unclasped his cloak and threw them on top of Geoffrey's. "It sure as hell is warmer in here than in the

Black Hart." Jean sniffed a few times and his nose swiftly led him to the food. "Ah, a second course, I see."

When Geoffrey asked about the Germans, Jean reassured him that they were in good spirits, but anxious to leave Ravenna.

"Then we should be off to the chapel," Geoffrey said. "With the first commission done, we should pray for success with the second one."

"Not bloody likely, Geoff! I just got here and I am ravenous. The Germans were not generous with their fare. You go on ahead and I will follow later. Or better yet, I will take the first watch here until you return."

"That will do," Geoffrey said. He donned his cloak and arming cap, and he was about to leave when he turned to Jean and said, "Give me your hood, since you will not be needing it."

Jean gestured at the garment.

"I should come with you," Niccolo said. "The commission is every bit mine as it is yours, since I must lead us through the *valli*."

"You can pray just as well here," Catherine said. "No one should see you, even at night."

"Especially at night," Jean added. He had already poured himself a cup of mead and loaded a plate.

"So can Geoffrey, but all the same he is leaving," Niccolo argued.

"I will be making devotions as well as praying. Now that I have a few coins in my purse, I can buy a few prayers and candles for my…father." Geoffrey had wanted to say the name of his friend Roger Swynford, who had been killed during a brawl, but instead 'father' came out. "I will do one for yours as well, Niccolo."

"You must be weary," Catherine said to the boy. "You may sleep here, if you wish, or we can retire to my room."

"I am not tired."

"Then read your Cicero." Catherine produced the tome from underneath Niccolo's satchel.

Geoffrey glanced at the book. "So, you are a reader as well as a lover," he teased. Suddenly his face became serious. "Is that Scripture?"

Catherine waved for Geoffrey to make his final departure. The boy had been battered enough by the squire's wit for one evening, she reckoned.

"It is Cicero, a Roman orator," Niccolo explained.

"I do not know him, but if he can make your tongue as smooth as silk, you will have enough of an arsenal to conquer your Marguerite with ease." He winked at Niccolo, who began to blush again.

"You are letting in the cold air, Geoff," Jean said. "Be gone with you!"

Geoffrey nodded and closed the door behind him.

"I would tell you to accompany him," Catherine said to Jean, "but I need you here, as regretful as that sounds. You could have brought at least one of the Germans with you."

"It is all or none with them. A funny lot, those Germans of ours, although I understand their reasoning perfectly." Jean shoveled a heap of mince pie into his maw.

"Would you care to explain it to me? I am a part of your English Free Company now, for better or for worse."

"Strength in numbers," Jean mumbled through his chewing. He swallowed hard. "They refuse to break up their lances for the sake of their own protection, and so they are all staying together at the Black Hart tonight. Are you worried that we will be found out?"

"I must be concerned at all times. What else have you learned?"

"What makes you think I know any more than you? This is not my city, after all." In truth, one of Jean's stops had been at the shop of the tailor, who had assisted him with deceiving Geoffrey.

"I know you well enough that you burrow like a mole, poking holes and peering into places that are closed to you."

Jean guffawed and nearly choked on a piece of bread. He sent a stream of mead to dislodge it, coughed a few times and wiped his mouth with his sleeve.

"Ugh!" Catherine exclaimed. "Do you and the squire *not* have a napkin for that? We have no time to launder your garments."

"Tear off a piece of your skirts, m'lady, and present it to me as a charmed token of your esteem," Jean quipped.

"I will bring you a rag and a washbowl if you answer my question properly. What do you know?"

"I know that Manfredi made it to Ferrara."

"Thank the lord for that. What else?"

"More importantly, Kate, I also know that someone from the Hospitallers told the *podestà* about our visit as the Voltana family to the count. What might come of that even *I* do not know." Jean loaded some marinated vegetables onto his plate.

"Then we had better leave in the morning."

"If we can."

The day was white. When Geoffrey stepped out of the lodgings he could hardly see across the street. The temperature had risen overnight, but great snowflakes continued to fill the sky. He went back in and informed his companions about the weather.

"At least we will not freeze to death," Jean said.

"The horses will have a hard time of it, though," Geoffrey said.

"How will we find the trails through the *valli* if they are hidden by mountains of snow?" Catherine asked.

"We cannot go," Niccolo declared. All eyes turned to him. "Not only will the trails be hidden, but the ponds and marshes as well, and I fear the ice covering them will melt. The eastern *contado* holds innumerable hazards at the best of times."

"Are you sure, Niccolo?" Geoffrey asked. "You say you know the land well, so can you not lead us through safely? I will follow."

"I know it if I can see it." Niccolo looked at the partially open shutters. He was thinking of the fear that had beset him when he nearly led his companions astray on the road to Faenza. He did not want to suffer that feeling again. "What can I see now?"

"At least we can assume that if we cannot move, nobody can, especially an army," Catherine said. "Let us hope the sky clears and another cold spell descends upon us soon."

Jean sighed. "I had better tell the Germans about this. Give me some silver, Kate." He held out his hand in front of her. When she continued to be unmoved, he explained, "They will need a little coin to calm them. They probably have realized that we will march out today, but we still need to keep them in good spirits."

Catherine produced two dozen *grossi* and Jean left to fulfill his commission.

"Shall we call on his lordship again?" Geoffrey asked.

"We have all we need from him," Catherine said. "We can visit the chapel today, perhaps, if attendance is low."

"Then I shall seek his audience alone," Geoffrey declared. "I had no chance to speak with Count Robert yesterday, and I would like to share counsel with him, if he condescends to see me."

193

"I will go with you," Niccolo announced and he leapt from his chair. "He might have counsel for me too."

"I am against it," Catherine said. "Did you not hear what your 'steward' said? The *podestà* already knows about us."

"Then there is no harm in going again, is there?" Geoffrey said.

"And I finished my Cicero last night," Niccolo added.

Catherine could see that the boy was enamored with the squire. "If we go, we go as a family. Niccolo: take your sword with you. You must look like a proper lord's son."

When the trio arrived at the hospice, they were greeted with disappointment. The clerk admitted them, but when they reached Count Robert in the library, they saw that his health had worsened. He was suffering from fits of violent coughing and he would shiver often. Because of this, the audience lasted less than an hour, when his lordship begged them to leave while he had a purgative and subsequent rest. They need not quit the hospice, however, for he would receive them again in a few hours.

"This is disappointing," Geoffrey said, "and not a good sign." They were standing in the gallery that bordered the cloister.

"I will tell you what is and what is not a good sign, squire," Catherine snapped.

"Well then, tell me," Geoffrey said.

Catherine thought for a moment before answering. "That he was well enough to receive us yesterday, when it was needed, suggests that our commission is favored. Beyond that, we must wait, and I will tell you more."

Geoffrey stared at the snow-blanketed cloister with disappointment. "Maybe you can find the signs that will tell us when the snow will stop. You can wait in the kitchens, if you like. I will remain here and pace the gallery. My legs are stiff from idleness. And besides, the kitchens are too warm for me."

Catherine nodded. Seeing that Niccolo had no intention of accompanying her, she took her leave.

"Show me your sword again," Niccolo said. "You boasted well about it last night, so now I want to see it in the light of day."

"My *couteau*? If I draw my sword, it must draw blood. That is the custom."

"Has it drawn blood?"

"It has." Geoffrey patted the pommel.

"Whose blood did you spill during your pass of arms last year? Catherine told me that you fought against the supreme pontiff and won. I have heard about feats of

194

arms performed by the Count d'Ivry, but none from you."

Geoffrey realized that the marquis had unwittingly caught him in a lie. He had brandished his sword at the battle near Orte, but he failed to draw blood. He had performed a feat of arms, though, so he decided to amend his previous declaration, hoping to distract the boy.

"Of course, a sword can be drawn for the purpose of training or mending." Geoffrey smiled. "This is natural. Listen, Niccolo, while we are waiting for his lordship to call us, let us display our skills with arms. The practice will do us good."

Niccolo was wary about crossing blades with the tall and very confident squire, but Geoffrey seemed so keen on fighting that Niccolo felt that he should agree. "Where? Do the brother-knights maintain a training hall in the hospice?"

Geoffrey looked around and, having come to a decision, spread his arms wide. "Why not here? The gallery has the breadth for close play, and with your short sword that is all we can do anyway."

Niccolo nodded and they set about clearing away snow and stone benches to create their lists. For barriers they marked the hospice wall, cloister colonnade and a pair of stone benches set at either end. When they agreed that they had produced a proper venue for their practice, Geoffrey and Niccolo met in the center of the lists to discuss rules. However, troubled by the vast difference in their respective heights, Niccolo decided to even things out.

"Let us trade arms," Niccolo said. He drew his short sword and held it up by the blade. "You will chop me to pieces otherwise."

"I cannot relinquish my *couteau*." Geoffrey's tone was the most serious Niccolo had heard yet.

"You mean you *will* not relinquish it. Fair is fair, Geoffrey, and my disadvantage here is too great."

"From what I understand, you suffer great disadvantage in the field, yet here you still are. No one gave me a leg up in the hall of squires, but I fought with skill and purpose and became the captain of a confraternity. I *found* advantage."

"But you said you that *couteau* of yours has been with you since birth. I would find easy advantage if I had such a blade, skill and purpose aside. All the same, we are not in the field."

"Very well, my lord. You hold the senior rank, so I cannot deny you. We will trade arms." Geoffrey took Niccolo's short sword and weighed it in his hand. It was considerably lighter than his *couteau*, even with the many jewels and bits of gold and

195

silver smothering it. He unsheathed his own sword and, with a solemn face, handed it to his opponent. "Now, let us have at it!"

Niccolo had trouble steadying the new weapon in his two hands, but he eventually found equilibrium when he leaned back and set himself in a low guard. He wanted to stand in Iron Door, but the hefty weight of Geoffrey's sword pressed down on him, so he had to bring his feet closer together for Half-Boar, which was less defensive, but it gave him enough leverage to allow him to make an easy parry of just about any strike.

"We will play to disarm, not to touch," Geoffrey said. "We will only draw the blood of our enemies." He held out Niccolo's sword with one hand and set himself in a middle stance.

"I have not been arms training for long," Niccolo said.

Geoffrey seemed not to hear. He advanced with a single step and twisted his blade to catch Niccolo's in a bind and thereby wrench it out of his hand, but the boy snapped it back, permitting nothing more than a scrape of steel. Geoffrey immediately repeated his move and again Niccolo withdrew, this time taking a few steps rearward towards the colonnade.

"Where is your counter?" Geoffrey asked. "You are lucky I did not finish with an upward cut. That would have sent you flying."

"I was thinking of one," Niccolo answered.

"Thinking? You think and you are dead. You must just step forward and strike. Who is your arms master? Your mother? Come now, I do not want to have to teach the basics. You are old enough to have mastered them."

Niccolo reaffirmed his grip and shuffled forward. He was about to make a simple thrust towards Geoffrey's chest when the squire swatted away the blade with a crosswise strike and then, anticipating an upward cut, brought down his sword and knocked the *couteau* from Niccolo's hand.

"You should have met my blade on the upswing," Geoffrey said. "I was expecting your counter. This really is beginner stuff and you have the better weapon."

Niccolo said nothing. He was desperately trying to remember what the arms master had taught him or anything from the many bouts he had witnessed. However, his hands hurt, causing him more difficulty to secure a fast hold of the *couteau*. He was to advance above all, he recalled, but if he had to retreat, then he must counter and advance again. The squire was taller, so any downward slice was out, Niccolo reasoned, but he feared that an upward cut would lack the necessary strength to achieve its purpose. This left him with few striking options and he began to regret taking Geoffrey's sword from him.

Setting himself in Half-Boar again, but leaning forward a little, Niccolo set the pommel against his hip and jabbed ahead, twisting his blade in order to at least lessen the squire's crosswise counter when it came. Then, maybe he could close into grapple and put pressure on the hilt, since Geoffrey was wielding his sword with just one hand.

The duelists clashed, but as before the force of the counter was too great for Niccolo to withstand and he staggered sideways, leaving the *couteau* to trail by its tip along the ground. Then, Geoffrey brought down another blow and sent the blade clattering away towards the library.

"Come now, that was no more than a gentle tap!" Geoffrey said.

Niccolo grew hot in the face. He thought about the icy fortress and faces full of snow from January. He wanted to charge the impudent squire and push him to the ground, but he knew that would be foolish. The enemy captain from January was his own size; the squire was not. Instead, he kicked the *couteau* along the gallery and gave Geoffrey a dirty look.

"I cannot play like this," Niccolo declared.

"I am not your arms master. I am not training you. I have every right to win this match."

They heard a door swing open and Catherine appeared behind one of the shifted stone benches.

"By Jesus's noble passion, what foolishness is this!" she said in a barely restrained voice. "Who is trying to kill who?"

Geoffrey was taken aback by the fierceness of the astrologer's question. "I was teaching his lordship a few skills," he said, hoping to ease her anger.

"No you were not! You said that you are not my arms master and so you have every right to win!" Niccolo cried.

"Well, you demanded an even match, and so I assumed you wanted to play in a proper pass of arms. Did I not hear you right?"

Niccolo frowned and could not think of anything more to say. He straightened his doublet and marched to the library.

"Have you gone mad?!" Catherine said. "Did you bring him all the way here just so he could be killed? Are you that desperate to draw blood?"

Geoffrey picked up his *couteau* and after dusting it off sheathed it. "Calm yourself.

He was in no danger, for all that is holy, we were not playing for touch. And besides, it is clear that he is sorely in need of arms training."

Catherine blocked Geoffrey as he tried to leave the lists. "And what if the count or one of the brother-knights had witnessed this spectacle? We could easily be forbidden from returning to the hospice and word of it would reach the *podestà*. This was very reckless of you, Geoffrey."

"Well, I suppose…"

"And now Niccolo is upset. My only hope now is that you were not stupid enough to wager with Niccolo on your foolish match."

"If he is to lead his own army, he must know how to wield a sword."

"He has Manfredi for that." She shifted as Geoffrey moved to avoid her. "He is still a boy."

"He looks every inch a man to me. You saw him ride and heard him speak, and I daresay he led us well to Ravenna and to his prospects for a grand marriage. His father, no doubt, would have had him more prepared for war."

"I am not his mother and you are not his father. Neither of us belongs here. Do not overstep your bounds, Geoffrey. You do not know Italy as well as I do."

The astrologer's words struck Geoffrey hard, yet he would not be put off. "His vassals must see him at the head of his host, be they loyal and not. That much I know, Kate. This Manfredi is his captain-general only; he cannot inspire fealty."

Catherine thought about this argument for a moment before saying, "Fealty or not, none of this is your concern. Your duty is your commission, which is to get the marquis home in one piece. And may I remind you that it was I who gave you this commission, Geoffrey, so your duty is to me as well as to Niccolo. I have had to tolerate this excursion to Ravenna, but no more diversions or you will receive nothing at the end."

Geoffrey stiffened. What the astrologer said was true and he was embarrassed. All the same, he believed he had taken the right path, especially now that the marquis had better prospects.

"No more diversions," Geoffrey said. "I give you my word." He handed Catherine Niccolo's sword. "Do not let his lordship forget this."

CHAPTER 13

The storm lasted the entire first week of March. However, the English Free Company and its charges were not idle. Catherine tutored Niccolo in reading and rhetoric during the day while Geoffrey taught the boy about arms and armor in the evening, and when the astrologer was not looking helped him master sword fighting stances.

Once, Geoffrey tried to teach Niccolo how to be courteous to noble ladies, considering that he would have to meet the beautiful Marguerite one day, and solicited Catherine's assistance. Although Niccolo had trouble looking at the mock Marguerite in the eye, the lesson was going well until Jean arrived and suggested that, to enliven the boy's humors, Catherine put on her black and red velvet gown. At those words Niccolo fled the courtyard, Geoffrey doubled over in laughter, and Catherine made sure that Jean's bad shoulder hurt for the rest of the day.

Jean, meanwhile, was obliged to hone his skills at victualing with the small allowance Catherine disbursed to him every other day, since the market stalls had little to offer other than rumor and idle chatter. It was there that Jean learned that Manfredi had joined Jean de la Salle's company of Bretons at the town of Maiero only a few miles northeast of Portomaggiore, which he made his main camp. Azzo, meanwhile, had made it back to Argenta.

The three German lances kept to themselves in the Black Hart, drinking, whoring, gaming, and sometimes polishing and mending their gear. At night, Geoffrey would join them in any one of these pursuits, returning home just in time to take his turn on watch.

Count Robert held only brief audiences with the squire and the marquis, sometimes together, sometimes separately, for the shift in the weather signaled a worsening of his health. This was just as well, since every visit to the Hospitaller hospice put them at risk of discovery by Polenta. Geoffrey gently prodded the count to tell stories about his and his ancestors' fight against the heathen, ostensibly to inspire Niccolo, but more for his own listening pleasure. The old man would try his best, but he would either fall into a coughing fit or simply nod off in mid-sentence.

Then at last the wind died, the skies cleared and the temperature fell far enough that the city's wells froze over.

"I do not recall it ever getting this cold in Avignon," Geoffrey said, although he had his cloak open and his arming cap on the table. "It should carry us to Manfredi faster." He and Jean were sitting in the front hall of their lodgings, waiting for their horses to be fed and watered. They were ready to leave Ravenna.

"Or to our deaths," Jean quipped. "Are you sure the boy knows his way around his own land? Following a well-traveled road is one thing, but crossing a load of wetlands is another, no matter how frozen they might be."

"I had the marquis list the villages and markers between here and Ferrara, and he did not hesitate on one of them."

"He could have made them up, for all you know, Geoff."

"I suppose, but he is a serious lad and I have yet to find anything false in him. All the same, we must ride northwest, and now that the clouds are gone we should be able to keep our direction true."

Jean went through a mental checklist of all the victuals and gear he believed he had set.

"Did you take your final leave of the count?" Jean asked.

"I did."

"What did he say?"

"He wished us 'God speed'."

"Of course he did, but did he tell you anything unexpected?"

"I claim no expectations from his lordship."

"Now I am finding falsehoods in you. You had expectations of him from the day you met him."

Geoffrey raised his eyebrows. "He is returning to Cyprus as soon as possible. His health suffers greatly here."

"Will he not wait for an answer from the boy's regency council? That is his reason for being here." Jean rubbed his lower shoulder. It was hurting more than ever.

Geoffrey thought about the Saracens and the Turks and the many threats to the Christian kingdoms in the Outremer, but he knew Jean would not want to hear about all that again. "He can wait in Cyprus just as well as he can here. His lordship met Niccolo, so he is content."

"Humph!" Jean suspected that Geoffrey was not telling him everything, but he could not be worried about that now. The only certainty was that they were leaving for Manfredi, which was most important. "I had better see that the Germans are ready, although I am sure they are. In truth, I am more worried that they might have wagered away some of their gear or still owe somebody silver. It would not be the first time."

"You would know the most about that," Geoffrey said.

Jean ignored the comment and went outside. The citizens were busy clearing the streets of snow, leaving a sheet of ice over the paving stones. For once, Jean was glad about his clogs, for while they did little to keep his feet warm, the web of nails he had pounded into their soles helped him stay upright. He doubted the squire had been clever enough to make the same adjustment to his precious buskins.

As he entered the lane where the Black Hart stood, Jean saw Tommasino Crivelli standing by the door of the inn. He was partially blocked by some horses, but there was no mistaking the odd Italian. Jean looked for a shadow to slip into, but the bright morning allowed him nothing. The intense sunlight seemed to blind Crivelli, however, because when he turned in Jean's direction he gave no indication that he recognized his erstwhile companion.

Jean casually retreated until he was out of sight. At first, Jean wondered if Crivelli was alone, that he finally had become fed up with Captain dell'Ischia and left the Company of the Rose, but the dozen or so horses he was apparently keeping watch over made that unlikely. And why would he be in Ravenna? No, Ischia had tracked them down. This was sound reasoning, since only Ischia knew Geoffrey and him with any degree of familiarity, and it was what he would have done in their place, if Azzo d'Este was the Gamesmaster and they were in Avignon.

Jean peeped around the corner – Crivelli was still by the door, though a few servants were milling about between the horses. Jean silently cursed his ill luck. He had to inform the others about this sudden misfortune, of course, but at the same time he was wondering if the Germans had been compromised. Before getting back to Geoffrey, Jean decided to learn if he could still rely on the main body of the English Free Company.

Keeping both eyes open for any other member of the Company of the Rose who might be searching the streets for the marquis, Jean found a circuitous way around the Black Hart to reach the inn's stable. He thought about simply killing Crivelli and scattering the horses, which would improve their odds of escaping, but Jean remembered that the lord of Ravenna was against the marquis and had almost certainly been informed about his likely presence in the city, which meant that Polenta's many men would be searching the city for Niccolo. So, Jean decided against what would be a pointless murder.

He peered into the stable and saw that the Germans' horses and their gear were gone. They must have already cleared off for the meeting point near the main gate, Jean reckoned. They might drink like a friar, Jean thought, but when those Germans had somewhere to go, they wasted no time getting there.

"Geoff! Geoff! Thank God you are ready!" Jean cried when he saw the squire, the marquis and Catherine ensuring that their gear was well set on their mounts. "We must leave now! Ischia is here and I do not believe he has come for the count."

Geoffrey's hand immediately went to the pommel of his *couteau*. "Did he see you? Is he alone?" He looked up and down the street.

"He brought his company with him, so he is not a messenger. He is at the Black Hart. Where is my nag?" Jean frantically looked around until he spotted his horse hitched to a post a few yards away.

"That explains why a rank of men-at-arms raced passed here towards the Hospitaller hospice. They might believe we sought refuge with Count Robert."

"Then we had better hurry. I doubt those brother-knights keep vows of silence." With some difficulty Jean worked his way into the saddle.

Catherine quickly mounted her horse and urged it forward. "What about the Germans?" she asked. "Are they still with us? Did you pay them?" She looked at Jean with suspicion.

"Yes, yes! All was done according to the *condotta*." He explained what he had discovered at the inn.

"Then let us be off!" Catherine ordered.

Geoffrey looked at Niccolo, who had said nothing up to this point. "By your leave, my lord," he said.

Jean and Catherine frowned, since they had to rein in their horses for the sake of this courtesy.

"Should we take the high street?" Niccolo asked.

"That would be the fastest way to the main gate," Geoffrey advised.

"We might avoid meeting men-at-arms if we take the alleys," Catherine suggested.

"Or we might get caught without a means of escape, or become lost," Geoffrey argued. "Regardless, such a path will slow us. We will take the shortest and swiftest way."

Catherine nodded her agreement. Niccolo put his horse into a trot, but Geoffrey spurred Saint George into a gallop and overtook him, throwing up a screen of snow as he went and obliging the rest of the group to follow him at that heady pace.

Since the Hospitaller hospice was not on the high street, they avoided the bulk of men-at-arms that had gathered there and easily reached the designated meeting point, which was a hundred years from the gate.

No one was there.

"What deceit is this?!" Catherine cried. She pulled her horse close to Niccolo's and held her arm protectively across his chest. Her eyes flitted along the street and at the windows above her, searching for crossbows that might be trained on them. "Where are your Germans?"

"No deceit, woman!" Jean shouted back. "After seeing Ischia at the Black Hart they probably decided it was safer on the other side of the gate. Or are you wanting to surrender his lordship to his enemy?"

"Enough!" Niccolo declared. "We must trust Master Hotspur and his company. We have no choice but to advance, and if someone tries to stop us we will counter with these." He patted his short sword.

"You are right," Catherine conceded. "Germans or no Germans, we must get through that gate."

"It is time to play the Voltana family again," Geoffrey said.

They trotted towards the gate: Geoffrey and Niccolo led, followed by Catherine and then Jean, who had to stiffen his neck to keep himself from turning his head around.

Geoffrey soon saw that not only was the main gate closed, even the small door in it was shut, which gave him cause to worry. At the guardhouse, he called for him and his family to be let out, but on one answered. After a tense moment, during which Geoffrey thought about where else he might take his 'family', a man emerged and stepped into the sunlight. Geoffrey slammed his hand on the pommel of his *couteau* when he saw that the man had a sword in his hand – it was one of his Germans.

"By the devil's own hellfire, what is the meaning of this?!" Geoffrey demanded. A shiver went down his spine at the thought that he had been betrayed.

The German man-at-arms smiled and explained that they had seen Ischia and the unexpected surge in the number of Polenta's men-at-arms marching through the streets, and so fearing discovery, they immediately went to the main gate. However,

EVAN OSTRYZNIUK

instead of waiting where they should have and risk arrest, they decided to seize the guardhouse until their party or a large force of men-at-arms arrived.

"Then open the gate and let us fly!" Geoffrey commanded.

At these words the remainder of the English Free Company appeared and soon the gate was pushed open just enough to let them all through.

"Now, where do we go?" Geoffrey asked Niccolo. They were gathered at the first milestone.

Niccolo sighed. He looked around for a landmark, but all he could see was snow. Then he bent his head back and squinted into the sun. "We need to ride north," he said. "We must reach Lake Comacchio. From there I know which *valli* to follow to Maiero."

The wind was stronger in the open fields, but it was not as fierce as when they had ridden into the city. They soon reached a canal that curved eastwards, like a moat, around Ravenna, and decided to follow it until they found a road that led northwards. And after about a dozen more miles they saw a wide bridge that Niccolo reckoned should take them into the *valli*. A toll booth and a few outbuildings sat on the opposite bank.

"Well, this is it," Geoffrey announced. He surveyed the terrain and saw nothing but a flat white plain broken occasionally by small copses or maybe a village. "You are certain this road leads to that lake?"

Niccolo nodded. "Few roads cross the *valli* and all lead to Comacchio."

When they reached the bridge a dozen men appeared from behind the outbuildings and formed a rank of four lances on bridge's northern end. Each lance of three men was armed with an Italian pike, which was a good yard longer than the customary four-yard French pike.

Geoffrey yanked on his reins, nearly causing Saint George to rear. He caught the eye of the senior lance head of his company; each seemed to question the other about what to do. They would be about an even match, Geoffrey reckoned, although if his Germans were as good as Jean said they were, they should be able to push these guards off the bridge with ease.

"We are still a family. Remember?" Jean whispered. He had noticed Geoffrey's suddenly fierce look and had quickly ridden up to him. "We can pay these bastards off and be gone. For once, we have silver in our purse."

Catherine appeared beside them and made the same suggestion.

Geoffrey relaxed his shoulders and furtively shook his head at the German to

204

indicate that he should stand down. He then spurred Saint George to meet the men-at-arms arrayed against him. The moment the first hoof struck the bridge a mounted figure with a black cap, long face and graying beard trotted out from behind the toll booth.

"Well, what a motley crowd we have here," Giovanni dell'Ischia said. "The Marquis of Ferrara, your lordship." Ischia touched his cap and bowed to Niccolo, who was several paces behind Geoffrey, "a wayward English squire, some lowborn German pikemen, a jumped up French villein, and…I cannot quite make out your home, m'lady, although if I were to guess, I would say Sicily. I might even wager on it."

Geoffrey drew his sword half way out of its scabbard. "Stand aside, Captain! You have no right to accost us, although if you are an agent of the wretch Azzo d'Este, then I shall have at you and crush you and your rabble as I did twice before!"

"*Once* before," Ischia corrected. "That first time…we can call it a draw. No matter. I have four lances with all points armed holding you, several more soon to return from scouting the rest of the canal, plus Polenta's men within calling distance."

"I do not see them," Geoffrey said. The Germans, meanwhile had dismounted of their own accord, collected their pikes from the pack horse and were starting to form a rank of their own. Catherine had drawn close to Niccolo while Jean pulled his horse nearer the Germans.

"You will. One blow of the trumpet and you are done for. Hand over the boy," Ischia demanded in a lower voice.

"The answer is no!"

"Then the answer is wrong. Listen, Hotspur, you have no cause to be in this land. Despite your being a man of Gaunt, I could kill you now and no one would be the wiser. Think about it. You are a stranger here. You cannot truly defend the marquis, and as a man of high chivalry, you should know that."

The seed of doubt Ischia was trying to plant failed to find purchase.

"I have vowed to bring his lordship to his rightful place," Geoffrey said with iron conviction.

"And you would die for him? He will not come to harm if I take him to his uncle. He is of noble blood. However, if he reaches Manfredi there is every chance he *will* die when his uncle brings him to battle." Ischia now appealed to the squire's compassion, or at least he hoped to confuse him about how Italy really worked.

"I am certain I will not die today, at least not by your weak hands." Geoffrey motioned for the Germans to advance to the edge of the bridge.

"Then you will die by the lord of Ravenna's hands, or one of his agents," Ischia said, although he realized that the squire had the confidence that he could defeat him again, and no amount of arguing would change that conviction. His and Polenta's men were indeed approaching, but Ischia could not be certain they would arrive before the squire committed a reckless action and shed blood on this miserable bridge.

"Do you know this man, Geoffrey?" Catherine asked.

Geoffrey gave brief account of their journey together on the Way of the Franks.

"The squire Hotspur is my guardian," Niccolo declared. "I will have no other and you will stand aside!"

"I have no love for Azzo, my lord," Ischia stated, "or Polenta. I could just as well escort you to Mandredi, assuming I had your trust." If he could sow a little uncertainty within the little band of fugitives, he might be able to win advantage *and* ruin the English squire.

"Explain yourself!" Niccolo demanded.

"He is playing for time, Niccolo," Catherine said.

Niccolo looked at Catherine and then at Geoffrey expectantly.

"You are the marquis, my lord," Geoffrey said. "You tell me to advance – I will advance; you tell me to hold – I will hold. I will remain on guard with all points armed, though, Niccolo."

"I believe you," Niccolo said and then called to Ischia, "I am listening!"

Ischia nodded and urged his horse forward a few yards. "My lord, my only interest is the Company of the Rose, and it is starving. Your Uncle Azzo has given me promises, but that is all. I am a free lance, in other words, and I offer you my sword for service as far as your captain-general." He held out his hand in a supplicating gesture.

"How can I be sure you will not murder me and *my* company and steal his lordship?" Geoffrey asked.

"You would let your guard down so?" Ischia said. "Doubtful, but I will tell you why my interest lies more with you, my lord, than with your uncle. If I take you back to Ravenna, no doubt Polenta will take you from *me* and tell all that it was he who captured you, leaving me with nothing but embarrassment. Of course, I could make for Azzo's camp by crossing the *valli*, but I do not know them well enough and I doubt you will tell me the safest path. And I cannot return the way I came, by the Faenza road." Ischia stopped to pique everyone's curiosity. Geoffrey bit.

"Why not?" Geoffrey asked. "We came by that road with fewer men than you and in poorer conditions, yet we got through."

"Yes, that was a neat trick you pulled in Bologna, Hotspur. The *podestà* and papal vicar are still arguing about what happened. To answer you, Conrad Altinberg has already moved out of Faenza and occupied a stretch of that road. Too dangerous for me now. This is what I give you to display my sincerity. Your army is coming together, my lord."

"Then how were you able to pass, as a part of Azzo's host?" Catherine asked. "They must have stopped you, if indeed what you say is true."

"I was stopped and searched, but, you see, I have nothing to suggest that I am with Azzo d'Este. As I said, he only gave me promises – no *condotta*, or a seal, or anything of his. Altinberg had no reason to detain me and my men. And he did not offer me a *condotta* either."

Geoffrey, Niccolo and Catherine looked at each other. Even the Germans began a discussion about the likelihood of Ischia's story.

Seeing that his words were at last finding purchase, Ischia increased his wager on Niccolo trusting him by ordering his men to withdraw and stand aside. From his vantage he could see a cloud of snow billowing from the direction of Ravenna. A group of Polenta's riders were coming.

"Do you think it is true about Altinberg?" Niccolo asked Geoffrey.

"I do not see why not," he said. "If we decided to march during the cold, clear weather, I expect he was wise enough to have done the same."

"Damn!" Catherine exclaimed. "We should have linked up with Altinberg when we had the chance."

"It was his lordship's decision to meet with Count Robert, which is more important," Geoffrey said.

"How well do you know this condottiere, Geoffrey?" Niccolo asked. "Did you really twice defeat him in a pass of arms?"

"Yes. He is a poor captain, from what I have seen, so in truth I do not fear him. His men are weak. If I may be permitted counsel, my lord, I reckon that joining him would be lesser threat than if we fight him here now and then fight Polenta's men later. However, I will fight him, if that is what you order."

"What do you want, Ischia?" Niccolo shouted.

The captain shrugged and said, "A *condotta*, of course, and a good one."

Jean rode up to the trio and asked, "What are we doing?"

Catherine asked Jean about the Company of the Rose and whether they should trust Ischia. "You were a debt collector. You have a better nose for lies and deceit than the rest of us."

"He does not like Geoffrey at all," Jean said, "but he brought the count safely from Assisi to Ravenna. His men might be weak, but they come from respectable families. In short, they are not brigands. We are even numbers, so if we keep the marquis close to us and arms at the ready, I reckon we should be fine with them. But then again, do we really have a choice here?"

An icy gust caused everyone to turn their heads away from the sea wind.

"No regency council here, my lord!" Ischia called out. "Time flies and into the arms of Uncle Azzo!"

"If you promise to stay close to me, Geoffrey, I will strike an accord with this man," Niccolo said, "but only if you all agree." He looked at the three adults each in turn. He felt good about making a decision, and saying the words aloud buttressed his conviction.

Jean scratched his beard and squinted with his right eye in the direction of Ischia. He thought he could see Crivelli lurking near the toll booth. "I will submit if Geoffrey does," he said.

"I will do as you order, Niccolo," Catherine said. She was thinking about how all her property was still in Ferrara.

"I am at your side no matter which way this falls," Geoffrey declared and he nodded.

Niccolo rode to the middle of the bridge and announced, "Let us go forth together, Captain dell'Ischia."

"These are my terms and they are not onerous." Ischia met Niccolo on the bridge. "You recognize me and the Company of the Rose as your armed escort to the camp of Astorre Manfredi and make this known to your regency council. You will offer me a *condotta* with you personally for three months with the right to recruit freely." He gestured at his men. "As you can see, the Company of the Rose is big enough to conduct high-born lords and ladies, but not so big to fill a full rank in a main battaile."

"It will be done." Niccolo extended his right hand and they shook on the deal.

"A wise decision, my lord. Now, let us be off!"

After Geoffrey brought over his men to the northern side of the canal, the two captains mixed their companies so that each English Free Company lance was paired with a Company of the Rose lance. The Germans and Italians jostled each other and neither group had any words for the other, but no blood was spilled or harnesses damaged. Geoffrey and Ischia rode side by side with Niccolo close between them, while Jean and Catherine were obliged to travel next to each other behind them. The column maintained a tense silence as they traveled at a steady pace northwards.

Niccolo had been right about the condition of the *valli* – most of the canals and creeks, ponds and wetlands were frozen over, which gave the horses more confidence to plow through the snow. They made good time, so that by mid-afternoon the column reached the southern shore of Lake Comacchio. From there they decided that the safest route would be to cross the Reno River into territory Niccolo was certain was still loyal to him.

"You should have taken the northern gate to make your escape," Ischia said after the column crossed the Reno. "You would have beaten me to the bridge. That was poor scouting on your part, although leaving by the main gate was unexpected and you might have stumbled on Altinberg with some luck."

"That might have looked suspicious," Geoffrey said after a while. "We came in through the main gate, and so we decided that it would be wise to depart by the main gate. We could not change the scheme when you arrived."

"All the same, a good captain keeps other schemes well at hand, like hiding a dagger in the boot. What say you, my lord?"

"I suppose it might have been to our advantage," Niccolo said.

"Yes, well, being a good swordsman is not the same being a good captain," Ischia noted. "Of course, being a foreigner does not help either. My lord: what is the next village and what vassal resides there?"

Niccolo scanned the horizon and gave a name.

"Is that near the Reno?" Ischia asked.

"Just a few miles north of it."

"This is good." Ischia sat tall in the saddle and grimaced. "Polenta has a company stationed near the Po River. We do not want to encounter any of his scouts, so let us hold to a northwestern course close to the Reno, assuming you are sure of loyal vassals there."

"Loyal vassals and my own dominium," Niccolo said. "I know this area well."

Ischia nodded and smiled.

Geoffrey had little more to say. Even though he had completed his commission with Count Robert and would finish the other with the Marquis of Ferrara, he had to admit that he had missed two opportunities to bring the marquis to the safety of his army, and this poor reckoning was weighing heavily on his conscience. He was a man of Gaunt, after all. Also, his pride was dented; Giovanni dell'Ischia had bested him. He should have spent his time in Ravenna scouting and planning several ways out instead of indulging himself and hiding.

Geoffrey began to grow despondent and he felt himself shrink in the saddle, a sensation that was intensified by the disorienting and isolating impact of the unfamiliar wintery expanse around him. He wondered if his lord and master, the Duke of Lancaster, had forgotten about him by now, and he recalled for the first time in several weeks the shock he received at Sansepolcro. He thought about the Blues and what deeds they might have performed in the past year, and how they would have elected a new captain in his long absence. Despite all, Avignon and the halls of Gaunt were his home and his fellow squires were his companions, and so he had better make his way to them before he was lost forever.

As they entered a village, Geoffrey felt a tap on his shoulder.

"Geoff, Geoff! Did you not hear me?" Jean said. "We must find lodgings."

Geoffrey looked up and was surprised to see that twilight had come. He slowly nodded at Jean and said, "I must stay close to the marquis."

The village belonged to Niccolo, or rather to the Este inheritance, but Ischia, Geoffrey and Catherine all agreed that it would better if Niccolo did not reveal himself to the villeins or anyone else, including the stewards who had remained after the lords left to serve in Niccolo's army. They simply occupied the village and billeted the men-at-arms at the best huts. Once they were settled in, Jean and Crivelli were sent to scout the surrounding area to learn what they could about the local situation.

"Manfredi controls the land between Ferrara and Portomaggiore," Jean said as they gathered for supper in the steward's house. "His main camp remains the town of Maiero, just a couple of miles up the road from Portomaggiore. Some say there was a battle nearby while others say that Germans and Bretons have been plundering neighboring villages. Of course, no one could give me a name, but you cannot expect anything more from villeins." Jean snorted and grabbed a roasted chicken leg the steward's wife had provided for the feast.

"Bretons?" Geoffrey said. "Must be just rumors."

Niccolo looked sheepishly at Geoffrey. "The main garrison in Ferrara is composed of the Breton company of Jean de la Salle," he said. "My father hired them and the regency council decided to keep them."

"That is something that must be remedied," Ischia said. "This is why Azzo has you on your heels, my lord. Bretons will only fight if they know they can win. Who else comprises your host?" Ischia was in no mood to use soft words with the marquis when foreign men-at-arms were concerned. He had the boy almost by the scruff of his neck, and so he pressed on. "Germans? Arabs? I pray you have not succumbed to hiring English to serve your cause!"

Niccolo was not about to list the condottieri in his host, even if he knew which ones had formally signed a *condotta*. "That is a question for my captain-general," he said. He turned to Jean and asked, "What is the mood of my subjects?"

"Forgive me for saying so, my lord," Jean said, "but all the men and not a few women we questioned are more afraid of the German and Breton companies coming than your uncle. They say that they hear the brother of Alberico da Barbiano fights alongside Azzo d'Este, and while I do not know who that is, he seems to have a high reputation amongst the people."

Niccolo nodded.

"Alberico da B-Barbiano drove the foreign m-men-at-arms from Rome when they th-threatened his grace the supreme pontiff m-many years ago," Crivelli explained. He has a reputation for b-being not only a talented c-condottiere, but also a d-disciplined captain, who refuses to give quarter to f-foreigners."

"Yes, it was the Barbiano that smashed the English and German companies that were ruining our land," Ischia said. "You will not remember what joy we felt when he ruined them, for you are too young."

"Better for your own to ruin you than for others to, eh?" Jean said and he smirked. "What does it matter who burns down your hut?"

"You do not understand all. The art of war has improved since the Barbiano became condottieri. Order, discipline and respect have replaced disarray, poor training and barbarism," Ischia said. "That is why the Barbiano and other Italian condottieri defeat foreigners. He is like our father...father of Italian condottieri. You ought to remember that, my lord, when you go to confront your uncle in a pass of arms."

"I am listening," Niccolo said. "Did you serve with Barbiano?"

"I did, as my father did." The second admission was a lie.

"Was this after he was thrown out of the first Rose Company?" Jean asked.

Ischia glanced at Jean and his mouth tensed. "Foreigners had ruined that company. My father did well to leave it when he could."

Ischia, Jean and Crivelli continued to discuss the companies of the past for several more hours, but Geoffrey was not interested. He approached Niccolo a few times with questions about his lands and his court, but the boy wanted to listen to the stories about the great condottieri, and so he gave the squire curt answers. Geoffrey then tried to raise his mood by thinking about how he had successfully completed Count Robert's commission and that soon Niccolo would have a wife that was fair, rich and of ancient nobility. This made him feel a little better, but his silence also increased his sense of isolation from the company around him. That night, Geoffrey dreamed about a clean sword and an evasive enemy.

The next day the column rode steadily westwards. The villages and landmarks became even more familiar to Niccolo, but the closer they approached Manfredi's camp, the more visible the depredations of the armies on the landscape: barns emptied of grain and livestock, trees felled for timber and fuel, and settlements inhabited by only the aged and infirmed. Even though the snow covered the worst of the ugly scene, the sight of his dominium so ravaged affected Niccolo. He had read and heard about the most horrible of devastations wrought by armies, but had never witnessed war in person.

"I would guess that this is the work of the Germans," Ischia said. He could see the pained expression on the marquis's face and wanted to do nothing to relieve it. "All in all, rather restrained. If Bretons had been here we would be seeing scorched huts and ravished women about, and a few hanged men for decoration."

"Must be Azzo's men," Geoffrey argued. "Manfredi would have ordered his lordship's men not to violate his lands."

"So, you are a close companion of the captain-general, are you? You know nothing, squire! I doubt he can control his lordship's soldiers as well as you think, particularly if they are foreigners."

Geoffrey also saw how the ravaging of his dominium troubled Niccolo. However, so long as the lords of this region were on his side, he should do well in the final pass with Uncle Azzo. The villeins will rebuild; one always appeared to take another's place. What Geoffrey hoped to see was the young marquis grasping the baton of command with both hands. Then his men, be they vassals, local condottieri or foreign companies, will obey his will.

"I would not be so sure of that, if I were you," Geoffrey said. "What do you think, Catherine? You know Manfredi and his lordship's regency council."

Catherine scanned the countryside, but it seemed to make no impression on her. "I have seen worse. What is for certain, though, is that we are near Portomaggiore, so we had better keep our wits about us. We must pay this ruin no mind."

After several more hours the group met with an advance scout belonging to Manfredi. Everyone breathed a sigh of relief and soon they were marching past ranks of cheering men-at-arms along the road into Maiero. Niccolo's mother and most of the regency council were in Ferrara, but Astrorre Manfredi and regency council head Alberto Roberti were on hand to greet the marquis with great ceremony.

After a medical inspection of Niccolo and interrogations of Ischia, Geoffrey and Catherine, whereupon they described the purpose and results of their prolonged journey, they all gathered in the parish church's refectory for a banquet and some happy news.

Ischia had not been lying. Conrad Altinberg and his fellow German condottiere Ugo di Monforte had struck camp when the weather broke and marched their six hundred-strong company of mounted heavy men-at-arms without rest directly northwards, taking the fortified towns of Lugo, Cotignola and Bagnacavallo, which belonged to the Barbiano clan, as far as Argenta, where they surprised Azzo and forced him to withdraw to Consandolo. The moment he heard this, Mandredi mobilized his companies with the intention of trapping Azzo between his hammer and Altinberg's anvil. They met just outside Consandolo, and while they inflicted a defeat on the pretender, he was able to slip around Manfredi's companies and retreat in good order to Portomaggiore, where they were now.

"Why could you not crush them at Consandolo?" Niccolo asked. "To me it does not sound like you were outnumbered. Did you believe that I was dead, and so was afraid to rout the man who would replace me?" Now that he was, for all intents and purposes, home, he was feeling more comfortable and confident.

"Of course not, my lord," Manfredi said. "In my haste to destroy them I outpaced my foot companies, which would have covered my flanks. The field found for the pass of arms was very wide. Your uncle and Giovanni Barbiano are experienced captains. They quickly saw that I would beat them, so they sounded the retreat and went around us. We gave chase, naturally, but their companies are well disciplined. They reached Portomaggiore before we could overtake them."

"So, the war is almost over," Niccolo said. "When will we take the city?"

Manfredi smiled. "Portomaggiore is strongly fortified and Azzo holds it with most of his army."

"How many?"

"Between four and five thousand men. And horses. We should be able to starve them into submission, since we are nearing the end of winter."

"Do you anticipate someone coming to relieve him?" Niccolo asked. "I am still at war with Ravenna and Modena, and Milan might yet declare against me."

"I am holding Polenta against the Adriatic near the Po River and Modena does not have enough men to overcome Roberti, Pio and the Boiardi to the west of here." Manfredi raised his glass to salute himself.

"So, I have missed it all," Niccolo said in a quiet voice.

CHAPTER 14

Maiero, near Portomaggiore

Niccolo d'Este was disappointed that his mother could not leave Ferrara for the several hours-long journey to Manfredi's camp to welcome him back. Her message, while expressing relief that he had finally arrived home safely, stated that she was receiving the *signore* of Padua, Francesco da Carrara, on an important matter, and so she could not simply leave the talks. However, she expressed confidence that Captain-General Manfredi and regency council head Alberto Roberti had met him with the courtesy appropriate to his rank. They had. And now they were seated on either side of him at the head table in the refectory of the parish church.

Both men had agreed that a banquet in his lordship's honor should be held as soon as possible so that the lords and captains of his army would see him, since he had been 'lost' for so long. To his right were Roberti, several other members of his regency council, and the head of the Maiero town council. To his left were Manfredi, Giovanni dell'Ischia, a couple of Manfredi's senior captains, Jean de la Salle, and Geoffrey Hotspur.

Two tables had been set perpendicular to the head table. The right one held the German condottiere Conrad Altinberg and his retinue, who had been able to ride around occupied Portomaggiore to each Maiero, as well as representatives of Ugo di Monforte and Conrad Landau, who were still with their respective companies south and north of Portomaggiore. The left table was occupied by the leading vassals and *raccomendati* who were serving in Niccolo's personal retinue in Ferrara: Antonio degli Obizzi and Salvaccio Bentivoglio and Giovanni Cavalcabo, as well as Catherine and the English squire's companion Jean, who the marquis noticed was still attired in his hideous mustard yellow jupon.

"Let us start, by your leave, my lord," Manfredi said. He called for the hall to be silent and asked his company priest to recite a benediction. Everybody stood up and bowed their heads. The refectory was already warm from the many bodies and steaming dishes covering the tables, despite the freezing weather outside. Niccolo had had time to have his white doublet embroidered with silver brocade cleaned and brushed and his linen chausses mended. No one had sent his wardrobe from Ferrara to Maiero, so Niccolo had little choice for his evening attire, but Catherine had been clever enough to find a decent pair of boots for him, borrowed from the local council head's son.

Alberto Roberti remained standing after everyone else sat down.

"By the divine grace of our Lord," he said, "his lordship the Marquis of Ferrara, Niccolo d'Este, has been delivered to us as whole as when he left us, and although in his absence his cause has prospered, and the fool and pretender Azzo d'Este languishes, trapped just a few miles from where his lordship's mighty host is gathered, his safe return only lends more credence to his right to rule Ferrara and receive the Este inheritance."

Roberti went on to salute the condottieri and captains who had chosen to fight on the right side, not least of all Captain-General Astorre Manfredi, and the cities of Florence, Padua and Venice, who remained as guarantors of Niccolo as the Marquis of Ferrara. After several more salutations and words of thanks, Roberti called on his lordship to tell of his adventure.

Niccolo was prepared for this. Just before the banquet Roberti had instructed him on what to say and who to acknowledge. So, with the images of Cicero and his tutor Donato degli Albanzani in his mind, he arose and gave a partial account of his escape from Bologna, his journey to Ravenna through a snowstorm and his crossing the frozen *valli* to Maiero. He was surprised by how strong and even his voice came out, as though he was sitting in the kitchens with the Whites and not standing in front of some of the most distinguished lords of his dominium.

From time to time he would look at Geoffrey and Catherine, both of whom had their eyes on him, although he was told not to mention either of them by name. He thanked the Lord and Savior for his deliverance and Manfredi and the regency council for their recent victories.

"For great service to me during my time of uncertainty," Niccolo continued after pausing to receive a leaf of parchment from Manfredi, "by leading me through many dangers to the heart of my dominium, I grant Giovanni dell'Ischia this *condotta*, which makes him an esteemed captain in my host with all the rights and privileges deemed appropriate to his rank." Niccolo held out the document for all to see.

The hall erupted with cheering and pounding on tables. Ischia stood, bowed to the hall and accepted the *condotta* from Niccolo.

"I also want to thank Geoffrey Hotspur, squire and man of the Duke of Lancaster, John of Gaunt, for his loyal assistance in guiding me here," Niccolo said, forgetting Roberti's counsel, but his voice was drowned out by the ongoing shouting and lauding of the first hero. Roberti gestured to Niccolo, who sat back down.

Ischia raised his hand and began to speak. His words were slow and measured, but powerful enough to subdue the hall. He said that he wanted to assure everybody that he had left the cursed Azzo d'Este of his own accord and that he had known the marquis was in danger, and so he had taken upon himself the commission of leading his lordship to his rightful place. Ischia mentioned the escape from Bologna and the blinding snowstorms that had affected his tracking, but he laid emphasis on how he deceived the *signore* of Ravenna, Obizzo da Polenta, and stolen the marquis from under his nose, and finally he described the dangers of riding through the *valli*. The names Geoffrey Hotspur, Jean Lagoustine and Catherine never left his mouth.

The moment Ischia sat down several of the younger guests approached the head table and began fingering the *condotta*, asking questions and nodding their heads in the marquis's direction. Ischia was glad to receive them all.

Niccolo saw that Manfredi was pleased with the attention his fellow condottiere was receiving; Roberti less so. The crowd at the head table obscured his view of the English squire, but he could see that his companion was wearing such a scowl that a shiver went up Niccolo's spine. Fortunately, the Frenchman was staring at Ischia and not at him.

Niccolo was almost afraid of what Catherine's expression might be, but to his surprise the astrologer's face was as placid as ever. He wished that she was sitting next to him, but Roberti had said that such a courtesy could not be extended to her, since his mother was not present. All the same, Niccolo felt his muscles twitch.

"Captain-general," Niccolo said, hoping that by drawing Manfredi towards another matter, interest in Ischia would wane, "my host appears to be well set to finish the campaign before the snow melts. How fare the men?"

"We are fortunate to still have ample supplies, my lord," Manfredi said to Niccolo, "so the men fare very well, indeed." He gestured at the plates loaded with roasted capons, mince pies, fish stuffed with rice, almonds and ginger, a range of vegetable pottages, and an assortment of marinated fruits and berries. Each guest had an Este eagle-embossed goblet filled with mulled wine. Its aroma of lemon, cinnamon and cloves overpowered all other scents in the tiny hall. "I daresay your Uncle Azzo does not dine as richly, and soon he is not likely to be dining at all!" Manfredi gave a dark chuckle.

"But he still holds Portomaggiore, captain," Niccolo said. "I suspect its larders and cellars are well-stocked with victuals. We should be prepared for a long siege."

Manfredi looked at Niccolo with surprise.

"We cut off all trade with Portomaggiore shortly after Azzo took it," Manfredi explained, "and I expect he has already plundered its stocks to feed his cold and hungry army. Also, my spies inform me that the city's walls are nearly bursting with people who fled both us and him, so victuals there are fast disappearing."

"Then one prick of the walls and my subjects will pour forth like the canals of the *valli* in spring," Niccolo said, "and it would seem almost all my vassals as well." He looked around and was saddened by the small number of liegemen present. "How many surrendered after your feat of arms at Consandolo?"

Manfredi sipped his wine. Over the rim of the goblet he glanced at Roberti, who met his eye but said nothing. After setting down the goblet and wiping his mouth, Manfredi said, "In truth, Azzo retreated in such good order that we were unable to capture more than a handful of his men, and no lords."

"I asked how many surrendered – not how many you captured. All of them are holed up in Portomaggiore?"

"All, my lord."

"And despite the likely prospect of defeat, none are willing to yield to me and accept their investiture by my hand?"

Manfredi nodded.

"Are you at least parleying with any of them." Niccolo's voice was strident, although it lacked the full force of a grown man. "I assume the Modenese lords are too stubborn and will fight on until I reduce their castles and take them in chains, but those of Ferrara, of the ancient Este lands, must be willing to talk."

Roberti decided to answer this time. "The regency council thought it prudent to wait until you were safely returned, my lord, before opening that channel."

Niccolo was surprised by this answer; such things rarely depended on him. However, he swiftly realized that it was important they knew if he was captured or dead before marking a course of action. Niccolo's felt a coldness wash over him.

"You will press the siege, though, I assume," Niccolo continued. "And their lands are forfeit. Before I left Ferrara I recall signing my name to documents that returned the land held by the rebellious vassals to my hand."

"You have an excellent memory, my lord," Roberti said.

"Have you been enforcing my will?" Niccolo thought about the rebellion against his father and how he had carefully selected estates that were the most critical to the rebels, thereby undermining their ability to wage war.

It was Roberti's turn to show surprise. "The council has been the force behind your will, my lord, and the council has let it be known that any vassal or *raccomendato* who supports the pretender in any manner will lose what property and privileges he holds."

"But you have not seized any of the land of my enemies?" Niccolo asked.

"I will speak plainly, my lord. We have had neither the time nor the men to commit to such a campaign," Roberti said, "and we had to contend with the possibility of you being lost." Roberti sipped his wine and tore a piece of bread from a nearby loaf.

"He means dead," Ischia interjected. "You were gone for so long that I wager your council thought about accepting your uncle in your stead!"

"Nonsense!" Roberti cried. "You have spoken out of place, Captain dell'Ischia. However, truth be told, we did fear the worst when we heard that you were not with Captain Altinberg."

"He is to blame!" Ischia said and pointed a greasy finger at Geoffrey. Then he chuckled, as though he had spoken in jest.

All eyes at the head table turned to the squire. Thus far in the evening Geoffrey had said nothing, setting his mouth straight and his jaw taught. He heard the pronouncements and listened to Ischia describe his feats of prowess. He thought he caught the marquis mention his name and patiently waited to be called to accept congratulations, salute and speak, but nothing had come of that. He held his spine straight against the back of the chair and let his eyes wander over the crowd, silently placing each man in relation to the marquis. The fare did not interest him, although the wine was to his taste and kept his lips and mouth from drying out in the sweltering hall. Only a slightly furrowed brow bespoke of the condition of his humors.

"The squire looks to be at prayer," Manfredi quipped. A few guests laughed, but Niccolo, Jean and Catherine did not. Manfredi turned to Roberti and asked, "What is his name again? Haute-peur?"

Niccolo gave the correct pronunciation of Geoffrey's name.

"Yes, that is better, although I have not seen him couch a lance astride a charger." Manfredi leaned over the table and turned back to Geoffrey. "What say you to this accusation, master squire?"

"I fulfilled my commission," Geoffrey said plainly. Perhaps now the marquis would announce his reward, he thought.

"And our Lord fulfilled His commission by being nailed to a Cross, and now he is dead. What is your excuse?" Ischia said sharply.

Geoffrey was at first shocked to hear irreverence come from the old condottiere, but then he recalled that such words were little different from those he and his fellow squires would exchange after a surfeit consumption of wine and whatever other spirits were at hand. They would often make a contest out of who could spout the rudest phrases without uttering heresies. All the same, for the sake of dignity and in the presence of esteemed company, Geoffrey refrained from making a rival obscenity. While much of the hall responded with laughter, when he glanced at the marquis he saw that the boy wore a sour expression.

"It was a matter of reading the signs," Geoffrey explained. "They did not lead us to Faenza."

"Bah!" Ischia cried. "You just did not know which way to go. The only road familiar to you was the one that led to Ravenna and into the den of the lion."

"It is true that I followed the Way," Geoffrey said. His frown deepened, but choler would not churn in his humors. "And it was the Right Way."

"But did you not know that Captain Altinberg was already lodged in Faenza, master squire?" Roberti asked. He was not keen on discord arising amongst the condottieri, so he offered Geoffrey a means of escape from public censure. "The winds were high and the snows were deep. Perhaps his was the proper way?"

"I had been thus informed, my lord," Geoffrey answered. "However, we had no knowledge of his intentions." Geoffrey would not cast aspersions on the German captain.

"Everybody knows that Captain Altinberg was and is with the young marquis," Ischia stated. "He would not have force marched his company from Tuscany to Ferrara had that not been true. You were as presumptuous as always." Ischia took a hard draught of wine.

"Let us ask the astrologer if this is true," Roberti said. "She is as clever as what we might expect from someone in her station." He gestured with his goblet at Catherine. She was wearing her green gown with silver stitching and a new wimple, from which she had suspended a ruby pendant. "Was it not your intention to bring his lordship the marquis to Captain Altinberg after your harrowing escape from Bologna?"

"It was proposed," Catherine answered. "However, as Master Hotspur was our guide, he chose a different route for us."

Geoffrey looked at Catherine and then at Jean, who he could see was gritting his teeth so hard that his jaw trembled.

"Then you erred in judgment, squire," Roberti said.

"As you say, my lord," Geoffrey said. He looked at Niccolo, who seemed to have his eyes on the far wall, as though he was in a trance.

"We all say so," Ischia said. A few cheers rose up from several places along the table, but on the whole the guests were already losing interest in Geoffrey. Other topics were broached and someone called for more wine. "Of course, one never knows where a German truly stands," Ischia mumbled as he took a draught of wine.

The name Count Robert d'Ivry came to Geoffrey's lips, but there they stayed. He was expecting Niccolo to declare his meeting with the Cypriot lord and announce his impending nuptials to the jewel of the East. He must have told the regency council all about it by now. That news would justify his actions before the entire hall, and they would laud him for his boldness and dedication to the true heir to the Este lands. It was not his place to say anything about the matter, unless he was directly asked, however, since he recognized the delicacy of marriage arrangements.

Melancholy continued its ascendancy in Geoffrey's humors, and mixed with his overall disappointment in the evening brought a gloom that enveloped the young squire. He drank again, but Geoffrey no longer had any taste for wine. Here was a hall full of lords and captains! He wanted to talk, so he turned to the one man who also had been silent for the better part of the evening.

"Captain de la Salle," Geoffrey said in French to the Breton after they had exchanged formal pleasantries, "we have yet to hear of your deeds of arms. His lordship the marquis spoke highly of your abilities when we were in the *valli*."

Jean de la Salle was a very thin man with short black hair and a face that looked as though it was made out of blocks. He was not as well dressed as the others in the refectory, but that might have been on purpose, Geoffrey thought, since Breton men-at-arms liked to separate themselves from everyone else, whether at war or at peace.

"Are you sure about that?" de la Salle retorted. "His lordship is too young to have seen me or anyone else fight." His voice possessed a stronger lilt that what Geoffrey normally heard in Avignon, and his 'a' and 'i' seemed to go on longer than was necessary.

"His lordship praised you all the same." Geoffrey was slightly put off by this curt response.

"That is all to the good, since we saved his city the other month. Praise be to God for keeping the land too soak with the sweat of Heaven for chargers to do their mean work." De la Salle raised his cup and took a long draught.

"Are you not a part of his lordship's retinue, then?" Geoffrey drank as well. He liked the Bretons almost irreverent turn of speech, as it reminded him of the Blues and their own humble banquets.

"Nah, we are just hired help. Only vassals and *raccomendati* get that privilege, although I will tell you that I would never want to be yoked to such a bond anyway." Geoffrey was surprised to hear this and asked why not.

"I realize that we are attending a banquet, but you have no intention of reporting our talk to the boy or Roberti, do you?" De la Salle pressed the lip of his goblet against Geoffrey's chest. "Because if you do, I will deny everything and I will be believed. You might be his companion, but I have been with him since his father ruled this land."

"I have no intention of telling anyone anything, unless you reveal a conspiracy against his lordship, or against me!" Geoffrey smiled to make himself more affable.

"Very well. As a Breton, his lordship would never grant me land or privileges, but aside from that, such bonds are an unsure thing, and I do not like being unsure."

"What!" Geoffrey was incredulous. "So, if his lordship wanted to make you his man, make you a knight, you would refuse!"

"I would," de la Salle said plainly, "unless I would not have to serve his lordship, but that would never happen, of course."

"You are a fool!" Geoffrey could not silence his tongue.

However, instead of being offended, de la Salle merely laughed and called for a servant to pour him more wine.

"We are all fools, Hotspur, but I am a fool who can leave these other fools behind, if need be."

"All the same, you are bound by your *condotta*, or would you refuse to fight if the fancy took you?"

"Bite your tongue! I swear on my family's good name to fight for whomever I pledge to fight, but I do not want to be burdened by all those other services or, God forbid, provide hospitality."

Geoffrey could not understand this attitude, but it seemed to be a common one amongst condottieri. He believed that any man would want to be close to a great lord and serve him in a manner befitting his station.

"But when your *condotta* ends, that is it! You are thrown to the wolves, so to speak," Geoffrey argued. "Why would you want to go it alone?"

"I would not go it alone. I have my company, and Italy has no shortage of *condotti* ready for me to sign. If I want to buy land, I buy land. If I wish to return to Brittany, I go. I am content."

Suddenly, they heard Alberto Roberti's voice rise above all others.

"Captain Altinberg! Tell us again how you routed the pretender. Not all of us have heard about your wondrous feat of arms." He raised his goblet to salute the German.

Knowing that it would be bad form to continue his conversation with the Breton captain, Geoffrey returned to his seat.

Conrad of Heidelberg was roughly the same age as Giovanni dell'Ischia, although his hair and beard were still mostly brown and he possessed more youthful features. Few would have guessed that had spent more than twenty years campaigning in Italy with some of the most talented condottieri of the age. Niccolo knew this, and he wondered why he did not ride directly to Faenza instead of listening to the English squire and risking his head even further. He also knew that Altinberg had a reputation for swiftness, and so he would have been more likely than any of his other captains to have been in Faenza on time. And Altinberg's *condotta* was signed before he fled Bologna.

Niccolo let his shoulders droop as he listened to the captain tell about his night march across the frozen plain to Argenta, where he surprised Azzo and forced him to retreat to Consandolo. There, the pretender was unable to regain the initiative because the German had been too fast in pursuit, forcing him to give battle beneath the walls of the city. His men fought well, Altinberg said, but Azzo outnumbered him and was able to withdraw to Portomaggiore. The captain was generous in his praise and circumspect in any suggestion that Manfredi had been too slow to react to his advance, and thereby failed to close the circle around Azzo.

Other captains and vassals peppered him with questions and Altinberg was not shy about answering them with a loquacity that impressed the Italians. Servants brought in more wine and cleared away empty dishes.

The more the German spoke, the less Niccolo wanted to remain at the banquet. The honor of the evening had shifted from him to Ischia and now to one of his captains. The men around him seemed to grow bigger and louder. He looked for

Catherine again and found her speaking with one of his vassals. She was smiling and making occasional gestures. He frowned.

"You will have a better escort to Ferrara, my lord," Niccolo heard someone say. He turned and saw that Roberti was speaking to him. "Your father's retinue."

"You mean my personal retinue," Niccolo corrected.

"Of course. They are set and ready to leave at first light."

"Tomorrow?"

"Tomorrow. The regency council asks you to tour the *contado* to show yourself to the loyal vassals and *raccomendati*. Even if they accepted the new investiture, they need to be reminded of their service to you."

"But what about the siege?"

"What about it?"

"I must see it through."

Roberti suppressed a chuckle. "You are not needed for that, my lord. Manfredi leads your host well."

Niccolo felt himself sink even further. The words 'not needed' seemed to echo around the refectory.

"So, now you are even," Jean said. He spat in the snow as he and Geoffrey trudged through the village to the stables Manfredi had assigned to them as their lodgings. Both men were staggering a little from the wine they had consumed, but the sharp icy gusts that pierced them from time to time made sure that they kept their wits about them.

"What do you mean? I have nothing." Geoffrey's sullen expression from the banquet remained unchanged.

"I mean Ischia. The bastard has bested you again now, after you set him on his arse twice. I can reckon, as can everyone in that hall, including the marquis." Jean flexed his good shoulder, which was growing as stiff as his bad one. "How was it you did not put him in his place."

"That would be true. However, I could not draw my sword in such esteemed company, so do not be as lacking as a lamp with no light. The marquis? The captain-general? The head of the regency council? How could I insult them by committing such an act?"

"You could have used your fists, or at least your voice, Geoff. You just sat there and let him steal your thunder! Were this a game, you sure as hell would have not sat so quietly."

"But this is not a game. His lordship is safe, and that is all that matters." Geoffrey's voice trailed off.

"Yes, it is a game. I know games. I worked for the Gamesmaster of Avignon, and he taught me all about games, so no need to tell me this is not a game. And do you know what the wager is? Do you, Geoff? It is your *name!*" He slapped Geoffrey on the arm in disgust.

Geoffrey stopped in his tracks and looked at Jean. His frown grew deeper and then his face softened. "God's dignity!" he cried, but said no more.

Jean cringed, but when he understood that the squire was not about to beat him, he relaxed and said, "That is right, Geoff, and Ischia shat all over it!"

The Frenchman was right, Geoffrey thought. For so many weeks now he had been so concerned about the names 'Este' and 'Ivry' that he had forgotten about his own. He had borne his two commissions on his own name just as in Avignon he had borne many wagers on 'Hotspur' as a squire in good standing in the halls of Gaunt. As he looked around the snow-frosted village, he realized nothing had changed in that regard. In truth, since that low point at Sansepolcro his name should have risen. Geoffrey felt his heart push against his chest. He was being cheated.

In Avignon, a fellow gamer had tried to cheat him – once. The man, whose name or station he no longer remembered, had given the young squire a pair of loaded dice after an exceptionally large wager. In the heat of his gaming fury, the man thought Geoffrey would not notice, but he did. As he ritually thread the dice between his fingers, he could feel that their weight was not right. However, instead of complaining to the landlord, Geoffrey smashed the dice against the wall to reveal their falsehood and then forced the cheating man to eat the pieces. The end result was a brawl, several days in gaol and a reprimand from Gaunt, but the ordeal had been satisfying. Here, though, the matter was not so simple.

"If the scoundrel Ischia had been alone, I would have thrashed him, but his lordship the marquis said nothing and I could see that Manfredi and Roberti were not about to gainsay one of their own. My hands were tied, Jean!" Geoffrey clenched his fists and showed them to Jean before turning abruptly and walking ahead.

"So, you are not humorless, after all," Jean said as he raced to catch up with the squire. "Well, at least they fed us properly, so that is some reward."

"I expect you had your ears twitching for any word of my reward, the one of silver," Geoffrey said, but he was also thinking about the knighthood Niccolo had promised him.

"And yours were not?"

"It was the marquis's duty to announce it. I remember the promise of silver very well, as well as a place in his host."

"The astrologer made that promise."

"And the marquis approved it. He is the man responsible for everything done in his name." They were passing a large number of men-at-arms and camp followers. Some were singing, some were laughing and some were just talking loudly, but all were in good spirits, Geoffrey noticed. Occasionally, a few men or women would glance in his direction as he kicked his way through the snow and comment amongst themselves. None approached him, however. Geoffrey's ears started to burn.

"He is hardly a man, Geoff."

"If he holds a sword and rules a land, then he is a man."

Jean would not argue the point, but he was intent on spreading the blame for his companion's stolen fame. "The astrologer deceived us. The reward might yet come, but she should have spoken the truth. She had the opportunity."

"Catherine spoke the truth," Geoffrey said, "just not all of it. You remember how she wanted to continue on to meet with Altinberg at Faenza."

"Yes, but the boy prevailed in his decision to ride onwards."

"I coerced him."

"You counseled him. It was as you said: his will is supreme. He could have followed Catherine's advice just as well as yours. You see how close they are. I know you do. Instead, he chose yours, which was the right decision, in my opinion."

This was not true, but Jean could see how very dark the squire's humors were, which made him unpredictable. With a snap of the fingers Geoffrey Hotspur could be at the gaming tables, in the parish church or riding hell-knows-where into the wintry darkness. And if the squire was lost, then he was lost as well. The English Free Company without its English captain was nothing.

"I know this: his lordship Niccolo should have announced my reward, Manfredi and Roberti be damned. Do not blame Catherine; blame the marquis!"

They reached the stable. Because it belonged to the local lord, the stable was large enough to lodge more than a dozen lances, mostly men-at-arms belonging to the Este household itself, and their horses. This, coupled with a few glowing braziers, made it almost as warm as the refectory. Jean looked around and saw that *their*

German lances were away. Altinberg could not have them back until they made a formal arrangement, so they remained as one company. Jean pulled off his hood, unclasped his cloak and threw himself on the blanket that was closest to a brazier.

"I should have taken a flagon of wine with me," Jean said as he wriggled to make himself comfortable. "I am feeling only mutton-drunk, which is not enough to ensure a good night's sleep with the mood I am in, and I daresay you are feeling about the same, Geoff."

Geoffrey did not answer. He carefully folded his cloak, unbuckled his *couteau*, which he carefully laid at the side of his bedding, and unbuttoned his doublet. The stable was too warm for him. He was restless and the renewed uncertainty of his position unsettled him even more.

To calm himself Geoffrey rummaged around his memories for times with the Blues, but the great disappointment of the banquet clouded his mind, leaving him with nothing but vague recollections of his companions. He did not want even to think about his lord and master, the Duke of Lancaster, although the name Gaunt led him back to the name Este, and then to the name Ivry, which brought a measure of calm to the squire's turbulent humors. Count Robert had not forsaken him, Geoffrey reckoned, and he wondered if he would have the chance to see his lordship again before he sailed for Cyprus.

"*That* is a very fine thing they can give us while we wait for our silver," Jean surmised. "Wine and victuals. We can do nothing else." He closed his eyes, but after a moment he suddenly opened them. "We are staying, I assume?"

"Yes. We will hold here until the marquis fulfills his commission, just as I did."

"And when will that be?"

"You are in a hurry to return to Avignon?"

Jean's blood froze. The squire had hit the nail on the head in a place where Jean had not expected. He was not at all anxious to return home, as much of a home as it was. The Gamesmaster was waiting for him and he had done nothing to secure his position, which meant begging for forgiveness or (most likely 'and') bringing his master a load of silver. Jean was not keen to do either, but he could not remain idle and without purpose. Yet, he had a purpose.

"We need to enroll the German lances anew," Jean said, "and maybe enroll a few more. If Ischia can, then why cannot we do the same?"

"You must be more than mutton-drunk to ask me a question like that, fool. That *condotta* the marquis presented to Ischia gives him the right to enroll free lances –

EVAN OSTRYZNIUK

you know that, since you are always banging on about such things. You also know that the marquis gave *me* nothing."

"Oh, come now. Maybe we cannot put up a stall and hire a crier to announce our intentions, but I cannot see the harm in talking to some of the men-at-arms – our Germans, at the very least. *And* they have friends in the other companies here."

"Those men belong to Elstinborg."

"Altinberg," Jean corrected.

"Altinberg. I remember very well that they only agreed to follow me as far as Manfredi's camp. So, here we are! They have no cause to stay with me, and what would I do with them on the journey back to Avignon? I doubt I will be hiring out my sword to a convenient caravan."

Geoffrey gave Jean a sharp look. Realizing he was still standing, he dropped himself down on a stool close to the brazier, dragged his *couteau* towards him and propped his chin on its pommel.

"Ahh...the return to the halls of Gaunt, where you believe no one has forgotten you, let alone forsaken you. And how will you answer his grace when he asks you what you have done in the year you have been away? 'My blade is as clean as the day my ship set sail, my lord, but look at this tiny purse of silver a boy gave me'." Jean mewled the mock conversation with the duke and limply held his hand to imitate dangling a small bag.

Geoffrey threw Jean a dirty look. "What do you know? Your service to your master is as a swineherd to a lord."

"I know that without a display of prowess, your chances of finding a decent lord to serve on campaign are slim and none. Maybe you can buy a place, but no knight worthy of the title would even consider putting you in the bottom rank. You saved the boy-marquis, although the feat is muddied now, but that is not enough, and you know that. Azzo d'Este is still out there, bloodied but unbroken. Keep the English Free Company whole and put it at the service of the marquis. A final pass of arms must be made at some time or another."

Geoffrey stared into the glowing orange coals of the brazier.

"I do not know if I can trust the marquis now," Geoffrey said, "or rather I cannot see him running his own war council. And besides, who knows if and when his uncle will come out to fight. I expect at no time soon, since I heard at the banquet that Niccolo is to leave to tour his lands. I missed my chance." Geoffrey thought about the battle at Consandolo, which was spoken about at the banquet as much as

228

the marquis's escape from Bologna. He did and did not regret his prodding Niccolo to meet with Count Robert, yet...

"All the more reason to keep the Germans with us," Jean said, although he could not explain why.

Geoffrey sighed. "Let them decide for themselves who to serve. No, wait, let them go. I cannot feed and lodge them as I should until I receive my reward."

Jean squinted at Geoffrey, but he did not press the issue. He merely nodded, lay back on his blanket and closed his eyes. He would talk to the Germans in the morning.

Geoffrey was still restless and no less dejected than he was at the banquet. His talk with the Frenchman only brought up more questions and provided no answers for him. And the stable was still too stifling hot for him to be comfortable. Seeing that his companion was now asleep and feeling himself sober, Geoffrey buttoned up his doublet and went for a walk.

He had no intention of returning to what remained of the banquet and instead hoped to meet with a merry band of men-at-arms or lords or even fellow squires who had found a place in the Este host. Geoffrey convinced himself that he was in need of good company, with fine ale, raucous laughter, giddy maidens, and – if Lady Fortuna favored him – games. However, each thought about spending such joyous time was accompanied by a fear that someone would be babbling about the battle at Consandolo or saluting the Marquis d'Este, which helped spoil his intentions.

Geoffrey followed the icy road back to the village. From time to time he would hear distant laughter and see a twinkling light, but he never approached them. Before he realized it, Geoffrey had reached the refectory. After a brief hesitation and a sour face, he pressed on to the parish church. Its considerable size for such a small town impressed Geoffrey and reminded him that he had hardly set himself to prayer since leaving Umbertide. He entered through a side door and was relieved to find the nave almost as cold as the street.

Along the wall Geoffrey found a row of folding seats normally reserved for priests. Seeing no one else around, he sat down on one and stared into the undulating flames of the few votive candles burning near the altar. He tried to see himself kneeling at the altar, ready to receive his spurs and say his oath of fealty as he was made a knight, but like the companionship he was seeking it all was distant and uncertain. Silence rang in the squire's ears and soon all thoughts and feelings left him. The flames blurred and eventually went out.

Geoffrey awoke with such a start that he slipped off his seat and fell onto the stone floor. The dream was the worst yet. The enemy did not retreat from him this time; they simply did not see him. Geoffrey had felt the impetus to advance and set upon those men-at-arms ranked against him, but their total disregard for his presence brought confusion, and with it a force that rooted him to the spot. He was trapped. He was invisible. Then he was beset by a fear that he would be seen and hacked down without the chance to defend himself, without the chance to bloody his sword, even in a futile last stand.

Geoffrey was shaken. As he lied on his back and stared into the darkness, he heard footsteps approach.

"What a strange manner of praying," Catherine said. "I do see you down there, Geoffrey Hotspur."

Geoffrey turned his head towards the eerie light and made out the figure of the astrologer. She was alone, it seemed.

"I saw you pass the refectory, so I decided to follow you. We are leaving tomorrow."

"We?" Geoffrey slowly made his way to his feet.

"Niccolo and I. We ride to Ferrara and then into the *contado*. The regency council will set your reward and I will deliver it to you, as I promised." As she looked at the squire closer, she frowned and asked, "You seem out of breath. Was the prayer so intense?"

"When you can," Geoffrey said, ignoring Catherine's question.

"His lordship, Niccolo, appreciates your service."

"Then he should make it known. He is the ruler of Ferrara, is he not?"

"You are right; he should have not let Ischia speak as he did. You understand my reason for speaking as *I* did, though?"

"You do not matter."

Catherine raised her head at this remark, but she let it go unchallenged. They were alone in the church and the squire's humors were clearly still very dark.

"So, you will wait for my return?" she said.

"I will." As he watched her turn to go, Geoffrey said, "Wait a moment! I want you to read a dream. You may charge whatever you like, but I do not want to wait to hear your words."

"If I determine the reading to be a simple one, I will tell you now, in this house of God, and ask not a penny for it. If I find much that is uncertain or difficult in your dream, then you will oblige me to wait for when I can receive you properly. A dream is a troublesome thing, and so I do not wish to mislead you. Agreed?"

Geoffrey nodded. He decided to give several accounts of the dream of his battlefield failure, including his most recent nightmare. When he finished, Geoffrey looked at Catherine with an expectant face.

"You are in luck, master squire, and so you can close your purse, for I read only one meaning for your vision of an unbloodied sword."

"Yes?"

"You must bloody it!"

CHAPTER 15

Portomaggiore

Azzo d'Este wanted to stab the messenger when he announced Captain dell'Ischia's defection. That he had little regard for the second-rate condottiere made the insult that much greater, since it betrayed an arrogance that was not remotely justified. And to think he had felt sorry for Ischia when he saw him for the first time in his piteous state, with a handful of lances trying to resurrect the Company of the Rose, so much so that he gave him that spy commission to Assisi. Azzo had never heard of Giovanni dell'Ischia, or his father, although others claimed to have and told him that they were not impressed by his reputation as a captain of men-at-arms.

However, Azzo had been swayed by the old man's passion and dedication to his purpose of creating a powerful Italian company of arms, and so based on that he had decided to trust him. As he watched the messenger scurry down the scarping of the citadel from his tower window, Azzo thought about putting a bounty on Ischia's head. If nothing else, it might sow some discord in the ranks of his enemy. However, vengeance was not in his blood and Ischia was not that important, so he decided to let it pass for now. This was not the first time a condottiere had changed sides in the middle of a campaign.

The loss of the boy was vexing, though. Glancing passed the unfortunate messenger at the crowded streets of the swollen city, Azzo rubbed his tired eyes and wondered what stratagem he needed to employ now in order to save his position. He had to admit that Altinberg had outwitted him. He did not think that the German would have the balls to advance on him without knowing where the marquis was, let alone at night during a heavy frost.

Of course, his position at the poorly fortified Argenta would have been untenable for long anyway, while Consandolo was simply a mistake. He had assumed that Polenta, the *signore* of Ravenna, would have taken advantage of Altinberg's departure

232

from Faenza to harass him from east, slowing the German and forcing him to bulk up his rearguard. That would have given him time to properly ordain the battailes and make a better showing at Consandolo and against the smaller force. Why Polenta had not reacted, Azzo could not understand. He had some men in the north near the Po River, but not all of them.

Above all, his army remained intact and in full, and he still controlled the most important city of the Este inheritance after Ferrara. If his nephew and his regency council wanted to defeat him, they would have to come and get him. And that would not be easy. Niccolo's own father had rebuilt the walls that now protected him and strengthened the citadel, and he was well-supplied. He could hold out against a long siege, although he would prefer not to. The longer he remained idle, the more difficult it would be to break out, since Manfredi would eventually cover the flatlands that surrounded the city with siege engines and sappers. In the meantime, Modena could send him the men and money its leading *signore* Lancellotto Montecuccoli had promised, while his old master, the *signore* of Milan, might finally openly declare for him. He had endured sieges before and won.

Azzo was most troubled by the former Este vassals, though, since he felt they had not done enough to bring about the collapse of Niccolo's rule. Most of them had small retinues and little silver, and while they were willing to fight beneath his banner, few seemed anxious to confront the Niccolo loyalists. He reckoned that the problem was that the most powerful Este vassals, with the sole exception of Ato di Rodiglia, had chosen to stay with the boy, and Azzo sensed that they had not fully committed to his cause out of fear of them. The Roberti, Pio and Boiardi had land and property throughout the *contado*, which was part of the reason why he wanted to grab as much territory as possible as soon as possible. He had to sap their strength. He had wagered that a winter campaign would be enough to fatally undermine the son of Alberto, and had it not been for the Germans and Bretons, Azzo was sure he would have.

Azzo chuckled. He had all the Italians while his nephew had all the foreigners. This was not quite true, of course, but he found it funny that the restorer of a true native Company of the Rose was with those whom he most despised. The presence of foreign captains and men-at-arms on Italian soil did not bother Azzo very much. In truth, he rarely thought about it. He had fought alongside German, Breton, English, Hungarian, and even a few Swiss captains in his many years of campaigning and found as many superior as he found wanting. All they desired was silver. Few were interested in ruling any scrap of land they might have conquered. It was a skill they could never master anyway. That was not their purpose. All the same, having his army dominated by foreigners damaged Niccolo's Guelf credentials. His family had always sided with the supreme pontiff against the German emperors and had been duly rewarded. True, that was a hundred years ago, but the people remembered.

Or maybe, the people should be reminded, Azzo thought. One of the reasons the streets below him had merged into a single mass of heads was that so many people had fled to Portomaggiore at the approach of the companies of Altinberg, Monforte, Landau, and de la Salle. Some might have abandoned their villages at the sight of Manfredi's Italian men-at-arms too, but that did not matter. He would make Ischia's dream his own and champion the cause of liberating the Este lands from foreign invaders with his all-Italian host. He would make the war cry of 'Guelf or none' heard across the *valli* and into the Lombardy plain. He would cause Niccolo to look weak by having to rely on men from beyond the Alps.

The news of Emperor Wenceslas coming to Italy after Easter should add fuel to that fire. The Este vassals should support this scheme, Azzo reckoned. They could dress their refusal to accept investiture at the hands of a twelve-year-old boy in the robes of Pope Gregory VII, who had once challenged a German emperor over the right to appoint bishops and control Church lands. The lords from Modena would love it. After all, Canossa is very close to Modena.

The appearance of Giovanni da Barbiano in his ranks was convenient now also and would lend credence to this new stratagem. His brother Alberico was famous not just within condottiere circles, but also amongst the common folk for the acts of *libertà* in Rome and Naples he performed against Breton and German companies. This new approach to victory should please Giovanni, Azzo believed, since the younger brother was sure to want to escape the shadow of the older more famous Alberico, as well as give a hard kick to Manfredi's backside. He was to meet the younger Barbiano at the war council session this evening, and this time around he would invite all the Este vassals so that they will understand how they had to spread the word about Azzo's new aim.

At the moment, Giovanni da Barbiano was inspecting the defences at Portoverrara, which controlled the main river crossing east of Portomaggiore. Azzo did not expect that Manfredi would attempt to seize that town, since the land around it was laced with canals and Barbiano was holding the bulk of his company there, but the great number of villeins camped in and around the town was worrisome. They are hungry and Lord knew how many were carrying a disease. He would like to send them all home, but that was impossible short of employing such violence that might set the cities ablaze. Portomaggiore too had more than its fair share of unwanted people, but at least the city was larger and better stocked.

Azzo had to admit, though, that the city's *podestà* was managing the situation well. His own retreat to Portomaggiore had coincided with a sudden influx of villeins and others fleeing the advancing companies – his and Manfredi's, so for a while chaos reigned. However, the *podestà* must hail from a family of accountants, Azzo reckoned, since he immediately set about dividing the shapeless mass of people, forming them into groups, each with its own captain, like companies of men-at-arms, and assigning them to the care of the guilds, confraternities and charities of the city.

Azzo had done his bit too, of course, by deploying his men on the squares and near storehouses to ensure order. The city was quiet now, but tense. A recent review of the victuals situation revealed that they had enough to last them until summer, assuming that disease and a breakthrough by Manfredi did not get to them first. This gave Azzo an idea. Amongst the thousands of common folk that lay at his feet, some of them must be former men-at-arms or had trained in village militias – Alberto d'Este had promoted arms training throughout his *contado*. If he could form these men into proper companies, he might have enough of an advantage to push Manfredi all the way back to Ferrara. Then he could deal with Altinberg and link up with Polenta.

As the armies stood now, they were about even in numbers in both mounted and foot men-at-arms. He also reckoned the experience levels were about the same. Azzo knew that his own company was the equal of any out there, while Barbiano commanded an impressive force of mounted heavy men-at-arms. What gave the new scheme its specific genius was that he would assign each vassal to equip and lead a band of militia. They had to be given something useful to do, since reports had already reached Azzo that in their idleness some had taken to gaming, whoring and other vices that he was sure would lead to brawls and sinking morale. All was fitting into place very nicely.

His new stratagem settled, Azzo returned to the question of what to do with the boy. Capturing him was out of the question now. His spy in Ferrara had reported that he was no longer in Maiero and should be kept out of harm's way for the remainder of the war. This was just as well, since it meant that they would no longer come face to face until he finally defeated the boy.

A servant entered and began stoking the fire in the hearth.

Azzo had had no illusions that the peace conference in Bologna would come to anything, especially since he had deliberately put forward outrageous demands that were sure to be rejected. However, he could not in his right mind ignore the wishes of Venice and Florence and expect those cities to support him once Niccolo was crushed. Padua was already a friend. He supposed they had been playing for time until Manfredi could be brought on the boy's side, but so be it. Once he had Manfredi trapped in Ferrara, Azzo expected those cities to make the appropriate shift in attitude.

As far as the fate of the boy was concerned, he would be allowed to live; Niccolo was an Este, after all. Azzo could force the boy to take the tonsure or give him a small patch of land on the edge of the *contado* to rule. The worst result would be if he managed to flee his lands, to a sanctuary, like Venice. Azzo recalled the exile of his family over seventy years ago. After a brief war between brothers, his branch of the Este had been allowed to settle in the northern part of the Ferrara *contado*. He would have to be very careful about the investiture, though, or he might cancel it altogether and lodge the whole of his company in Ferrara...

Well, he was getting ahead of himself. He felt the warmth of the revitalized fire on his back and it soothed him. He looked towards the horizon and saw that dusk was fast approaching. Smoke from the fires in Manfredi's camp rose in black wisps and a line of his own horsemen was meandering along the southern bank of the river towards him. Barbiano should soon be coursing them. The time had come to send his criers into the streets to assemble the vassals.

Since March came in like a lion, it went out like a lamb. Spring descended on the Este lands with all the speed of a hawk finding its prey. The snow seeped into the earth and the ice on the rivers and canals dissolved within days. The whole of the *valli* was transformed from a white wasteland into a churning brown mass as the melting snow from the southern mountains swelled the newly freed waterways and flooded the lowlands. The question on everybody's mind now was when the ground would be dry enough to start the 1395 campaign season.

Geoffrey had not been idle during this change in season. Although his heart remained heavy and he had yet to decide what to do after he received his reward, he had spent his time in Manfredi's camp recreating the life of a squire for himself. Every morning he would brush his pourpoint, polish his hauberk, oil his *couteau*, tighten the rivets in his helm, disassemble and reassemble his leg harness, test the points, and consider what other pieces of armor he needed to complete his harness before arming himself with the ensemble. He could not don his fighting attire alone, of course, so he borrowed a manservant from one of the lances that shared his lodgings.

He then would spend several hours sword training, sometimes alone with a pell, sometimes with one of his fellow lodgers, although he was disappointed to find them far less skilled than himself. Occasionally, he would ask Jean to join him on the pike, especially after Geoffrey became friendly with some of the Este lances, but Jean refused, citing this task or that problem needing his attention. Eventually, he stopped asking and instead told Jean to learn the going rates on Armorer Row.

Much to Geoffrey's surprise, the presence of a tall English squire who could outfight anyone with a broad sword attracted the attention of the local children. Once Jean was out of the stable and beyond sight, about a dozen boys and girls would crowd on a stone wall to watch Geoffrey cajole and eventually defeat his opponents. They were particularly interested in his *couteau*, especially the mystery of its mottled ruby pommel, and Geoffrey was not above spinning stories about its history whenever they would ask. Geoffrey would have preferred for a row of maidens to serve as his audience, but he enjoyed the juvenile distraction, since nobody else seemed to want to talk to him. After while, the men-at-arms lodged in the stable began calling them the English Flea Company.

In the afternoons Geoffrey would groom Saint George and walk him around camp. The land was as yet too wet for proper riding and the palfrey was not suitable for lance training. From time to time he was tempted to saddle up and make his way to Ravenna. He had heard nothing from Count Robert since his hasty departure from that city, and his occasional questioning of passing messengers yielded nothing. He once thought about writing to his grace the Duke of Lancaster about where he was and who he was with, but before he found scribe Geoffrey changed his mind, since he believed that such news was of no consequence to anyone. As his dream clearly demonstrated, he had performed no true feat of arms.

The dream returned to him several more times after Niccolo's departure, though never as dramatically as during that night after the great banquet. Rather, it was Catherine's final words in the church that continued to haunt him: 'You must bloody it!' every time he gripped his sword, struck the pell, met with men-at-arms, or thought about Avignon. The campaign season in France should be starting soon, he would think, and in the Outremer. Geoffrey even thought about pledging himself to one of the Este vassals, but he never had the opportunity to meet one, despite his having made acquaintance with a few Italian squires.

What was more troubling, though, was that none of the vassals, *raccomendati*, condottieri, or local lords had invited him to share their table. Surely, Geoffrey reasoned, if the Marquis of Ferrara and the heir to the vast Este lands had accepted him at his table, so then should everyone else. By the time April arrived, Geoffrey had learned why.

"I wish I knew what we are getting," Jean said as he met Geoffrey at the head of Armorer Row. He was wearing his customary yellow jupon, brown chausses and thick-soled boots, but he also had on a scarlet brimmed wool cap instead of his usual coif. "Always be precise when it comes to silver. And do not tell me that you cannot count, because I have seen you cast dice and play at tables."

"The number belongs to the regency council, and I doubt Catherine planned to spill her own purse. Why do you need to know? His lordship arranged for us to be fed and lodged until his return." Geoffrey then spotted Jean's new apparel and said, "Where did you get that? And it is not a helm, I see. You have not returned to your old occupation, have you, and been earning a penny or two by beating the odd coin out of debtors?" He flicked Jean's hat with his finger.

"Nothing of the sort." Jean pulled off his new headwear and began fingering the brim. "It is because we are sucking at the teat of the captain-general that I can afford such luxury. Here, feel it. That is as fine a quality as I have ever touched." He handed it to Geoffrey, who nodded in agreement after closely examining it. He popped the cap on his head and let the brim fall down over his eyes.

"Fit for a lord, but not for me," Geoffrey declared. He yanked off the cap and tossed it to Jean. "However, the fittings I am after I can see from this vantage. What prices for plate have you discovered today? If Italian harnesses are as fine as Italian hats, I would do well to complete my kit before I return to Avignon. One of my training companions told me yesterday that the rates remain unchanged, even though mongers are demanding more for victuals, the scoundrels."

Jean was surprised to hear the squire reveal insight into the cost of things. "Why do you say that? No more men-at-arms have entered camp since we arrived."

"Campaign season is almost upon us, and I remember how his grace's knights would complain every April about how dear arms and harnesses had become, and that the armorers, smiths and mongers should be thrashed for their avarice."

"They should have bought during the winter," Jean sneered and carefully set his purchase on his head. He then gave Geoffrey an account of the latest prices for plate armor, chainmail, gauntlets and sabetons, gambesons and pourpoints, swords, pikes and falchions, including the cost to mend and sharpen them, and pavilions. He would not waste words on the squire by telling him about the less esteemed items, like leather jacks and bows. Jean finished by saying that Geoffrey's friend was right – prices had changed little since they had arrived.

"All to the good. What about chargers?" Geoffrey rubbed his hands. In the distance he saw riders kicking up mud behind them.

"Chargers? What has happened? Did Saint George throw you off during one of your training exercises? I cannot see us having enough silver for such a luxury, no matter what the size of the reward." Jean squinted at the rider and made a dismissive wave of his hand.

"Why do you say 'us'? That silver was promised to me. I will spend it on what needs for me."

"And why do you say 'me', Geoff? You accepted that promise on behalf of the English Free Company, not as a squire of John of Gaunt. I was there, and so were the three German lances *we* enrolled. They must get their due, and so must I. They have been remarkably patient with us until now."

"The Germans are no longer with me, or the English Free Company. And besides, I do not recall signing a *condotta*, which seems to be so important to these condottiere companies."

"Listen, Geoffrey, those boys helped you get the marquis out of Bologna and covered us in Ravenna. They were even ready to hew down Ischia and his band at your slightest command, so it does not matter where they are now. We got the boy home as the English Free Company, so you had better acknowledge that. Sure, you can take the lion's share as captain, which is also so important to these condottiere companies, but every man will get his proper share too." Jean did not raise his voice or make threatening gestures. He just told the simple truth as plainly as possible.

"There is wisdom in your words," Geoffrey said after pausing to let the Frenchman's words soak in. "I always pay my debts, and I am indebted to them for their help, English Free Company or not. However, *I* will give them their due."

"You are the captain," Jean said, "but all the same you will not have enough to buy yourself a charger."

"I am just curious, the truth be told, for until I am made a knight I have no need

239

for one." His words reminded Geoffrey about Niccolo's promise, although he should not expect such an honor now.

"I did hear that some of the Este vassals are selling a horse or two," Jean said. He was already thinking that if the squire bought himself a new mount, he could claim Saint George and use his own nag to carry baggage. "They brought too many, and now with fodder growing dearer feeding them has become a burden. Maybe if you talk to them and tell them a story about Gaunt, one of them will be generous to you."

Geoffrey frowned. "I have not been introduced to any lord or vassal since the banquet," he said. "I have not received a single invitation to share a table…from anyone! I find this very strange. All humility aside and even his grace the Duke of Lancaster aside, I did perform a rather impressive feat by leading his lordship the marquis to this very place."

Jean sighed. "Yes, well, I am afraid that you are not popular, Geoff." He placed a hand on the squire's shoulder. "It is Ischia. He has been telling just about all who will listen that the marquis is alive only because of him and that you put the boy in danger."

"What? This is outrageous! God's bones, what other falsehoods has he been spewing?" Geoffrey inhaled deeply and grabbed the pommel of his *couteau*.

Jean hesitated before saying, "That you might be a spy for Count d'Ivry, which would explain why you took the boy to Ravenna."

"How is it that you know all this and not I? I have not heard anything and my training partners have said nothing of the sort. Are you certain about these lies?"

"Crivelli told me about what his captain has been up to."

"Who?"

"Tommasino Crivelli. Ischia's man. The one who stammers."

Geoffrey nodded.

"He told me that Ischia has been visiting every lord and vassal he can find, and recruiting whom he can. He hates Ischia, so I trust his word. He receives the lowest pay and his position has been reduced. I think he might bolt from the Company of the Rose any day now."

"Very well, but is he your only tongue? If you are aiming to deceive me again, then by the grace of God I will make you pay for it!"

"Why would I deceive you? Do you find any gain for me on this account? Because as sure as the Devil shits in my soup, I do not! The other men-at-arms will not talk about you in front of you, Geoff. For one, you are a captain and a squire of some distinction. For another, you are very tall and skilled enough in arms to slay them on the spot, should you wish it. And for yet another, quite honestly they like you."

"Has the entire camp been flooded with his lies?"

"It would seem so. If you follow me down Armorer Row, you can discover what I already know." Jean stepped back in readiness to ward off a blow, should the squire's humors compel him to strike.

Geoffrey grimaced and again looked at the chargers prancing on the sodden fields. "This cannot stand. The lies must be overturned."

"How? Listen, I have sung your praises, but my voice is weak. You should have said something at the banquet. I sure as hell was ready to!"

"The marquis should have. It was not my place."

"We have already talked about this. Giovanni dell'Ischia is every bit your peer, so you could have spoken against him and not offend the boy, or Roberti, or Manfredi."

"Maybe."

Jean waved his hand and sighed. "That is in the past. I cannot say what we can do about it now. Ischia is not liked by many of the lords and captains, but he does have their ear."

"I will challenge him to a duel." Geoffrey tightened his fist around the pommel. "He says we are even, that each of us has bested the other twice. Well then, let us break that deadlock with a final pass of arms!"

"Ischia will refuse."

"Then he will be a coward and *I* will make it known!"

"He has already proven his worth, and *that* is known. And besides, he is old. Your besting him at arms will impress nobody, truth be told, Geoff."

"Then what can I do? Remain insulted?"

Jean shrugged. "Display your prowess, as is your desire, with the English Free Company."

"How can I do that?" Geoffrey swiped his arm across his body. "You can see by the mud in the fields that ordaining battailes is well-nigh impossible. When? I do not even know if I will remain after I receive my reward."

Jean wanted to say 'we', but he thought the better of it. He had resolved not to return to Avignon and the Gamesmaster, which meant that he had better keep the

English Free Company intact for as long as he could. That the squire seemed to have again relinquished the issue of his and their finances to the former debt collector boded well.

"Then I suggest you continue training until the marquis returns," Jean said.

They did not have to wait long. Within the week Niccolo returned to Manfredi's camp, accompanied by the *signore* of Padua, Francesco da Carrara, and his company of one hundred and fifty mounted men-at-arms. No banquet was held to welcome his lordship back this time. Instead, Niccolo went straight to his lodgings behind the refectory.

The moment Geoffrey heard about the marquis's arrival, he announced that he would seek an audience with him immediately.

"He must have my reward and I expect he wants to bestow it upon me," Geoffrey said loudly so that everyone in the stable would hear. "It is proof of great service." He mounted Saint George and left.

For a very brief moment Geoffrey was surprised to see that Jean had beat him to the main square of Maiero, but he remembered who the lowborn French was and accepted the acquisitive reasoning behind his presence. They marched together up the steps of marquis's lodgings and announced themselves. Jean closed his eyes and covered his face with his hand when Catherine appeared.

"His lordship is not receiving today," she said. She was modestly dressed in a grey taffeta gown with narrow sleeves and little embroidery.

"You know why we are here," Geoffrey said bluntly. He was in no mood for courtesy.

"I do, but that is of no consequence. His lordship will call for you."

"Then I will wait." Geoffrey straightened his posture and looked down at Catherine.

"Then you will be waiting in vain." After glancing at the guards, she drew close to Geoffrey and whispered, "He has gone hawking, near the copse just north of town."

"Indeed?"

"You should meet with him there, away from the eyes of Roberti and Manfredi."

"And Ischia," Jean added.

Catherine threw Jean an annoyed look before returning her attention to the squire.

"The tour did not go well."

"And how well did his mother receive you?" Jean asked. He would not be put off.

"I want to know that too," Geoffrey said and folded his arms across his chest. "What did you tell her about me?"

"Her ladyship received me well enough. I told her all about you as a seasoned man of Gaunt with many friends throughout Christendom, so her son was never in danger."

"And she believed that?" Jean asked.

"Yes. I have her trust and she is very busy. Who is there to confirm or deny it, at least for now?"

Geoffrey and Jean looked at each other.

"You are certain his lordship will receive me?" Geoffrey asked.

"I am certain. He talked about you several times. He is sad about how the banquet ended."

"And he should be!" Geoffrey declared.

"Keep your voice down, fool! He is still a boy, but I believe he needs someone to talk with him like a man. So far, only you have been so bold, or daft. Regardless, I feel his resolve waning and it must be restored. I expect you are departing soon, so you must do this now, for his sake, if not for yours."

Jean looked at the astrologer with suspicion. "You will add silver to our chest for this manly task?"

"Jean! Be silent!" Geoffrey ordered.

"I am wondering why she is so interested in the boy's mood. I suppose you lose a pretty penny if the boy fails, eh, Kate? Still, the other side would take you on, in one station or another." He leered and snorted.

"Niccolo will make a good ruler," she answered, refusing to dignify the coarse innuendo with a response. "Good rulers can be good friends, and we all need good friends, especially those without land or hall."

Geoffrey nodded. He took the astrologer's reasoning at face value, for it touched him at the core of his own ambitions. "I will go," he declared, "and I will go alone."

A mounted guard stopped Geoffrey at the edge of the field, but when Niccolo noticed the commotion he ordered that the squire be let pass. The boy was standing with his right arm outstretched. The arm was encased in a leather sleeve. His eyes were on a great bird circling overhead. The closer Geoffrey approached, the lower the creature flew. It landed on Niccolo's arm at the same time Geoffrey made his greeting.

"Do you hawk, master squire?" Niccolo asked in a formal voice. He hooded the magnificent white and grey bird and bound its feet.

"Of course, my lord. His grace trains his squires properly. I excel in hawking as well as I do in sword play."

Niccolo glanced at a dour-looking man standing a few yards away. "This is my arms master," he said. "My sword play has improved, although it as yet falls behind my mastery of hawking." He gave the bird to the arms master, who took it to a rack laden with other hawks.

"Do you want me to fight him?" Geoffrey asked.

Niccolo cracked the briefest of smiles. "I want you to accept a purse of silver from me. I pray it will not be the last reward I grant to someone who serves me as he should. In my saddle bag is one thousand silver florins. It is yours."

Geoffrey dropped to one knee and bowed his head. "Thank you, my lord," he said. After a respectful wait, he looked up and said, "It fairly warms the cockles of my heart to see you again, Niccolo."

Niccolo embraced the squire and bade him stand.

"If indeed you fear the loss of your wealth, I will return to you every penny of my reward. I know war is costly."

"I fear the loss of everything, Geoffrey." Niccolo's face fell and he began to remove his leather sleeve.

"But the war is nearly won. Everyone says so."

"Everyone in Maiero says so. But out there…" Niccolo gestured to the north, "the tale is much darker."

"I am listening."

Niccolo told Geoffrey almost in a whisper that he was greeted like a hero in Ferrara, but as he traveled through the loyal parts of the *contado*, the reaction to him steadily changed for the worse. Common people started to complain about depredations done by the companies and demanded *libertà* from the foreigners, a word he had only heard with regards to the cursed Modena. The Bretons in his escort suffered several attacks. He even uncovered rumors that he was planning to sell the Este inheritance to the German emperor, thus betraying his forebears. Many vassals and even *raccomendati* received him coldly. After several days, it was decided that for the sake of security, he should only hold audiences in the houses of Este factors and stewards.

"The worst moment came near the end, when we were already near Ferrara," Niccolo explained. "As our column was passing through some village I heard someone cry 'Azzo – Guelf! Niccolo – whelp!' Soon, the whole crowd was chanting those awful words. They could not be less true, yet people believe. I do not understand what has happened. My father suffered betrayal, but not such insults. This is worse that the revolt of 1385. I was so upset that I nearly ordered my escort to decimate the village!" He walked over to the hawks and stared at them.

Geoffrey followed. "I hope you hanged a few of the blackguards anyway!" he said. "Villeins are not hard to come by!" He slapped Niccolo on the shoulder.

The boy sighed. "I fear not. Many of them have fled their villages, out of fear, I reckon, since victuals still seem to be plenty and I saw no signs of plague. Even with his defeat at Consandolo, it would seem that my uncle still holds the advantage. He took the war to me and has yet to be expelled. More men-at-arms have gathered on my land. I should have taken the battle to him, near Modena, the moment he raised his banner against me."

"You will still drive him out. Your men remain in fine spirits and are eager to fight for you. Just say the word and they will arm all points before you can cry 'havoc'!"

"Perhaps, if we have time. But even if I force Uncle Azzo to yield, I may not be left with anyone to rule! If everyone believes that I have betrayed the family, another pretender will appear, or the fire of rebellion will consume the entire dominium. That happened to my father, and no one claimed that he was not Guelf through and through. Or Venice and Florence might give up on me and let Milan have Ferrara for want of a marquis who can rule." He turned fully to Geoffrey and whispered, "I am thinking of abdicating."

"Niccolo!" Geoffrey's eyes grew wide. "I see no cause for such dark thoughts."

"I will take the Cross," Niccolo declared. "I will join Count Robert at Ravenna and sail with him to Cyprus. If the Hospitallers will take me, I will enter their order. You and Count Robert spun many stories about the struggle against the heathen, about how it is the supreme duty of a knight to defend the True Faith. Let it be! We can all sail east together." Niccolo smiled and grabbed the squire's arm.

"But what about Marguerite? I daresay his lordship will withdraw the offer of his daughter if you withdraw from your duty to serve your family and your dominium as marquis! I doubt you will be welcome in Cyprus because of it, let alone be allowed to accept the crown of Jerusalem."

"Oh, I expect nothing will come of that marriage offer anyway. My mother and the *signore* of Padua are arranging for me to take his daughter someday. You know he led my tour?"

"*You* led your tour, Niccolo." But that was all Geoffrey could say. He was stunned by the rejection of the Ivry countess.

"I suppose. The regency council is still formally considering the offer, but I very much doubt it will come off."

Geoffrey felt the yellow bile of choler grow in his humors. Excellent opportunities were slipping away, yet all he could see was uncertainty and idleness. He looked at Niccolo squarely in the eyes and said, "Mercy of God, *you* must set this right!"

"I cannot! If my regency council, Roberti and Captain-General Manfredi along with all the money Venice and Florence have given cannot repair all these holes that continue to appear in the dike, then what can I do?"

"You can lead. You are the marquis. How many times have I told you that?"

"I would rather take the Cross and follow our Lord and Savior."

"Your rightful duty now is to lead. You can take the Cross later. Remember Frederick Barbarossa." Geoffrey recalled how Jean had explained to him the foolishness of taking the Cross as a pauper and without a proper company of men-at-arms. "I saw you in Bologna. Your words had the force of a king!"

"I failed at Bologna, Geoff. The peace conference collapsed because of my fury."

"You do not know that. What is more important is that you assumed the place your father and God gave you."

Niccolo frowned and looked away. The sun shone brightly and the spring breeze was cool against his neck. He thought about his mother and Catherine and wondered what would become of them should he abdicate. He thought about all the books and parchment he had read about his dominium and the glorious Este history. He thought about Cicero and how he used rhetoric to convince. He thought about his father.

"I need your advice, Geoffrey," Niccolo said. His voice was steady.

"As a companion or as a counselor? As a counselor I must be privy to more knowledge than otherwise."

"As a counselor."

"I accept. How goes the siege of your uncle?"

"Well, I suppose. I have not heard otherwise."

"Well! Have you not seen for yourself?"

"No…"

"Then you had better." Geoffrey motioned to the servant who was holding Niccolo's riding gear. "By your leave, my lord marquis!"

CHAPTER 16

Geoffrey and Niccolo galloped southwest passed Maiero and across the two canals that formed the defensive perimeter of the territory Manfredi controlled. No one stopped them until they reached the command pavilion of the siege, where they dismounted and searched for the man in charge. They found him – a veteran sergeant belonging to Manfredi's company –speaking with a band of muddied sappers near a pile of brushwood.

He did not recognize the marquis at first and thought that the two young men were scions of some local lord out for an adventure, but when he saw the Este eagle on the broach of the younger boy and the high quality of his attire he dismissed the sappers and bowed accordingly.

Niccolo wasted no time in getting to the point. "Give me a tour of the siege works!" he commanded.

The sergeant asked if Captain-General Manfredi or Alberto Roberti was with his lordship, and looked around expectantly.

"No, and nor will they," Niccolo said.

The sergeant looked suspiciously at Geoffrey.

"This is Captain Geoffrey Hotspur, the newest member of my war council. If we are to ensure my inheritance and put the pretender away, we must know every inch, every stone, every ditch and tunnel of this siege. Now, let us go!"

The sergeant, seeing that he had no choice but to obey, led Geoffrey and Niccolo across a damp field to a line of wooden screens facing the massive walls of Portomaggiore.

When Geoffrey peered through a small window in one of the screens, his first impression was that they were in the wrong place, for he saw nothing but a few fascines scattered about and a couple other screens protecting no one at all. Frustrated, he looked over the top of his screen and surveyed the area. A wide river ran flush along the curtain wall, leaving no berm, curved around the western wall and then straightened to flow eastwards as far as Geoffrey could see, which was another smaller walled town no more than a few miles away. He saw evidence that a large bridge once spanned the river from the city's closed northern gate, but beyond that Geoffrey saw no signs of ruin or fighting. The walls were unscathed by fire or catapult shot and the surrounding fields appeared to be ready for spring planting.

Now that he was thinking about it, Geoffrey found no catapults or siege engines of any kind. He could see clusters of pavilions belonging to Niccolo's captains and vassals to the west and to the east, but little activity to speak of. A few men-at-arms were sitting on likely river or canal crossings, so at least Manfredi was keeping *some* presence at the gates of the enemy, Geoffrey surmised.

"What is there to stop a conrois of horsemen from setting forth from around the corner over there and sweeping you away?" Geoffrey asked the sergeant and pointed passed the gate. "And where are the mangonels and trebuchets?"

The sergeant explained that the numerous canals coupled with the wet ground were enough to inhibit anyone from mounting a large scale attack on their works. And besides, they had only just started constructing a siege, so there was really nothing for anyone to demolish, he added.

"Still, more could have been done," Niccolo said. "The battle at Consandolo was weeks ago."

"This mess would not frighten anyone," Geoffrey said and spat in disgust. "Men should be ranked from here to as far as the eye can see, shouting curses and threating havoc!"

Niccolo stepped back to afford himself a better view of the battlements. He was dismayed to see the pennons of so many of his former vassals fluttering from the towers. Uncle Azzo was flying the Este eagle, which held pride of place, flanked by the gonfalons of Barbiano and Rodiglia, but Niccolo also recognized the arms of the Montecuccoli and Montegarulli of Modena, the Sassuolo, whose paterfamilias Roberti had killed in battle last year, the Savignano, the Flesso, the Luciolo, the Pocaterra, the Magnani, the Montanari, and the Spinelli. Where were his pennons? Several miles back. How these recently defeated men could still hold out against him Niccolo could not understand, although the poor preparations of the siege informed him that the war was likely to continue for some time.

"Come, Geoffrey, let us leave this place," Niccolo said forlornly.

The ride back to Maiero was much slower than the gallop to Portomaggiore.

"I might as well return to Ferrara and wait for the regency council to tell me when the true siege begins," Niccolo said. "That is their custom, and mine, it seems. Besides, I have missed so many lessons with my tutor that I am sure he has forsaken me already."

"Well, your captain-general certainly has made a bollocks of it, if you want my counsel. He should have rushed siege engines and sappers here the moment your uncle seized the city, or stormed the walls before the blackguard made himself at home."

"We only hired Captain Manfredi during the peace conference, so he could not have had enough time."

Geoffrey frowned. "That is true. Well, whoever was leading your host at the time should have done something. What am I saying? *You* were leading your host. You still are. What for run to Ferrara? You were just there, and what purpose did it serve? What previous lessons did you learn?"

"I learned that my serving as the head of the Este family is not welcome, from the lowest of my subjects to the grandest of my vassals, but I do not *know* those men. At least, not like my father knew them."

"Nonsense! They are just waiting for you to show them that you are their father now."

"What do you mean?" Niccolo looked at Geoffrey in surprise.

"Now that I am your counselor, I no longer need to hold my tongue. Your subjects and your vassals – they do not know any better. They are hearing to all sorts of stories and rumors and do not know what to believe. No one rules them; no one leads them. Your dominium is like a house without a paterfamilias; a place of chaos and uncertainty. Your Uncle Azzo understands this, which is why he set upon you in the middle of winter."

"You cannot expect me to lead an army, even if it is my own?"

"Why not? My lord and master, his grace the Duke of Lancaster, was in the saddle with sword in hand fighting alongside his father against the Scots, against France, against whoever dared to stand against him!"

Niccolo was startled by the squire's quickness. Nevertheless, he listened to every word he said. "But I have not completed my arms training. I ride well, but never in closed ranks. As much as I would like to, I cannot join a pass of arms and expect to come out of it alive!"

"I find reason in that. All the same, you can still *lead* your host. You can still issue forth and ordain your battailes. You can still arm yourself and hold your banner aloft as you order the ranks to set on. Manfredi can be your sword. *I* can be your sword, Niccolo!"

Niccolo raised his voice to meet Geoffrey's. "This could have been done at Consandolo! You caused me to miss that fine pass of arms, and I do not see the armies ordaining for battle now or on the morrow."

"I admit this. Had I known the purpose of your German captain, then I might have followed him, for I too regret forgoing the chance to bloody my blade. But we all have our commissions. I fulfilled mine. Why will you not fill yours?"

"How!? By Jesus's noble passion, Geoffrey, how will I lead my army if none will oppose it on a field in a proper pass of arms? How can I be father in my own house if no one sees me as such? I must wait…wait until the regency council…No! I will *tell* the regency council to create a scheme that will demonstrate my authority."

"You want to wait? Until when? When Azzo breaks out of the castle back there and again takes the battle to you? You said yourself that few vassals came back to you after Consandolo and your subjects are restless and disrespectful. It is time for you to take the lead."

"But how?"

"By an act of prowess," Geoffrey said with all the conviction he could muster.

"An act of prowess." Niccolo stared across the canal-lined fields. He could already see Maiero and the pavilions of so many men-at-arms that comprised his army, but he also saw few banners belonging to his vassals and *raccomendati*. "But that would require a feat of arms, and as I said, I see no one ordaining battailes."

"Why should it? I agree, performing a feat of arms best demonstrates a man's prowess, but that is not all. A display of arms would work just as well, I reckon. At least for you, Niccolo."

"Are you suggesting that I hold a tournament?" A shiver ran down Niccolo's spine as he recalled the death of Azzo da Castello just three months ago. "That would be a foolish act in the middle of a war. Also, my subjects might be offended by such a luxurious display of arms. More rebellion might ensue."

"In truth, I did not have a tournament in mind, although I would not oppose it. No, rather I counsel you to display your arms beneath the walls of your enemy. Gather your host, Niccolo, and march them to the river's edge! There, call out the pretender, shout the names of your treacherous vassals and demand they open the gates to you and yield to the true lord of this land! You read all their pennons. You know your house better than anyone, I daresay. And the field is prepared for an army, not for a siege, as we saw."

"Have you lost your wits, Geoffrey? They will not come out! Why should they? You give poor counsel."

Undeterred by this rebuke, Geoffrey turned to Niccolo and smiled. "Of course, they will not come out! That is not the purpose I propose. You must issue your demands in person. You must humiliate your false vassals by showing them that you stand at the head of your army. *They must see you!* Arm yourself with your father's sword! Some might yield. Some should yield. They should know they are lost, and they will know after they hear you speak."

Despite his exhortations, Geoffrey was thinking that such a confrontation might somehow offer him the opportunity to demonstrate *his* prowess.

Niccolo felt his heart beat faster. Warmth spread throughout his humors and his head began to swim. He did not want to become lost. "I will order Manfredi to call for arms the moment we reach camp!"

They were crossing the final canal before camp when they were met by a conrois of horsemen belonging to Manfredi. The man-at-arms in charge of the conrois informed Niccolo that he had been sent by the captain-general to escort his lordship back to Maiero and then on to Ferrara.

Niccolo nodded, and he and Geoffrey soon found themselves surrounded on all sides by mounted men-at-arms.

As they approached the hall of the *podestà*, Niccolo said to Geoffrey, "Why do you support me so? You have your silver, so you can return to Avignon." He was suddenly unsure of himself and worried about meeting Manfredi and Roberti.

"Because you are the legitimate ruler. And I say this not because of the accident of your birth. Count Robert d'Ivry would not have offered you his daughter had he not believed you to be the true Marquis of Ferrara. I bow to his judgment. I bow to the law that makes you lord of this land. Now, let us see how you uphold that law!"

When Niccolo walked into the hall, he saw that not only was his war council in full session, the faces of the men who comprised it were somber.

"My lord," Manfredi began softly. "Your arms master informed us that you fled your hawking exercise and rode to Portomaggiore. Please tell me this is not true."

Niccolo immediately noticed that the captain-general was bereft of that convivial disposition he had showed in Bologna and at the banquet that was held in this very hall last month. "This is true, captain. I went to inspect the siege. I was not impressed." Niccolo's voice was steady but cautious.

Manfredi looked at Roberti and then at the other captains.

"I would rather you not take such impetuous actions, my lord," he said. "It is very dangerous. If you want to tour the works, I can arrange it, although it is unnecessary. We almost lost you once. Your capture would end this venture in short order." He glanced at Geoffrey, who was standing just behind the marquis.

"How would that be? I saw no one at the works but a few tired sappers!"

"You are not fully aware of the circumstances, my lord," Roberti said. "In books these things are laid out in perfect order, and so the whole can be seen with a single glance, but this history has yet to be written."

"Then tell me" Niccolo pulled off his hat and dropped it onto the table. Bits of mud flew off the brim and spattered the surface. "The regency council excels at giving instruction."

Roberti nodded at Geoffrey and said, "This is for the ears of the war council only. Master Hotspur will have to leave." He turned to Geoffrey and said, "You received your reward, I assume? Very good. You are free to depart at your discretion. The regency council thanks you for your service."

"He is my counselor, Alberto, and he can stay," Niccolo announced.

A guffaw erupted from the back of the hall. Geoffrey and Niccolo's eyes immediately fell on Giovanni dell'Ischia.

"That man cannot be a member of the war council!" Geoffrey accused, pointing a finger as Ischia. "I remember very well the accord made with his lordship."

"Captain dell'Ischia is here on another matter and will be asked to leave as well," Manfredi explained coldly.

"Tell me," Niccolo said and he folded his arms across his chest.

"The matter does not concern his lordship," Roberti. "What is of consequence here is your appointing counsel without consulting...your council."

"I am the Marquis of Ferrara. I am the *generalis dominus*. You witnessed the investiture. I will appoint whoever I like."

Roberti raised himself to his full height and put on a very solemn face.

"My lord. Your own father, may the Lord grant him eternal rest, created a regency council on very specific terms for the benefit of your rule. New elections to the council are not for another month and the electors must come from certain places and stations of your realm. It is not our place to amend his lordship's will. Our situation is grave enough as it is without adding more uncertainty."

"His lordship has spoken," Geoffrey said as he placed his hand on the pommel of his *couteau*. "His will is set."

"Squire!" Manfredi said sharply. "Counselor or no counselor, I will have you thrown out of my camp if you continue to interfere! You do not know this land like I do!"

"But I do," Niccolo said. "I saw no danger. The fields were empty."

"You rode from the north," Manfredi said.

"Why is that of consequence?"

Manfredi and Roberti went silent.

"Alberto," Niccolo said, turning to the head of his regency council, "I am not attempting to defy my father's will. I am not trying to bring chaos. The squire Hotspur is my personal counselor – not a member of the war council or any other council in Ferrara. He is neither a vassal nor a *raccomendato*. He does not even have a *condotta* with me or the captain-general, so he cannot trouble you. He stays. This is my will and it will be obeyed." Niccolo put on such a stern look that the men around the table leaned back.

Roberti sighed. "The squire can stay as long as he knows his place, which is to remain silent unless we say otherwise."

"If the Englishman stays, so do I!" Ischia declared.

"Why *is* Captain dell'Ischia here?" Niccolo asked.

"He was caught poaching lances from other captains," Manfredi explained. "His *condotta* allows him only the right to find free lances. He is being rebuked."

Ischia nodded.

"Let him stay," Niccolo said. "He can lead his company alongside me to Portomaggiore."

"My lord?" Manfredi and Roberti said in unison.

Niccolo quickly explained his plan to shame his vassals and challenge Uncle Azzo, recounted the failure of his tour and stated that his army had lain idle long enough. The sun was warm and the weather had opened the way to renewing the war.

Geoffrey nodded. He caught eye of Ischia, who appeared to seethe with contempt.

"A bold scheme, my lord," Manfredi said, "and I understand your desire to stand at the head of your host and rule in your own name. I would be leading an assault against the city right now if I could, but you do not fully know your situation."

"This is the second time you have said this. Explain," Niccolo commanded. He leaned over the table and looked at the several maps lying open. "I know that the ground is still too wet for horses to ordain and charge. I know that a siege is the best stratagem at the moment. All the same, I want to show that we are prepared to meet Uncle Azzo. I want to show that I am prepared to defend my inheritance."

"And you will," Roberti said. He took a deep breath before continuing. "Your tour was not a complete failure because we now better understand the true nature of the forces ranked against you, my lord. Captain Altinberg succeeded in getting a messenger through to say that militia companies are drilling on the fields between Portomaggiore and Portoverrara. Not local militia, but over a thousand villeins and other subjects. I am surprised you did not see them. The popular reaction to your tour suggests that similar mustering might be underway elsewhere in the *contado*. If those companies move against us, it will be in concert with Azzo, and we might be outflanked. We are considering pulling back your army, my lord, to Ferrara."

Geoffrey was aghast and he could not restrain himself.

"Are you mad? Give me a hundred men and a hundred good horses and I will drive those beggars back to their proper lords! Then you can get on with your siege!"

"Silence, boy!" Manfredi shouted. "I will make good on my threat if you interrupt us again. Altinberg is unsure of the numbers and my spies are quiet. As I said, we are only considering moving back. Venice has promised you men as well as money, my lord, and we have collected the whole of your retinue from Ferrara. We could try to squeeze Azzo out of Portomaggiore before this militia host issues forth, but as you saw, the siege works are far from complete, and I fear even a brilliant demonstration of your authority beneath its walls will not bring about the desired pass of arms. We could easily find ourselves between the hammer of this unexpected militia and the anvil of Azzo's companies if we are not careful."

"My counselor may speak, captain-general," Niccolo said. "I understand the situation. However, I will not retreat. I missed Argenta and I missed Consandolo. I was refused at the investitures and I was refused at the peace conference. And now I am being overturned by my own subjects. You have done great service for me and my family, Alberto, but I must lead now or be lost."

"He must display his prowess," Geoffrey said. "He is the marquis."

"I agree," Ischia said. "His lordship must show himself at the head of his own army – his *Italian* army, preferable made up of his own vassals, *raccomendati* and local men-

254

at-arms. Send the Germans and Bretons to Ferrara or against Modena, but make the villeins know that they will have to fight against their own kind if they continue to threaten his lordship. Their hatred of foreigners runs deeper than you think, my lord marquis, my lord Roberti, and captain-general."

"And how would you know more about this than us?" Roberti asked.

"Because of my crime. The Company of the Rose has been casting its net wide, and so we have measured the depth of discontent in the marquisate."

"That should not matter," Geoffrey countered. He was surprised by the captain's support of him, but it was but a single thread to mend the rent trust between them. "Italians or no Italians, his lordship needs to show himself as their true ruler, for that is the order as set by God. He has done nothing for anyone to question that inheritance. Germans, Bretons or bands of trolls standing behind him, what matters is that he display his right to rule!"

"I have heard your arguments," Roberti said, "and I see merit in both of them. However, his lordship has never stood at the head of anything more than a band of boys in a walled garden. Now is not the time to try his mettle. The stakes are too high and our knowledge too poor." Roberti turned to Niccolo. "Our scouts must learn more about your uncle's intentions. Azzo has tightened control of what territory he has left, so I am not sure if his messenger can pass around the lines as easily as his captain did. So, for the sake of order set by God, we strongly counsel you not to stand at the head of our army until the full regency council, including your mother, can be convoked, which will be in Ferrara. Please wait for us there, my lord."

"I want a word with my private counselor." Niccolo stepped back from the table, took Geoffrey's arm and led him to near the entrance.

"What say you, Geoffrey? These men are set against me and they have the law on their side. I must respect my father's will. He set Ferrara right after he was nearly overthrown, and now I am in his place but without full control of...anything!"

Geoffrey looked at the desperate face of Niccolo and saw that he was more than ready to wear the mantle of a ruler. Yet, he considered what the head of the regency council had said about his lack of experience.

"I agree that you must submit to the will of your father, even if he no longer walks the Earth. I am still for you bringing your uncle to battle sooner than later, but the wet ground and uncertain dangers of these militias might be signs for you to wait. Manfredi is a well-seasoned soldier, so we must respect his judgment. Therefore, my counsel to you is to rule in concert with these men. Inspect the ranks. Tour the camp.

Drill the lances. Know the faces of the men you will lead into battle, if not today, then soon. Also, commission me to scout the enemy. You can trust me to give you the truth."

Niccolo thought hard about Geoffrey's words. The squire was asking him to compromise, which the squire himself rarely did. He nodded and turned back to the war council. "I withdraw my demand to demonstrate before the walls of Portomaggiore," he said. "However, I will remain in camp for a time. With my loyal arms master already here and the fields clear, I can train with the lance."

Roberti agreed, provided he keeps his retinue close.

"I will. From what I understand, Captain Altinberg has his company south of Portomaggiore, so he is blocked from scouting territory north of the city. I will give Captain Hotspur one hundred of my men to coast the mustering militia from our side."

"This task would be better for an Italian captain," Roberti said, "for if what Captain dell'Ischia says is true, then the sight of an Englishman at the head of a column of your men might aggravate their ranks."

"I would be happy to take the commission, my lord," Ischia said.

"It is yours," Roberti answered. "Confer with Captain Manfredi about the positions."

Geoffrey was outraged. Here was a great chance for him to demonstrate his prowess and it had been snatched away from him, and in front of the marquis, lords and senior captains of the army yet. He clenched his fists and scowled.

"But my lord," Geoffrey said with barely restrained anger, "Captain dell'Ischia is not fit to serve. He is under arrest, so he cannot be trusted to carry out a commission of such importance."

"It is done, master squire," Roberti said. "And the captain is not under arrest; he is being reprimanded. He will pay a fine and that will be all. Now, I conclude this audience, by your leave, my lord." He looked at Niccolo for a moment before starting a conversation with Manfredi.

Geoffrey stomped out of the hall and marched to Saint George. He was already mounted when he saw Niccolo running towards him.

"I am sorry, my lord, but I cannot abide such an insult," Geoffrey said. His scowl remained. "Perhaps I should resign my brief service with you and be on my way. The mountain passes should be clear of snow by the time I meet them."

"Geoffrey, Geoffrey, listen! I do not release you from my service, although I cannot stop you if you want to leave. I will not give Ischia any men; he can risk his own company. However, you heard Roberti: I must keep my retinue close at all times, and it needs to be a strong band of men-at-arms. The English Free Company is not engaged, is it?" Niccolo looked worried.

"Give me until dusk to consider your offer, my lord." Geoffrey's manner was officious. He whipped his reins and set Saint George on a course for the stable, but he had only gone a few dozen yards when, remembering the desperate face of the young marquis just moments ago, he turned around and waved. His face softened. "Niccolo. Just a couple of hours."

By the time he reached the stable Geoffrey had decided that he would accept Niccolo's offer. The young marquis was so close at taking his rightful place at the war council that he could not leave him now. He could not walk away from the heart of leadership. And then there was the likely knighthood to consider. Faithful service was one step towards that honor. The privilege would also show Ischia that the old condottiere had not bested him again. He could coast the canals in search of a pass of arms all he wanted, but he would never be close to the Marquis of Ferrara.

Pride would not let Geoffrey immediately inform the marquis of his decision, however, so instead he went in search of Jean. After asking several of his training companions about the whereabouts of the Frenchman, Geoffrey eventually found him in a nameless cellar tavern on the edge of town sitting with Catherine the astrologer.

"Where the bloody hell have you been!" Jean cried. "Back to the siege?!"

"What do you know about that?"

"She told me." Jean nodded at Catherine.

Geoffrey looked at Catherine in surprise.

"Niccolo came straight to me after you left him. He was not short on words to describe your adventure, and I daresay the council was right to chastise you."

Geoffrey called for a pint of ale and sat down at the head of the table, putting Jean and Catherine on either side of him. "What else did he tell you? He was not in any danger, I can tell you that!"

"About the confrontation with Manfredi and Roberti, and about the offer to captain his retinue."

"You did not mention that!" Jean exclaimed and shot an annoyed look at the woman.

Catherine ignored the outburst. "I counsel you to accept Niccolo's offer. Everyone will find advantage in it."

Geoffrey nodded.

"Where is the *condotta*? Now, this *is* a proper hiring!" Jean asked excitedly. "What terms did he give you? What about lodgings? The stable is not as attractive as when we first arrived."

Geoffrey ignored the questions. "You must get the German lances back, and more if you can find them. The marquis wants a strong retinue, and one that he can trust. That bearded bastard Ischia has soaked up all unattached men-at-arms, I am told, but I know you are cleverer than him, Jean."

"You reckon rightly, my friend." Jean tapped the side of his nose and winked. "Truth is, I never let the Germans go. They would have had a difficult time reaching Altinberg's company anyway, what with all the men-at-arms moving about on old Azzo's side of the river."

"Villein militia?" Geoffrey asked.

"The same."

"How do *you* know this, Jean?"

"Because I talk to people. This is how it works: you fight with your companions; I talk with mine. We drink too, but that does not enter into this bit of babbling."

"I suppose you were talking with the Company of the Rose fellow you like so much, the stammerer," Geoffrey spat. "I would like to know what those lads say about me."

Jean leaned back and looked at Geoffrey carefully. He scratched his beard and ground his teeth before answering. "You mean Crivelli. Yes, we share ale from time to time. He is not as dumb as you might think. Ischia is using him all wrong and–" Jean cut himself short and pointed his finger at Geoffrey. "You saw Ischia again, did you not, at the war council?"

Geoffrey gave a halting yet brief account of his confrontation with the condottiere. When the serving lass brought his pint, he downed half of it in a single swig.

"You are right, Geoff. He is a bastard and the son of the Devil, so we had better keep clear of his Company of the Rose. It is full of the dregs of the army anyway. That special *condotta* clause he won has not served him well. Crivelli admitted that few good or well-armed lances want to serve with him."

"His reputation betrays him," Geoffrey said. "I had thought he wanted to keep proper order in his company and find the best knights to serve him, but after Ravenna, the banquet and this enrollment scandal, I can now see that he is simply an untrustworthy son of a whore!"

"The man is black through and through, that is certain," Jean said. "He will only take Italians, no matter who, and so he has offended the Germans and Bretons. Also, since meeting and training with you, Geoff, many of the men-at-arms are offended by the way Ischia has tried to ruin your name. Me and Crivelli have been working to put that right. The lad knows the pain of a poor name."

"Good! I will be sure Niccolo learns this." Geoffrey turned to Catherine. "How well do you know Giovanni dell'Ischia? You ever read for him?"

"Not in the least. The name is Tuscan, but beyond that dell'Ischia has no fame attached to it. You said that he was ordered to scout the strange militia gathering. What are they doing?" Catherine asked. "I mean, are they on the march?"

"They are a swarm, but poorly armed and without good captains," Jean explained. In truth, he knew less that he was letting on and was simply recounting his own childhood experience with village militia. "Why? Do you want to join the English Free Company?"

"I am leaving for Ravenna today, and so I need to know how far I must travel eastwards to ride around them. I have a commission from her ladyship, Niccolo's mother, to Count Robert."

"Excellent!" Geoffrey exclaimed. "The nuptial negotiations are proceeding apace, then, are they? I was worried that they had been forgotten" Geoffrey recalled Niccolo's sad words on the matter, but now Geoffrey reckoned that his dismissive attitude must have been affected by his darkened humors.

"I cannot say more. I only allowed myself to tell you that morsel of news should you wish to pass on a message to his lordship."

After listing several customary greetings and questions about his health, Geoffrey asked Catherine to tell Count Robert that he had not forgotten his desire to take the Cross and liberate the Holy Land from the heathen.

"Nothing from me," Jean said, "but I advise you to follow the same course that led us from Ravenna here. The eastern *valli* should still be flooded, and so should not hold many men-at-arms. It is reasonably safe for the likes of you."

Catherine thanked both Geoffrey and Jean, and after telling them to stay close to the marquis, took her leave.

"You should have done a reading for us!" Jean called after her. "It would have been the least you could have done for us poor souls!"

"You should have asked me earlier." Catherine's voice faded away as she climbed the stairs.

Geoffrey chuckled. "A damn sight more useful to us at this moment would be to raid Armorer Row! Come! The jangle of my new silver sings a song about my harness, and yours too." He untied a lace from his belt and threw his purse onto the table.

Jean, being careful not to spill a single *grosso*, examined the reward.

"Looks like enough to pay for about two dozen lances for maybe two or three months. Italian lances, even. Well done!"

"Do not forget about the harnesses, and I suppose I should get myself a pike. We have not trained together for a while. I will wait on the charger, although since I am leading the marquis's retinue, I should—"

"Slow down, Geoff. I will place this silver in the company treasury, but I will not spend a single penny on a harness for me. There is no need."

"What do you mean? I realize that as the lance anchor you stand at the tail of the pike, not the head, but all the same you cannot fight in that ugly jupon of yours. You might not need a hauberk, let alone a breast plate, but a sturdy leather jack should do you nicely, and a proper helm. You are strong enough to wear a coat-of-plates, so maybe that sort of armor is for you. I have the silver. Did you see a coat-of-plates anywhere on Armorer Row?"

"Coat-of-plates or no coat-of-plates, our lance is at an end, Geoff. I cannot fight. I am rubbish with a pike or a sword. And besides, now that you have finally agreed to form a proper company, somebody must be its steward, and that steward will be me."

Geoffrey frowned and looked at Jean askance. "You cannot be in earnest. Bah! You are having me on, but I forgive you. Now, pay for the ale and gather your gear."

"I am serious. My shoulder aches something fierce and I have not had your arms training, nor am I likely too. You see how I walk. I got no support to give a pike to do it right and I am not about to risk being slain to prove myself wrong. Someone needs to reckon the accounts, sit on the parchment and arrange…everything else. I am the treasurer. I am the records keeper. I am the master victualer. I would be the keeper of the seal, if we had one. That is enough. I do not need the title of lance anchor."

"You are as fit as any man here, and what is to say that you cannot do all those tasks *and* fight alongside your captain? I do not understand you, Jean. I know you were born a villein, but I should think Avignon would have stripped you of such rustic…habits."

"Rustic habits or none, with me behind the pike I would only drag you down." Jean shook his head.

260

"So be it. You will have time to train, though, so I leave the place open for you." Geoffrey downed the remainder of his ale. "You are coming with me to Armorer Row, though, now." He grabbed the purse and shoved it down the front of Jean's jupon. "You know the traders. You know the prices. I know what I need. Once we are down there, once you are blinded by all the glare of all that polished steel and amazed by the keenness of the arms, I am convinced you will change your mind about fighting."

Geoffrey wasted no time establishing himself in his role at captain of the guard for the Marquis of Ferrara, and to ensure that his wardrobe befit his new station he not only completed his harness with new pieces of armor, he had his gray-blue doublet lined with satin and its sleeves widened, ordered a pair of light blue chausses and bought a purple roundel hat with a tassel. He would wear this ensemble when he went hawking with Niccolo and then would change into his pourpoint for the few times he replaced Niccolo's arms master between the barriers.

However, for the week of Easter all arms training and like pursuits were dropped in favor of attending Mass every day. Manfredi forbade gaming, ordered taverns to close and seized all wine and ale stocks. The men had to wait until the Tuesday after the holiday to resume normal camp life. That was when Geoffrey took Niccolo to the cellar tavern in the evening after arms training.

"Seems like a year since I last held a tankard," Geoffrey said. "All the same, celebrating the Holy Father and Son on the greatest of holidays fairly warmed the cockles of my heart. I feel good, cleansed even. The year has started afresh."

Geoffrey looked around for a serving lass. The tavern was full of men-at-arms, including a few from the English Free Company. Geoffrey now had eight lances in his pay. In addition to the three German lances, Niccolo had given Geoffrey five of his own lances, bringing the English Free Company up to twenty-six men. "You will have a pint too, Niccolo?"

"Wine for me, Geoffrey." Niccolo removed his green and white chaperon and placed it on the table. His hair was as long as the squire's and he had taken to combing it in the same fashion, with the locks draping around his ears.

"I have been waiting all day to ask you something," Geoffrey said as he leaned over the table. "What news from the war council? I am pleased that Manfredi and Roberti let you attend the sessions, although I should be at your side."

"They cannot deny me. I may not be allowed to appoint members to the regency council or order the army about, but I can go where I like."

Geoffrey nodded and smiled. He was glad to see that the marquis was seeing no need to ask for permission to assume his right. "Easter is over and we are not retreating. I take this to be a good sign."

"I should not tell you the decisions of the war council. I would like to, but the walls have ears, as Catherine once told me."

"Can you not tell me anything? I am the captain of your guard, after all. I should be prepared."

Niccolo was about to speak when a serving lass at last appeared. Geoffrey gave her the order and then doubled it.

"She is very busy," Geoffrey said by way of explanation. "Even the Marquis of Ferrara must wait for his wine sometimes. As you were saying…"

"I cannot tell you anything about the siege, but I can say that the *signore* of Padua is bringing a company of Venetians."

"Crossbowman?"

"I do not know. Doubtful, since their pay will not be usual crossbowman pay."

Geoffrey shook his head. "Your army could use some crossbowmen. Shooting across these flatlands would be like Heaven for them. A band of English archers would be better, though, but Lord knows where to find any on this side of the Alps."

"True. I have read about the glory of English archers. Little about the glory of English knights, though." Niccolo smiled.

"Fie! Such talk is dangerous around a man of Gaunt!" Geoffrey mock warned.

"Yet, it is only talk."

"Had you agreed straight away to marry the beautiful Marguerite, Count Robert d'Ivry would have brought a thousand knights from the Holy Land to fight for your cause."

"When? Next year? I need men now, not after I have been driven from my own lands."

"Blasphemy! Never speak of defeat unless it be that of your enemy. Never call ill fortune upon yourself because it might hear!" After a short pause to look for the serving lass, Geoffrey said, "So, Manfredi wants to give battle soon, then. This is good and none too soon."

"I said no such thing."

"It was there in your words. Regardless, I still think it is a good idea for you to demonstrate with your army within sight of your uncle. They must be starving behind those walls by now. Tell the war council again. If you bring just one treacherous vassal back to your side, it will be a victory."

"I agree."

"Commit more and more feats of prowess and soon the number of banners in his host will dwindle to none!"

"That would be a very fine thing. You know, Geoffrey, I would also like to see your gonfalon flying next to mine."

"Mine? I cannot raise the banner of his grace the duke, since I do not serve him here, or the gold lions of his majesty King Richard. Of course, if you grant me land and a title, I am certain that I could find an impressive banner."

"I mean the English Free Company. Your company. All the other condottieri have gonfalons to make themselves known to friend and foe. Where is yours?"

Geoffrey cocked his head and stared at the marquis. "My company does not have a banner, or a charge or a badge. Is it truly necessary?" Geoffrey did not expect the English Free Company to survive his service with the Marquis of Ferrara, so he was dismissive of the idea.

"I appointed you *and* your company to lead my retinue. Your lances would gain more confidence knowing that they can rally to something of their own. It is awkward, otherwise. And speaking of a sea of banners, the more I can show in my ranks the better."

"There is reason in your words." Geoffrey caressed the brim of his roundel hat. "I cannot think of what my banner might be, though. I will ask Jean to make something up. He had my special surcoat for taking the Cross done up, so he knows something about it."

The serving lass appeared with two large tankards of ale and a silver goblet filled to the brim with red wine. Geoffrey grabbed a handful of coins from his purse and dropped them on the table. He gestured to the girl to take what she needed, which she did. Geoffrey smacked her bottom when she turned to go, but she did not seem to notice.

"She is wearing too many skirts," Geoffrey said. "She should have felt that."

Niccolo blushed and averted the squire's gaze. The girl had reminded him of Catherine. He began to poke around the pile of silver when his finger touched something sharp. He dug further and pulled out a rusty rowel.

"Where did this come from?" Niccolo held up the rowel in the light cast by an oil lamp lodged in the sconce next to them.

Geoffrey squinted at the odd bit of metal and frowned. Some time passed before a look of recognition softened his face and he snorted. He told Niccolo about the hut near Umbertide and his encounter with the local children.

"Mountain children are a rough lot," Niccolo said. "I enrolled a few of them in the Whites and within a week they had despoiled my mother's garden. Now, about your gonfalon. What sort of device would you like? Mine is the while eagle. It is a fairly common device, I know, but there is a story behind it. Many years ago the cry of a white eagle warned the father of the Este clan of a surprise attack as he was approaching his first pass of arms. He was wise enough to recognize its meaning, and so he used that knowledge to win the battle."

"That was quite a marvel." Geoffrey sipped his ale.

"Yes. So, what demonstrates the power of your family?"

This was a very difficult question for Geoffrey. He had no family. He really did not have a name. 'Hotspur' had been given to him as a child by one of the wives at court when he tried to chase after a mounted knight as he was riding out for a campaign. He could not in good conscience take the device of his lord and master, let alone his king. And besides, arms had to be granted to him. Also, the gonfalon under discussion was for a company of men-at-arms and no more.

Geoffrey stared at the rowel, which was still in Niccolo's hand, until a glint from it struck his eye. He blinked and in that instant he saw himself astride a charger with all points armed. Geoffrey made a wry smile.

"Let it be the rowel," Geoffrey said.

"The rowel? Well, a rowel belongs to a spur, so I understand, although as a device it is very uncommon." Niccolo examined the rowel again before he cried, "Wait! Look at it, Geoffrey! Is this not the sun? I have seen in books of heraldry this device employed to mean the sun. I believe this will work. Now, tinctures."

"Gules?"

"Hmm, too close to that of your king. And besides, red cloth is very expensive and fades quickly, I am told. Pick another color. Not white, though, pilgrims and crusaders use white."

"Which? You have already removed two tinctures."

"Something meaningful. The color must display the key attribute of your company."

Geoffrey rolled his eyes to the ceiling and leaned back. He understood the purpose, and so he would have to make it right. After a lengthy pause, he declared, "Blue!"

"From your confraternity?" Niccolo shook his head. "I suggest you pick again."

"No. Blue for fidelity."

"I like that. However, a darker blue, not Este blue. Divisions? Bends, fesses, chevrons? Divisions are very popular these days."

"No, none of that. My head already aches from the details. Let it be the sun on a field of blue. That is quite enough for my tastes."

"So be it! Azure, sol Or. That is the way to say it."

Geoffrey nodded. "Indeed. I will get Jean to do it up the moment I see the lazy blackguard."

The marquis and his captain of the guard continued to drink and discuss knighthood until Geoffrey noticed one of his German lances opening a gaming board on the table next to his. He became distracted and intermittently listened to Niccolo. Geoffrey thought about begging leave of his ward so that he could play and letting one of the senior men-at-arms in his company take his place for a few hours. Niccolo was expected back in his lodgings before compline to resume his studies anyway.

No, that would not do, Geoffrey reasoned. If word got out that he passed off the Marquis of Ferrara for the sake of a game, Ischia would blacken his name so deeply that it would reach the bowels of Hell. He could return Niccolo early and then backtrack to the tavern. That might be the best course of action, Geoffrey thought as he worried the fringe of his purse. His fingertips had started to tingle for want of a pebble or a pair of dice.

"Are you practicing the tanning trade?" Niccolo asked.

"What is that you say?" Geoffrey clenched his hands.

"You are wearing the leather of that purse something fierce, or are you expecting me to refill it?"

"No, of course not. Your generosity has been greater than what I deserve." Geoffrey hastily gathered his money and the rowel and scooped them into his purse. "I just saw my men playing at tables over there and I was deciding whether or not I should put an end to it."

Niccolo leaned over the table and scanned the cellar until he saw Geoffrey's distraction. He recognized that some men were playing nard, judging by how two players were sitting at one board, casting dice and moving pieces along the inlaid triangles of the board's surface. Closer to him Niccolo saw a chequered board being laid out and a member of his retinue dumping a load of pebbles next to it.

"Quek," Niccolo said.

"Well spotted. Do you play?" Geoffrey asked.

"Of course. I do not just read books and pretend to master arms."

Geoffrey raised his eyebrows. It would do for the Marquis of Ferrara to be proficient in more than reading and fighting, he reasoned. A lesson in wagering would serve both their interests right now.

"Come, Niccolo. Let us muster our company at tables!" Geoffrey grabbed the full tankard with one hand and his purse with the other and stood up, sending the bench tumbling backwards.

Niccolo was excited, although he refrained from showing it. He remembered how he and Catherine had played at tables in Ferrara, as well as how he taught the game to the Whites and then won all their money. He followed the squire to the tables without his silver goblet.

The assembled players immediately fell silent and bowed their heads when Niccolo appeared in their midst, but he waved off the formality and called on them to continue setting up the game.

"Should we draw lots to determine the first setter-on?" Niccolo asked. "What is your custom?"

One of the Germans said that they would be pleased and honored to play by the custom favored by his lordship.

"That is gracious of you, but I want to learn your rules, although if I do not like them I reserve the right to change them at will."

The players nervously looked at one another, but when Niccolo laughed, they all laughed with him.

"A man through and through," Geoffrey said and he clapped Niccolo's shoulder. "Set the game as you like," he told the players.

"So, who is in?" Niccolo asked.

"You may cast first, my lord," Geoffrey said. He recalled how Ischia had set the order of casters when they played on the Via Francigena.

"You are the better player, captain," Niccolo said, echoing Geoffrey's sudden formality of address. "You cast first. And you have the silver."

The tingle in his fingertips grew into a throb. He inhaled deeply to calm the quickness rising in his body. If he would not allow himself to play, then he would watch and counsel. Geoffrey handed his purse to Niccolo.

"I should not wager today. As the captain of your guard my duty would be questioned, and I know as well as anybody here how my name has suffered of late. You cast."

The rules were the same as those when Geoffrey had played against the Company of the Rose. Niccolo understood and said that he was ready.

When the board was finally set up and cleaned, Geoffrey snatched the leather casting pouch and loaded it with dice. He hesitated. If he asked, Niccolo would return his money and allow him to make the first cast. A good cast would be a good sign for him and the marquis, Geoffrey reasoned, while a bad cast would mean they should quit the hall and make for the books. Geoffrey shook his head. Niccolo wanted to play, and it was bad form to defy a lord. *That* would be a bad sign too. They had committed. Geoffrey handed Niccolo the pouch.

Niccolo stepped to the mark. He shook the pouch several times and looked uncertain. He knew that all eyes were on him, yet he kept his own on the chequered board ahead of him.

Geoffrey noticed Niccolo's hesitation. "What is your lucky number, my lord?" he asked.

"Should I have one?" Niccolo answered.

"Sure! Take mine!" Geoffrey leaned over and whispered 'nine' in the boy's ear.

The players and watchers laughed. Niccolo felt a wave of relief wash over him. He cast the dice onto the board.

"Seven!" someone cried.

It was the same result as Geoffrey's first cast on the Via Francigena. This is a good sign, he thought.

"Are we wagering at one or two pennies a hit, do you reckon?" Geoffrey asked the players.

"Pennies!" Niccolo cried. "That is dull. I will wager by the *grosso* and nothing less. Who is with me?"

A few players began to grumble. A *grosso* was worth twelve times a penny and twenty *grossi* made a full silver florin.

Geoffrey smiled at the bold gesture. Without question Niccolo should stand at the head of his army, he reckoned.

"Well, you blackguards?" Geoffrey said. "Show your mettle to the marquis." Then, seeing that no one was stepping forward, he added, "I will stand anyone who joins the player circle for the first round." Geoffrey grabbed a handful of coins and slapped them onto the table next to the pebbles.

Two German men-at-arms from Geoffrey's own company and one Italian took the squire up on his offer.

The wagering began. When it reached Niccolo, Geoffrey again leaned over and whispered, "As this is the first round, I suggest you accept the last wager of twenty stones at a *grosso* a hit and make your number in two pitches instead of one. It is allowed. It should be easy money."

Niccolo accepted the counsel and made it known. He counted two sets of ten pebbles, gathered one set in his hand and returned to the mark. Thinking back to how he was able to beat Catherine those many weeks ago, he rotated his wrist several times and pitched. The pebbles flew in an arc and all landed on the board. Seven hit white squares.

"Remarkable!" Geoffrey exclaimed. He collected the coins from the losing players and gave them to Niccolo.

"Keep them," Niccolo said. "If you will not be a player, you can be a treasurer. And besides, you will need the silver to pay for the gonfalon and badges of the English Free Company."

New players entered the circle, but this time men belonging to the retinues of Niccolo's vassals. Niccolo knew them and greeted them appropriately. The lords themselves, the new players explained, were dining together.

The explanation raised Geoffrey's ire, but he buried it. He gave the casting pouch to the man he reckoned was the least experienced of the lot.

The new caster threw a 'twelve'.

"You could be in for a big win," Geoffrey told the man. "I do not believe we need to set a hit ceiling for this turn."

The wagering started off very high with thirty-five and forty stones at one *grosso* a hit, but the stake eventually settled at twenty stones at three *grossi* a hit. When the wagering came back to Niccolo, he startled everybody by proposing that the player pitch just fourteen stones in exchange for an *accomandigia*.

The player hesitated. Geoffrey saw that he was nervous and uncertain. Niccolo had picked the right man to challenge for a large wager, he thought.

The player asked what his stake should be.

"Investiture," Niccolo answered. "When you capture one of the rebels, you must force him to accept investiture at my hand."

A solemn murmur swept through the crowd. Some left the table to tell others about the surprise wager.

When the man started to waver on accepting the stakes, Niccolo began to harangue him, dropping bits of sensitive information about his lord's family and arguing about the necessity for a man to be bold and demonstrate his prowess. He quoted Cicero several times, which the man did not recognize but understood. Others soon joined in the coercion until the player relented. He and Niccolo shook hands and the man prepared to pitch.

Geoffrey stayed silent throughout the negotiation. He had heard Niccolo speak with passion and eloquence before, but this display of rhetoric astonished him. If only he had had such confidence at the banquet. If only he will find such words when he has his battailes ordained against Azzo.

The man did not make his 'twelve'.

CHAPTER 17

Easter had gone as well as Azzo had expected. Mass was said in every church and every chapel under his control. Bells tolled for days. Relics were paraded through the streets of Portomaggiore and the surrounding towns still under his control. Larders were opened to all regardless of rank or station. He had thrown his own money to the poor and especially to the villein militia he had armed and mustered. Although still under siege and with hunger, disease and pestilence ever present threats, the people were smiling. When Azzo had made his address from the balcony of the hall of the *podestà*, thousands cheered him from the square below. Even the Este vassals, who had expressed resentment over their having to captain the militia companies, saluted him, especially after he made several of them knights. All were celebrating victory even though they had yet to take the field. However, that was about to change.

Terce hour of Friday, April 16 had arrived. By now the sixteen companies of militia led by more than two dozen Este vassals and their retinues should be just about in position. He had ordered them to march out of Portomaggiore and Portoverrara before dawn, while at the same time he ordered his sappers to reassemble the bridge that led from the northern gate. The sight was a marvel to behold. Although equipped with a motley array of arms, including pikes, halberds, falchions, spears, and axes, mostly seized from the local armories or expropriated from the cities' guilds and confraternities, he had had the villeins drilled well enough so that they could form ranks and files without poking each others' eyes out.

Their aim was to seize a three-mile stretch of canal between Portoverrara and what was called the Big Canal, which flowed north-south and eventually fed into Lake Comacchio. That should prevent Manfredi from outflanking him and keep much of his army engaged. Then, when the time was right, he would signal the vassals to push forward and envelop Manfredi's camp, forcing him to surrender or retreat. The militia advance should also ignite the fire of revolt throughout the Este lands against Niccolo, assuming that he had prepared the kindling well enough. Azzo believed he had, if the reports of the boy's troubles during his tour were true and the villeins maintained even half of their rebellious enthusiasm.

Azzo recognized the dangers of his scheme – a popular revolt could engulf him too, but he was confident that the Este vassals could keep their companies under enough control to maintain the tide of battle. A few hundred or even a thousand angry villeins were not worth the effort of throwing into battle, as they would break easily against the mighty pike of a proper company of men-at-arms, but eight thousand such common men he believed would form a wave big enough to swamp his enemy as deeply as the melt-water had flooded the *valli*.

Azzo called for the gate to be opened. Behind him were one-and-a-half thousand mounted men-at-arms and the same number on foot with all points armed. An hour earlier he had sent two hundred of Barbiano's men to sweep away Manfredi's pathetic siege works and chase away the guards that were assigned to protect them. Soon, they would be in Maiero telling Manfredi, the German condottieri and Niccolo's regency council that the pretender had sallied forth and was ordaining battailes for a great pass of arms.

Azzo knew Manfredi would be swift to react, and so he was expecting to see his vanguard before noon. Or Manfredi would flee to Ferrara. The poor state of his siege works suggested to Azzo that he was contemplating this action anyway, since just before Easter one of Rodiglia's scouts had reported that Captain dell'Ischia and his suddenly inflated Company of the Rose was coasting the canals near Portoverrara and had witnessed the drilling of the thousands-strong militia in the half-sodden leas. It was a shame that none of the rebellious villeins had brought a crossbow with him, Azzo thought. Then he could have shot that traitorous captain out of his saddle.

To cover a retreat, Azzo had discovered that Manfredi had stationed the six hundred mounted men-at-arms of Conrad Landau on the road between Ferrara and Portomaggiore. If he were to engage this company, the action might slow Manfredi long enough to either draw him into battle or for the militia to sweep from the east and smother him.

Of course, Manfredi was a selfish enough condottiere that he might consider sacrificing the German to get his own company back to Ferrara without letting it shedding a drop of blood. Either way, Azzo would be victorious and his nephew would be left with a greatly reduced host to make a last stand in Ferrara.

Azzo, meanwhile, would leave no one to cover a retreat. To ensure that his host matched that of Manfredi's he would keep no reserve. This was one of the riskier aspects of his scheme, he knew, so he would have to rely on the order and discipline of his men to hold their ground at all costs. But just to make they did, the river would be at their backs.

As the great oak doors creaked open, sunlight crawled along the ground until it bathed the captain-general in a golden hue. He was alone, since neither his fellow captains nor the Este vassals were present to share the glorious moment. Barbiano and Rodiglia had taken their companies south and west to hold Altinberg and Monforte in order to give the impression that Azzo was intending to break out towards Modena. They only had mounted men-at-arms, so their action should be swift. Once Azzo had engaged Manfredi's main battaile, they would be called to join him. Together Barbiano and Rodiglia had a thousand men, and so if that impressive force did not give Altinberg cause to worry, then nothing would. The remaining vassals, including Lancellotto Montecuccoli, were leading small companies out by a side gate in order to hasten the advance.

Azzo fingered his white baton of command. Any moment now he would signal for the trumpets to sound the advance. Then the drums would start to pound as the feet of three thousand men and the hooves of fifteen hundred horses were set forward. Behind him near silence reigned, which was good. A babbling army was a nervous army.

The die is cast, Azzo thought as he watched his scouts take up positions on the Ferrara and Maiero roads. He was retaking the initiative and wagering heavily on its outcome. The house of Este was in chaos; he now must be the paterfamilias that returns the natural order.

The captain-general checked his gear one last time. Even though he did not expect to fight himself, nonetheless he was armed with a near-full complement of gear. The old hauberk still fit, although no one could see it because of the light blue surcoat blazoned with the white Este eagle. The surcoat had rather wide sleeves, he thought, but apparently this was the fashion these days, and he had to appear as though he understood the present as well as he understood the past. The leg and arm harnesses were reshaped and riveted anew for the same reason. His spurs were wholly new, being an eve-of-battle gift from Montecuccoli. A helm he decided to forgo, preferring to wear his dark blue velvet hat trimmed with ermine.

Although the sun was shining, a chill still permeated the morning air. Azzo inhaled deeply and raised his white baton. With all the force he could must, he yelled for the army to advance.

"They number no more than two thousand," Captain dell'Ischia said. He was speaking to Manfredi, who was staring at a list of men-at-arms. The war council had called Ischia back to restate his findings from the scouting commission they had given him the previous week. "Altinberg exaggerated the numbers because he assumed more villeins were training further to the east, where he could not see. I saw, and as I reported to you no one was in the fields with even a spade, let alone arms. The area is flooded. And while it is not for me to say, but I suspect the good captain is not inclined to release any of his men to you for fear of being overwhelmed, should Azzo try to push through to Modena."

Reports had come in from scouts and spies that a great revolt of villeins was underway. Rumors that Azzo d'Este was coming to liberate the lands of Ferrara from foreign occupation had reached Manfredi's camp and would soon spread throughout the *contado*. The council had yet to hear anything from Altinberg, but a messenger from Landau had just arrived to announce that some of his men had met with Azzo's vanguard on the Ferrara road north of Portomaggiore.

"Crush the militia and Azzo will have to return behind the walls of Portomaggiore," Ischia suggested. "If he chooses Modena instead, we can squeeze him dry like a lemon."

"Thank you, Captain dell'Ischia," Manfredi said. "We asked you for your report, not your counsel."

Ischia nodded, but before ceding the floor to the next speaker, as said, "I assume you will put me in the bottom rank when we meet Azzo on the field, as was promised."

"It shall be done. Has your company armed all points?"

"It has."

Manfredi nodded and turned to Alberto Roberti. "Shall we have deeds of arms today?"

Before the head of the regency council could answer, the main door to the refectory opened and Niccolo strode in, flanked by his captain of the guard.

"I have heard all," Niccolo stated. "Have you sounded the clarion, captain-general?" "The men are mustering, my lord," Manfredi answered. "The question is where to send them. We cannot remain here."

"And we will not. I have already ordered the *carroccio* to be readied. Show me the map."

"We must first consider the safest route for you to take to Ferrara, my lord," Roberti said.

Niccolo gave Roberti a hard look. "No. We must first consider our course of action. I defer to the captain-general to create a scheme, if he has not done so already."

Geoffrey stood in proud silence as he watched Niccolo defy the head of his regency council. Once he caught the eye of Ischia, and he could almost feel the contempt with which the captain was regarding him. They would reckon once the battle was won, Geoffrey decided.

"If you remain with us, my lord," Roberti explained, "then our best scheme would be for Manfredi to remove the army and you to Ferrara and wait for additional men from Venice and possibly Florence."

"That is a foolish scheme and one I doubt the esteemed captain-general has put forward," Niccolo countered. "I will not lead my host walking backwards. Then I am lost for sure, and so you are you, Alberto. We will advance. The question is: against whom?"

"His lordship is right," Manfredi said. "We pull back to Ferrara, the whole of the Este inheritance will be on fire."

"You just want to have a go at Barbiano for seizing your towns," Roberti said. "I will not risk losing the war for your interests."

"I do not deny that I want to meet Barbiano on the field, but he is with Azzo, and we can destroy them both now. If we fall into a siege, we are lost and not relief will save us. Looking at the numbers, I see we can dispatch the militia and then turn our attention to Azzo's main. Landau can hold him off for as long as we need. If this is a diversion and his intention is to set forth to Modena, we can retake Portomaggiore and suppress the revolts. We can press him in Modena later, if we do not capture him first."

Roberti sighed and frowned at the map. "You are certain about the numbers, Astorre? I still see us at a disadvantage."

"*I* am certain about the numbers," Niccolo declared. "Yes, the bands of villeins make my uncle's host look bigger, but they are stretched. We can take them piecemeal. The canals keep them apart and the wet ground slows them." Niccolo was thinking about his father's strategy during the 1385 revolt.

"His lordship's presence at the head of his host will more than even the sides," Geoffrey declared. He could not help himself. Here was an opportunity to perform a feat of arms, to bloody his sword, to display his prowess, and so he could not let it slip away because of the war council conspiring to keep Niccolo away from actual battle.

"You may address the ranks before we march out and stand beneath the Este gonfalon in the *carroccio*, but your marching in the battailes is out of the question," Roberti said.

"He should be with the men," Ischia stated. "If the villeins and vassals see him on the field with all points armed and ready to spill blood for his own cause, they might think twice about advancing against him."

"I have already told you, captain, that your counsel is not welcome," Roberti said through gritted teeth.

"I agree," Geoffrey said. "Without his lordship present they are just fighting against men-at-arms, not against their lord and master."

"*Foreign* men-at-arms," Ischia corrected.

"There is something in that," Manfredi said, "and I know that your fate, Alberto, is tied with his lordship's fate."

"Let us put this to a vote," Roberti suggested, "to the war council only." He glanced at Geoffrey and Ischia in turn.

Everyone agreed. Manfredi, as the captain-general and head of the war council, was to make the resolutions. First, he asked for all those in favor of an orderly retreat to Ferrara to raise their hands. Roberti, two other members of the regency council, Carrara, and Jean de la Salle raised their hands. Then, Manfredi asked for all those in favor of advancing against the pretender by a scheme created by him to vote. Manfredi, Niccolo, Cavalcabo, Obizzi, and Bentivoglio raised their hands.

"We are split," Manfredi announced. "Suggestions?"

"The other captains have not voted," Roberti said. "They are members of the war council too."

"We cannot wait for them to somehow sneak passed Azzo to reach us," Niccolo said.

"Why do you not vote on their behalf, my lord?" Geoffrey said. "When his grace

275

the duke is not holding court in Avignon, which is often, the highest ranking knight in the hall decides everything. This is no different."

"But does this knight decide on when to spill blood?" Roberti challenged.

"If need be, yes. That is the custom."

"Done!" Niccolo shouted triumphantly.

Manfredi nodded.

Roberti, realizing that he had been outflanked, relented.

The glorious chime of the clarion call rang in Geoffrey's ears all the way to the stable, where his newly completed harness was waiting. Along the way he saw men pouring out of houses, halls, taverns, and pavilions. He heard criers announcing mustering points. He dodged riders galloping up the high street to the refectory for orders. Traders were already pulling down Armorer Row and packing carts.

However, Geoffrey saw nothing that suggested panic. Rather, he felt he was witnessing the proper reaction to an approaching pass of arms. At the stable he met the head of one of his German lances, who informed Geoffrey that his men would be ready within the hour and asked where the English Free Company was to be deployed.

"With the marquis at the head of the main battaile," Geoffrey said and then asked where Jean was.

Before the man could answer, Geoffrey heard the Frenchman's cursing in the depths of the stable.

"You still refuse to fight?" Geoffrey said when he saw Jean in his yellow jupon, packing gear that had nothing to do with arms. "I can get you a harness, since Niccolo's retinue keeps many spares."

"Oh, I will fight, Geoff, but only when I have to. This little brawl is all yours." Jean locked a new chest and fastened the key to his belt.

"You will not sit in the baggage train with the women and cripples. You are enrolled in the English Free Company at your own insistence, and as captain I cannot allow you to shame me or the company. I have suffered enough on that account!" Geoffrey kicked the chest.

"Do you want to lose all your silver again? Who can keep it safer than me? Hmm? No one but me; that is who!" He kicked the chest back and looked around. "Did you get yourself put in the bottom rank?"

"We are with the marquis in the main. I am his captain of the guard and he did not dismiss me."

"Very nice. I hope you will get a chance to bloody your sword. I will have one of the children who trail you to clean it when you return."

"I will be cleaning it between the halves of your arse if you refuse to join the rest of the company, you blackguard!" Geoffrey tried to seize Jean by the shoulder, but because his lower shoulder was towards the squire, Jean was able to duck away.

"Listen, captain!" Jean held out his hand between him and Geoffrey. "I am the master victualer, treasurer, recruiter, and many other things for this company, but man-at-arms I am not, nor should be. You put me in or anywhere near one of the lances and it is sure to be chopped to pieces."

"So, you are a coward, Jean."

"I am honest, Geoffrey, for once, which you no doubt do not believe."

Geoffrey was about to pounce on Jean again when he stayed his hand. There is truth in his words, he thought, yet Geoffrey still did not like the idea of having even one man away from him. He still had to collect the other lances, which he had left to protect the marquis, and he was worried that he might have to give them back, now that the sides were about to set on. Geoffrey rubbed his chin and looked around him. His eyes fell on their gear and in particular his harness. Time was fleeting. He was about to give Jean one last chance to come to his senses and do right by his captain when he caught a glimpse of blue cloth tied in a bundle.

"Since you are a collector of titles," Geoffrey said, "I will give you one more: standard-bearer. You can hold the English Free Company gonfalon with the others *behind* the main battaile."

"As honoured as I am, Geoff, I will have to decline. Sword, pike or banner, this bad shoulder of mine cannot take the strain and—"

Geoffrey would not let Jean finish. He went to each of his lances that was still in the stable and announced: "Jean Lagoustine is our standard-bearer! Jean Lagoustine is our standard-bearer!" When he returned to Jean, he said, "It is done. If you fail in your duty to keep our banner aloft as we fight for the marquis, one of the men will make you pay for it in your own blood. That is the custom."

"You are a bastard through and through Geoffrey Hotspur." Jean spat near Geoffrey's harness. "Let it be so, but you had better do right by the gold sun on a blue field." He went to the cloth bundle and began to untie the leather straps.

"You can hire some of the village children to haul our gear. I know how well you get on with them."

"Yeah, yeah, I may be daft, but I am not so daft. Now, tell me: where shall I make the sun rise?"

"What?"

"Now look who is daft. Our gonfalon, the rag with the big yellow blotch blazoned in the middle. Where are we to muster?"

Instead of directly answering Jean's question, Geoffrey explained Manfredi's battle plan while simultaneously changing into his harness. As he stripped down to his tunic, he said that the captain-general had split the great host into two unequal divisions. Niccolo, under Manfredi's guidance, would lead the larger division against Azzo north of Portomaggiore, where all reports say he is assembling the bulk of his army. This larger division would be ordained in three battailes on a field between the Ferrara and Maiero roads. Because Conrad Landau should meet Azzo's vanguard ahead of Niccolo and Manfredi, his German company should become the bottom battaile.

After putting on his pourpoint, with its numerous points and eyelets, Geoffrey continued the lecture by saying that the main battaile would comprise Manfredi's company of three hundred mounted men-at-arms and a mix of mounted and foot men-at-arms from Niccolo's own retinue. He reckoned it to be double the size of Landau's company. The Lord Carrara of Padua would command the top battaile with his own retinue and the remainder of the Este men-at-arms. The captain-general estimated that the sides should be even, although his side possessed more experienced captains.

Geoffrey was about to pull his hauberk overtop his arming jacket when he realized that in his excitement about reciting the battle plan, he had forgotten to lace his leg harness. He picked up a sabeton and with a look of frustration called for a manservant to help him arm.

"What about the other bit?" Jean asked. He was busy with his own arming by working to affix the gonfalon to its staff and yardarm.

"What other bit?" Geoffrey again called for a manservant.

"The smaller division. You have said nothing about it. And stop yelling. The one thing you forgot to buy was a servant and no one has time to lend you theirs."

"Then you help me. I will tell you what to do." Geoffrey held out the sabeton.

"Ask one of those urchins who follow you around to arm you. Put the flea company to good use, since their fathers do not seem to be able to."

"Ah, so you heard the jest."

"Of course. No one pays me any mind."

"They have vanished. There is no one."

"Very well, let me play servant. I cannot leave my captain standing in a stable half-armed, after all." Jean snatched the sabeton out of Geoffrey's hand. "Now, about the smaller band of men who are about to see blood."

"And the more glory to them." Geoffrey explained the order of arming his leg harness: sabetons, greaves, cuisses, poleyns. "Manfredi is sending the Bretons after the villein militia crawling over the leas to the south. The ground is too soft for horses and those lads know how to deal with such brigands."

Jean stared at Geoffrey. "That is all? I hear those militias are brimming over with men; de la Salle has only seven hundred in his company. Sure, on the field a single Breton is worth two, maybe three villeins armed with axes, but this might be a bigger tankard of ale than they can swallow!"

"Calm yourself. The Breton de la Salle is leading that division with his own company as well as the retinues of Cavalcabo, Obizzi and Bentivoglio. Confidence is high."

"Thank the Lord for small mercies." Jean was examining one of the arming points while Geoffrey held a cuisse against his thigh when Jean said, "You will have to show me how to tie the points. They keep slipping."

Geoffrey had Jean hold the piece of armor in place while he made the proper knots in the two points that held up the cuisse, and then he buckled the strap behind his thigh. In short order they had the other half of the leg harness armed. After a walk around the stable and flexing his joints, Geoffrey called for his hauberk. Jean helped him pass it through his arms and over his head and pulled point cords through the mail where necessary for them to fasten the arm harness.

"I hesitate to ask this, Geoff, but where will Ischia be? You did not mention the wretch. I assume he will be in the bottom rank of the main, if his *condotta* remains true."

"Yes he will – in the vanguard with Landau! He will ride out to meet Landau and lead him to the field. Bastard though he is, I must respect him for that commission."

"I wonder if Crivelli will be with him. I have not seen the lad for over a week. Perhaps he finally withdrew his lance from the Rose Company and went home. Ischia would not miss him if he has gone, although he would still kill Crivelli if he could find him." Jean buckled a couter to Geoffrey's elbow. "Come to think of it, I have hardly seen Ischia's company at all, except at a distance when they are riding out on scouting errands. Strange lot. Keep to themselves mostly."

"He should be fighting, regardless of the captain. A man is nothing if he fails to show his mettle."

"Or display his prowess, such as you have not. Does holding a blue banner count, I wonder?"

"Your friend comes from a manor; you come from nothing. Now, hand me my cap. We are almost ready to take the field."

"Almost, yes. Now, show me the *condotta* the marquis drew up for you and we will be on our way. The lads should know what to expect after they 'have deeds of arms', as you would say, or has he already made you a knight? I heard great lords do that sometimes on the eve of battle." Jean gave the fully armed squire his padded cap and helm. He then rolled up the gonfalon and slung it over his shoulder.

"I am his lordship's captain of the guard. That is my commission," Geoffrey said, "and that of the English Free Company," he added after a pause.

"No *condotta*! Are you mad! Not having a pot to piss in is all very well for yourself, but the rest of us…" Jean dropped his head on his chest and sighed. "As the treasurer of this company it is my duty, nay, right to join you in any consideration of a new commission. This is a new commission. What am I to tell the men? That they might get a share of the booty, if any? Leading these men means more than just knowing which is the sharp end of a sword."

Geoffrey drew his *couteau* and brought its tip to within an inch of Jean's nose.

"I vow to bloody my blade today. Let it not be yours!" Geoffrey declared in a solemn voice. He then turned around the sword, took hold of the blade and brought the pommel down hard against the lock of the new chest.

The brass hinge split with a loud crack. Geoffrey kicked open the lid, leaned over and pulled out his purse. "Give them this!" he said and tossed the purse to Jean. "It is fat enough to feed all. Niccolo is as good at wagering as he is generous. Now, let us put on our surcoats and be off!"

The mustering point for the main battaile was the driest field near the first canal west of Maiero. As the day was fast approaching noon, the sun against the clear sky was warm, although a slight cool breeze was enough to prevent the men from sweating in their armor. The march was slower than expected because the first few conrois of horsemen had churned up the road ahead of the foot men-at-arms.

For the Bretons and the rest of the smaller division the going was much tougher.

Only a handful of trails led directly south and many of those were still sloshed with mud, so the rank and file as well as the captains cursed every step of the way. No one could be certain that the fields and leas were dry enough for large bodies of men to pass through them.

Geoffrey collected his company and found the marquis in very good spirits astride his mount with Roberti and members of the regency council.

"You look ready to do battle with the worst of my enemies, Geoff," Niccolo said. They shook hands. The English Free Company fell into place around the marquis.

"I should turn around and go home," Geoffrey said as he smiled. "You do not need me, since your harness has the strength to withstand a thousand blows."

Niccolo preened a little as he showed off his gear. Beneath his light blue surcoat blazoned with the Este eagle Niccolo had armed himself in a shirt of densely woven mail. The pieces of plate that encased his arms and legs had been polished to blinding perfection. He was wearing a mail coif, but his helm, which tapered at the back and was without a visor, was large, so it was strapped beneath his chin to make it secure.

"Where is Captain Manfredi?" Geoffrey asked. He glanced at Roberti, who seemed not to notice the squire.

"He and Carrara are leading the main. We will ride with the *carroccio* ahead of the foot companies. I am told that seeing the gonfalons it bears raises the morale of the men." Niccolo looked behind him and saw a thousand men-at-arms pouring through the narrow streets of Maiero towards him. One in particular caught his eye, since he was without a weapon or a helm and was desperately pushing his way through the mass of men. When he at last broke free and began to splash through a ditch towards him, Niccolo saw that he was a slight man with plain features that had recently been beaten.

Geoffrey saw the man too. He called for one of his men to accost him.

"Crivelli?" Jean exclaimed when the confrontation caught his attention.

"Is that your friend the stammerer?" Geoffrey asked.

"It is. Tom! Has Ischia forsaken you that you chase about in such a mad fashion?"

Crivelli, out of breath and with his hand clinging to his side, was brought before the riding party. Jean explained to Niccolo and Roberti who the stranger was and why he was no threat to the marquis's person.

"Are you fleeing the battle?" Niccolo asked Crivelli. "I consider that a threat to my person. I need all the men I can find."

"Trust me, my lord," Jean said. "This man is no threat to anyone."

"M–My lord," Crivelli sputtered. "I–Ischia had b–betrayed you."

"Give him some water!" Niccolo shouted to one of Niccolo's servants. "The man can barely speak!"

Crivelli shook his head. "Eight th–thousand," he said.

"Tom! Slow down and whisper, for all that is holy!" Jean advised.

Crivelli took a deep breath, spat on the ground and then looked straight at the marquis. "Captain dell'Ischia lied to you, my lord. The militia is not fewer than two thousand men; they are eight thousand strong!"

CHAPTER 18

"If I did not need the men, I would put you in chains and ransom you to your family," Azzo d'Este said as Giovanni dell'Ischia approached him. They were meeting on the Ferrara road half a dozen miles north of Portomaggiore.

"If not for me, you would be the one in chains, if not now then later when your city falls," Ischia responded. He was surrounded by Azzo's men.

"Indeed?" Azzo surveyed the land around him and caught sight of the Company of the Rose waiting about two hundred yards up the road. "Your company has grown, Giovanni. You must be doing well. All Italians, I expect. Your obvious success only feeds my suspicion."

Ischia gestured behind him. "That was not difficult. Once they understood my purpose, these true Italian men-at-arms begged to enroll in my company. I now place them under your hand."

"I once gave you a purpose and you spat on it. A great lord might raise his sword against me, but not someone like you, captain. You have as yet said nothing to convince me not to follow through on my threat, and that threat is very real. Beneath Portomaggiore lies a very fine dungeon." He gave Ischia a hard stare.

"I was placed at a disadvantage with regards to your nephew," Ischia lied. "I, he, Polenta, we all might have been slain had I not sought a temporary alliance with the boy. Now, he rides to you for a final reckoning. He is yours for the taking. And so, as you can now see, I have not betrayed you." Ischia craned his neck back and looked down his nose. He was wearing his customary black hat and cloak, while on his red surcoat he had emblazoned a white rose over his heart.

"Is that why Polenta refused to ride against Altinberg's flank when he left Faenza? You are to blame for that too?" Azzo pointed at Ischia's chest. "I should slay you myself!"

"Polenta himself is to blame for that folly," Ischia said quickly, seeing how Azzo now had his hand on the pommel of his sword. "He failed to see that the boy was right under his nose. He cannot be relied upon. Recall his failure to force the Po."

Azzo stroked his beard and contemplated this twist of reasoning.

"This may be true, Giovanni," Azzo said as he released the grip on his pommel, "but my nephew riding alongside Astorre Manfredi to his defeat cannot be your doing, so you still have brought me nothing."

"I have brought you victory."

"How? Did you spread plague in camp?"

"You have eight thousand Italian villeins in your militia spread along the canals to the east of here. I know because I scouted them thoroughly."

"Yes, and what of it?"

"Manfredi believes you have only two thousand."

Azzo raised his eyebrows and glanced at his neighboring vassals, who began to exchange words with one another.

"I deceived him. The captain-general has deployed a small force of despicable Bretons and a few petty vassals against your militia as a result. They will be crushed and the villeins will sweep north into the heart of the *contado*. Manfredi and Niccolo will be lost! Consult your scouts if you do not believe me, Azzo."

"I will. All the same, this does explain why Manfedi is rushing to meet me." However, it did explain why Altinberg and Monforte were not rushing to meet this threat, Azzo thought, for he had just received messengers from Barbiano and Rodiglia respectively, who informed him that they had encountered the enemy, but no clashes had yet occurred. The German captains were maintaining defensive attitudes and blocking all roads leading south. Azzo decided to trust Ischia, for the time being.

"What is your aim now, captain?" Azzo asked.

"I wish to enroll under your banner, my lord," Ischia said as he doffed his hat. "You promised me a *condotta* and possibly an *accomandigia* if I delivered you the boy. I have."

"Not quite, but I will enroll you all the same. However, you will obey my every command and fulfill every commission I give you. Should you decide that your will supersedes mine, I will seize your company and blacken your name. What say you to these terms?"

"I accept. I serve loyally, despite what you might think."

Azzo called for one of his factors to arrange for a *condotta* to be drawn up in the name of Giovanni dell'Ischia.

"And the Company of the Rose," Ischia added.

Azzo nodded and ordered the factor to include all the usual clauses about supplies, booty, prisoners and ransoms, preparedness of arms and armor, and the option for further service after the term of the *condotta* expires. When Azzo asked about the size of the Company of the Rose, Ischia said "fifty lances".

"Fifty! I do not see so many before me. You have not left some behind, have you?" Azzo asked with a hint of suspicion.

"I have thirty now and you will give me twenty more."

"Twenty more! God's dignity, Giovanni, you are presumptuous! I have none to spare, but after we win this pass of arms I will grant you the right to find lances from amongst the prisoners." Azzo then declared that he would give a monthly pay rate of twenty silver florins in white money per lance, which was more than his own men were earning, but the *condotta* would be for only one month starting today. Ischia himself, as captain, would receive four hundred florins.

"A thousand florins even," Ischia said. "Done!"

They shook hands and Azzo had the vassals around him serve as witnesses to the deals. Ischia called for his men to join him in the ranks and proceeded to describe the battle plan of Manfredi, the strength of his companies and where he could expect to find them, and the reported mood of the Este subjects.

"And what about my nephew? I should like to capture him myself this time."

"He should be with Alberto Roberti and other exalted fools at the top of the main. He has a large retinue now, though, led by an obnoxious English squire, who is very meddlesome." Ischia spat to the side.

"This would not be the tall English lad who rescued the boy at Bologna, would it?" Azzo made a wry smile.

"The same. I should like to slay him, should the opportunity arise. I have already blackened his name."

"Do not be so hasty to kill, Giovanni. Killing leads to vengeance, and this squire is a man of Gaunt, I hear. I should very much like to meet him!" A chuckle rippled around the group, save for Ischia.

"This is a ruse!" Alberto Roberti said. "Azzo knows we have the advantage, so he sent this fool to deceive us. I will have the truth beaten from him." He ordered his men to seize Crivelli.

"Wait!" Jean said. "I know this man. Let me speak with him." Jean handed his gonfalon to one of the Germans and dismounted.

"Tom! Speak the truth! What is the meaning of this?" Jean saw that Crivelli was not only unarmed, but his clothes were torn and his face was swollen.

"Ischia has set out on a campaign to rid Italy of foreigners, so when he saw that he could cause the defeat of the German and Breton companies by falsely reporting the number of men ranked against them, he did so. I have no reason to lie." He coughed several times and winced in pain.

"I mean what about the cuts and bruises. What happened to you?"

"The other day I realized that I would not rise in the Company of the Rose, so I ended my service with Ischia, which did not trouble him in the least, but when I told him that I would seek a place in the English Free Company, he flew into such a rage that, well, this was the result. The moment he was done, I fled to the *valli* and hid, but I found neither food nor shelter. The moment I saw that the army was on the move, I returned. Ischia has the Devil in him now!"

Even after Jean related the story to Roberti and declared that he would vouchsafe Crivelli's name, the head of the regency was still not wholly convinced. He ruled against torture as a means to learn the truth and instead ordered that Crivelli be bound and taken with them to the battle. Roberti then ordered one of the junior members of the regency council to remain where he was and to bring to him any news from the remaining scouts who were still coasting the eastern *valli*.

"I must ride ahead and inform the captain-general," Roberti continued. "If all this is true, we might indeed be obliged to seek sanctuary behind the walls of Ferrara. You stay with the main, my lord."

Geoffrey sighed loudly, but he said nothing. He exchanged glances with Niccolo and then looked at the injured Crivelli.

"But what about de la Salle and the vassals who accompanied him to meet the militia? Should we call them to stop or return to camp?" Niccolo asked.

"It might be too late for them," Roberti said solemnly, "but even if they can pull back, we might need a screen to cover our retreat. Prepare yourself for sacrifices, my lord."

Niccolo decided that he would not prepare himself for sacrifices. He reckoned that the loss of even a few loyal vassals, especially at this critical time, might cause the defection of yet more vassals and *raccomendati*. He had to know for sure the size of the militia companies. His rule now depended on it.

"We must send more scouts and we need to inform de la Salle," Niccolo declared. "I will go," Geoffrey said. "I brought the wretch Ischia into your camp. I am responsible. Let me coast the enemy and know their true strength."

"Let him go," Roberti said. "You no longer need a private counselor anyway." After ordering some men-at-arms to stay close to the marquis, Roberti spurred his horse and galloped ahead.

"I await your command, my lord," Geoffrey said. "Give me this commission, Niccolo."

"It is yours. I trust no one else to ride into the teeth of the enemy and count heads."

Niccolo and Geoffrey shook hands and embraced. After Niccolo rejoined the main battaile on its march to Portomaggiore, Geoffrey gathered his company and gave the order to return to camp.

The *signore* of Padua's top battaile was still forming columns as the English Free Company rode passed them into Maiero. The town was quiet. The baggage train was parked in the commons and a few servants and camp followers were silently but intently packing the last of their belongings. Geoffrey asked a carter which route the Bretons had taken and was duly directly towards a crooked brown line dotted with pools of water in the shape of boot soles.

"I know that every chance exists that you will thrash me as badly as Ischia thrashed Crivelli for saying this, Geoffrey, but we can return to Avignon now," Jean said, making sure to hold himself more than an arm's length away from the squire. "After all, you can now boast that you were captain of the guard for the Marquis of Ferrara, you rescued him from certain capture, you lead the English Free Company…"

"You told me that you have no intention of returning to the Gamesmaster or to France," Geoffrey said. He had his eyes on the horizon. "Changed your mind?" He was already feeling a mixture of sanguine and choler rising in his humors, and so he could not be bothered by his companion's daftness.

"That is true. What I really want to say, or rather ask, is what will we do if we encounter a seething mass of eight thousand villeins bent on rape and ruin? And I am certain we will see such a spectacle, since I know Tom, and he has nothing to gain by lying about such a thing." Jean suddenly felt cold around the legs. When he looked down he saw that his chausses had become soaked from all the mud the horses were kicking up.

"I am certain too, but we must also learn how they are being ordained, if they have horses, bow or crossbows, and we must tell all this to Captain de la Salle, if he already does not know, and then to his lordship."

"And if the situation looks hopeless, we can take our company and go elsewhere," Jean said. "You do not have a *condotta*, so we do not need to be here, according to law and custom."

"I will fulfill my commission and then we shall see," Geoffrey said sharply. "All the same, I am not leaving this battle until I have bloodied my sword!"

They followed a narrow path southwards through the *valli*, but the muddy path soon turned into a brown stream, and Jean feared that their horses would become bogged down.

"There must be another way," Jean mumbled.

"Ask them." Geoffrey pointed to a band of villagers, who were picking their way through a nearby field. "They are probably going to watch the glorious pass of arms."

"Or plunder the corpses afterward." Jean hailed a villager he recognized from Armorer Row and asked which way to the battle.

After a short while on the correct trial, Geoffrey heard the clash of arms and set his eyes to follow their direction. What he saw when he found the Breton company thrilled and awed him in equal measure: a thousand men ranked along a front of at least a mile in length and thousands more setting against them.

Geoffrey spurred Saint George towards the gonfalon of Jean de la Salle, which was very close to the top rank of his division. Geoffrey saw no reserves on his side while across the canal he spotted several columns, each led by disloyal Este vassals, marching to support their engaged companions.

"Are you here to help us?" de la Salle asked Geoffrey as soon as he was beneath the gonfalon. "I asked for more reinforcements than this!" He gestured with a bloody hand at the eight lances of the English Free Company.

"I am here to scout," Geoffrey shouted. The sounds of battle seemed to grow louder. He heard the shriek of a man and looked in time to see a villein being pierced by a pike. He also noticed a few wounded being tended to on the ground not far from the rallying point and even more bloodied men-at-arms returning to the ranks.

"A scout! What is there to scout? Get your men in the ranks. Where are your pikes?" A messenger approached de la Salle and his attention shifted.

Geoffrey took the opportunity of de la Salle's distraction to get a better view of the battle. The Breton captain had deployed his men so that his right flank was protected by a narrow canal that ran north-south and his left flank was covered by a village, although Geoffrey reckoned that these minor obstacles could be easily overcome by a determined counter-attack. To buttress his own lines, de la Salle had mixed his men-at-arms and those of the Este vassals. Horses were wandering the fields behind the ranks. Geoffrey gripped the pommel of his *couteau* and he had to struggle to keep it sheathed. His commission was to scout and report, although he was feeling himself being drawn to the field.

A great cheer went up to his right. Geoffrey turned his head and saw a band of villeins armed with halberds crossing the narrow canal. Behind them on horseback was a disloyal Este vassal exhorting them to cut down the Breton bastards.

Geoffrey wanted to spur his mount and meet this traitor in a single pass of arms, but he looked at the canal and the muddy meadow next to it and realized that Saint George would break his legs before he had crossed half the distance to the blackguard. But help was already at hand. Even before de la Salle was aware of the danger, he saw two dozen of his pikemen pull themselves from the top rank and go to throw back the new threat. Breton lances usually consisted of only one or two men per pike, Geoffrey knew, and so he reckoned that their relative lack of strength was made up in numbers.

"Geoff! Geoff!" Jean yelled. "Give us an order. Please!"

The squire felt his shoulder trembling, but when he tore his eyes away from the battle he saw that it was the Frenchman shaking him.

"Blast you, Jean, what is it?"

"Lead us out of here!" Jean shouted.

Geoffrey stared at Jean for an angry moment before realizing that his commission had barely begun. He asked de la Salle about the number of casualties he had sustained and was shocked by the low number he received, considering that Geoffrey could see twisted bodies lying in and between the two sides. He told Jean the figure and then impetuously promised de la Salle that the marquis would send reinforcements shortly. After ordering one of his men to immediately report about the course of the battle to his lordship the marquis, he shouted for his company to follow and galloped eastwards.

The ranks of men seemed to never end. Seeing that none had bows, crossbows or slings, Geoffrey coasted almost within spitting distance of the enemy. All had crossed the long east-west canal and mustered. Some companies were heading in a northwest direction, which would eventually take them behind de la Salle or to Maiero. They were moving slowly because of the wet terrain, but without major rivers or woodlands or gullies to slow them even further, let alone a company of veteran men-at-arms to throw them back, Geoffrey reckoned that the militia would reach Niccolo before vespers. That was assuming de la Salle and the vassals could stand firm, but Geoffrey was doubtful. Looking back, he measured the ground they had given to the furious militia by where most corpses were lying, which revealed that the top rank of the enemy currently engaged with de la Salle were now trampling those bodies lying closest to the canal.

Geoffrey and the English Free Company rode on. They passed the end of de la Salle's line at the village and into the open country. The leas here were sloppier than those farther west. The spring melt was still gathering closer to the Big Canal, Geoffrey reckoned, and he slowed Saint George to a trot.

"Crivelli was right," Jean said after he caught up with Geoffrey. "I count at least a dozen companies, maybe more, since the fighting back there is a right bloody mess. There must be over eight thousand of those beggars, Geoff." Jean sighed and squinted at the mass of militia marching towards them. "I see no reason to ride on."

"Nor do I. Let us return to de la Salle and tell him what we saw, then back to Niccolo!"

When they reached the rallying point, one of de la Salle's servants informed Geoffrey that Cavalcabo had been killed, and so the Breton had joined the ranks to take command of his retinue. More dead and wounded were lying nearby, Geoffrey noticed. He surveyed the undulating ranks for a final time. The Bretons and their companions were still holding the line, but the ranks of militia had grown thicker since he last observed them.

A whoop caused Geoffrey to jerk his head to his left, where he saw that a band of militia had broken through and were imploring others to follow them.

"Let us have at them!" Geoffrey cried. He ordered his company to draw swords and form two ranks. Because they were only scouts and the ground was too soft for a massed mounted charge anyway, the men-at-arms had brought neither lance nor spear with which to run through the enemy.

"Pick your man!" Geoffrey said once he had his company in order. Because the Germans had been with him the longest and they had fought together before, Geoffrey placed them in the bottom rank. He had the Italians form the top rank and ordered them to catch villeins who tried to flee.

"I should make for the marquis and tell him all that we have seen," Jean said. He was hoping to be forgotten, since Geoffrey now knew that he was useless with arms, but when the squire turned and looked directly at Jean, he saw the familiar gaming fury in his eyes. "Time is of the essence."

"I agree," Geoffrey shouted. "You must go alone, however. I have work to do here and the men have formed ranks and drawn to the field. God speed, Jean!"

"What about the gonfalon? Should I plant it with the others?" Jean shook the golden sun to make it shudder.

"Carry it to the marquis so that he will recognize you. You might be slain otherwise." Geoffrey spurred Saint George and took his place at the head of his company.

Jean shuddered at the word 'killed'. He took a final glance at the raging lines of men and arms and grimaced before whipping the reins and guiding his nag back to the trail. His greatest fear now was that a militia company had already reached Maiero and the baggage train. A bout of plundering might slow them down for a while, long enough maybe for Manfredi to send someone to hack them to pieces, but all the same many goods and much silver would be lost. Jean had entrusted the property of the English Free Company with the steward of the baggage train, since the company had no servants of its own to protect it. A chill ran down Jean's spine when he thought about the potential loss of all he had gained in the past two months. Jean reined in his nag. Fear suggested that he cast aside the gonfalon and make straight for the baggage train. There, if all was still safe, he could reclaim the company silver and flee to…where?

Jean stood up in his saddle and squinted in the direction of Maiero. He could make out the contours of the church and the refectory, but he was still too far away to see if the town was being looted. He looked up at the English Free Company gonfalon and back again at Maiero. Damn! He had worked too hard to create this company – and it finally was a genuine company of men-at-arms – to lose it now. He had given birth to this strange thing; without it he was nothing with nowhere to go.

Jean made a wry smile as he recalled his final words to Catherine the astrologer before she left for Ravenna: "The next time you write to the Gamesmaster, Kate, tell him from me that he can go fornicate with the Devil! I am not coming back!"

After swallowing hard, Jean set his horse towards Niccolo d'Este.

Geoffrey was shocked by the obscene fighting skills of the villeins. When his company set upon those that had broken through, instead of using their halberds to engage his men they began stabbing at the horses. The Germans lost three mounts in the first pass as a result, but by aiming for the beasts the villeins had their arms out of position, and so when the Italians rode in they were able to bring down their swords on a dozen heads with ease. Geoffrey himself was able to knock down one man by kicking aside his halberd and turning Saint George into him. However, the palfrey had trouble finding his footing and he stumbled backwards, nearly throwing Geoffrey from his saddle. By the time he righted his mount, the melee was over and all the attackers lay dead and the Bretons had sealed the line.

"Rally to me!" Geoffrey yelled. "Well done, lads," he said when they gathered around him. They had suffered a few wounds, but none had been killed. They had lost six of their twenty-six horses, however.

Geoffrey looked at his sword; it was clean. The blade even glinted in places where the oil he had applied to keep the rust away remained. He wondered if he should return to Niccolo's side and to where the main pass of arms would happen. He was captain of his guard, after all, and the field near Portomaggiore promised more ransoms and more witnesses to any displays of prowess. However, it was clear that he was needed on this sodden field. Geoffrey looked at the mass of struggling men and saw the banners of several disloyal Este vassals. They should be the target, he thought. Geoffrey ordered his company to dismount.

"Find a pike and form your lances," he ordered. He picked up a discarded Breton pike and was surprised by how light it was. "Two to a pike! We need as many lances as we can to impale these bastards!"

Geoffrey jabbed the pike into the ground. It sank deep into the mud before falling over. When he walked his soles made a sickening squishing noise and his sabetons were soon heavy. He thought about remounting Saint George, but he could not effectively lead his men from the saddle on this day. All the men-at-arms around him were on foot. Only some of the traitorous vassals were on horseback and Geoffrey could see they were having a difficult time keeping their mounts stable.

"Well done," Jean de la Salle said as he approached Geoffrey. He was wet and filthy from the waist down. "I am glad for your return. Where are the rest of your men? You promised reinforcements."

Geoffrey watched with envy as de la Salle wiped his bloodied sword on the surcoat of a dead villein.

"They are on their way," Geoffrey lied. "My man is leading them here."

"And none too soon." De la Salle was breathing hard. He bent over and spat into the mud.

"A company of the militia has nearly reached the village over yonder." Geoffrey pointed towards the east. "Your men are holding the line there, but more rebellious bastards are coming. Shall I take my company there?"

"No! I need you here. I need you to plug the holes as you just did. How many lances do you have? A dozen? Do what you can!" He grabbed Geoffrey's arm, looked him in the eye and nodded solemnly before returning to the battle.

Geoffrey watched de la Salle push his way into the ranks and take his place behind the third rank next to the trumpeter. He then scanned the lines and found Obizzi and Bentivoglio. All three men were near the bottom rank, shouting orders, shoving men into position, and constantly searching for where the next push of pike might come from. They were fighting a defensive battle, Geoffrey reckoned, and if reinforcements did not come soon the line would break. Even though many villeins had been slain, they were showing no hesitation filling the gaps of their ranks, urged on by the vassals and their retinues, who were standing behind them.

One of the Germans asked Geoffrey what they should do.

Geoffrey turned and inspected his company. They looked determined. He knew the Germans had fighting experience, but the Italians were strange to him. However, they were an older lot; Niccolo mentioned that these men had served his father during the 1385 revolt. Geoffrey was confident that his company would not flee as long as he led them properly. He again surveyed the battle and spotted a band of militia preparing to strike the right flank.

"To the canal!" Geoffrey cried. "A florin for the man who can skewer the most meat!"

Geoffrey ordained his ranks as before and placed himself in the center with his *couteau* drawn. His fingers tingled and his head felt as though it wanted to fly from his neck. The field in front of him narrowed. However, the advance through the mud was stubbornly slow, and several times the lances slipped, forcing them to stop and reform ranks. The closer Geoffrey approached, the farther away the sounds of battle seemed to be, as though they were receding into the distant horizon. A chill went up his sweaty spine. This was not unlike the dream. His eyes went to his clean sword and his stomach turned. This had to be true, Geoffrey thought.

Then he stumbled; one of the points holding his right sabeton in place had come

EVAN OSTRYZNIUK

undone. A wave of panic swept over the young squire. This was a new sensation for Geoffrey. His humors felt as though they wanted to break through his skin, yet he continued to trudge forward, carried by his own ranks of men-at-arms.

The sabeton slipped off Geoffrey's foot and started to drag. One of the Italians in the top rank stepped on the metal shoe, pinning the squire's leg to the ground. Geoffrey felt the jerk throughout his body and he nearly flew into the German lance to his right, but the man-at-arms heading he lance was swift and he shouldered his captain back upright.

The jolt revitalized Geoffrey's clarity. The canal was very close now and he could make out almost every detail of the faces of the men who were trying to cross it. Just ahead were the steel tips of thirteen pikes, each a mix of brown and crimson. One point even had a torn piece of leather stuck to it. Geoffrey raised his sword higher. With each man-at-arms slightly stooped over his pike, the squire towered over his company, so nothing obscured his view. He could see that the left end of his company was now touching the top-most rank of the defenders. He could see the many ranks of the enemy pushing forward so that the bottom ranks of both sides were tangled. The mud grew deeper and water filled his boots and soaked his chausses. Geoffrey called out to the sergeant commanding the ranks.

"Where do you want us?" Geoffrey shouted. His voice was loud and clear. His ears popped and suddenly the roar of battle filled his skull, drowning what uncertainty that remained.

The sergeant did not appear to be surprised to see Geoffrey or his men. He simply grabbed the pike nearest to him and pointed it at a man who had just been slashed by a halberd.

"We are to have deeds of arms today, men!" Geoffrey shouted. He lowered his sword in the direction the sergeant had indicated. Dozens of villeins had finally crossed the short north-south canal and made it up its eastern bank to support the first setters-on. "Let us keep our purpose to hold this ground for his lordship, the true and only Marquis of Ferrara!"

A cheer went up from his men.

"Now, close ranks! Ready to advance! Company, forward!"

Every man leaned into his pike as the English Free Company stepped ahead through the mud and the blood and into the face of battle.

Chapter 19

The report from the attack across the long east-west canal was not as encouraging as Azzo would have liked. The Bretons were putting up a more spirited resistance than he had anticipated and those militia companies that remained unengaged were moving very slowly towards Maiero. The messenger stated that the reason for this measured pace was that the ground was still very wet and they had more canals to cross than they had anticipated. The day was well passed noon and Manfredi had ordained his battailes about half a mile from him. However, neither side had parleyed and neither side was moving.

Azzo had advanced his army as far as he thought safe. He was within striking distance of Manfredi, yet he could still return to Portomaggiore without much trouble, if need be. Azzo was disappointed that Manfredi had chosen the field and not him, but the condottiere was nothing if not swift when he had to be. Although the land was perfectly flat for as far as the eye could see and the only walled towns were ahead and behind them, Manfredi had found probably the best location to set Niccolo's army without fear of being outflanked, unless either the militia bored down on him from the east or Barbiano defeated Altinberg and appeared from the south.

Manfredi had strung his ranks from the bend in the Po di Primaro River that was closest to the Ferrara road and the Ferrara road itself. Beyond that was a web of canals and salt marshes that made fighting there impossible. So, in order to turn Manfredi's left flank, Azzo observed, he would have to cross the river, which was impossible without suffering heavy losses. Azzo was sure Manfredi was holding a company of horsemen in reserve to thwart such an attempt. What he really needed to do was control the Ferrara road. That way he could turn Manfredi's right flank and open the way to the great city, forcing his foe to either retreat through the sodden fields or surrender. Glorious!

But how strong was his own position? On the whole, it was not as good as Manfredi's, Azzo reckoned. His own left flank was anchored by the Ferrara road, but his right flank was secured by nothing more than open land for about a half a mile. Were the ground firm, his men could be turned by a single charge of a few hundred knights, but the soft fields offered him protection from that.

However, a determined rank of men-at-arms on foot would cause him a lot of difficulties, and this was Azzo's greatest fear. Eventually Manfredi would signal his battailes to set on and use his greater numbers to take advantage of that weakness. Unless the militia companies smash the Breton lines and fall upon Manfredi's left flank or Manfredi weakens his own force by sending a stream of reinforcements to throw them back, thereby losing his numerical superiority, it was back to Portomaggiore for him.

No horses, no arrows, no crossbow bolts. All Azzo could see was five thousand pikes pointed at each other. The question now was how long he should wait before deciding whether to advance or retreat. The day was slipping away and still no sight of his militia companies or men departing from Manfredi's host. He needed something to hasten events.

"Captain dell'Ischia!" Azzo shouted.

"Yes, my lord!" Ischia was with the other vassals and captains waiting alongside Azzo.

"Take your company and thirty of my lances and give the militia captains a good hard kick in the arse!" Azzo then informed Ischia of the situation along the east-west canal. "If you find any company not locked with the enemy, seize command of it at once! I will have a sealed order drawn up. If any of the vassals troubles you on this account, shove it in his face."

"I thank you for this honor, my lord. Might I select my own lances?" Ischia tried hard to suppress a grin, but it came out beneath his beard all the same. He knew immediately that he would take over the whole operation and lead the Italian militia companies to victory over the foreigners. He had the authority now and he had the will.

"Take those men over there." Azzo pointed to a conrois of young men-at-arms in the top rank of the main. "They are good enough for you."

Montecuccoli asked why he was not being given the honor and dropped a few careful phrases about how Giovanni dell'Ischia had little command experience.

"It is because I can spare him and not you, my dear Lancellotto. Manfredi, Roberti and my nephew need to see you. They need to see that Modena still wants its *libertà* from the Este." Azzo swept his arm from the Po di Primaro River to the Ferrara road.

While they waited for the sealed order, Azzo took Ischia aside out of earshot of the others.

"Do whatever it takes to get those villeins to push forward with all speed, Giovanni," Azzo said. "Half of them are probably looting whatever they find instead of keeping ranks. The vassals do not share your passion for ridding this land of foreign companies, and so I doubt they can rally such common folk with much effect." He looked back at Montecuccoli and the others. "But ignore them. Those villeins and others who have suffered under the boot of the German and Breton soldiers know why they are here, but they are a simple people, as all those in the lower stations are, and so they are easily distracted if they are not bashed on the head with their purpose. Keep them to their purpose, Giovanni."

Ischia nodded. He did not need reminding about why he had chosen to cross the field, but all the same Azzo's words bolstered his confidence. He could see that he was Azzo's man now, and so he could expect lucrative service with the house of Este. Soon, everyone will forget that the Company of the Rose was once led by blackguards from the barbarous north; they will only know that its captain was the Italian and liberator Giovanni dell'Ischia.

Geoffrey thought it a marvelous sight to see his company push the line of militia into the canal. He whooped and yelled and doubled the rewards for the spit contest. When a second band tried to secure a foothold on the western bank of the north-south canal, Geoffrey slapped his men on the back and ordered them to show no mercy.

"I will send their heads back to their lords as trophies!" Geoffrey cried as he swung his *couteau* to try make one himself. He missed because he was too far back in the ranks to reach anyone but his own men, but the thrill of wielding his sword in battle was producing enough bloodlust in his humors that he did not care.

For a while the English Free Company suffered no casualties. The halberds, falchions and spears of the enemy were too short to reach his men with their four-yard long pikes. One brave soul might knock a lethal tip away only to be pierced by another. All his men had hauberks and helms, although few had the complete leg and arm harnesses Geoffrey was wearing, but the only armor the villeins could find for themselves were leather jerkins or fustian gambesons – or nothing at all. It was a poor man's army, but an army with the weight of numbers on its side.

After a third and fourth wave of militia crawled up the bank towards them and were beaten back, Geoffrey's war cries grew less frequent. He started to breathe heavily and he stopped holding his sword aloft. Another company of militia appeared on the opposite bank and began to organize for a crossing. The Este vassal who captained them was standing on the lip of the canal ordaining his men into ranks.

Geoffrey realized that this would be no pell-mell crossing. To his right he could see men moving in anticipation of outflanking him. Already the English Free Company was holding the very end of the line. If anyone got around him, he would be turned, and without support…well…Geoffrey did not want to imagine what might happen then. He *could* not imagine what might happen then.

"To the right, ten paces!" Geoffrey ordered. This would leave a gap on his left, he knew, but he hoped that de la Salle would see it and fill it with whatever men they could find.

The company shifted position with ease. Geoffrey thanked the Lord and all his angels that he had been blessed with men-at-arms who had done this before. He almost stumbled again on account of the swiftness of their movements, but unlike previous near-fall, he was able to recover before someone needed to nudge him into place.

While Geoffrey was watching what would be the fifth and likely the sixth and seventh rank to taste the pike of his men, several survivors from the fourth wave gathered their courage and fell upon his left side. The fury of the assault caused one of the German lances to go down after its pike split and a man got in close enough to strike the lance head. True to form, one of the Italians stepped in and closed the breach, but the company had shrunk all the same. Geoffrey suddenly felt as though a large part of his company had disappeared. If another lance went down and then another, he would soon have to face the wrath of a thousand villeins alone.

"Captain Hotspur!" Geoffrey heard de la Salle call out. "Come to me!"

After giving his men assurances that he would return before the next assault, Geoffrey extracted himself from the ranks and slogged his way to the gonfalons.

He, Jean de la Salle and Antonio degli Obizzi gathered on one of the few patches of grass remaining on the field.

"We have lost *signore* Bentivoglio," de la Salle announced.

No one said a word. Geoffrey looked at each man. All were dirty and exhausted.

"I assume we have lost the village by now as well?" Geoffrey asked.

De la Salle said that he had heard nothing from the village for some time. What he did know was that about a hundred men of his men had gone down, but more troublesome was his company's strength. They had been fighting for more than three hours without respite and the Breton captain could not be certain they could withstand very much more, unless he could tell them that reinforcements were within moments of relieving them.

"Well, Hotspur?" de la Salle asked. "Are fresh men on their way?"

Geoffrey opened his mouth to promise that they would see a full company of knights riding towards them if they would only look over their shoulders, but he held his voice. Jean must have reached Niccolo by now and told him of the desperate situation, and Geoffrey believed that Niccolo would not deny him the additional men.

"They will come," Geoffrey said in a raspy voice and he coughed. So much shouting had come out of his mouth and so much mud and filth and gone into it that he sounded far from like the young squire that had entered Manfredi's camp just over a month ago.

"That is not good enough," de la Salle said. "We can no longer hold our ground. We must withdraw or offer terms of surrender, or we will be overrun. If what you said is true, Hotspur, more militia companies will soon arrive. I propose to parley. What say you all?"

"I sent a man specifically to bring reinforcements," Geoffrey lied. He refused to contemplate surrender. He would obey Jean de la Salle as the captain-general of this field regardless of what he decided, but he could not see himself bending a knee to a rebel Este vassal. "They will come."

"You have said that, but unless you are a conjurer your words will not get them here any faster. Now, I will signal for parley. You, Hotspur, take over Bentivoglio's company. *Signore* Obizzi already has Cavalcabo's men. If they agree to parley, you should have enough time to merge the companies and secure the right flank as before."

De la Salle ordered his trumpeter to blow the signal for parley. They waited in silence for an answer. De la Salle had the signal sent again. After another tense silence they heard the response: the other side was willing to talk. De la Salle called for a messenger.

"Find a white bit of cloth and a horse. Look for a rider on the opposite bank also bearing a white banner and find a gap in the line to pass through. Around the right flank where Hotspur has his men should do. The captain will lead you. There is enough of a berm between the canal and the flooded field for you to pass. I do not know who commands the militia, but find him and tell him that we are willing to withdraw. Now, go!"

Geoffrey found Saint George and escorted the messenger to the end of the line. More villeins had massed on the opposite bank, but none looked about to plunge into the canal and wade across to support their brethren huddled in ragged ranks no more than a couple of yards from the bloodied tips of his men's pikes.

Geoffrey gave the order to hold arms and explained that de la Salle had agreed to parley. Servants appeared and began winding through the ranks to give the men-at-arms water and bind their wounds. Geoffrey counted the men still standing in his company: twenty. He learned that Bentivoglio had about the same number of heavy men-at-arms left in his retinue before he went down with a falchion slice across the neck. Still, while the attacks had desisted, the numbers of armed villeins were still growing on the other side. Geoffrey had no faith in the parley. He could see no reason why Azzo would let the Bretons and Este vassals withdraw.

A rider bearing a white flag emerged from the ranks of the militia and picked his way along the canals towards Geoffrey. De la Salle's messenger urged his horse down the bank of the north-south canal and was let through on the other side. The meeting was not long. Geoffrey could see de la Salle's man mouth his message. The other rider nodded and galloped back the way he came while de la Salle's man waited.

Geoffrey's humors would not allow him to remain idle. After surveying the enemy ranks and noting where he believed were weak points, he rode back to the Breton lines and picked Bentivoglio's men out of the congested ranks.

Some of the late vassal's men, a few of whom were knights, objected to the young squire taking over, but when de la Salle reminded them that Hotspur was his lordship's captain of the guard, they dropped their opposition and quietly joined the English Free Company.

"They are still not here," de la Salle reminded Geoffrey.

Geoffrey felt embarrassed, but he would not expose his lie for fear of humiliation and disgrace. Yet, the uncertainty was grinding at his conscience.

"Let me ride out to meet them, my lord," Geoffrey said. "I know you cannot spare a scout. I know the path."

"I think you had better," de la Salle said. "Your company is in good hands with Bentivoglio's men."

Saint George carried Geoffrey away from the battle northwards. He decided that he would travel one mile before turning back. Abandoning one's companions is one of the worst crimes against chivalry, Geoffrey knew. He had never let the Blues down and he would not let his company of men-at-arms suffer another onslaught without him.

Along the path Geoffrey passed wounded men hobbling back to camp, bands of children trying to sneak close to the battle, groups of villagers with carts and empty sacks waiting...

After the designated mile Geoffrey yanked on the reins and scanned the terrain. Empty marshes and fields laid to the west, although for a moment he thought he could see the battle between Manfredi and Azzo, but he knew he was deceiving himself. To the north Maiero looked tranquil. Shifting his gaze eastwards Geoffrey observed that the water on the flooded fields was being whipped up by the wind and forced to roll in waves towards the sea. A pang of disappointment struck his heart and he bowed his head. Geoffrey frowned and raised his head for another look around. A cool breeze was caressing his face, but from the east, and it was hardly a wind.

Geoffrey stood up in his saddle and stared hard at the flooded fields. The roiling waters were not waves, he realized; they were a column of riders. Geoffrey's heart leapt. They had to belong to the marquis, he reckoned, so he spurred Saint George and crashed into a sodden field towards them. For once Geoffrey was glad he was astride a palfrey, for if he had had charger beneath him, armed as fully as he was, then the immense weight of the beast and rider almost certainly would drag them down before he got within shouting distance of the column.

Dodging ponds and leaping over ditches, Geoffrey was able to guide his mount close enough to the strange riders that he could make out the two gonfalons fluttering at the head of them: a white eagle on a light blue field and a golden sun on a dark blue field.

"Jean! Jean!" Geoffrey cried and he brandished his *couteau* over his head.

The column stopped and Jean trotted into the field to meet the squire.

"Is the battle lost?" Jean asked. "The marquis gave me a hundred lances when I told him about how the Bretons and the Italians were being mauled and more companies were on their way to finish them off. Manfredi ordered that I lead these lances to the far left flank to meet the greater threat. He believes that de la Salle and the vassals can hold their ground."

Geoffrey saw that the riders were fully armed with pikes and swords. They were not scouts. "The battle is almost lost. Jean de la Salle is parleying with the other side for a withdrawal, but that is doubtful. Two of the vassals lie dead. The Bretons cannot hold. I am taking these men south to support them."

Geoffrey rode passed Jean to the head of the column, where he ordered the sergeant in charge to follow him.

"Manfredi was very specific about where he wants these men," Jean said when he caught up to Geoffrey. "He is the captain-general and he knows how to conduct a pass of arms."

"Manfredi does not know all, Jean. Our situation is worse, now, and I am the senior captain here. The threat from the east can wait."

Jean shrugged. "As long as you take the blame, it is all the same to me, Geoff. How is our company doing? Performed many feats of arms, have the lads? I see your blade is not yet bloodied."

Geoffrey looked at his sword with a frown and sheathed it. He then gave such a comprehensive account of the English Free Company's actions that Jean wondered if it had not fought three battles since he left.

"I am not pleased about the losses, but I suppose the Italians would have had to return to the marquis anyway, and I doubt that the villeins will offer much in the way of booty or ransom." Jean squinted southwards. He could just make out the militia marching on the far bank.

"Our thoughts coincide, strangely," Geoffrey said. "I still might be able to get my hands on a vassal or two before this day is done, though, but let us be off! We have over a mile to ride before that."

Geoffrey looked around and spotted a band of children wielding sticks in a mock battle. He hailed them and brought Saint George about. As he approached, he recognized several as belonging to the flea company.

"A florin for whoever can find the trails leading south to the canal where the true battle goes. I am in haste and my company is large." He pulled out a silver coin and flashed it above his head. "You know our purpose and I know yours, boys."

A girl no more than a year younger than Niccolo stepped forward and declared her intention to win the florin. Geoffrey remembered her as one of the few children who would watch his training nearly every day.

"Then sit with me and we shall ride."

The girl asked for the florin first.

"Just grab her by the scruff of the neck and let us be gone!" Jean said.

Geoffrey ignored the suggestion. "You are clever, poppet," he said in a friendly voice. "Tell you what: if you can snatch this coin out of my hand and flee, I will not chase you; if I grab you first, you will climb onto old Saint George here and lead us through. What say you?" He held out his hand. In its palm was the florin.

The girl did not answer and she lunged for the silver. However, the moment her finger was on the coin Geoffrey closed his hand around hers. She tried to pull away, but it was no contest. Soon, the girl stopped struggling and nodded. Geoffrey lifted her and placed her in the saddle in front of him.

"Now show us the way," he ordered.

As they slogged through the sodden fields, Geoffrey asked Jean to tell him what was happening between Manfredi and Azzo.

"Nothing. They are just staring at each other. Niccolo is impatient and so to keep him quiet Manfredi sent a band of skirmishes to challenge Azzo's men to fight, but nothing came of it. No chance to display your prowess with those lads, Geoff." Jean's final words were trimmed with sarcasm.

"Then I am where I should be," Geoffrey said. "Still, once we are done here, I expect Niccolo will set on there."

The column arrived at the rallying point as de la Salle was ordering his trumpeter to sound that the parley was over.

"Thank the Lord you have arrived, Hotspur!" de la Salle said and he looked at the column. "This is all? It will have to do. Their captain refused our offer to withdraw and instead is demanding our immediate surrender."

"Such great arrogance from such a lowly vassal," Geoffrey asked. "Show him to me and I will press on until I have him beneath my boot!"

"No vassal – condottiere. Giovanni dell'Ischia. Can you believe it? How the hell did he get there, is what I want to know. The devil's in it, I say!"

Jean gave the Breton captain an account of the betrayal and the intentions of Ischia, as well as of the idleness of the armies to the west.

"Yet, this is all the men his lordship, Manfredi and Roberti can spare? They will allow us to continue fighting for another hour at most."

"Then we had better place these men where they might inflict the most harm,"

Geoffrey said. "Surrender means slaughter, from what I can see, and Ischia is not a man to give quarter when he has the advantage. He sought my ruin even after he had bested me."

"Then I will take care to place rightly," de la Salle said and he began inspecting the one hundred new lances, or three hundred men in total.

The girl tried to get off Saint George and accidentally kicked Geoffrey in the thigh.

Geoffrey was startled and looked at the small creature wriggling in front of him as though he was seeing her for the first time.

"I will set you down, poppet. Just wait." He repositioned the girl so that she would not fall.

"And do not forget to share your florin with your companions," Jean warned. "They will do anything for you for the sake of a coin, for I have seen the likes of you miserable ragamuffins before."

Jean's words coupled with the radiant sun of the English Free Company banner beaming down on him reminded Geoffrey of Umbertide and the rustic urchins who at first taunted and then helped him find the way to a sanctuary on the Via Francigena. They had been a useful lot when set right, he thought.

Geoffrey bolted upright.

"Might I suggest a scheme, my lord?" Geoffrey said.

"You have earned the right, Captain Hotspur," de la Salle said.

"We cannot throw back the militia companies that oppose us and many more will soon be upon us, so let us rid ourselves of the second threat. At the same time we set the whole of the fresh company on a single point to break the enemy ranks. Once we collapse one rank, others will tumble. Villeins do not fight wars. The threat of defeat will put the fear of God into them and they should break. I am certain the Bretons will find the energy to fall on them. I know their fierce reputation."

"So, how do we rid ourselves of the thousands soon to be ranked against us, Hotspur?"

"We send the children after them!" Geoffrey turned the girl around to face him. "I will give you another florin and another to each of your companions if they fulfill a little task for me. It will be as easy as pie! What say you? You have already earned my esteem."

The girl looked unsure and said nothing.

"What jest is this?" de la Salle demanded.

"I think I understand what the squire has in mind," Jean said. "Diversion."

"I will enroll you and your companions in the famous English Free Company if you do as I say, nay, command." Geoffrey set the girl down on the ground. He then pulled a handful of coins from his purse and showed them to her.

The girl stared at them, but she did not try to grab them or flee.

"You must have many companions," Geoffrey said, "a clever and brave girl like you. Find them and have them run to the men that are marching towards here from the east. They must tell those men that many soldiers are coming from the north to kill them, and so they must kill those soldiers first. Some of your companions' fathers are with those men, are they not?"

The girl nodded.

"Then your companions must save their fathers." Geoffrey poured the coins into the girl's outstretched hands. "If you fail to complete your commission, my sword will find you. You remember how I bested all those knights who set against me, do you not?"

The girl smiled and promised to obey her captain. She then ran back into the fields.

"Can you be certain she will do as told?" de la Salle asked.

"No, I cannot, your lordship, but I am willing to wager on it," Geoffrey answered.

"Children like him, for some reason," Jean added.

"Very well. I will inform de la Salle and Obizzi that we will press to break through. Even if the children fail, a single great push of pike might shatter the lines and in the confusion some of us might be able to escape the wrath of the villeins."

"The push should be made where my company stands," Geoffrey said. "We can throw the blackguards into two canals and turn their flank."

"I agree, so now take them there! When the trumpet sounds to push, then push!"

Geoffrey led the one hundred lances to the end of the line, where his company was readying arms to hold back a strike that was only moments away. The lull in fighting during the parley had given enough time to the Este vassals to bring some order to their militia, and so they too were readying arms in densely packed ranks along the east-west canal and in the newly supported ranks on the western bank of the small north-south canal that the English Free Company was defending.

The Germans, Italians and Bretons all gave Geoffrey a welcome cheer. He made a brief account of the newest scheme and ordained the new company just behind his own. They formed a square twenty lances across and five ranks deep aimed at the point where the small canal flowed into the east-west canal. Geoffrey told the English Free Company that once the new men broke through, they were to finish off those in front of them and then follow the new company into the gap.

"What should I do?" Jean asked. "I suggest waiting at the rallying point."

"Dig that gonfalon into the ground and pick up a pike!" Geoffrey yelled. "And no excuses! We will make a lance together, since I need as many as I can find."

Both companies heard Geoffrey, inspiring the men-at-arms to jeer at Jean and threaten all manner of reprisal if he did not join them.

Jean realized that if he did not comply, he would be lost. None of the men-at-arms that he had enrolled would pay him any regard, silver or no silver, because they would no longer trust him.

Jean gave Geoffrey a hateful stare and stabbed the staff a yard deep into the mud. The men cheered.

A trumpet sounded, but from the other side of the line. A great roar went up and the villein militia started to advance. Within moments, de la Salle gave the same order.

"Niccolo in Ferrara!" Geoffrey cried and he hunched over his pike.

The sides crashed into each other with such force that pikes shattered, spears broke and halberds twisted. From the start the greater numbers of the reinforced militia steadily overpowered the now thinly ranked Bretons all along the line, pushing them back on the slippery ground. The vassals exhorted the men to destroy the foreigners once and for all. One man, though, in a black velvet hat and a black cape sat on his mount and watched the crush of men in silence. He was smiling.

The English Free Company too was drawing ever closer to being overwhelmed. Now knowing how skilled Geoffrey's men were, the militia was more cautious about advancing and put more pressure on the end of the line in the hopes of turning it. A few villeins were wading upstream with the intention of going around the men-at-arms altogether, but the deep water was giving Geoffrey's men a little more time.

"Did you bring your sword?" Geoffrey asked Jean. They felt the pike shudder as a halberd strike glanced off it.

"I did, but I cannot handle two arms at once." Jean was struggling to anchor the pike. His hands were being rubbed raw, since his gloves were in the baggage train, and his shoulder felt like it was about to pop out of its socket.

"The line is breaking. It will be every man for himself soon!"

Seeing that the villein wielding the halberd was preparing for another blow, Geoffrey cried, "All ranks! One step! Steady, push!"

Twenty pikes lurched forward, pressed into the bellies of a dozen men, and then returned to their previous position. Geoffrey and Jean succeeded in knocking back their man into his rank without piecing him. Another man came around him and tried to swat their pike away, but Geoffrey held firm and was able to jab the foe in the arm. So many men were now crowded on the bank that the force of the top ranks was propelling the bottom ranks forward before they could properly ready their arms.

"This is madness!" Jean shouted. "We should make a run for the horses and leave this lot to their fate! The English Free Company will be no more in a quarter of an hour!"

From his left Geoffrey heard a series of heavy splashes. He swiftly turned his head and saw that the new company was driving the enemy ranks into the smaller canal. One after another, men from the militia companies were falling and drowning in the rushing water. They would be passed the Bretons soon if they did not turn into the enemy's left flank, but Geoffrey had to put his own part of the scheme to life. No matter how many men were standing against him, he had to push forward and not stop until either they were standing on the edge of the bank with not a living soul in front of them or be overwhelmed in the effort.

"All ranks!" he shouted. "Full advance!" He looked back at Jean and saw that his eyes were closed, but he still held fast to the pike. "This is it, Jean. For all that is holy, brace yourself!" He stared ahead at the massed foe. After inhaling deeply, Geoffrey ordered. "Steady, push!"

The forty-two men of the English Free Company tramped forward and immediately made contact with the bottom rank of the militia. Their progress was slowed by the resistance of flesh, but the men-at-arms continued to grind their feet, inching forward as the force of their pikes crushed one rank against another and then against yet another until they started to crumble. The militia had no space to raise their halberds, lower their spears or strike with their falchions. They could hardly move at all and soon men from the top rank also began tumbling into the canal.

All of Geoffrey's lances knew they had to press their advantage now, and so they pushed harder until they started to feel the resistance slacken. Their pace steadily grew.

Villeins began to give up hope of turning Geoffrey's company and were searching for ways to flee the deadly pikes, but the only escape was to cross the canal. Arms were dropped and a headlong flight began.

When he saw that no enemy remained standing on his side of the canal, Geoffrey turned his attention to supporting the relief company. His men were too exhausted to cheer their victory, but they remained in ranks because they knew the battle was far from won.

"Form two ranks!" Geoffrey ordered. When this was done, he commanded, "Company, left!" Once the men-at-arms had aimed their pikes anew, Geoffrey announced that they would make for the point between the relief company and the Bretons. He saw that the fresh Italians were in the midst of finishing off anyone who remained on the wrong side of the smaller canal and turning to plunge into the side of the militia line.

Marching with greater confidence than at any time during the battle, the English Free Company swiftly crossed the short span of ground that led to the point of attack and joined the weary Bretons. Together they easily repeated Geoffrey's success at the smaller canal and began to turn the line even before the relief company was fully arrayed and engaged.

The enemy ranks began to collapse into each other. The relief company, English Free Company, and soon the Bretons and Obizzi's men were throwing back the villein militia. More men went into the canal while others fled to the closest bridge in order to reach the safety of the southern bank.

"Let us go after one of the vassals!" Jean yelled. He pointed at a man on horseback.

"We must keep the company together," Geoffrey said. "They might try to rally. Lord knows they have enough men still armed to try!"

The bridges over the long east-west canal were contested, but once most of the militia was routed, de la Salle was able to bring enough men to bear on them to force the defenders with little trouble. Soon, Geoffrey and his company found themselves on the southern bank unopposed.

When Geoffrey looked back to where they had just fought, his eyes fell on the hundreds of bodies sprawled for over a mile along the northern bank. He found the scene strangely dissatisfying.

"He has already got one!" Jean said and he pointed at de la Salle, who had standing next to him two vassals with their hands bound behind their backs.

"We must keep watch for a rally," Geoffrey said. "The point should be close." He looked over the heads of the scattered mass of men and found Giovanni dell'Ischia.

"There!" he said. "If we are taking anyone today, we are taking him!"

Ischia was in the midst of a crush of men, arguing with the surviving vassals about how to rally, when he saw Geoffrey and his company coming towards him.

"The day is lost, captain!" Geoffrey shouted. All around him men were surrendering. A detachment of Bretons was approaching to cut off any escape to Portomaggiore. "Submit to me or be slain!"

The defeated vassals declared that they would surrender to Jean de la Salle only.

"Agreed!" Geoffrey said.

"What?" Jean cried. "That is a lot of silver to give away, fool."

"They will not submit to me without a fight, Jean, and if I force them, I might lose Ischia."

As the vassals moved to abandon the militia, Ischia spurred his horse and tried to push through the sea of men.

"Take the pike, Jean!" Geoffrey unsheathed his *couteau* and ran after his prey.

Ischia did not get very far. After freeing himself from the crowd, his horse had trouble finding its footing on the soft ground and stumbled. A band of Bretons saw the attempted flight and closed in.

When Geoffrey caught up with Ischia, he pulled him off his mount, threw him on his back and placed the tip of his sword on the captain's throat.

"Yield or die!"

"As an Englishman, I expect you to kill me anyway," Ischia spat. His beard was matted and muddied.

"On my honor, I cannot kill and unarmed man, no matter how faithless, so I amend my demand: yield, knave!" Geoffrey pushed on his sword until a small circle of blood pooled around the tip.

Ischia gasped. "Were you a knight, I would consider submitting, but to a squire? You are nothing! Bah!"

Geoffrey clenched his jaw. He could feel anger well up inside his chest and pour into his arms. This was not like the passion that had overtaken him at the clash of arms against the militia. This was more akin to hatred, or rather disgust. Geoffrey could not look at Ischia's face without wanting to crush it. Instead, he lifted the blade back and inch and pulled it a foot to his right.

"I would only permit a great lord, or my father, to speak to me in such a vile manner. As you are neither, I must defend my dignity." Geoffrey replaced the tip of his *couteau* to a spot just below Ischia's ear and drew a long, red line across his neck to the matching spot on the other side.

Ischia stared at Geoffrey with contempt and let his body go limp.

Azzo heard the news about the defeat of the militia at the canal and the disappearance of the other militia companies from the *podestà* of Portomaggiore. So many men were flooding back to the city that the gates could not be closed.

However, all was not lost, Barbiano had returned with most of his company while Rodiglia was now in Portoverrara to guard against a possible attack from the Bretons. He was about to order his bottom battaile to advance when he saw something that made him go pale. Riding into the field between the ordained armies was his nephew. He was bearing the Este gonfalon. Behind him trailed most of the vassals he had assigned to the militia companies and Giovanni dell'Ischia. They too were bearing gonfalons, although their own, and they were unarmed.

"By the grace of God and good arms!" Niccolo shouted. He was facing Azzo and his host. "These men have submitted to me, the Marquis of Ferrara and son of Alberto d'Este, and they have agreed to accept investiture of all the lands and privileges they and their families were holding from the Este as of the day of their rebellion against me from my hand and from my hand alone." Niccolo surveyed the ranks of his enemy. He could see the banners that were still set against him, but they were far fewer in number than on the day he inspected the siege works. This gave him confidence to continue. "I call upon those amongst you who still refuse to accept the true Marquis of Ferrara to lay down their arms and also receive investiture from my hand. To those who submit now I will grant full restoration of land and privileges. To those who refuse – exile!"

Niccolo's army cheered and shouted encouragement.

"*Libertà* has been won!" Niccolo continued with the full force of his young voice. "*Libertà* from the pretender and from all those who aim to destroy the legacy of my father, and his father, and all the great men of the mighty Este clan!"

Azzo recognized Alberto's voice in Niccolo, although it still belonged to a boy. However, he had to admit that it was more measured than in Bologna. His words were more reasonable too. Azzo shook his head. Any chance he had of overthrowing his nephew would soon disappear if he did not act soon. He had to advance.

After giving several final orders, Azzo took a last look at the field and saw to his horror several of his vassals leaving the ranks for the other side. He shouted for the trumpeter to signal the attack, but the sickening feeling churning in the pit of his stomach told him that he had lost the Este inheritance.

Epilogue

Ferrara

Geoffrey was sitting alone on a bench beneath the loge of the walled garden in the citadel watching several court ladies and their maids plant flowers. The brilliant light of the May morning obscured his sight somewhat, but if he squinted he could recognize a few from both stations that he had met at one or another banquet held in honor of the great victory that he was proud to have been a part of. After Niccolo and Manfredi had captured Portomaggiore and taken Azzo, Montecuccoli and all the remaining defiant vassals prisoner, Geoffrey had accompanied the marquis around the *contado* suppressing rebellion and ensuring that the Este inheritance was wholly and firmly in his hands. Now, not wishing to make the same mistake as he did last autumn by delaying his forward journey too long, Geoffrey was enjoying one final day as a guest of his lordship before departing for Avignon and the halls of the Duke of Lancaster.

"You have no need to hide in the shadows, my Lord Voltana. I believe that some of those ladies are not yet married, so you may approach them."

Geoffrey looked up and saw Catherine in the loge above him. She was wearing a yellow gown, to match the season, Geoffrey assumed, and a ruby pendant shone from her pale wimple.

"Of that I have made certain, mistress astrologer. I am just waiting for them to end their labors before I commence mine."

Catherine stepped around the loge and sat next to Geoffrey.

"You are brightly attired for such a campaign, I see." She ran her hand along the length of the ivory-colored doublet Geoffrey was wearing.

"Niccolo gave it to me as a present for joining the Whites. Not a bad lot. They should serve him well, when the time comes." He was also wearing his purple hat, grey linen chausses, and brown buskins.

"You did not challenge any of them between the barriers, did you Geoffrey?" Geoffrey chuckled and shook his head.

"I just showed them a move or two. No bloodying of swords, I promise." Geoffrey looked at Catherine and saw that she had placed a square package on her lap. "Bought yourself something, I see," he said and pointed at the brown canvas wrapping, "or did you receive a gift from his lordship as well?"

"No, my wardrobe suffers no shortages, unlike yours. I am sorry you lost all your silver and possessions. Although, I am not surprised that those militia companies fell on Maiero instead of attacking the Bretons or Manfredi. I suppose they lost their way in the *valli*, and no doubt once they saw the baggage train, their mouths started to water and they forgot all about their war for *libertà*."

"I suppose." Geoffrey thought about the children he had sent to mislead their fathers and wondered if they had survived the looting. He never looked for them after the battled ended. "However, I have my harness and I have my *couteau*, so I am not so troubled by the loss. Jean was mad as hell, though, as you can imagine. He has spent the past week petitioning the regency council and anyone who will listen for recompense."

"Has anyone listened?"

Geoffrey shrugged.

Catherine thought as much. Now that Uncle Azzo and Modena were no longer threats to Niccolo, the regency council probably felt no need to hurry with paying its men-at-arms, not least the tiny English Free Company.

"And what did you win for your feat of arms, aside from a silk doublet?" Catherine asked. "I have only just returned from my commission to Ravenna."

Geoffrey lolled his head before saying almost dismissively, "I should receive a few ransoms from the noble prisoners I took. Captain dell'Ischia was the biggest prize, although he is poor, and I was given my share of the captured vassals when we took Portomaggiore. It will be enough to get me back home."

"And a knighthood, perhaps?"

Geoffrey frowned and turned away from Catherine.

"No," he said flatly. "His lordship cannot make me a knight because he is not yet a knight himself, and no one else will. He did promise to fulfill his pledge to me just as soon as he is granted spurs and his waist is girded, so I have that."

"You also have this." Catherine shifted the square package to Geoffrey's lap.

"You recovered something from the baggage train?" He lifted the package; it was soft and light.

"I recovered something from a friend." Catherine assumed a solemn expression and looked into the squire's eyes. "Count Robert d'Ivry did not live to see the spring, Geoffrey. He died in his sleep in the hospice of the Knights Hospitaller a week after I arrived, and there he still lies."

Geoffrey turned pale and slumped against the wall of the loge. He closed his eyes and raised his face to the sun.

"Was he murdered?" Geoffrey asked in a quiet voice. "The *signore* of Ravenna had him almost under arrest, and now that his side has lost…"

"No, our Lord decided that it was his time to return him to Paradise."

Geoffrey sighed. "At least I fulfilled his commission. This brings me what little joy I can muster."

"I told him that and he was grateful to you. That is why he wanted you to have this, Geoffrey. He said it belonged to him and that his family would no longer need it." Catherine tapped the canvas package.

"What is it?" Geoffrey dropped his head onto his chest and blinked several tears from his eyes.

"It is yours, so you must reveal the contents."

Geoffrey turned over the soft package and opened the folds that secured it. At first glance, he thought that the plain black cloth was a shroud or funereal garment, but when his eyes fell on the white cross sewn onto it, Geoffrey felt as though someone had squeezed his heart for an instant. He leaped up and bathed the fabric in sunlight to display its full glory.

"By Saint Mary's holy countenance, it is a surcoat!" Geoffrey cried. He held the garment outstretched and turned it around several times.

Catherine was equally astonished.

"That is not just any surcoat, Geoffrey," she said. "It is the surcoat of the Knights Hospitaller." Catherine stood up to have a closer look at the marvelous present. "The fabric is worn."

Geoffrey also closely examined the shirt. He not only found places of wear, but also stains and neat tears, almost like slits, and he immediately knew where, when and how this damage had been done.

"I must thank his lordship," Geoffrey said quietly. He carefully folded the surcoat and with trembling hands placed it on the stone bench.

"You heard me say that Count Robert has passed on, did you not? I suggest you buy a prayer for him. He will know."

"He will. All the same, I should see him. It would be the least measure of respect I could show him. He was to leave for Cyprus when spring came, so I expect he will be gone soon. His companions would not bury him in this land."

"Ravenna is not far and the roads are safe, now that the war is ended. Manfredi is still in conflict with the Barbiano over Lugo, Cotignola and Bagnacavallo, but that has nothing to do with you."

"I should ask his lordship the marquis to accompany me," Geoffrey mused.

"As much as he would like to, Niccolo is on his way to Milan to witness the emperor make the *signore* of Milan a duke, as am I."

"The emperor... Niccolo asked me to escort him there." Geoffrey recalled how he had escorted Count Robert through the mountains with the deceitful Ischia. "First – Ravenna; then – Milan!" he declared. Geoffrey reached for his *couteau*, but he only grabbed air. He had left the sword in his lodgings in the citadel.

THE END

Glossary

Arms & armor:

couteau	French broad sword
pourpoint/gambeson	padded arming jacket worn beneath a hauberk
hauberk	chainmail armor shirt
surcoat	cloth shirt or tunic worn over a hauberk or other types of armor; often blazoned with a coat-of-arms
aventail	chainmail scarf to protect the neck and shoulders; suspended from the helm
sallet	type of helm that tapers at the back
points	leather or cloth strips sewn onto an arming jacket to which pieces of armor are affixed
pell	wooden post used as a target for sword practice

Arm/hand protection:

spaulder	metal plate armor to protect the shoulder
couter	metal plate armor to protect the elbow
vambrace	metal plate armor to protect the arm
gauntlet	metal glove to protect the hand

Leg/foot protection:

cuisse	metal plate armor to protect the thigh
poleyn	metal plate armor to protect the knee
greave	metal plate armor to protect the shin
sabeton	metal plate shoe to protect the foot

Legal terms:

accomandigia	type of contract with an established lord for loosely specified military services; not based on land; less stringent arrangement than traditional vassalage
contado	adjacent territory controlled by a city in Italy
condotta (pl. condotti)	type of limited written contract given to a mercenary captain to conduct war on behalf of the giver of the contract; the word 'condottiere' – mercenary captain – derives from it
dominium	all the land under the control of a single lord
podestà	type of independent magistrate elected by a city to administer its affairs other than justice; usually candidates had no ties to the city in question
raccomendato (pl. raccomendati)	subject of an accomandigia
signore (pl. signori)	Italian lord
valli	region east of Ferrara dominated by shallow lakes, rivers and wetlands where the economy was dominated by fish, salt and water-borne trade
villein	common word for serf or peasant

Military formations:

battaile	division of men-at-arms or knights for a battle; an army usually consisted of three 'battailes' – vanguard, main, rearguard
conrois	squadron of 20-50 horsemen
miles	medieval foot soldier
top, bottom rank	'top' rank of any military unit was the rearmost rank; 'bottom' rank was the foremost rank

Other:

carroccio   Italian wagon that served as a command or rallying point for an army in the field; often stored gonfalons and money; sometimes held an altar

grosso (pl. grossi)   basic monetary unit in Italy roughly equivalent to the British shilling or French sou; although exchange rates and terminology varied greatly, the rule of thumb for determining relative values is: 12 denari (pennies) make a grosso; 20 grossi (shillings, sous) make a florin (pound, livre)

Outremer   Old French for 'overseas', general name given to the medieval Crusader states, although it could refer to any lands in the Eastern Mediterranean

routiers   common French word for brigands or bandits, though usually made up of ex-soldiers, often English

THE
ALTARPIECE

BOOK ONE OF THE CROSS AND CROWN SERIES

SARAH KENNEDY

KNOX ROBINSON
PUBLISHING
LONDON • New York

CHAPTER ONE

May 1535, North Yorkshire

Mount Grace Priory was cold as a crypt, despite the gold-shot tapestries on the stone walls. Sister Catherine gathered the woolen shawl around her shoulders. The candle on the oak infirmary table guttered, and she cupped her hand around the flame. When the light steadied, she stepped to the window and tucked cloths between the shutters. She placed her ear against the wood for a moment. Nothing. It must have been the wind. The soldiers had surely gone to the inn for the night. She had a few hours at least.

Catherine tiptoed to the door and peered down the long corridor, but her eyes could not adjust to the blank darkness beyond her workroom, so she turned once more to her task. She laid out her receipt books and measured them with her eyes. They could be hidden easily enough. She ran her palm over the worn leather covers and opened one. She had drawn the herbs and flowers herself, and her finger traced the bright veins she had penned into the daffodil leaves on one page. She had copied details of their altarpiece in a corner of each page. The Magdalene with her golden jar of ointment. A cherry tree with Joseph reaching to pluck the fruit. A Christ child, sitting in the crook of his Mother's elbow. The Madonna, always in the upper right-hand corner.

The script was black and firm, and Catherine read through a few of her receipts. Yes, she had them by heart. She could do without the books. For now. If only she could find a way to practice physic without losing her head. She stacked them, lifted the pile, and unlatched the door. Stepping into the darkness, she slid along the interior wall of the nuns' walk until she reached the dormitory. She hesitated, listening. An animal rustled along the garden's edge, a weasel or a rat, too low to be seen. Not a man. Not yet. She had already loosened this latch and she slipped inside without a sound.

The other nuns were sleeping under heaps of blankets, and Catherine crept to her own pallet, where she knelt and arranged the books in the hole, easing the loosened stones back into place. The last one clunked as it dropped, and she froze, her heart banging loud inside her ribs. But no one stirred as she slunk back out.

Her taper still burned in the infirmary, and Catherine took it up before she stepped softly into the walk again, turning the other way this time. She hurried around the corner to the narrow steps leading up to the reading room. Catherine's head grazed the low ribs of the vaulted ceiling, and she went straight to her knees, reaching under the scriptor's desk. Her fingers found the wrapped manuscript, tied tight with string, and she lifted it onto the small table. Her hands were icy, and she trembled as she tested the knots. The parcel was intact and she lifted the candle to go.

Voices. Men's voices. Catherine stiffened. Boots on stone pavers. They were in the church. She should have written out the will first. If Catherine fled right now, she might make it back to her infirmary unseen. But a door whined below. The door from the church into the convent. Too late. Catherine blew out the flame and sat holding the ends of the string and breathing the sweet smoke. She was sweating under the heavy woolens, but her feet were cold, and she began to shiver. They would surely hear her gulping for air.

At least two of them, right below. Someone seemed to complain, and a wisp of yellow light flickered past the steps. Her scalp prickled. Another door, farther off, at the back of the convent, opened, and the voices faded. Thump of wood against wood, a metal latch coming down. All was blackness now. Her feet went numb, but she squatted without moving. All was silence. She was afraid to show her face at the window, but after an eternity of quiet, she flattened herself to the wall and raised herself to the sill. The interior of the convent seemed at peace. No soldiers in sight. Catherine snatched up a few pigments pots and, balancing them on the pages, teetered down the steps. The door into the church, usually locked, stood open. Fear knotted her limbs, but she clenched the goods and ran back to her infirmary, where she skidded inside and bolted the door, chest thudding like a rabbit in a trap. She pulled the stopper from a bottle of perfume and inhaled. Essence of lily of the valley, said to heal the heart. She let the fragrance fill her, but her ribs still ached.

Before she set to work, Catherine lifted her skirt to wipe her damp palms. Her shift was embroidered with red and yellow birds that seemed to lift their beaks and trill from the cloth, and blue-eyed, many headed flowers that sprawled and twisted the tendrils of their stems. She could not see the colors, but she ran her fingers over the slick threads. Would they tear the very clothes from the women's bodies? She'd heard stories of worse. She sat until she could no longer hear the terror whistling in her ears, then she held the candle's wick to her bowl of embers again.

Catherine had already prepared her egg whites and quills, but when she laid the parchment open, she faltered. Latin or English? English, she decided, but still she postponed the beginning. The page lay before her like creation and she stared into its surface as she had stared up into the clouds as a child, searching for God. Her hand trembled. She must not err. It might be the last document she would write. Her fingers cramped from clutching too tightly in the frigid air, and she laid the tool aside. The sharp nib pointed at the parchment like the lean muzzle of some fiend. Like the point of a soldier's sword.

Catherine touched her breast. *Breathe.* A drop of sweat trickled down her forehead and landed on the parchment. She had copied a hundred receipts. The uses of borage for jaundice. Mint for the stomach. She had drawn saffron. Roses. *Loosen yourself to the work at hand.*

The quills continued to deride the young woman. She began again by picking one, but chose instinctively with the left hand and hastily returned it to the jar. No. She must not make a mistake. She selected again, whispered *Sweet heart of Mary, strengthen me*, and wrote out the page in perfect script with one inkhorn and one penknife, dipping and mending precisely. *This is the will and testament of Catherine Havens, twenty years of age, foundling of Mount Grace Priory, Yorkshire, England, adopted daughter of Christina Havens, Prioress of this Convent. I have secured Receipt Books written in My Hand under the Seventh Stone from the West Wall of the convent dormitory for their safekeeping. We are to remove from our Home at the order of King Henry VIII and I leave these Goods with intent, God Willing, to return and claim them. I have made and illumined the Books with my Own Hands and have tested the properties of all the Herbs listed therein. I have found them good. I have worked physic as a practice of my gifts from God. I have done this with the Blessing of my prioress and my priest and for the Good of my Immortal Soul.*

The list of contents covered the entire page, and when she had finished, Catherine switched to her left hand and signed her name at the bottom. She added a flourish of ink, as she had done in her books, and was pleased with the royal look of it. Catherine opened the jars of pigment and swirled colors into the shells of egg white and water. Closing her eyes, she began to see feathers and leaves. The birds and beasts and imagined faces of the saints filled her margins, and vines and acanthus leaves twisted themselves under her hand into ferociously serpentine windings. She bloodied her initials, adding around the text miniscule drolleries and grotesques, a monkey face grinning from a daisy head and a blue-faced clown playing a silver pipe, with canaries for ears. On the top right corner hovered the Madonna, who made all things well. She held the light over the page and, seeing the work was good, scattered sand over the words. Now she could rest her eyes for a few minutes before the storm of the morning struck them.

When the door rattled, Catherine was slumped with her head on her arms, sleeping. The candle had burned down to a puddle, and she jolted awake. The parchment lay dry before her, and she covered it with her arms.

"Catherine, are you in there?" It was Sister Ann.

Catherine's arms went weak with relief and she unlatched the door. "Come in. Quick."

Ann stood in her sleeping gown and a thick shawl, the dark nimbus of her hair disordered around her ears. She was a big woman, but she glided inside without a sound. "What are you doing out of the dormitory? And alone?" Ann took up the parchment and held it to the shrinking flame. Her brown eyes looked almost black. "Is this wise? You have put your name to it." Ann could not read, but she knew the fancy signature well enough.

"It's my will. There is nothing to shame me in it. I do not intend to be taken for a witch. And if someone else should find it, I will likely be dead."

"No talk of that now. What will do you do with it?"

"Put it somewhere safe."

Ann lifted the wrapped manuscript. "Is this the work of that Margery Kempe woman?"

"I mean to keep it." Catherine stretched to her full height. She was almost as tall as Ann, though of a thinner build.

Ann huffed out a laugh. "No one will want it. You may leave it in plain sight. That woman was lunatic."

"I will have it. It's too delicate to leave to chance."

"It may not go well with you if you are thought to be an admirer of hers."

"It will not fit under the floor. But I mean to keep it."

"As you wish."

Catherine pulled a bag from a shelf and emptied a heap of coins onto the table. "Is it enough, do you reckon?" She shuffled the gold. "I will add all the printed books. They are almost a library now."

"You could add the gift of your sweet green eyes and it wouldn't be enough, Catherine. Keep your books and stow them where they won't be burned. He will take the altarpiece, whatever you offer him. He will take whatever he wants. Hide your money, too. You'll want it before the snow falls again."

"I could make the offer. He may prefer ready coin."

"Come, Robert Overton keeps that much in his purse for tidbits. Hide your money and put your books away. He knows good and well how much that Madonna is worth. Let it go. If he is content with Her, he may not see us so clearly."

"She means more to me than all these books together. I have prayed under Her eyes all my life."

Ann rubbed her thumb against her fingers. "That money will feed you for a while. Mary will not." She palmed a gold piece and let it fall. "I tell you, save your wealth. Your Madonna is already gone."

The cock sang a few choked notes outside the window, and Catherine placed the coins, one by one, back into the bag. "Is there light yet?"

"No. Why? You're surely not eager to see this day begin."

"There were men in the church tonight. I want to see what villainy they've wrought."

"Soldiers?"

"I only saw their torches as they went past the reading room. I thought they were coming for us, but they went on through." Catherine folded the parchment twice, tied it with string, and sealed the bow with a button of soft wax. "Mother Christina says she will barricade herself in her chamber if they come into the convent."

"We'll see how firm she stands when a blade's at her throat. She's the one who has brought us to this."

A pain wormed across Catherine's forehead. "The king's secretary has done it, not Mother."

Ann shrugged. "Don't be angry. Cromwell doesn't act without the forms of law. All he needed was a word of suspicion. I don't blame her. I just say how things are."

The pain went flat. Ann was right. "You're free to go if you want."

"Go where? With the others?" Ann shook her head. "What a choice these men give us."

"Devil and the deep blue sea. I am decided. If I am not allowed to practice physic, I have no life. And I have promised Mother Christina to stand by her."

"You had better hide that parchment, then. Even the drawings could put you under a charge of dealing with the devil these days."

Catherine pushed her stool to the outside wall and stepped up onto it. A door hinge squeaked somewhere outside and Ann pinched the light to death. A flicker. A footfall, steps hurrying by. A swish of cloth. Then nothing. Catherine clung to the stone, and after a few minutes in the dark, Ann lit another candle with her flint, but she tented it with her shawl. She pushed her ear against the doorframe.

"Is anyone in the walk?" whispered Catherine.

Ann shook her head.

"Was that a man, do you think?"

"No telling."

Catherine stretched to the seam where the wall met the curve of the roof. There was a narrow gap in the corner, just wide enough. She pushed the will in as far in as it would go and hopped down. "Is it concealed?"

Ann nodded. "Now, show me where these men were."

"They came from the nave, but they went the other way out, toward the river. Either through the refectory or the garderobe." The two women inched the door open. They were alone. Catherine trotted around the walk, Ann close behind, into the dark church. It was still full night.

"I cannot see my hand before my face," Catherine whispered, and Ann raised the candle, but its small halo was lost in the vast shadows of the nave.

They skidded from pillar to pillar. The space was empty, the double front doors barred, as they always were at night. Catherine pulled at the latch, but the bar was solid. The rooster tried out his morning song again.

"Are you certain they came from the church?" said Ann.

"I thought so. I was sure so. But perhaps my ears deceived me in the dark."

"I see no way a person could have entered this way."

"They went out the back. Maybe they came in that way."

"Did they have a key?"

"I saw nothing but the light as they passed by."

"It makes no sense." The flame trembled in a sudden breeze and went out. They felt their way across the nave to the sanctuary, where the air was still, and Catherine held the candle while Ann sparked it to life once more. The flame cast its circle of gold as high as the carved angels above them, who threw long winged shadows across the arches, their slender arms grasping at nothing. The saints stood, palms clasped together, in their niches, and the stained glass of the windows winked.

Catherine said, "All seems well, thank God. For now."

"If all is well, we should go back. Perhaps it was only the sexton."

"That was not the sexton in the walk just now."

"Come on to bed." Ann tugged Catherine's sleeve. "We will need our strength soon."

Nodding, Catherine turned, but she glanced up and the candle dropped from her hand. Flames splattered and bubbled across the pavers. "My God," Catherine cried out, leaping backward.

Ann gasped. Even in the dark, they could see the gap above them, a great blank space. Their altarpiece, with its blue Madonna and Child, was gone.